Praise for

DEVIL OF THE DEEP

"Beautifully evocative and wonderfully queer, *Devil of the Deep* is a swashbuckling and captivating tale. Falencia Jean-Francois is an author I know I will be returning to again."

—A.K. Mulford, bestselling fantasy author of The Five Crowns of Okrith series

"*Devil of the Deep* is a profoundly soulful story of mermaids, pirates, and lost gods—where the bonds of family (both blood and chosen) are tested by forces of tyranny. As action-packed as it is poignant, the novel expertly navigates themes of acceptance, regret, passion, love, and loss and demands we closely examine what it means to be in community. This is necessary reading."

—Leslye Penelope, award-winning author of *Song of Blood & Stone* and *The Monsters We Defy*

"Lush in worldbuilding, explosive in action, and steeped in culture, this achingly compelling fantasy is a love letter to queer people of color who deserve to be the heroes of their own story."

—Natalia Hernandez, author of the Flowers of Prophecy series

"*Devil of the Deep*—Queer. Black. Mythos for the culture. If you're into pirates, mermaids, and burning corrupt systems to the ground—or in this case, flooding them while having an adventure on the seven seas—this one is for you."

—E.A. Noble, author of *When Blood Meets Earth*

"A clever mix of creation myths and colonizers, *Devil of the Deep* dares to bring shadows to the surface through action-packed adventure, compelling characters, and emotional depth. Falencia Jean-Francois is a rising voice among the tides, submerging readers in themes as lyrical as the songs woven into the heart of the story."

—Robin Alvarez, author of *When Oceans Rise*

"*Devil of the Deep* gripped me from the very beginning. It's an exciting tale filled with adventure, Haitian culture, unashamed queer characters, and a little bit of deconstruction from oppressive belief systems. What more could you ask for?"

—Kay Synclaire, author of *House of Frank*

"Falencia Jean-Francois has filled her richly imagined world with complex characters to create a propelling story with timely social commentary about the danger of blind faith in corrupted power. I'm an instant fan!"

—Mona Tewari, author of *Burn the Sea*

"Falencia Jean-Francois's debut is a triumph for the fantasy genre and literature at large. Not only is queerness, Blackness, and Caribbean heritage front, center, and the norm in the magical world where this gripping mermaid-pirate adventure unfolds, Jean-Francois beautifully explores the human condition and expertly indicts systems meant to harm and diminish. Rest assured, you haven't read anything like *Devil of the Deep*."

—Talia Cadet, book influencer

DEVIL of the DEEP

DEVIL of the DEEP

FALENCIA JEAN-FRANCOIS

This book contains depictions of graphic violence, execution, child death, child abuse, implied pedophilia, transphobia, alcoholism, and a cult.

Published by Left Unread Books, an imprint of
Bindery Books, Inc., San Francisco
www.binderybooks.com

Acquired by Michael LaBorn
Edited and designed by Girl Friday Productions
www.girlfridayproductions.com

Cover design: Charlotte Strick
Cover painting © Jasmine Green

ISBN (paperback): 978-1-967967-04-9
ISBN (ebook): 978-1-967967-05-6

Library of Congress Cataloging-in-Publication data has been applied for.

Printed in China

First edition
10 9 8 7 6 5 4 3 2 1

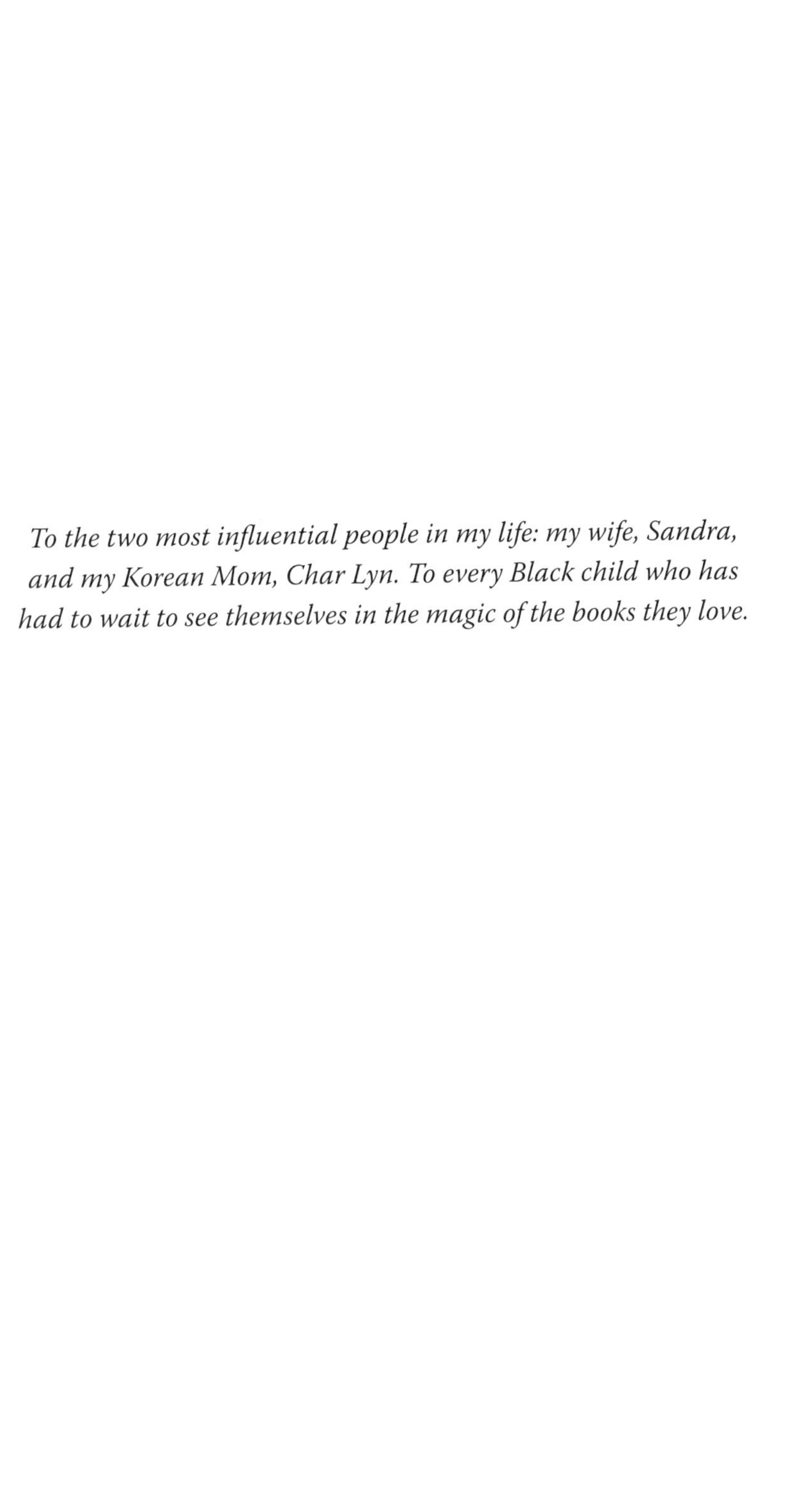

To the two most influential people in my life: my wife, Sandra, and my Korean Mom, Char Lyn. To every Black child who has had to wait to see themselves in the magic of the books they love.

One

THE FISHERMAN

Twenty years had passed since the fisherman's wife had returned to the sea, yet he still reached for her every morning before the sun opened his eyes. With a sleepy smile on his face, he would slowly slide his fingers across the bed they had shared since their wedding night, eager to feel her warm skin, only to find empty air. All wounds healed with time, proclaimed the ancient adage, but what chance did time stand against the power of his dreams to unravel any healing? Under the moon's eye, he was with her again, and every time the dawn pulled him back into the land of the living, his heart broke anew.

The fisherman found work to be the only remedy for his heartache, so he rolled himself out of bed, stretched, and pretended not to hear his joints crackling like stones in a sack. As he relaxed his body, he inhaled deeply and brought his palms together before his chest, twisting them in opposite directions before exhaling and dropping his arms to his sides. His silent communion made, he lifted the heavy wool sweater—a gift from his wife—from the bedpost and held it up to the light.

"Should've paid more attention to your mending," he murmured, shaking his head as his brown finger slipped through a new hole.

But then, you would need to learn how to sew, my darling, his wife answered in his head. *That is something even I could not teach you.*

He chuckled, pinching a white hair from the sweater's stitches before throwing it on over his shirt. His hair hadn't been gray when his wife was alive.

"You won't be able to recognize me," he said to the empty room.

Silly man, she laughed, *I would know you under any circumstance.*

For breakfast, he ate the last of the week's bread, trying not to remember the first loaf he and his wife had shared at their wedding. He tried not to remember how, as they had broken the bread and sung to each other, the two parts of their song had come together to make a beautiful melody, promising them a lifetime of happiness. Failing, he splashed cold water on his face to rid himself of whatever dreams remained.

"I'll have to remember to buy more when I go to the village to sell the day's catch," he muttered.

Make sure you get some oil, too, for your joints.

"Of course, love," he sighed.

By the time he crossed the threshold of the scrubbed wooden shack that had once proudly housed his little family, dawn was already breaking over the horizon. Were he a young man again, he would have long been on the water by now, pulling in his first or, even, his second catch, but he had grown attached to sleep in his old age.

The wind whipped his white hair as he trudged down the

long, winding path that led through the tall grass between his doorstep and the pier that jutted stubbornly out into the crystalline sea. He heard his little fishing boat calling to him as he crested the last hill, knocking rhythmically against the pillar to which it was tied as the soft waves carried it back and forth.

"I'm coming. I'm coming," he muttered.

He struggled to untie the knot that fastened his boat to the dock, wondering vaguely if fatigue or old age was getting in his way. He chose the former, though he knew what his people would say. Eventually, the knot yielded, and the fisherman sighed, relieved to have delayed his retirement one more day.

Careful not to aggravate his bad knee, he lowered himself into the boat and pulled his fishing net onto his lap. While his hands ran over the mesh, checking for loose weights and holes, the song he always sang before he embarked upon a sea journey rose in his heart. The original words told the story of a fisherman who cared only about material possessions and was pulled into the deep for his selfishness. Still, the song was rumored among fisherfolk to protect those who sang it from the selfish fisherman's fate, so the fisherman hummed the melody. Inwardly he prayed for whoever might be listening to accept his offering in exchange for peace while he ventured on the waters. On a whim, he pulled a painted shell from his pocket, one of the many he had taken to collecting and painting from the beach. He kissed it and tossed it over his shoulder as an additional show of genuflection.

As the shell plunked into the water, the fisherman heard another voice join his, creating a harmony that swelled and died on a single note. He jerked his head this way and that, but he saw only the sea and the sand, the dock and the dawn.

"Just the wind playing tricks on an old mind," he chuckled, but he did not take up the song again.

When he was certain his net would still hold more fish than it let through, the fisherman unfurled the fishing boat's single sail. It caught the wind at once, billowing out and carrying the boat and its only passenger out to sea. He rode the undulating waves just short of the point where the land beneath the water gave way to deep ocean, and, reaching a spot he knew to be fruitful, he used the rudder to angle the vessel against the wind and dropped the anchor. He cast his net into the sea and waited to hear it slip into the water with a soft hiss. Instead, a whisper caught the fisherman's attention.

"Who's there?" he called, looking all around as though he expected to discover someone standing on the water.

He saw no one but, inexplicably, felt the urge to take up the ancient song, again. Wary, he resisted the call, wondering if, perhaps, a spot closer to the shore would suit him better.

He yanked hard on his net—once, twice, not caring whether the fish entangled within it flopped into the boat or flailed back into the sea. On the third pull, he felt the net catch on something. Frustrated, he pulled as hard as his old bones would allow. It would not budge. Finally, he dropped it, sighing in exhaustion as he prayed he would not have to cut it free. As he bent to take it up once more, the length of net he had managed to retrieve suddenly leaped from the deck and slid back over the side of the boat.

"No!" the fisherman cried, lunging after it. A moment too late, he leaned over the rail and peered into the water just in time to see his livelihood disappear beneath the surface.

The song from his heart returned and the desire to sing with it, made stronger by the other voice rising slowly from the deep. It circled the fisherman's boat as it grew louder, clearer, and more irresistible. He did not need to understand to know he should fight, but doing so felt like holding back the tide. Before he could stop himself, he opened his mouth and poured out his soul into the water. A shadow appeared just beneath the surface of the water, as though the fisherman had called it. As it drew closer, the fisherman saw its colors: blue and white and pale brown with bright green eyes.

Both he and the creature stopped singing. He squeezed his eyes shut, muttering to himself that he must have fallen asleep in the boat, that he was dreaming. But when he looked again, the thing had moved closer to the surface of the water and was using its webbed hands to beckon him forward.

The fisherman looked around again, certain that this was some kind of trick, and, as he searched for another boat and another soul to explain what was happening, the tender notes of a different song slipped into his ears, wrapping themselves around his heart. He froze. Tears welled in his eyes as the song carried him back to the day that he and his wife had first joined their voices and their lives together.

It was not until he heard the splash and felt the cold seep into his clothes that he realized he had thrown himself over the side of the boat. Though his old joints and weathered lungs protested, he pushed through the water, propelling himself deeper into the darkness, his eyes wide open and stinging as he searched for the creature. In the end, it was the creature who found him. It swam circles around him, a graceful blur of glistening light brown skin and shining blue and white scales. The fisherman got his first good look at the wiry old man who had not legs but the tail of a fish. His gray hair floated in thick tendrils around his narrow, pointed face. Even as the fisherman's lungs began to burn for breath, he fought to keep his place in the creature's presence.

"You carry great longing in your heart."

The creature's mouth formed the words, and his voice rang through the fisherman's mind, recalling images stronger than memories of his wife's face, her sparkling eyes, her beautiful smile, that both warmed and lanced his heart in equal measure.

"You wish to see her again."

The fisherman strained against the fading of the memories, but they disappeared all the same, and he was soon left with only darkness. Somehow, this was worse than being awoken from his dreams.

He nodded fervently. The creature wasted no time. He took the fisherman's face between his cool, smooth palms.

"What will you give?"

Anything, the fisherman thought desperately, placing his hands over the creature's as his chest seized painfully. *Everything.*

The creature brought his face closer and closer to the fisherman's, and, as their foreheads touched, the fisherman sighed, finally giving up his last breath.

Two

NNENNA

Nnenna slipped her sword into her adversary's belly and watched, with a satisfied smile, as his expression shifted from surprise to agony to despair in a matter of seconds, his life spilling freely onto his boots. She could have left him there on the deck—he'd be dead in minutes—but she couldn't resist the urge to toss him overboard before going off in search of her next fight.

The battle for the *Reverence*'s hold had been closely fought, but their victory had been all but ensured by a sudden stroke of strategic brilliance on her part. Most of the *Reverence*'s crew were dead, their bodies either strewn about the deck or swallowed by the sea, but there was still an annoying dozen or so fighting as though they had a chance at changing their fate. Nnenna was only too happy to relieve them of that misconception.

She stood only five feet and seven inches but cast as imposing a shadow as any man on her crew. Her skin was the same deep, dark, sun-kissed brown that most of the people of the Seven Isles bore, but her hair, finger-sized crimson locs that dangled over the lapels of her cotton shirt, stood out. She wore it loose as a display of her confidence that no enemy could get close enough to use it against her without paying dearly for the attempt.

She took a handful of strides toward the quarterdeck, where her captain was squaring off against two assailants. She had intended to help him, but stopped short when he executed a clever bit of swordplay that left the two assailants' blades in each other's chests. She must have looked impressed, because he cocked an eyebrow in her direction and flashed her his most arrogant grin. Without hesitation, she raised her hand to respond with her favorite rude gesture.

As she and Captain Delva shared their moment of triumph, a song rose in her heart, singing a malaise into her chest that tempered her spirit. Something was amiss. She turned to observe the deck just in time for an enormous fist to slam into the side of her head. The blow knocked her to the deck, and her cheek exploded with pain as it scraped against the scrubbed planks. Her ears rang so fiercely she could scarcely hear her thoughts, and the floor beneath her swayed violently, as if threatening to throw her into the abyss. She was tempted to let it, but if she stayed down, she was a dead woman, and she'd be damned if she would let herself be killed by a filthy Fleet captain whose ship she'd already conquered.

She rolled onto her back and forced her eyes open. The captain, a brute by the name of Hidalgo, stood over her, his weather-beaten face contorted with the rage and desperation of a man with nothing left to lose.

"Burn in Agwe's Wrath, pirate," he growled, his blade poised above his head, ready at any moment to slice Nnenna open from neck to navel.

Her eyes widened as her survival instinct surged. She jumped to her feet, brandishing the cutlass she managed to hold on to. His blade connected with hers with such force that all the bones between her hand and her shoulder threatened to shatter. But she held firm and fended off his attack. He came at her again, beady eyes ablaze and teeth bared, bloodlust rumbling from him like the low growl of a hungry beast. She parried again and again, deflecting every surge of his blade. Each strike sent a shock wave rippling through her arm, rendering bone, muscle, and sinew into jelly.

Shit, Nnenna thought as her numb fingers lost their grip and her weapon clattered across the deck. She jumped back to narrowly dodge an attempt to decapitate her. *Shit! All right, don't panic. Don't—fuck!* She twisted away from a jab that would have severed her arm at the shoulder.

Hidalgo was a giant of a man, that much was obvious. He was more than two heads taller than her, and had at least twice her strength, but he relied too heavily on it, attacking wildly while leaving himself unprotected. His movements were also—she ducked under a swing aimed at her ear—stiff and awkward like he was trying to avoid using—she leaped over his blade as he swung it back at her ankles—one side of his body. He must have been injured.

Finally, she thought, the smile creeping back onto her lips, *something I can use.*

Hidalgo raised both arms to deliver a fatal strike. Nnenna spun into his reach, then rammed an elbow into his ribs. She found the exact spot where one of her crew had stabbed him earlier. The ogre howled in pain. Nnenna drew one of her daggers, reached back, and plunged the blade into Hidalgo's throat, cutting his cry short.

His last words were lost to the choking, gurgling sounds of his death. He clutched at his neck in a last-ditch effort to stop the bleeding, but his legs buckled beneath him nonetheless. Nnenna knelt and pulled out the dagger, releasing an arterial fountain that shot high above her head. She waited until the spurts of blood quieted to a steady stream and his massive twitching body finally lay still. Then, she stood and turned to her captain, blood-stained and sweat drenched, chest heaving, smiling exultantly in the midday sun.

"Captain Delva," she called breathlessly into the hush that had fallen over the *Reverence*'s deck as she and Hidalgo had fought. A smirk tugged at the corner of her mouth. "I believe this ship is now ours!"

Once the crew of the *Medusa* were back on their ship and the *Reverence* was safely in tow, Captain Delva gave the order to set sail for Yamaye.

"I owe you a great debt," Delva said to Nnenna as he poured her a generous cup of whiskey in his cabin.

"I thought you didn't like being in debt," Nnenna said, leaning back in her seat and resting her booted feet on the smooth lacquered tabletop.

"I don't," Delva replied, knocking her feet back down and placing the drinks on the table instead. "That is why I'm doing something completely mad."

Nnenna took a sip and shivered as the fine liquor washed over her tongue. "Are you telling me so I can talk you out of it?" Nnenna asked cheekily.

"No, I'm telling you so you can grovel at my feet."

She snorted into her drink. "I beg your pardon?"

"The take from the *Reverence* is the biggest we've ever seen," Delva went on. "My share alone could keep a man comfortable for the rest of his life. And that's exactly what I intend to do."

"Captain?" Nnenna asked, her eyebrows drawing together.

"I'm an old man, Nnenna. The fight for the *Reverence* nearly took it all out of me. Better that I walk away as the beast that brought in the biggest haul any pirate has ever seen, than die the old fool who did not know when to say when."

"What about the *Medusa*?" Nnenna asked, sitting bolt upright. Delva said nothing but gave her a look that told her everything she needed to know. "Truly?" she asked in utter disbelief.

"You're a fearsome pirate, the absolute scourge of the Fleet, and the best first mate a captain could ask for. No one deserves this more than you. It would be an honor to hand the *Medusa* over to your safekeeping. We'll have to put it to a vote, of course, but I think the crew will agree with me."

"Thank you!" she said, launching herself at him and throwing her arms around his neck.

"Careful!" he said as she nearly knocked his glass out of his hand. "This whiskey is older than you are!"

Nnenna laughed. "I'll make you proud."

"If you want to make me proud, keep giving those Fleet bastards hell."

This was not an order that Nnenna needed. She picked up her glass and raised it to her captain. "To the *Medusa*!"

The vote among the crew was unanimous and, when they reached Yamaye, the pirate stronghold of the Seven Isles, twenty-year-old Nnenna Delahaye gave her first order as captain of the *Medusa*: Drink the island dry.

Three

PEARL

Pearl Highwater was desperate to attend Viceroy Seastead's funeral. She thought she had made peace with her uncles' decision not to let her go, inexplicable though it was. But then her friend Amos Stilltide, a boy she had known since they attended nursery school together, had swam up to her window and bragged that he would be in the front row for the proceedings. He had turned sixteen just one month prior and had already enjoyed enough of the fruits of full adulthood to inspire a new jealousy in Pearl that required nightly repentance to reconcile. Now, indecision twisted her insides as she contemplated further sin. The oblong opening to the outside looked to be just large enough for her to fit through. She could sneak away and return before her uncles noticed her absence.

The thought of adding a lie on top of the secret she was already keeping from them turned her stomach sour with guilt, and she bowed her head in apologetic supplication. Viceroy Atlas Seastead, her community's leader and their god's mouthpiece, had passed away only one week ago and, already, she was forgetting to live by his example. She let out a frustrated breath. Being trapped in her home for days was making her crazy. But the only way to get what she wanted was the right way. She trusted that Agwe would provide.

"Where's Uncle Rain?" Pearl asked as she descended from her nook. She had claimed it for herself when she had grown too old to share sleeping quarters with her uncles. Her Uncle Wade was preparing the first meal. He was not her uncle by blood, but for as long as her care had fallen to Rain, her father's brother, Wade had loved her as though she were his own.

Their home was a three-chamber cave, one of dozens dotting the upper walls of a great chasm in the sea. The central chamber, which housed their living spaces, was the largest and acted as a throughway between the two inner chambers—her uncles' sleeping quarters and Pearl's nook—and the outside. The larger room where her uncles slept could be entered through a doorway from which her uncles hung a curtain of woven kelp for privacy. Pearl's nook sat above the main chamber and was accessible only via a short tunnel in the ceiling just wide enough for Pearl to fit through. They had fewer possessions than most in the Settlement—only the mid-tail length, rough-spun shirts that the temple provided to cover their torsos, the tools that Pearl's uncles used on their expeditions, the treasures Pearl rescued from the Shallows, and the driftwood trident head Pearl had brought home from her lessons in the temple. But their home still felt like a home to Pearl.

Her tail twitched in anticipation as she waited for her Uncle Wade to respond. Unbothered, Uncle Wade gently turned the headless fish over onto its clean side and resumed scraping off its scales with his favorite sharpened stone.

"He is meeting with Secretary Stormcoast in the temple," he said, finally.

Surprised by this answer, Pearl swam closer to her uncle. “Why?” she asked him, twisting so that she was within his sight.

He turned his head to her and gave her the half smile that meant he could not say. Pearl let out a frustrated groan. “This isn’t fair,” she whined.

“He wants to tell you himself,” Wade said.

Pearl froze.

“Tell me what?” she asked.

“It’s not my place to say. When he gets back from the funeral—”

“I want to go!” Pearl exclaimed.

“Pearl—” he started in the tone Pearl hated to hear.

“Please!” she begged. “Everyone in my class is going. I should be there!”

“The number of people who partake in something does not determine how right it is,” her uncle replied.

Pearl rolled her eyes. “I have done everything you’ve asked since Viceroy Seastead died. I’ve stayed within sight. I haven’t visited the temple. I’ve barely left my room! I am almost a woman grown. I deserve to know what is happening!”

Wade sighed and handed her the fish. Pearl looked at it and considered refusing, but it was her favorite. He had even cut it open for her and pulled out the bones.

“There are things at work that you don’t understand,” he answered as she took the offered meal and bit into the deliciously squishy fish meat. “Rain wants to tell you himself.”

“Does it have anything to do with him campaigning against the secretary for viceroy?” Pearl asked around her second mouthful of fish.

Uncle Wade set his rock down slowly. “How do you know about that?”

"You two don't speak as quietly as you think you do at night. Your voices carry right up into my room."

Pearl could not tell if the look that came over Uncle Wade's face was exasperation or disappointment. Perhaps it was both. Either way, it made Pearl feel as though she had something to prove.

"Do you really believe he can defeat the secretary?" she asked.

"He and Viceroy Seastead managed to find common ground," Uncle Wade answered carefully, "and he has since gained much support."

Pearl thought of the secret she kept from her uncles, of the decision she had made without consulting them. She was tempted to tell it now, but the possibility of her Uncle Rain as viceroy kept her quiet.

"I want to vote for him," Pearl said instead, and this time, she easily read her uncle's surprise. Satisfied, she went on. "I'm old enough. I want my first sustaining vote to be for Uncle Rain."

"You know we don't believe the way you believe," Uncle Wade said tentatively.

It was the first time either of them had said this aloud, though both knew it to be true. Her uncles did not find the same comfort in Agwe's teachings that she did but gave her freedom to observe on her own. Pearl suspected they had hardened their hearts to Agwe after many in the community had turned their backs on them once Uncle Wade became part of their family, but it had never felt right to ask. Instead, she strove to embody what she learned from her temple lessons and hoped her example would help them find their way back into Agwe's kingdom.

"Agwe knows Uncle Rain's heart," she replied. "If He chooses Uncle Rain to lead our people, I have faith in His plan."

Uncle Wade brought a hand to his stubbly chin. Pearl stared

at him, holding back a smile as she silently watched his resolve melt before her eyes. Finally, he sighed again and closed his eyes as though already regretting his decision.

"Finish your food," he said. "If we hurry, we can make it."

Minutes later, Pearl floated in the glass-domed outer atrium of the temple in a large crowd of people, with her Uncle Wade by her side. They were dressed like the rest of the attendants, in the ceremonial green robes that tickled the fins that ran down the back of her tail. With her hood raised to show respect and to contain the untamed, dark coils of hair trying to float freely around her head, she looked around, trying to find her Uncle Rain.

"Do you see him?" she asked Wade.

"Not yet," Wade answered, looking around himself.

Pearl frowned at the facade of the temple built into the rock-and-coral cliffside and sighed when Uncle Rain failed to materialize. He did have a flair for the dramatic. She supposed he would make himself known when he was ready.

The temple was the grandest building in the Settlement. Hewn from the cliffside that towered over the chasm, the edifice boasted a large central opening with a carved balcony through which only the viceroy and his secretary could pass. All other temple workers, those who had dedicated their lives to Agwe's service, came and went through the lower entrance, a smaller opening at the building's base. A pair of guards stood sentry at either side of both entrances, dressed in the green-and-gold uniforms of the temple guards and armed with gold-tipped spears.

As Pearl wondered, for the hundredth time, what it would be like to be allowed within the temple's innermost chambers, she saw a pair of hands waving to her. She smiled as she caught sight of Amos Stilltide, who had indeed secured the best spot and was beckoning her to join him. She tapped her uncle.

"Can I go with Amos?" she asked. "I can barely see anything from here."

Uncle Wade looked around nervously.

"I'm sure he's just making a dramatic entrance," she said. "All the more reason to be front and center."

Wade laughed. "Go on," he said.

Pearl took off, weaving through the crowd of waiting attendees to the front row.

"You made it!" Amos said excitedly.

When Amos had come to Pearl's tiny window, she had only been able to see his face, and now that she could see the whole of him, she wondered what happened on a week-long expedition that could change a person so much.

"Agwe's word!" she exclaimed when she reached for his hand to greet him and he pulled her into a hug. She disentangled herself from his arms at once. He was closer now to a man than a child, and with her on the verge of adulthood, she did not want to invite any insinuations.

"I'm sorry," Amos said, quickly. "I didn't think—"

There was a flurry of agitation among the crowd and, relieved, Pearl turned her attention to the balcony that jutted out from the temple's higher opening. The two guards flanking the entrance uncrossed their spears and the secretary, the viceroy's second-in-command, emerged, dressed in the lavish golden regalia that marked his station. He wore a look of consummate sorrow as he placed two webbed hands upon the decorated railing. As he stared down his nose at the masses before him, the furor died down to silence.

"My brothers and sisters," the secretary called grimly, "on this, the darkest of days, we bid farewell to our cherished leader, Viceroy Atlas Seastead. For fifty years, Viceroy Seastead has carried the well-being of this Settlement, the last remaining members of the holiest line, descended directly from Agwe Himself, upon his shoulders." He brought his gnarled hands to his own shoulders, holding the final sound in a long hiss. "His time to rest has come. May he find peace on the other side of the divide, and may his soul join with those of our ancestors whom Agwe saw fit to thrust into the heart of the sea to protect them from the devil's wrath. Brothers and sisters, we invite the children's choir to raise their voices in sacred song to honor Viceroy Seastead."

A ripple moved through the crowd as six children separated themselves from their families and floated into a circle before the congregation. Pearl joined them, thinking ruefully of how this might be her final performance with them. Brother Marshwind, her teacher and choirmaster, floated off to the side, his arms raised and ready to direct them. Once Pearl had found her place in the circle, she raised both hands to the level of her chest, like the other singers. Brother Marshwind brought his arms down, and all seven singers began their song.

The choir sang the first verse of the familiar hymn, their voices entwined, high and clear in a simple melody. Their hands moved as one, making the signs that accompanied the song. Just as the verse ended, the secretary raised his own hands to his chest and every member of the congregation did the same. When the second verse started, dozens of voices joined in. They offered up their praise through song. Their hands moved through the spaces before them in unison, creating the sacred signs that would help their words reach Agwe's realm. This was always Pearl's favorite part of school, and it would be her favorite part of temple service when she finally became an adult. She closed her eyes and felt peace swell within her chest. The song was brief, but the feeling remained, even as she let her arms drop back to her sides.

"Agwe be praised," the secretary called.

"Agwe be praised," Pearl repeated with the congregation, her eyes still closed to the outside world.

"Through his rising tide, all things are possible."

Nodding silently, Pearl placed a hand over her heart and let the truth in the secretary's words fill her until he spoke again.

"We give thanks to Brother Marshwind for guiding these gifted singers. May their purity help our songs reach Agwe's ears."

The six children dispersed and resumed their places with their families. Pearl returned to her spot next to Amos.

"Brothers and sisters," the secretary went on, "though our hearts are heavy with grief, tradition dictates that a new viceroy must be named." He brought his hands to his chest and adopted a look of prostration. "I humbly submit myself for your consideration. As is the custom of our people, anyone else who feels moved by Agwe's grace may also submit their name."

Murmurs rippled through the crowd like waves. Pearl looked around for Uncle Rain. Surely this was the perfect moment for his grand entrance. She felt someone's fingers curl around her upper arm. Looking up, she saw Uncle Wade frowning down at her, the intensity of his grip catching her by surprise.

"What is the matter?" she gasped.

Uncle Wade opened his mouth to speak, but the secretary raised his hands over his head, drawing everyone's attention.

"Brothers and sisters, I ask you to close your eyes and open your hearts to Agwe. Let Him speak to you and tell you if I am worthy of leading you to His kingdom!"

There was another ripple through the crowd. This time, it was one row of congregants after another bowing their heads in contemplation. Pearl hurried to do the same, but the only voice she heard when she closed her eyes was the secretary's.

"Agwe has spoken," he pronounced slowly. "Brothers and sisters, I thank you for your support. Agwe's legacy shall live on through me!"

"We need to go," Uncle Wade whispered into Pearl's ear, his grip on Pearl's arm tightening as he pulled her toward him. She opened her eyes, and together, they wove through the crowd of fellow attendees. As they broke free of the crowd and swam to one of the arches in the dome that led outside, Pearl wrenched her arm from Wade's grasp. She was nearly a woman grown. She did not need to be escorted anywhere, especially not by the arm.

"Pearl, we do not have time for this!" Wade said through gritted teeth.

"What is happening?" Pearl demanded. "Why are we leaving? You said Uncle Rain was—"

"We need to get you home, now!" Wade said sharply. He had never spoken to her like that before. What had she done to earn his ire? He noticed her hurt confusion and he softened. "Darling girl, I sometimes forget that you are no longer a child. This place is not safe. We must leave, at once. And it would be the greatest tragedy if anything were to happen to you. Please, come with me."

Pearl did not understand. What did he mean this place was not safe? This was the temple, her favorite place aside from their little home. She wanted to ask, but he was frantically scanning the crowd again, his jaw tense. She had never seen her uncle so scared. Slowly, Pearl nodded her assent. They took off, Pearl furiously pumping her tail fin to match her uncle's quick pace. They crossed the plain of seagrass and dove into the deep chasm from which they had come. Neither said a word until they had crossed the threshold of their dwelling and Uncle Wade had pulled shut the thick stone door that would keep prying eyes and ears at bay.

"Uncle Rain?" Pearl called out, her voice quavering as worry built up in her chest.

There was no reply.

"I told him not to go to that meeting," Wade muttered under his breath, swimming past her to the entrance of where he and Uncle Rain slept. He sat on the tattered sofa and ran his hand over the fraying red fabric that covered the arm, no doubt thinking of the day Uncle Rain had brought it home from the Shallows. Pearl thought he might curl up on the cushion. Instead, he sniffed hard, his face settling into a steely resolve, and straightened to his full height. Uncle Rain had often told Pearl stories of his and Uncle Wade's adventures as scavengers, braving the unknown depths of the sea to bring back supplies for their people. She had only ever seen Uncle Wade as Rain's softer half, but the man before her now was every bit as mighty as Uncle Rain's stories told.

"There are things at work in our settlement that you do not understand, Pearl," Wade repeated as he swam into the living area, where Pearl hovered and watched him. "Your Uncle Rain and I have tried to shield you from it, and perhaps that was our mistake, but you are on the cusp of adulthood now, and you deserve to know the truth." He sighed heavily, and Pearl waited for him to continue. "The stories we've been told . . ." he said slowly. "The ones about our ancestors—"

"Where is he?" Pearl interjected. "He was supposed to be at the funeral."

A pained look came upon Uncle Wade's face that Pearl understood but refused to accept. Then, it was gone.

"The stories we've been told are not entirely true," he went on.

"They told me you would do this," Pearl said, rubbing her stinging eyes.

"Do what?"

"Try to get me onto your thinking," she said. "My teacher said that now that I am almost an adult, you would try to convert me. Uncle Wade, you and Uncle Rain may not believe in Agwe, but I do, and nothing will ever change that!"

"Darling girl, listen to me," Uncle Wade said, and Pearl could tell he was trying hard to speak carefully. "You are being manipulated. The secretary has been working to make sure no one learns the truth, but Uncle Rain and I have—"

"That doesn't make sense." Pearl glided back from the living room and up against the wall. "The stories of our ancestors, of Agwe—they're the words we live by. They can't be . . . lies."

"I know it is a great matter to take in," Wade said gently, moving toward her and reaching out a hand.

Pearl looked down at it but did not take it.

"If what you say is true, why haven't you told me until now?"

"That was your Uncle Rain," Wade said. "He wanted to wait until you were old enough to understand. He wanted to give you the choice to decide what to believe for yourself."

Pearl thrust her fingers into her hair, digging her nails into her scalp as though doing so would keep her from being lost to the uncertainty swirling around the place where her faith used to be. She searched her mind for signs but saw no difference between the stories her uncles told her about their ancestors and the stories she had heard in school. She had believed what she had been told. What other choice had she had?

"This can't be," Pearl whispered, more to herself than to her uncle. She closed her eyes, held her hands at the level of her chest, and began moving them, making the intricate signs she knew to be the most direct way to commune with her Lord. When she reached into her heart and found only fear, she broke.

Uncle Wade swam up to her, took her hands in his own, and held them to his heart.

"I am doing this all wrong," Wade stammered, momentarily bringing her back to reality. "Let me try aga—"

"Wade Brinebottom!" called a stern male voice from the other side of the stone door. "Viceroy Triton Stormcoast would speak with you!"

Wade's voice dropped to a whisper.

"Damn it! They must have seen!" he hissed.

Pearl's heart began to pound.

"Pearl, go hide in your room. Do not come down until I tell you it is safe, no matter what you hear. Do you understand?" Pearl nodded. "I have to let them in. Go, now, Pearl!"

Without another word, Pearl pushed off from the rocky floor and swam up the narrow passage in the ceiling that led into her little room. There was just enough space for a bed made of scavenged fabrics and a small beaten-up chest that Uncle Rain had retrieved from the Shallows for her. There was nowhere for her to hide in the room, so she pressed her back against the cool stone wall and stayed quiet.

As she settled into place, she heard the newly sustained viceroy's voice carry up the tunnel from the living room, his words muffled but still audible.

"I thank you, Brother Brinebottom, for permitting me to intrude upon what I imagine was a tender moment with Brother Highwater's family," he said. "I had hoped to find you after the procession, but you had already left."

"Yes," Uncle Wade answered. "After the sustaining, Pearl became quite emotional. She was very attached to Viceroy Seastead. But, of course," he added quickly, "she feels nothing but the utmost joy at your assumption of his position."

"Of course," the viceroy repeated. "It is expected that the natural-born nurturers among us will feel loss more deeply. If young Sister Highwater grows half so fond of me as she was of Viceroy Seastead, I shall consider my tenure a success."

"I will be honored to pass along your concern, Viceroy."

"And where is Pearl? I thought I saw her at the funeral as well."

"At the Shallows, collecting trinkets with her uncle," Wade lied. "She said it would bring her peace to find something to remind her of Viceroy Seastead."

"Ah, yes, the infamous Rain Highwater. I was surprised not to see him with you today. Perhaps I simply missed him?"

Pearl could almost hear a smile on the new viceroy's lips as he spoke, and she wondered why he would be pleased by her uncle's absence.

"No," Uncle Wade replied stiffly. "He arrived too late to attend."

"Such a devoted servant of Agwe's must surely have a good reason for missing such an important occasion."

"You'll have to ask him when he gets back."

"Indeed," the viceroy said, and something in his tone gave Pearl the impression that he was not satisfied.

"I was hoping to have the whole family here," the viceroy went on, "but no matter. I'm sure you'll want to share the happy news when she returns. After laying Viceroy Seastead to rest, I retired to the Divine Chamber to commune with Agwe for the first time, to ask Him what my first act as viceroy should be. I received a vision, in answer, of myself leading our people toward their holy destiny with Pearl by my side."

"What?" Pearl and Wade both gasped.

There was a moment of silence during which Pearl held her breath.

"She is wise beyond her years, she is obedient," the viceroy went on. "Blessed with beauty, yet she resists the devil's temptation to vanity. She is a dutiful servant of Agwe and a gifted singer. She will make a perfect wife."

Wade cleared his throat. "Forgive me, Viceroy," he stammered nervously. "I must still be in the throes of my grief. Pearl is much too young and has no desire for temple service, noble work though it may be."

"Oh, no?" the viceroy asked almost playfully. "Is she not on the cusp of womanhood? She turns sixteen in just two days, if I am not mistaken. Brother Marshwind has already submitted a petition for initiation on her behalf. Perhaps it was a mistake?"

There was no mistake. Pearl had confessed to her teacher her desire to devote her life to the service of Agwe, had begged him to petition the viceroy on her behalf. She planned to perform the sacred rites that would bind her to the temple on her sixteenth birthday. Doing so would grant her access to the sacred texts by which her people lived. She had thought she would have had more time to prepare her uncles for her departure.

"It is very rare for a young woman to become a servant of Agwe," the viceroy went on. "We typically discourage them from petitioning at all in the hope that they choose to serve Agwe by strengthening our numbers. But Brother Marshwind says that Pearl is a rare jewel possessing a sharp mind and unshakable faith in our Lord of the Sea."

"Then, I am sure she will be honored to be considered."

"Not considered," the viceroy corrected. "Chosen. Called by Agwe Himself and when Agwe speaks, we must heed His word, lest our devotion to Him be called into question."

"Of course," Wade said quickly.

"Tell Pearl she is to report to the temple at first light."

"I thank you, Viceroy," Uncle Wade said with unfamiliar deference.

The viceroy said nothing in return. Pearl heard the faint sounds of movement coming from the lower level and assumed the viceroy was leaving, but she remained in her place, as she had promised she would. Half a dozen heartbeats later, her uncle's voice called to her from below.

"Come on out, darling girl!"

She swam through the little tunnel and joined him in the main room. He was smiling, but it was the same kind of smile her Uncle Rain had once used to reassure her that there was nothing to fear in the dark, the same smile that no longer worked on her.

"I don't want to marry him," she said quickly. "I want to work in the temple but I don't want to be his—"

"Never mind that," Uncle Wade replied. "We need to leave."

"Leave? Why?" Pearl asked as her tail fin brushed against the rocky surface.

"Because Stormcoast will know very soon that we lied. He may already know," he answered, looking deeply concerned.

"But where will we go? There is nothing but wilderness beyond the Settlement!"

Uncle Wade sighed. "West and then . . . the surface. Land. It's the only place they won't think to look for us, the only place they fear to go."

"But the curse!"

"Everything we've been told about Agwe so far has been a lie. It stands to reason that 'Agwe's Wrath' is just a story meant to scare our people away from traveling to land."

Pearl's upset must have shown on her face, because Uncle Wade straightened, swam across the living area, and took Pearl's face into his hands.

"I'm so sorry, darling girl," he said softly. "This is not how I wanted you to learn the truth."

She twisted out of reach. "Your truth," she said after putting some distance between them. Uncle Wade's eyes widened.

"I *know* Agwe lives," Pearl asserted.

"You heard what the viceroy said," Uncle Wade pleaded. "You know his intentions."

"People are fallible," Pearl said resolutely, "but Agwe is perfect and through Him, all will be made whole."

Uncle Wade was silent for a moment, breathing slowly as he considered her words.

"Your uncle met with Stormcoast to convince him not to submit himself for consideration," he said softly, his lip quivering slightly. Pearl knew what he was fighting, because she felt the same painful urge rising in her, too. "He wanted to offer Stormcoast a chance to preserve his dignity. He was supposed to be at the funeral, but I don't think—" His voice broke as a sob forced its way out of him. He quickly collected himself. "I don't think . . . he made it out of that building."

Pearl did not know what to say. Her uncle's insinuation about the viceroy's hand in Uncle Rain's disappearance was clear, and as much as she wanted to refute it, her own experience made it impossible. It was not just the way his eyes had lingered when she finished her lessons in the temple that gave her pause; it was the way he ordered the temple servants about when he did work on Viceroy Seastead's behalf, the way he looked down at them, as though already claiming his place in the highest seat. It was easy for Pearl to imagine him doing anything to ensure he reached his ambitions. She was certain if she tried to express all this, to accept this reality, she would fall apart. Thankfully, Uncle Wade spared her.

"I'm so sorry, my love," he apologized again. "We must get moving. They could come back at any moment."

"I'll pack my things," Pearl said, turning her body to push off the ground once again, but her uncle stopped her, placing a hand on her arm.

"We can't take anything with us," he said. "We can't arouse any suspicions."

"Let me take one thing," Pearl insisted. "I promise it will fit inside my robes."

Her uncle sighed, but eventually nodded his head in assent. Pearl pushed off the ground and climbed back into her bedroom. This time, she lifted the lid of the chest, reached in all the way to the bottom, and pulled out a weather-beaten conch shell that sat perfectly in the palm of her hand. Pearl squeezed her fingers around the shell and swam back down to her uncle.

"Uncle Rain gave this to me," she said, holding it out so Wade could see. "Do you know what it is?"

Uncle Wade's eyes went wide as he peered at the shell.

"He found it!" he whispered breathlessly. "When did he give this to you?"

"Two days ago," she replied. "He said it was an early birthday gift. What is it?"

"If it is what I think it is, it's the key to everything our people have worked toward. It was thought to have been lost since the time of our ancestors." His voice trailed off. "I can explain more when we get to the surface. For now, keep it hidden. It's not safe for anyone to know you have it."

Pearl did as she was told, stashing the shell in her robes' pocket.

"We need to leave now, while the coast is clear," Wade said as he stood watch by the rocky home's main entrance.

The reality of her situation began to creep through her brave face, and she felt the sour taste of fear on her tongue.

"Can we sing?" she asked as though she were a child in search of comfort from the shadows of the night once again. "I know you don't believe in the stories and Agwe"—her voice quavered at that realization—"but can we please sing—just one verse—like we used to?"

Her uncle swam toward her and put his hands on her shoulders.

"Of course, darling girl," he said. "You choose the song. I will follow your lead."

With the comforting weight of her uncle's hands on her shoulders, Pearl closed her eyes and tried to dig past her fear to find the song that would carry her through this ordeal. It was a quiet thing, sitting at the bottom of her heart, but she drew it out and filled her voice with it. Uncle Wade recognized the song at once and joined his voice with hers. Together, they sang the first verse of Pearl's favorite hymn, filling their home with a semblance of the peace they used to know. When the verse came to a close, Pearl placed her hands on her uncle's and held them still. She looked into the kind brown eyes that had watched over her for as long as she could remember.

"I love you," she said softly.

The lines around his mouth were just beginning to appear as he smiled, but quickly faded as Pearl saw his jaw tighten.

"Are you all right?" Pearl asked.

A thundering boom shook the house as something solid collided with the door. Pearl watched in horror as a web of cracks appeared in the center of the stone slab, reaching toward the edges like cracks in a mirror. Before Pearl could gasp, Uncle Wade took her face in his hands, forcing her to look at him. "Go! Swim west! Keep the shell safe! I will find you!"

He pushed her toward the ceiling in their living area. Pearl hit the stone as a second blow shattered the door and a wave of green-and-gold-clad guards rushed toward her uncle. She forced herself to look away and scrambled through the tunnel that led to her bedroom. Then, she hurled herself through the little window. Her skin and scales scraped against the edges of the opening the whole way, but she made it out.

"He is fine," she told herself as she swam frantically across the chasm and away from the Settlement. "He will find me. Keep swimming."

The words became a mantra that held her panic at bay long enough for her to navigate the miles of wilderness beyond the rim of the chasm. As she approached the edge of the shelf that gave way to the nothingness of the open sea, the panic caught her. Her Uncle Rain was likely dead, her Uncle Wade, fighting for his life against temple guards she had trusted all her life to keep her people safe.

She threw herself over the edge and let the darkness below swallow her, diving until she could not tell if her eyes were open or closed. Her hands itched with the urge to pray as she held fast to the craggy cliffside. She did not know if Agwe could even see her signs this far away from home, but she made them.

"Please," she begged, bowing her head and pressing her palm to her chest. She moved her hand in a circular motion again and again as she spoke the rest of her prayer. "Let him live. Let him find me."

There was no time to wait for peace to settle over her. She would have to settle for faith. With her arms outstretched, she beat her tail as hard as she could, propelling herself forward into the open ocean.

Four

LU

A single bead of sweat escaped from an eager Lieutenant Lu Ortega's temple. It traced a line down his dark brown skin to his jaw, where it hung until it could no longer bear its own weight and it fell to his shoulder. Sweat seeped into the chest binder he wore under his uniform as he stood dressed in his full captain's regalia. The noonday sun shone like a white-hot jewel against the clear blue sky. His body crackled with anticipation inside, but he stood with his back straight and his gaze hovering slightly above the small crowd of well-dressed spectators who had gathered for the ceremony. There were more eyes on him than he was comfortable with. The only alleviation was that he was not alone.

He was on a raised platform in the anterior courtyard of the Citadel, headquarters of the Fleet and his home for the last eight years. This space was usually reserved for the midshipmen's practice drills but had been transformed into an elegant outdoor reception hall in light of the special occasion. It was Conferral Day, and an unprecedented four of the Fleet's top lieutenants were rising to the rank of captain. Lu had only learned that morning that he would be counted among the conferees.

He had skipped breakfast in favor of riding down the mountain on which the Citadel perched to the Cape in search of a reputable haberdasher who was willing to make alterations to his newly acquired dress uniform in less than half of the usual time. Unsurprisingly, all had turned him away, and Lu had turned, instead, to old friends. The results were indistinguishable from a professional job, as far as Lu could tell, but he did not want to draw any more attention to himself than was absolutely necessary.

The commodore spoke at the lectern at the front of the platform, enthusiastically recounting the Fleet's long and storied history as the purveyors of law and order across Ayiti and in its surrounding waters. Lu had nothing but the utmost respect for the man but desperately wished he would just get to the important part. But each new captain's accomplishments in service to the Fleet had to be named before they could receive their medals.

Lu let his eye wander about the crowd of unfamiliar faces. An elderly woman in a bright pink dress and matching bonnet stood in the front row. Sweat poured from beneath the bonnet as she beamed with pride, and she stared not at the commodore, but at the lieutenant to Lu's right, Rochefort. This must have been his mother. Lu wondered how far the woman had traveled to see her son become a captain. He remembered Rochefort saying something about his family being fisherfolk on the southern end of the country. What must it be like to be so loved by one's blood?

Lu's toes began to ache in his too-small, borrowed shoes. He started to surreptitiously shift his weight from one foot to the other to alleviate the pain, but as he did so, he caught sight of an unfamiliar face at the back of the crowd. His blood ran cold. The man had pitiless dark eyes set deeply into a brown face whose upper half was painted bone white. Most of the guests wore polite smiles but this man's grin stretched wide, taking up the bottom half of his face and revealing an impossible jumble of teeth. As he stared at Lu, he slowly brought a hand to the tattered top hat he wore upon his head, took it by the brim, and doffed it in Lu's direction.

An elbow connected with Lu's side, and Lu turned to find Rochefort leaning ever so slightly toward him.

"Close your mouth," Rochefort hissed. "You look like an idiot!"

Embarrassed, Lu hastily righted himself. When he looked back at the crowd, the man was gone. The commodore eventually made it through each of the lieutenants' accomplishments, eventually pinned their medals on their uniforms, and eventually pronounced the lieutenants as official captains. As the crowd erupted in applause, Lu swelled with pride as a song rose in his heart and he forgot all about the specter he had seen.

The ceremony came to a close, and the ensemble composed of four men and three women took up a tune that Lu recognized but could not identify. Then the reception began. It took place under a large white tent that offered merciful shade, and the captains were released to join their loved ones. Rochefort went straight into the arms of his mother, who received him with a face full of kisses and heavily scented perfume. The other two captains found their families, as well. Lu, however, made his way to the refreshments table. He drained a glass of champagne, which did nothing for his physical discomfort, but it did alleviate some of his embarrassment, and he piled his plate high with sandwiches and cakes. All at once, he knew the song and grimaced slightly at what the singing group's bouncing voices had made of what should have been a somber melody.

"Quite the appetite, there, Ortega!" said a voice from behind him.

He whirled around and nearly dropped his plate of food.

"Commodore!" he gasped. Commodore Christophe was a man of nearly seventy years, though his carob-brown skin bore few signs of his age. His eyes were small and dark, barely a shade darker than his skin, and always seemed to sparkle as they sat on either side of his wide, hammer-shaped nose. He, too, had dressed for the occasion, sporting his heavily brocaded jewel-green-and-gold coat despite the heat. His commodore's cap sat neatly atop his head, covering his salt-and-pepper hair.

Lu cleared his throat. "I'm sorry, sir. I missed breakfast because I was—"

"No need to apologize, my dear boy!" the commodore said, waving away Lu's next words. "In fact, it is I who should apologize to you!"

"Whatever for, sir?" Lu asked.

The commodore's gravelly voice dropped to a conspiratorial whisper. "For the last-minute nature of your conferral," he answered. "I do hope you will be kind when you write to your family to tell them the happy news."

Lu did not know how to explain to the commodore that he had no family to write to . . .

"Between you and me," the commodore went on, "your name has been on the list for conferral for quite some time, especially with that glowing recommendation from Captain Abernathy in your first year as a lieutenant. So, when I received word of the unexpected, er"—his eyes shifted this way and that as he searched for the right word—"opening among our ranks, I seized the opportunity!"

He grabbed the air in front of him as though the opportunity were a tangible thing.

"Was it him, sir?" Lu asked, dropping his voice to a whisper as well. "The Devil of the Deep?"

"I believe so, though one can never be sure with pirates," the commodore replied with a slight incline of his head. "Now, tomorrow morning, you and the other new captains shall accompany me on a little excursion. No need to mention it to the other officers. Don't want to cause a stir."

"Yes, sir."

"Very good! The carriage will leave promptly at seven!"

At that moment, the commodore spotted one of the other conferees. With a final congratulatory pat on Lu's shoulder, he walked away, leaving Lu teeming with excitement.

The reception showed every sign of continuing through the night, but as soon as the sun began to dip below the horizon, Lu slipped away from the party and took up his mount once again. He rode down the winding mountain road to the nearly deserted streets of the Cape, stopping only when he reached the harbor that separated the city from the sea. Lu dismounted his horse and tied her reins to a post. Then, he knelt on the wooden slats and began the painstaking work of unlacing his boots.

He breathed a sigh of relief when his feet were finally free of them. The scrubbed wood felt cool and rough under his bare feet as he walked along the planks that were so worn by salt water and time that they seemed to bounce with his every step. Lu walked by one fishing boat after another until he found the right vessel.

"Permission to come aboard?" he called to the kneeling figure in the boat.

A gray-haired man dressed in tan fishing clothes jumped to his feet and leaned over the side of the boat.

"Well, well, well! Look at what the tide's brought in!" Emmanuel Millet, whom everyone knew as Manou, gestured to an imaginary audience. "A *captain* of the Fleet has seen fit to grace the fishermen's side of the harbor!"

His voice was throaty and rough. Hearing it made Lu break into his first genuine smile of the day. Lu held up the boots.

"I'm returning these!" he announced.

"Don't just stand there," Manou said. "Bring them aboard and let me have a look at you!"

Lu did as he was told, vaulting over the fishing boat's rail to join his friend on the other side. The moment he stepped foot on the vessel, Manou took hold of his shoulders and angled him toward the dying light.

"You did it! You really did it!"

"I wish you could've been there, Manou," Lu said.

"No room for fisherfolk at fancy Fleet to-dos," Manou chuckled. "But you, my boy! You are the real deal!"

Manou took the boots from Lu and placed them on the deck.

"Thank you, Manou," Lu said, "and please tell Mai I said thank you for the alterations."

They shared one more embrace and Lu felt a song rise in his heart. Without thinking, he brought his hand to his chest.

"You feel it, too. Don't you, son?" Manou asked when he released Lu.

"No," Lu lied quickly. "It's just the bones in this old binder poking me in the chest. I might need a new one, soon."

"Well, you let Mai know when you need it and she'll have it ready for you," Manou replied.

"You know, now that I'm a captain, I make more than enough to pay her for—"

"Family doesn't pay," Manou said sharply.

Lu smiled. "I have to get back to the Citadel," he said.

"Of course," Manou replied. "Don't forget about us fisherfolk on your way to the top of the Fleet."

Manou saluted as Lu made his way off the boat. The old

man made two fists and drew them together at his navel. Then he brought one hand, with two of his fingers extended, to his forehead, trailed the hand down his nose and back up and out toward Lu. Lu returned the sign, beaming with pride, and turned to leave. As Lu walked away, Manou's voice, deep, low, and as beautiful as a dove's call, followed him all the way back to his horse, singing the old fisherman's hymn that he had taught Lu on their first voyage together. The Fleet's band had played this same song with the fanfare of drums and horns, but it was this version, simple and quiet, that touched Lu's heart. The song he had denied feeling on the boat came back to him, and he could not help but hum the old tune throughout his return to the Citadel.

Five

PEARL

"I don't think I can do it, Uncle Rain!" Pearl called to her uncle. He floated above the rocky terrain on the other side of the chasm that separated their property from the rest of the Settlement, his tail flipping back and forth to keep him aloft. He was miniature in the distance, but Pearl could see him smiling wide enough for two deep dimples to form in his pale brown cheeks.

"It's all right, darling girl," he called back. "I won't let anything happen to you."

"It's too far and too dark and . . . I just can't," she said, her eyes fixed on the nothingness she was certain would swallow her whole.

She had spoken too softly for him to have heard, but somehow he had known she needed him. When she tore her eyes away from the chasm, he was already swimming across the divide to join her.

"Sing with me," he said.

"That's not going to work," Pearl replied.

"Try it," her uncle insisted. "Trust me."

He took her hands in his and raised them to the ready position. Even though she refused to make eye contact with her uncle, Pearl kept her hands where he had put them. She let him choose the hymn, and when he began to sing, her hands moved almost of their own accord to make the signs that went along with the song. It was her favorite hymn, the one that told of Agwe's promise to His sea-dwelling children.

She felt the song swell in her heart and joined her uncle on the second verse. Her body began to sway, and before she knew it, she and her uncle were floating above the ground. The song carried them over the great chasm, all the way to the other side.

"I did it!" Pearl exclaimed when she realized what she had done.

"You did it, darling girl," her uncle said, smiling with pride. "Your parents would be proud to see how you've grown up."

Pearl frowned as tears welled in her eyes. She had not even thought of her parents while she sang.

"What's wrong?" Uncle Rain asked, tilting up her chin.

"I'm starting to forget them. I can barely remember Ma's face anymore, or Da's voice."

Uncle Rain sighed. "Worry not, darling girl. What you carry of them will be enough. You will know them in whatever awaits us after this life."

"But what if I get to Agwe's kingdom and there is nothing left of them in me? What if I have already changed so much that they will not recognize me? I was barely a child when they died."

"That will not happen," Uncle Rain said firmly.

Pearl wanted to ask how he could be so sure, but she read the worry behind his kind smile. He wanted her to be comforted, and so she decided she would be.

•••●•••

Pearl had been a child, then.

She was fairly certain she was an adult now. How many times

had the moon and the sun chased each other out of the sky as she swam? At least twice, she thought. She could barely keep her eyes open, could barely move her arms and tail to keep herself afloat, but even as she stared at the sunken part of a landmass that could be her refuge, she froze with fear.

She was closer to the surface than she had ever been. If she reached out, her hand would cross the divide. One push and she would breach the veil. The scriptures said death awaited those who wandered beyond the boundaries of Agwe's protection. Her Uncle Wade said the scriptures were lies and Agwe was not real. But Pearl had felt Agwe's love. It could not have all been lies.

"If I die, I'll be with Agwe and the ancestors. And my parents," she reasoned. "And if I live, I'll be safe on the surface."

It was a hope in either direction. Before she could talk herself out of it, she pushed herself upward and broke through the water.

The gills behind her ears sealed shut the moment they touched the air, and Pearl gasped as they knitted painfully into scar tissue. Something inside her chest expanded painfully. New muscles strained against the pull. Clutching her chest, Pearl fought to keep in whatever was forcing itself out of her. The longer she held it, the tighter and more painful her chest grew. When she could no longer hold it back, she exhaled, pushing an agonizing current of air and water from her body.

Pearl threw herself back under the waves and tried to swim down, but her body was changing too quickly. The webs between her fingers dissolved. Her tail split before her eyes, shedding its scales as it mutated into two long, gangly flesh-covered legs that flailed wildly under her robes. A massive swell of water took her up and carried her toward the shore. Her new limbs buckled when she hit sand, and she instinctively dug her hands in, desperately swallowing air as she hunched over on all fours. The water receded, and Pearl feared it would pull her along with it. She scrabbled up the beach to where the wet, packed sand gave way to soft white powder—far from the waves' reach—and threw herself onto her back.

Sunlight nearly blinded her, and when she threw an arm up to block the glare, Pearl noted with disgust how the air raised little bumps all over her skin. It had lost all of its slickness, and she was now soft and brown all over, with feet instead of a tail fin and legs instead of her beautiful green tail. Her lip quivered as tears stung her eyes. She quickly sat up, wiping her face, and raised her hands to her chest. Her body may have been strange, but she was alive and she would give thanks. A song rose in her heart at once, as though she had called it, and she readied her hands to make the signs that would allow her to commune with Agwe.

"Lord of the Sea, my god, my king," she signed, but when she tried to push out the hymn's melody, her throat tightened and she made no sound.

"No!" she tried to say, grasping her throat with one hand.

The word never made it past her lips. She could not speak. She could not sing. Uncle Wade had been wrong. Agwe's curse was real, and it was much worse than death.

Six

LU

The Citadel was a stone fortress that topped Ayiti's tallest peak. Its thick gray walls stood in stark opposition to the soft greenery that surrounded it, ever prepared to face any oncoming threats. Occupying over a hundred thousand square feet, the stronghold housed every member of the Fleet in the north district of Ayiti, from the commodore, who led the organization, to the lowly midshipmen, who were just beginning their journeys in order and justice.

At a quarter to seven in the morning, Lu dipped a knee before the golden trident affixed to the wall above his door and walked out of his dormitory suite on the fourth floor. Exhausted, but proudly dressed in his dark green captain's coat and crisp white trousers, he descended the spiraling stone staircase until he reached the main floor. When he emerged from the double front doors, he found the carriage the commodore had promised would be waiting. Its wide black body sat atop four sturdy wheels, gleaming as its golden trim caught the light of the rising sun. The coachman sat in a shallow seat at the front, hunched over his clasped hands and staring at a string of four of the most magnificent horses Lu had ever seen.

Ignoring the envious looks from passing midshipmen, Lu approached the carriage. The coachman sprang to life, while the footman jumped to the ground and took the door in one hand. He pulled it open, and Lu was greeted by a smiling Commodore Christophe.

"Please, pardon my late arrival, Commodore," Lu said as he climbed onto the luxuriously upholstered bench seat, sliding all the way to the end to sit directly across from the commodore.

"Nonsense," the commodore replied. "The other new captains could do with taking a page out of your book!"

"I must say I have looked forward to this trip since I was a midshipman, sir," Lu offered.

"Naturally," Christophe laughed, "but I promise you the rumors do not do this experience justice."

It was well-known among the lower ranks that once a lieutenant achieved the rank of captain, they received much more than a ship and a new title. Lu could count the number of captains he had seen conferred on one hand, and they all kept whatever transpired on this trip to themselves. Lu had his theories, of course, and some of what he had guessed was confirmed by his captain's manual, but neither whispers nor written words could complete the picture.

Two of Lu's comrades, Toussaint and Boyer, arrived within minutes. Lu was not surprised to see them both looking exhausted. He had overheard their celebration continue long after the reception had ended. They looked as though they had managed to pull themselves together, but the smell of rum that wafted into the coach as Toussaint followed Boyer in was strong. Lu fought not to react. Once they were settled, Lu could see they were both a bit pale in the face. He smiled sympathetically until he noticed the commodore frowning and quickly righted his face.

The fourth captain and last to arrive was Rochefort. He ran down the steps just as the clock struck seven, frantically tucking in his shirt under his unbuttoned coat and stepping awkwardly due to his unlaced boots.

"My sincerest apologies, sir," Rochefort huffed as he climbed into the carriage.

The commodore said nothing. When the door finally closed behind Rochefort, Commodore Christophe knocked on the carriage's ceiling twice, signaling for the coachman to depart. It had been a long time since Lu had ridden in a carriage. He had lived in the dormitories at the Citadel from the day he had joined the Fleet, but prior to that, his life had been drastically different. Lu did not like to remember those days.

The carriage wound down the mountain path and trundled onto the irregular dirt roads that crisscrossed through Milot, the rural commune composed of humble stone-and-straw dwellings that housed Ayiti's fisherfolk and sugar farmers. Lu knew this area. He had visited one of these houses just the day before. He wondered if they were stopping to see someone here, but the carriage continued its steady progress. Eventually, the houses became farther and fewer between as they neared Gonaïves, on Ayiti's western shore.

"Have you invited us to a day at the beach, sir?" Rochefort asked, laughing.

"Show some respect, Rochefort," the commodore scolded. "This is a most sacred matter."

"We're going to the temple," Lu muttered in a moment of realization as he stared out the window.

"The temple?" Toussaint asked.

"Don't be silly," Rochefort laughed as Lu was about to repeat himself. "There are no temples in Ayiti."

"It's in the manual," Boyer said, and Lu was glad not to have been the only one who had read the captain's manual that was on his desk after the ceremony. Boyer leaned back in his seat with his eyes closed. It seemed Toussaint had recovered, but Boyer still looked as though sickness could overtake him at any moment.

"Well spotted!" Commodore Christophe exclaimed, clapping once. "You've already started learning the Fleet's true history!"

Unlike the manuals he had studied as a midshipman and a lieutenant, the captain's manual was a soft-covered, leather-bound tome with gilded pages. Intrigued, Lu had flipped through the introductory chapters. He had expected to find rules and regulations, but the first chapter had been a story. There was a man from long ago, a fisherman, who lived in a shack on the western shore and was taken by the sea. His people thought he had drowned, but on the day they gathered at the beach to sing to his soul, he washed onto the sand on a swell.

"I have seen Agwe," the man said. "I have seen our destiny!"

Lu understood from his lessons that the Fleet performed Agwe's work, keeping the land orderly for His return, but never knew that it had been Agwe Himself who had inspired the fisherman to found the Fleet.

Before Lu could ask for more information, the carriage ride came to an abrupt halt.

"We carry on from here on foot!" the commodore announced. The door opened, and the company climbed out of the carriage. Lu was the last to exit.

Commodore Christophe bid the company to follow him. He stepped not down the road, but into the tall grass growing along its edge. There must have been a path, but it was perceptible perhaps only to those who knew it well. Commodore Christophe seemed to be one such individual. He led the company through the winding path of the grass that tickled their elbows. Boyer and Toussaint flanked Lu, and the three of them fell behind as Rochefort stayed in step with the commodore.

"Lieutenant Ambroise said Captain Hidalgo once let slip that the ceremony was a human sacrifice," Toussaint said in a hushed voice. "She said everyone took off their clothes and—"

"Antoinette!" Boyer gasped.

Toussaint tutted. "I'm simply preparing you for what's to come. Wouldn't you rather know, Stephan?"

The familiarity with which they addressed each other made Lu wonder if there was something more than comradery between them, and he felt an old wound ache as he remembered that he, too, had once felt friendship bloom into love. But she had been lost to the sea long ago.

"There probably won't be any sacrifice," Lu said, chuckling. "The manual tells the story of the fisherman, the Fleet's first commodore. We will probably sing praise and honor him as we recommit ourselves to doing Agwe's work."

"Fine," Boyer said, keeping his eyes on Toussaint, "but if I catch even a whiff of a knife, I will walk back to the Citadel if I have to."

Lu and Toussaint laughed. Eventually, they caught up to Commodore Christophe and Rochefort at the remains of a thatched-roof seaside hut.

The commodore had stopped, admiring the little building. "Magnificent," he breathed in wonder. Lu spotted Rochefort and Toussaint exchanging glances. Rochefort looked skeptical. Toussaint looked concerned. Of course, they would not understand. They had not read the manual. But Lu had. This was the fisherman's home, from which he had spread Agwe's message. The fisherman's devotion to Agwe was so powerful that he was able to convince others to join him and form the Fleet. He was a true prophet.

Lu walked past the other three captains and stood beside the commodore. “And though the fisherman had long returned to the sea, his humble home stood tall in his memory,” he recited.

Both men bowed their heads in a moment of shared solemnity.

“Ass kisser,” Rochefort muttered under his breath.

Lu ignored him.

They walked around the shack, and Lu was surprised to see that the front door was still intact, but rather than going inside, the commodore gathered them before it. He stood with his back straight, ready to address the small company. Lu attempted to stand behind his fellow captains but froze when Commodore Christophe laughed.

“Don’t be silly, Ortega! With me!”

Lu did not know whether the flush that crept up his neck and to his face was from pride or embarrassment, but he took the offered spot next to his commanding officer, avoiding the looks from the other captains. Rochefort pushed his way to a spot in the center of the three remaining captains, standing directly in front of the commodore.

“Be careful you don’t trip over your creatively laced boots, Rochefort,” the commodore said, glancing down at the man’s footwear. Laughter erupted from everyone except Lu and Rochefort.

The commodore turned and ran a hand over the time-softened wood to the side of the door.

Then he grasped the handle and pushed until it groaned open, wood scraping against wood. He stepped through the doorway without preamble, and arriving at the center of the small one-room shack, he motioned for the others to join him. Lu attempted to cross the threshold next, but a large hand on his chest pushed him back, and Rochefort, Toussaint, and Boyer entered before him. As he finally took his turn, he pulled the door closed behind him.

"This is where it all happened," the commodore said, his voice hushed in awe. "The fisherman returned to his empty home after his days in the sea with Agwe to create the Fleet."

"But, sir, how can that be possible?" asked Rochefort. "No one can survive three days in the sea."

"If Agwe willed it so, then it was," Christophe answered sternly. "Through the might of the tide, all things are possible."

Lu looked around at the cramped space. He expected to see signs of someone having lived there—a bed, a table, old linens, wooden dishes—but there were only the four walls made of the same scrubbed wood as the exterior and a wardrobe that stood painfully out of place with its lacquered modernity. It felt unnatural for a fisherman's home to be so devoid of the warmth he knew fisherfolk homes to contain. Quilts and fishing nets should have hung from the walls, fishing supplies should have littered the floor, and the smell of fresh fish should have permeated the air. Instead, the cabin was clean, as though someone had cleansed it of its former purpose in favor of this uncomfortable sterility.

The commodore pulled the door of the wardrobe open and drew from it a length of white-and-gold fabric. He threw the garment over his shoulders with a flourish, pulling a hood over his salt-and-pepper hair, nearly obscuring his face. "You may think that the most prestigious duty of a Fleet captain is the command of a ship and the performance of Agwe's work upon the sea," he said excitedly, "but *this* is the true honor." He reached into the robes and grabbed the handle of one of his daggers. It was only then that Lu noticed that it had been replaced with something far more ornate than his usual service weapon. “The time has finally come for you to learn the truth of our destiny, but first, you must demonstrate your devotion.”

He pulled the blade from its sheath with a swish of metal against leather and held it in the air, smiling expectantly at the confused faces looking back at him. A line from the manual floated into Lu’s mind as he gazed at the golden blade.

“‘The true God of the Sea, Agwe, will bless with greatness those who sacrifice that which is most precious,’” he recited softly, but the commodore heard and his smile broadened.

“Precisely, my boy,” he said. “You have heard that the Fleet are the might of Agwe, but have you never wondered exactly what that might is for?”

“For the promotion of law and order throughout Ayiti and its waters,” Rochefort recited verbatim from the lieutenant’s handbook.

“That is far from the whole of the truth,” the commodore replied. “Today you will learn the true meaning of devotion.”

The commodore reached his empty hand into the robes and pulled out a pure white scallop shell the size of his palm.

“Oh, Agwe, great God of the Sea!” he intoned to the ceiling as he held the objects at arm’s length toward the captains. “I bring you four more souls, ready and willing to sacrifice to you the precious gift of their blood as a covenant of service.”

Without looking down, the commodore passed the dagger to Lu, who took it by its handle. It was lighter than expected, and the tip of the blade was needle sharp.

It’s just a bit of ceremony, he thought. *Harmless pageantry, that’s all.*

Before he could talk himself out of it, he ran the tip of the blade across his open palm. At first, he felt nothing and saw only the empty line he had carved into his hand. Then, the blood came, thick and dark, pooling in his palm. Suddenly, his hand stung. He quickly passed the dagger to Toussaint on his left, and took hold of his own wrist to steady his bleeding hand.

Toussaint took the knife and ran it across her palm, just as Lu had done. She gasped as her own wound opened. Rochefort was next, and with all the foolhardiness of a man with something to prove, he took the knife and pressed the blade into his palm, uttering not a single word, even as his blood dribbled to the wooden floor. Boyer was last. His light brown face turned a nasty shade of puce, and he stepped back from the group.

"You may walk away, Boyer, but, should you refuse to make this covenant, the doors of the Citadel will be forever closed to you," Commodore Christophe said. "It seems too high a price for a little bit of blood."

For a moment, Lu thought Boyer might run, but the conflict in his eyes settled into resolve. He stepped forward and took the dagger from Rochefort, grimacing as he carefully sliced into his own palm. Then, he handed the blade to the commodore, who nodded and smiled with fatherly affection. Steeling himself with a deep breath, Commodore Christophe raised the shell high above his head, and Lu watched, wondering if he was supposed to do something next. Then he felt the tingling in his palm; the blood in his hand was moving. He looked up to see if anyone else's blood was behaving in the same way and found his three fellow captains gawking at their palms. The tingling grew stronger. Lu felt a pull from the center of his wound.

"Agwe be with me," he heard Boyer whimper from the other side of the room.

Their blood floated in thin crimson lines, reaching from their hands to the shell as though it were being called. The commodore dropped the shell to the height of his chest. He stepped to Lu, dipping his thumb into the pool of blood in the shell's hollow, and Lu noticed the sheen of sweat across his brow.

"Make your oath," the commodore said, his voice quavering slightly, as he pressed his bloody thumb to Lu's forehead.

"All that I am is Agwe's," Lu whispered.

The commodore placed his hand over Lu's injured one.

"Agwe will make whole those in His service."

Lu felt the invisible tingle intensify in his palm. When the commodore lifted his hand, neither a drop of blood nor a scar remained where Lu's wound had once been. He let go of his wrist and watched the commodore visit Toussaint, Rochefort, and Boyer in turn. Each made the same promise and received the same reward.

"You are now bound to Agwe," the commodore said, returning to the center of the room and placing the shell on the floor. "Everything you do, from this point forward, will be in service to Him. Beneath Ayiti's very waters, there exists a hidden people. Over the last several decades, the Fleet have become their ally. We have provided them with resources and, in doing so, we earn our place by Agwe's side when he spreads His kingdom throughout the world."

None of the captains answered. Christophe turned back to the wardrobe, this time opening both doors and standing aside to reveal the interior.

"So, what's that, then?" Rochefort asked bluntly.

There was a large circular mirror fastened to the back wall, gold and ornate, just like the handle of the dagger.

"This is how we communicate with our brothers and sisters in the sea," the commodore answered.

"How does it work?" Lu asked.

The commodore took his place in front of the mirror and made a series of gestures that forced Lu to stifle a gasp. He had used a sign of the fisherfolk, the secret language of the sea. Lu had never seen anyone outside of the fisherfolk use it. When the commodore completed the sign, his reflection disappeared, replaced by the image of a dark, cave-like room. He stood aside for the others to see.

"This is where the viceroy comes to me with messages," he said, "where he states his need for weapons, clothes, and any other resources he and his people might need. They are the Chosen of Agwe, and they await His return."

A pale face appeared in the mirror, narrow and weathered with bulging eyes. He bobbed slightly, and his slicked-back gray hair seemed to float around his ears. He wore a set of robes identical to the commodore's. Commodore Christophe noticed the man's arrival at once and resumed his place before the mirror.

"My brother," the commodore said, "our most sacred work continues. These four new captains have made their sacrifice and pledged themselves to Agwe."

"The induction will have to wait, brother," the man in the mirror said. "We need your help!"

"What has happened?"

"We have found Agwe's conch—"

The commodore's eyes widened. His body stiffened.

"Show it to me!" he demanded.

"It has been stolen by a young girl from the Settlement named Pearl Highwater," the man in the mirror said, looking away momentarily. "She absconded with the shell two days ago. Our guards are tirelessly searching the waters, but we fear she may have fled to land! Use your ships to find her, brother!"

"We will apprehend this thief and retrieve Agwe's treasure!

In the meantime, prepare your people. Once we find the conch, we shall finally bring about our destiny!"

"I thank you, my brother," the man replied. Lu assumed this meant the end of the conversation, but the man's hands began to fly before him, making more fisherfolk signs. "When you find the girl, make sure no harm befalls her. Agwe has promised her to me."

The commodore raised his eyebrows but said nothing. He made a fist and thumped it over his heart. The man in the mirror mimicked the gesture, ending their exchange before he disappeared. The commodore made another gesture, and the mirror returned to its original state. He turned to face the company.

Lu closed his mouth, which had fallen open as he had watched their conversation, to hide the fact that he had understood every word.

"Men, we have a mission on our hands!" the commodore proclaimed. "We must retrieve a sacred object from the hands of a thief! She was traveling toward the Seven Isles by sea, and has likely taken refuge on one of the islands of the eastern archipelago. Rochefort, as soon as we return, you will take the *Adoration* east to find this girl. Handle her with care. She is something of a protégé to the viceroy."

"Yes, sir," Rochefort replied, snapping to attention.

"And, of course, all of what you have witnessed here is of the utmost sanctity! Not a word to anyone, am I clear?"

The four captains answered in salute, and Lu's stomach turned.

"Return to the carriage. I shall meet you there shortly."

Lu made to follow the order with the others, but the commodore's hand upon his shoulder kept him back.

"How are you feeling, Ortega?" the commodore asked as he removed the ceremonial robes.

"Truthfully, sir," Lu answered, "I don't know how to feel. The things I have seen today . . ."

"Today, you have learned the truth! The world is not as mundane as it may seem, and you, dear boy, are in the heart of it all. You have more potential in the nail of your littlest finger than they have combined." He waved a hand at the door, referring to the other three captains.

"Sir?"

"As commodore, it is my right to name my successor. Between you and me, I've already found the man. If it is Agwe's will, I will have years and years to train him so that when I join Agwe's kingdom, I know I'll be leaving the Fleet in safe hands."

Lu could not believe what he was hearing. He had been a captain for one day, had only just come to grips with the reality of his new responsibilities. Now the commodore, the man whose career he had idolized since he had joined the Fleet, wanted to train him to be the next commodore one day. The excitement Lu had tamped down in preparation for this trip threatened to burst out of him.

"Surely, there is a better man for the job," Lu said.

"Are you questioning my judgment, Ortega?"

"Of course not, sir."

"Then, the matter is settled. I have kept a close eye on you since Commodore Graves named me his successor. You have the makings of a great captain and an even greater commodore, as long as you commit yourself fully to Agwe. Can you do that, son, or have I wasted my time?"

"I—I can," Lu stammered, almost too stunned to speak. "I can."

"Then, I have more to ask of you."

Lu straightened. "Sir?"

"You will learn more of this in your manual, but the sacred object alone is not enough to bring our destiny to fruition. Agwe also needs the purest voices raised in adoration to break through the barrier between our world and the Unknown. It is one of the captains' responsibilities to find such singers so that, when the time comes, Agwe may call upon them."

Lu thought of the seven singers at the conferral ceremony. "Can we not hire singers when the time comes?" he asked.

Commodore Christophe chuckled, patting Lu on the back. "Not just any singers will do," he explained. "These voices must be truly extraordinary. They must be able to reach into the soul."

This piqued Lu's interest, for he was no stranger to song. All of the fisherfolk sang. Lu had grown used to Manou's singing, but he was certain no one had a voice like his. He was not sure about his soul, but he was certain Manou had, on multiple occasions, gotten to the heart of the matter when Lu was upset more quickly with a song than with a spoken word. What better way to follow through on his promise to Manou than with a chance to sing for Agwe Himself.

"I know of someone, sir," Lu said excitedly. "He is a friend of mine. Man—I mean Emmanuel Millet. He is a fisherman, and his voice is exactly as you say!"

"Indeed?" the commodore asked. "Would this friend of yours be opposed to a little performance?"

"Surely not," he answered, thinking of how pleased Manou would be to learn that he would be performing for the commodore.

"Then, send a message with my secretary tonight! Tell your man to expect us tomorrow morning."

"Yes, sir!"

When the company returned to the Citadel, just before

dinner, Lu did not wait to put pen to paper. He hastily scrawled a note explaining the commodore's intention to visit their home and addressed it to Manou and Mai. Then, on his way to the senior officers' dining room, he found Christophe's secretary—a striking young lieutenant named Ambroise—and handed her the note with instruction to leave at once.

Later that night, when Lu was finally able to retire to his suite, he devoured every page of his captain's manual, desperate to learn everything he could about Agwe and the Fleet's great destiny.

Seven

NNENNA

Nnenna sat stiffly upon a makeshift throne on the porch of Yamaye's rowdiest tavern. Celebratory drums and horns filled the night air in her honor. She was freshly washed, her sun-darkened brown skin and recently retwisted bloodred locs finally free of all traces of the filth that had accumulated since her last furlough. She had also traded her usual sweat-stained shirt and worn black trousers for a sumptuously silky corseted red gown that she had claimed from the *Reverence*'s hold. What any Fleet beetle would be doing with such fine clothing was still a mystery to her.

"To the Devil of the Deep!" her first mate, a dark-eyed, dark-skinned, muscular, and devastatingly handsome young woman by the name of Tinou Olivier, toasted over the din. The rest of the crew, scattered around the bonfire blazing on the beach, raised a motley combination of pilfered receptacles that ranged from wooden steins to crystal goblets. Nnenna laughed as she spotted her boatswain holding aloft what was clearly a recently emptied urn and hoped to the seven that he had cleaned it before filling it with wine.

Nnenna's seat, a straight-backed chair with leather cushions and gilded legs, was her crew's tribute—a place of honor for their "Queen of the Sea" while they brought her treasures from their latest haul to inspect. She could have done without all the ceremony. She was exhausted and certain she could trust Tinou to ensure that the treasure was divided properly among the crew. But this was Yamaye, the hidden island refuge known only to those who made their living on the sea, and certain customs had to be observed.

"You've made rich men of us all," Tinou's deep voice murmured into Nnenna's ear as she stood beside her and replaced her captain's spent ale with a fresh one.

"And what will you make me in return?" Nnenna asked playfully.

"Very, very happy," she replied with a knowing smile, and Nnenna instantly perked up.

"What do you know?"

"There's talk of a Fleet ship roaming the eastern archipelago."

"Another one?"

"They say the Fleet is searching for a pearl."

"A pearl?" Nnenna asked, perplexed. "The ocean is littered with pearls. What pearl could be so precious that they would risk coming into our territory?"

"I don't know, but I'm eager to find out."

Nnenna smiled and drank deeply from her cup. "Tinou," she said upon resurfacing, "once again, you've been true to your word. I am, indeed, very happy." She got to her feet. "Spread the word: We set sail at dawn!"

"And why must I be the one to spoil their revels?" Tinou asked, wincing at the thought.

Nnenna turned from her first mate and glanced at the petite young woman with whom she had been exchanging flirtatious looks—the one whose bright red rouge made her lips all the more enticing—as she had danced around the fire. Her voice had risen above the beating drums like a bird soaring over crashing waves, adding a sweet melody to the cacophony. She had drawn Nnenna's attention again and again for the last hour. No longer able to resist the call, Nnenna tilted her head toward the tavern door. The young woman smiled and started walking.

"Because I shall be indisposed," Nnenna said, her gaze set firmly upon her companion as she handed her half-drained cup back to Tinou. She strode over to meet the young woman.

"That is a lovely shade," Nnenna purred, tracing a finger along the gentle curve of the woman's plump bottom lip.

"I heard the most fearsome pirate of all the Seven Isles has a penchant for red. I wanted to make sure he noticed me."

"And what do you think, now that *she's* noticed you?"

The woman turned her head so that Nnenna cradled her cheek, and smiled. "I think I'd like to take you upstairs and show you what else I have on that's red."

"What's your name?"

"Aline."

"Come with me, Aline."

With a wicked grin, Nnenna took Aline by the hand and led her through the tavern door, weaving through the dining room and up the stairs that led to the rented rooms. She walked right past the budget-rate rooms and straight to the one at the end of the hall, the best the tavern had to offer.

"A room fit for a queen," Aline said, turning to face Nnenna.

Nnenna took two steps forward and closed the gap between them. "And what about a devil?" she asked.

Aline smiled. "I'm sure a devil could make do."

Nnenna leaned forward and pressed her lips against Aline's

in exactly the way she had imagined doing all evening. Without breaking their kiss, they let themselves into the room, and finally behind closed doors, Nnenna relieved her new companion of every stitch of clothing on her person, red and otherwise.

Aline's body was a bright spot of beauty in the grimness in which Nnenna had lived since the last time she made landfall. Absent the layers of fabric and stiff underclothing, Aline was a paradise of sweet-smelling smooth skin and soft curves. As Nnenna freed herself from her own clothing, she feasted upon Aline with her eyes, eagerly consuming Aline's delicate features, stoking her own desire. The moment Nnenna stepped out of her gown, now a red pool of satin on the floor, Aline reached for her, and Nnenna closed the divide between them to kiss Aline once more.

They fell into bed together, their bodies undulating atop the luxurious bedding, already seeking to connect their tender flesh. The yearning Nnenna kept at bay while at sea suddenly demanded satisfaction.

"I want to taste you," she purred into Aline's ear as she gently laid the woman's arms over her head.

She pressed her lips to Aline's neck and shoulders first, relishing the way her ministrations made Aline's breath hitch and her body writhe. Inspired, Nnenna moved to Aline's chest, cupping Aline's small breasts and running her tongue in slow circles over each of her dark nipples in turn. Nnenna's adept hand ventured downward to coax Aline's thighs apart in search of the treasure that lay between them.

The moans and sighs Nnenna's fingers elicited could have been music, another song just as beautiful and intoxicating as the one that had first drawn her to Aline. Every stroke drew a new note, and every sound made Nnenna desperate to hear more. Unable to hold off any longer, Nnenna traded her hand for her mouth, working her way down Aline's body until she could bow her head over Aline's waiting heat. Nnenna's tongue danced within the slick warmth of Aline's beautiful folds' tender flesh, and when Aline's cries grew louder and more insistent, a new song rose from deep within Nnenna.

"That's it," Aline breathed, her voice high and quavering as Nnenna was especially attentive to the now swollen knot amidst her folds. "There!"

Nnenna strummed Aline with her tongue as though she were her instrument, deft strokes extracting note after delicious note of pleasure in the moonlit room. When Aline took Nnenna's head in hand, burying her fingers into Nnenna's hair, Nnenna knew Aline was near to her undoing. The desire to sing pulsed in Nnenna's throat, and this time, she indulged, releasing the lilting melody in sighs. The gentle vibrations of Nnenna's humming against her sex pushed Aline over the edge. She crumbled, gasping and trembling, singing Nnenna's name over and over as she fell into the throes of satisfaction. Nnenna was steadfast in her duty, lapping up every bit of Aline's pleasure before lying next to her on the bed.

Nnenna was no novice to lovemaking, but this was something new to her. Never had she felt such a pull to someone she had met only hours before. "Who are you?" she asked, half delirious with wonder.

Rather than answer, Aline pulled Nnenna into a deep kiss and moved her hand to where Nnenna was still wanting, teasing the tendrils of desire that remained. Nnenna knew this was a diversion, but, as Aline climbed atop her to return the many favors Nnenna had paid her, Nnenna could not find it in her to worry. The two women filled the night with their songs and, when they were both thoroughly satisfied, fell asleep in each other's arms.

••••●•••

The room disappeared. Eyes closed, Nnenna tried not to feel the gentle swaying that signified she was in the belly of the ship she had called home for months. Instead, she tried to feel the sun, warm on her face. Tried to smell the sea and hear the songs that had comforted her in her childhood.

A loud banging, clanging—metal on metal—startled her, forcing her to open her eyes. She tried to meet the gaze of one of her captors. He was a midshipman, just barely out of childhood, and yet he had been sent to perform a grown man's task.

"They want you on the main deck," he said, avoiding her eye. His voice cracked and squeaked with the remnants of adolescence.

The order was not solely for Nnenna but for all the prisoners who occupied the cell. Nnenna considered putting on a show for the others, giving him a fight just to see what he would do, but he was just a boy. It was not his fault his masters were without humanity. Without a word, Nnenna rose to her feet, struggling slightly, for the awkwardness caused by her bound hands. Upon her compliance, the other prisoners stood. The boy opened the cell, and Nnenna led the company forward.

When Nnenna emerged from belowdecks, the sunlight burned her eyes. How long had it been since she had seen the sun? Since she had breathed fresh air? Squinting, she could just make out the shapes of several people standing on the quarterdeck. She blinked several times as the face of the captain, standing at the helm, came into focus. He wore a look of disdain.

Another member of the crew materialized and took her by the arm, leading her and the others to the middle of the deck and rounding them up like a herd of sheep.

"Nnenna Delahaye!" the captain called from aloft. "You stand

accused of treason against the captain of this vessel! You have committed the heinous crimes of insubordination and mutiny! The punishment for these crimes shall be no less than death!"

Nnenna expected as much, knowing how much the Fleet depended upon its soldiers' loyalty. She was not shaken. In fact, she was not even listening to the captain's words as he pronounced the same sentence upon the rest of the prisoners. Her eyes were trained on the lieutenant standing to his right.

Look at me, you coward, *she urged as she glared in his direction.* Look at me!

But his eyes never lifted from his shoes.

She never took her eyes off him, even as heavy chains wrapped around her ankles. Understanding dawned on her at once. She had expected a sword through the belly, or a pistol shot through the heart. Not this.

"On my signal!" the captain called, his arm raised in the air.

The moment he brought his arm down, three muscle-bound members of the crew lifted an anchor onto the ship's rail and tossed it overboard. They moved out of the way as the chain attached to the weight went with it. The sound of the chain following it over the side was almost musical until it was cut by the sound of screaming. They had chained all the prisoners together by the ankles. Each mutineer on the line would be pulled across the deck and over the rail.

Each splash was deafening, and fear rose in her as her turn approached, but she kept staring at the lieutenant.

Look at me, *she begged in her mind.*

He never looked. She felt the pull at her ankles, and before she could gasp, her shoulder slammed against the wooden boards of the deck. She slid faster than expected, but she still managed not to scream. Her body hit the side of the rail, crumpled, and then went over, just as the others had done.

The waters were unsettlingly warm, close enough to her body temperature that, for a mad moment, she wondered if she had somehow managed to avoid them. She had not time to even take a final breath before she was sucked into the deep. The light that had blinded her only minutes ago disappeared slowly, then, all at once, as though the darkness itself pulled her in.

•••●•••

Nnenna woke with a gasp that threw her forward, jerking her eyes open. She clutched at her chest and was surprised to find herself unbound and dry, except for the sweat that stuck the bed linens to her body. Her heart thundered as she took deep, shaky breaths and scanned the room, an attempt to familiarize herself with her surroundings.

Someone stirred in the dark. Nnenna glanced at the other side of the spacious four-poster bed to Aline's sleeping form. Her lips slowly curved upward as memories from the night before pushed the bad dream from her mind. She was close enough to touch her, to run her fingertips along the gentle curve of the other woman's exposed back, but she resisted. Instead, she threw the linens from her legs and crept out of bed.

If Nnenna remembered correctly, her shirt, trousers, and jacket were in the wardrobe, where she had stashed them when she had swapped them for the red dress. Her boots, however, had been unceremoniously tossed aside as the night's activities had grown more . . . enthusiastic. Nnenna had not a clue where to find them.

She tiptoed to the wardrobe on the other side of the room and prayed to whoever was listening that the creaking door would not wake Aline. The clothes she sought were piled in the corner. She grabbed the lot with one hand and took them to the undressed window, holding each garment up to the weak predawn light to confirm its identity. Even with the light, she slipped her trousers on backward and had to give it another try.

"Giving the island a show?" Aline's sleepy voice said from behind her.

Nnenna chuckled as she put the trousers on correctly. "I'm sorry. I tried not to wake you."

"No need to apologize."

Aline stretched, raising both arms above her halo of dark curls to elongate her back, and the sheet that had been covering her chest slipped down to her hips. Nnenna's mouth went very dry.

"Breakfast?"

Nnenna could not tell if Aline was referring to actual food or more pleasurable activities. Either way, she did not have the time.

"I'm already late," Nnenna said, tearing her eyes away and continuing to dress.

"Then, let's have breakfast on your ship," Aline said.

Nnenna chuckled as she pulled her shirt on over her head. "My ship is no place for a lady."

Aline snorted. "You'd be hard-pressed to find a lady on this island."

"You're a lady to me," Nnenna said, tucking her shirt into her trousers. "And you're not getting on my ship."

She threw the jacket on and began the search for her boots.

"They're by the fireplace," Aline said. Nnenna chose not to acknowledge the disappointment in her voice.

"Thank you," she sighed, walking over to them and putting them on her feet.

"I can cook!" Aline suddenly exclaimed.

"We have a cook," she said, kneeling to lace herself up.

"Then, what don't you have? I have many talents!"

"You're certainly persistent," Nnenna muttered.

"At least, get me off this island. You can take me anywhere. I have some gold saved. I can pay!"

Nnenna sighed again. "What's wrong with Yamaye? It's practically a paradise."

"Practically a prison, more like," Aline said, pulling the sheets back up and tucking them under her arms. "Every day, I watch ship after ship bring sailors to Yamaye. I hear their stories of life on the sea and all the different islands they've seen. Then they leave and I'm still stuck here. I was born on this island, you know, to a mother who was stuck like I am now. She died having never stepped foot off this island. I don't want to suffer the same fate."

"By the seven," Nnenna groaned.

"It's easy for you," Aline went on. "You can come and go as you please, but I—" Her voice grew thick with emotion. "I am trapped here with no hope of escape."

Nnenna knew she should hold firm, but she could not stop herself from remembering the night she and Aline had spent together, the way they had connected to each other, almost at once. It was possible that Aline had targeted her. She, too, knew what it was like to be alone and helpless, but Aline had no way of knowing that. Nnenna also had no explanation for the feelings Aline evoked in her, the songs she had brought out of her. She knew that it was probably best to stay away, but she wanted to know more.

"Fine!" Nnenna said.

"Fine?" Aline perked up.

"Get dressed," Nnenna sighed. "Quickly."

Aline released a squeal of delight that was certain to have

woken the tavern's other guests as she shot out of the bed and gathered her surprisingly few possessions from her own room. Mere moments later, she sat at the stern of a dinghy while Nnenna rowed them toward the *Medusa*.

"One trip. Then, you're on your own," Nnenna said, pulling on the oars of the little boat and propelling them over the morning's gentle waves.

"Of course," Aline said, nodding.

Aline stared out at the sea, grinning from ear to ear. All of a sudden, the rouge she had worn last night seemed gaudy. As the sky exploded into a pink-and-orange sunrise behind her, Nnenna could see that Aline was a true beauty.

"I can't guarantee your safety," Nnenna continued, trying not to imagine the hell Tinou would rain down on her for this loose interpretation of her captain's prerogative.

"I would never ask you to," Aline replied.

At least the woman had some sense.

Eight

PEARL

The sun's rays beat down upon Pearl in a way they never could when she lived in the sea: drying her clothes until they were stiff, shrinking her long hair into tight coils, baking her new soft skin. She sat in the sand for hours, staring at her legs. She knew enough about them to know that the ancestors had used them to get around, but had only ever seen them depicted on the tablets upon which her people's scripture was written. These things attached to her body in place of her beautiful tail were grotesque in comparison, yet strangely, her body knew what to do with them.

She controlled her legs as effortlessly as she had her tail, pulling them close to her chest and extending them outward, shifting her weight on her backside to really feel how her legs joined at her hips. Now that she knew she was not dying, her curiosity began to nibble at her fear. What would it feel like to walk? To run? To leap into the air and fall back down? A glimmer of excitement bloomed to life inside her. Then, it quickly withered in the wake of her guilt. She should have been watching the waves for any sign of Uncle Wade. He had said he would find her, and if he had escaped from the temple guards not too long after her, he could join her at any moment. The chances of his finding this island were already near to nothing; she wanted to make sure she was the first thing he saw when he emerged from the water.

This is where we will make our new life, she thought wistfully.

Pearl waited. The waves continued to crash and stir, offering up no sign of Uncle Wade, and the sun traveled across the sky. Eventually, it disappeared behind the trees at Pearl's back, taking with it its blanket of warmth. The air turned cool, and harsh winds blew in from the ocean, whipping at her skin through her robes' thin fabric.

Agwe, be with me, Pearl prayed as she wrapped her arms around her body to keep the heat from escaping.

Agwe was nowhere to be found. He had taken her voice, had severed her connection with Him and the ancestors because she had disobeyed Him. But what about the viceroy and the temple guards who followed his orders to hurt her uncles? Had they not also violated Agwe's law? Were they not also deserving of punishment? Or, perhaps, their sins were somehow less egregious than hers? It hurt Pearl's head to try to make sense of it all. As she felt her frustrations rise, she closed her eyes and brought her palms together, twisting them in opposite directions and bringing them sharply down by her sides as she breathed deeply. It was seven iterations of this ritual before she felt her mind quiet, and Pearl wondered if it took so long because she could not sing.

The cold seeped through her thin land-dweller skin, into her bones, and her body quaked uncontrollably. She fell onto her side and lay shaking against the sand for hours. She thought her torture would never end, but, as the first rays of light bled into the sky, the wind relented, her muscles relaxed, and she fell into a dark, dreamless sleep.

Warmth had been unfamiliar and intoxicating. The heat that woke Pearl was punishing. It had leeched every bit of moisture out of her body while she had slept, leaving her skin stinging and the inside of her mouth feeling as though it were coated in sand. She needed water.

Sore from her tense night, Pearl gingerly got to her feet and tottered toward the ocean. Cool water kissed her feet when she stepped into the lapping waves. Hungry for relief, she ventured deeper and deeper into the ocean, fighting through the undulations, until they rose past her waist. A wild thought passed through her mind. Maybe she could ask for forgiveness and go back. It was impossible, but she made the signs nonetheless, bowing her head and brushing the fingertips of her right hand along the length of the palm of her left hand. When nothing happened, she tried again, rubbing her palm in a circle against her chest to show Agwe how truly sorry she was. Nothing. Agwe was not listening. She let her hands fall into the water, cupped them together, brought them to her mouth, and drank.

Each mouthful stung her throat, but the water was so cool and wet, she was thankful for the relief it brought. She drank deeply, gulping the liquid down until she could feel her belly stretching under her clothes.

Pearl waded out of the water and resumed her place in the sand, but as she lowered herself to her seat, her stomach twinged painfully. She rubbed circles over her belly, trying to soothe herself the way her uncles had when she was a child, but the pain only grew worse. Sharp spasms forced her to lie on her side, clutching her abdomen helplessly. Pressure rose from her stomach to her throat. She tried to get to her feet but only managed to make it to her hands and knees before she retched.

Seawater poured out of her in one continuous stream that

broke only when there was no more water to release. Pearl expelled half a dozen wet coughs before throwing herself onto her back in the sand to wait out the dizziness that had suddenly overcome her. Even the sea, which had once been as much a part of her as her own blood, now rejected her.

Pearl did not want to cry anymore—she wanted to be brave—but the tears came unbidden anyway and silent sobs racked her body. She missed her home, her family, her life. She missed the sound of her own voice. She missed feeling safe, being cradled and suspended by the sea. She cried until the world stopped spinning, and it was only then that she remembered the shell she had stashed in her pocket.

Pearl reached into her robes, struggling slightly with the dampness of the fabric. She pulled out the shell and held it up to the sky. It was unremarkable, a sand-beaten conch that was white on the outside with pink rays reaching out from within, but it was the last thing she had of her life in the sea. As she cradled it, she thought of the last time she and Uncle Rain had gone to the Shallows together.

"What are you doing, Uncle Rain?" she had asked him when she had seen him floating with his arm outstretched. His fingers danced dangerously close to skimming the ever-undulating veil that separated them from the land dwellers. He had not answered right away, and so Pearl had waited, watching him and counting her heartbeats until he had finally lowered his arm.

"Just checking something," he had replied, still very taken with the object in his hand. "Come over here, Pearl."

Pearl had dropped the shoe she had been considering adding to her collection and had swum to her uncle's side.

"What's that?" she had asked as she touched down on the sand next to him.

He had held it up so that she could see. The shell had been disappointingly unremarkable.

"It's . . . a key," he had said, though his tone had given the impression that he might not have been sure himself.

"I've never seen a key that looks like that," Pearl had said.

"Have it," Rain had said suddenly. "Call it an early birthday gift."

"Thank you," Pearl had said tentatively, taking it from her uncle.

When she had gotten home that day, she had put it directly into her treasure trunk and had not thought about it again until . . .

Why hadn't she thought to ask more questions? But, of course, she had elected to cut that trip to the Shallows short so that she could be back to the Settlement in time to watch the return of the scavenging expedition, hoping to catch sight of Amos Stilltide. It all seemed so silly, now.

Rain had said the conch was a key. She had not thought about it then, but it seemed strange now. Their people did not use keys. They knew them as land-dweller devices. There was only one door that needed to be unlocked, and that was the door into Agwe's kingdom. But she did not see how an old shell would do that.

Still breathing heavily, she held the shell up to the clear blue sky and waited for something to happen. The minutes passed slowly, longer than even Uncle Rain had waited, long enough for the muscles in her shoulder to ache. She tried a different tack. The conch had a small opening on its end. She brought it to her lips and blew. Not even a weak tone. She sighed and let her arm drop to the sand.

At the same time, her stomach released an angry gurgle that rattled her bones.

Pearl groaned. She had not eaten since before the funeral, and she had no idea what land dwellers ate. She would have given her tail fin—or, rather, foot—for a plump flounder to sink her teeth into. Her teachers had always been tight-lipped about how land dwellers lived, but some information must have slipped into her lessons. The voice of Brother Shellreef floated into her mind.

"And as the land-dwelling usurpers grow fat upon their breads and meats, every day, our people grow closer to our destiny."

Pearl did not know what breads were, but she understood meats to be animals. If there were animals in the sea, then there had to be animals on land as well. Perhaps she could find one somewhere on this island and . . . catch it? Kill it? Her Uncle Wade always made sure her fish were dead and deboned before they made it to her.

Agwe's heart.

A few steps away, the sandy beach became a wall of thick, lush green plants, and Pearl immediately thought of the small fish that would tuck themselves away in the kelp fields that grew all around the Settlement. If there were animals on this island, they would surely be found in the cover of this brush.

Pushing through the wall of green was more difficult than she had imagined it to be. Far from the pliable kelp leaves, these plants contained stiff inner workings with barbs that tugged at and tore her clothes. But she persevered and made it through to the other side. She had no words for the world she had entered. Gone was the sand, and in its place was something rich, dark, and warm that she had never before encountered. She was surrounded by tall plants with long, thin stems that reached high into the sky and culminated in green explosions.

There was something of a path before her, a slight depression in the ground that led farther into the trees. Maybe there were others on this island. Her stomach gurgled once again. Maybe they had something she could eat.

Pearl walked into what felt like the heart of the island, to a place where the plants grew so thick over her head that they blocked out the sky. She was soon tripping over roots jutting out of the ground. Her foot caught on a particularly prodigious tuber and sent her careening to the ground, face-first. Cursing inwardly, she flipped over onto her back and looked up at the crisscrossing branches above her.

A black creature, covered in hair everywhere except its small heart-shaped face, landed on the branch directly over her head. As she stared at it, it stared back at her. Curious, she started to move toward it with her hand outstretched, but before she could get close to it, it bared its teeth and hissed. She jumped back, ready to run. Then, she decided she would not let such a small creature intimidate her. With her eyes trained on the small animal, she felt around the ground next to her for something she could throw. Her fingers lighted upon a large rock. She seized it and turned over to get back onto her feet. The animal tilted its little head and continued to stare at her. Pearl slowly raised the rock, but before she could get it to the level of her shoulder, the creature darted to another branch and then another, swinging from tree to tree with its long arms and tail.

She had no time to think—it would be gone in the blink of an eye—so she took off after it, running under the branches and doing her best to avoid the roots while trying to keep her eyes on her prize. The canopy thinned and the sky returned, limiting the creature's options for escape. Just as Pearl thought she would have the creature cornered, she tripped over yet another root and crumpled to her hands and knees.

The animal chirped from somewhere above her. When she looked up to find it, however, she found herself staring into a man's dark brown face. She gasped and scrambled to stand, but the man was faster with his shining silver blade than she was with her unfamiliar feet. Two others flanked him, sporting the same dark brown skin and dressed in the same green and gold that made Pearl wonder if they were somehow connected to the viceroy.

Fear caught her by the throat and stopped her breathing. Her eyes darted nervously from one man to the next as she forced air in and out of her body. The leader held his sword tip to Pearl's chin and made an official-sounding pronouncement, but his land-dweller tongue was incomprehensible. Pearl waved a hand and used it to tap her throat in the hope that he would understand. Instead, he frowned. Without removing the sword, he turned his head to his two companions and spoke more words in the land-dweller language. Suddenly, the two people behind the sword-bearer jumped into action. One pulled her to her feet while the other patted her sides, hips, and legs. He found the shell in her pocket, reached in, and pulled it out to show to his superior.

"No! No!" she tried to scream, reaching for the shell, but her throat tightened around the words.

A pair of strong hands caught her wrists and wrenched her arms behind her back.

Agwe, please, be with me, she begged in her mind, but without a voice or hands to make signs, she feared her prayers would never reach Agwe's ears.

The sword-bearer sheathed his weapon and exchanged it for the shell. Then, his thin lips spread into a smile that made Pearl shudder. He gave another order, and before Pearl could take another breath, the two guards marched her toward the beach. Pearl walked in silent awe as she caught sight of the massive ship bobbing unnaturally atop the water in the distance.

Nine

NNENNA

Nnenna drained her requested cup of ale that replaced her breakfast upon her arrival onto the *Medusa*. Tinou had kept her mouth shut when Nnenna boarded the ship, late and with a passenger in tow. But now that said passenger was bent over the bulwark on the starboard side, offering up the contents of her stomach to the sea, Tinou had plenty to say. Aline had been a ray of sunshine from the moment she stepped foot on the deck, flirting playfully with the crew and ignoring Tinou's disapproving glare, but they had not been on the water for more than a few minutes before the novice to the sea had suddenly gone pale in the face.

"I knew this was a bad idea," Tinou muttered from Nnenna's side.

"Shut up," Nnenna muttered back, whacking her first mate's firm abdomen with the back of her hand. "Go find a bucket."

"Aye, Captain," Tinou replied.

They went their separate ways, Tinou belowdecks to retrieve the requested receptacle and Nnenna to Aline's side. She caught the sick woman just as she tried and failed to right herself, and they both fell against the bulwark.

"Shall I have the cook hold your breakfast plate?" Nnenna teased.

Aline groaned and raised a hand to Nnenna's mouth. "Please, no talking about food."

Nnenna kissed her hand and took Aline by the arm. "Come with me," she said, coaxing Aline to her feet.

She was much shorter than Nnenna and therefore had to stretch to allow Nnenna to support her. Together, they hobbled to the mainmast. Nnenna had intended to take her to her cabin, but a particularly large swell had her clutching the base of the rigging, refusing to budge.

"You'll get used to it," she tried to reassure Aline while rubbing circles on her back.

The most Aline could manage in response was a moan of misery.

"Tinou, where the hell is that bucket?" Nnenna called.

"I've got it!" Tinou's voice called back. She jogged to meet them at the mast and set the wooden bucket down next to Aline. "Captain, may I have a word?"

Nnenna knew what was coming, but stepped away from her seasick companion nonetheless.

"What is it?" she asked.

"She can't stay here," Tinou said.

"I'm well aware, Tinou," Nnenna replied tensely. "As soon as she is feeling well enough, I will escort her to my cabin."

"I meant on the ship. She can't stay. We're not too far from Yamaye. We can turn around and—"

"We will do no such thing!" Nnenna snapped.

"You would put your crew in danger over some strumpet—"

"Hold your tongue, Tinou," Nnenna growled, stepping to the woman and glaring up at her. "My fondness for you affords you many liberties, but I will not tolerate your questioning my decisions. I am the captain of this ship, and you will obey my orders. Do I make myself clear?"

Tinou had a hard time meeting Nnenna's eye. "Aye, Captain," she said tersely.

"Good. Now, help me get Aline into my cabin."

Together they lifted Aline to her feet and supported her while she embraced the bucket with both arms. They helped her across the ship to the great cabin at the stern and lowered her onto the spacious bunk where Nnenna normally slept.

"This was not what I had in mind when I vowed to get myself into your bed, Captain," Aline said with a weak smile.

"Hush," Nnenna chuckled, stroking Aline's forehead. "No need to worry about all that, now."

"Perhaps we should give the . . . lady some time to rest," Tinou said from behind Nnenna.

Aline let out a laugh. "Your friend does not like me much."

"Pay her no mind," Nnenna said, scowling over her shoulder.

"No, she's right." Aline shifted up so that she sat with her back against the clapboard wall. "I refuse to be a burden. Go about your business. I have my bucket and more than adequate accommodations. I shall remain here and find you once I am recovered."

"There, see? She's fine," Tinou said, no longer pretending to be concerned. "Let's go."

"Ring the bell if you need anything," Nnenna said, pointing to the captain's bell affixed to the wall next to the bunk. "I'll come running."

Aline laughed again. "Careful. You'll have me thinking you care about me."

Just then, the ship crested another swell, sending Aline diving into the bucket. Nnenna and Tinou took that as a sign to take their leave. The great-cabin doors were barely closed behind them when Tinou stopped Nnenna with a hand on her elbow.

"What will we do when we come upon the Fleet ship we came out here to find?" she asked gently. "The girl is no fighter."

Nnenna assured her first mate. "She won't be a problem. She—"

"Can you not hear yourself? In the heat of battle, when she needs you to come running, whose lives will be lost in exchange?"

"As I said, she will not be a problem. She will be locked away, safe, in my cabin. If our crew of a hundred men cannot keep the Fleet off our decks, then all our lives are forfeit."

Nnenna could tell Tinou wanted to respond, but her first mate wisely remained silent.

"Go inventory the food stores," she ordered.

"I did them yesterday," Tinou replied.

"And I am certain Sven had a very hearty breakfast! For the sake of the crew, please do them again!"

The corner of Tinou's mouth twitched upward into the barest suggestion of a smile. "I did tell you never to trust a thin cook."

Nnenna sighed, a smile crossing her lips as Tinou walked away. Her first mate was the closest thing to family she had, and Nnenna knew she was probably right, but she would be damned before she ever admitted it.

Perhaps there *was* something odd about Aline. Nnenna found herself suddenly too ready to bend to her desires, despite having known her for only a handful of hours. On more than one occasion, Nnenna had tried to resist her, but something in Aline's voice had changed her mind. Time away from her would be good. It would give Nnenna a chance to clear her head.

With her cabin in use, Nnenna elected to retire to the crow's nest, her second-favorite refuge on the ship. The way the little basket at the top of the mainmast pitched back and forth, exaggerating the movements of the ship, sent most members of the crew running when it was their turn to be on lookout, but Nnenna loved it. She did not know whether it was the sensation of being close to the sky or the solitude the crow's nest offered, but she took every opportunity she could to spend time there. When Delva had been the *Medusa*'s captain and Nnenna had only just joined the crew, she opted to sleep in the crow's nest rather than the crew quarters.

She climbed up the mainmast rigging in a matter of seconds. When she finally entered the cramped wooden enclosure, the first thing she did was lean against the side and breathe in the fresh sea air. The sun was still rising over the horizon, and the water sparkled as rays of sunshine bounced white light into her eyes.

A black shape shimmered into being amidst the brightness, and Nnenna, believing the anomaly to be in her eyes, blinked several times. When the black shape remained, Nnenna extracted her spyglass from her belt and peered through it. She immediately recognized the shape of sails.

"It can't be," Nnenna muttered, watching the ship come into focus. She read the name plastered across the bright green bow in shining golden paint: HFS *Adoration*.

"Shit," Nnenna cursed.

It would not be long before the two ships' paths crossed. She had to think fast. Throwing caution to the wind, Nnenna grabbed the rope that she had climbed up and used it to rappel down the wooden shaft, landing with a loud thud on the deck seconds later. She stopped long enough to steady herself, then ran to descend the companionway to the deck below.

"Tinou!" she called as she strode through the hold. "Tinou!"

Tinou stepped out from between two tall shelves, a sheaf of

parchment and quill in her hands. "Found some more useless tasks for me?" she asked sarcastically.

"It's here," she said, ignoring Tinou's bad attitude. "The Fleet ship is here, coming at us from the north, maybe fifteen minutes out."

Tinou raised her brows, all traces of her annoyance gone. "I'll have the crew ready the guns."

"No guns," Nnenna said, stopping her.

Tinou stared, perplexed.

"I don't want to risk . . ." Nnenna paused, knowing she would only stoke the fire she had just barely managed to put out if she told Tinou the truth. "The ship. I don't want to risk the ship."

Tinou narrowed her eyes.

"Trust me," Nnenna said. "We do it the way we did the *Reverence*. Do you remember?"

Tinou smirked. "How could I forget?"

"Good." Nnenna returned the smile. "Tell the crew to come about into the wind and luff up, run up the old colors, and get belowdecks and wait for my signal. Then, you meet me in the bows."

"Aye, Captain!"

For the second time that morning, they parted ways, this time fully aligned in purpose. Nnenna returned to her cabin, where Aline was fast asleep (and would hopefully stay that way), and found the red dress she had worn the night before. She quickly exchanged her captain's garb for the finery. It was quite the risk, giving up all her weapons except the dagger that she could secrete in the gown's pocket, but the reward would be well worth it.

Tinou was already waiting at the bows when she arrived. The *Medusa* had come to a standstill and the *Adoration* was fast approaching.

"Make it look good," she said to Tinou.

"I always do," Tinou replied with a smile.

The first part of their feint worked like a charm. A humble merchant ship afloat in the sea demanded curiosity, at the very least. When the *Adoration* drew alongside the *Medusa,* Nnenna sprang into action.

"Help!" she screeched at the top of her lungs, running toward the starboard side, making sure that she was visible to the other ship's occupants. She tried to make eye contact with at least one man as she screamed a second time. "Help, please!"

Just as she caught the attention of one of the men—the officers—on the quarterdeck, Tinou approached her from behind. Growling like a true menace, Tinou took her by the shoulders with two hands, and threw her down. Nnenna heard cries of surprise and concern come from the men on the other ship. She fought to suppress a smile and screamed once again as Tinou pantomimed throttling her within an inch of her life.

Even as she screamed, she could hear the commotion rising as the *Adoration*'s crew scrambled to assist the damsel in distress. Nnenna needed only one chivalrous fool to take matters into his own hands.

Come on, she silently urged.

Not a moment later, she heard the telltale thunk of a grappling hook finding its home on the ship's rail. Within seconds, someone was climbing over. Nnenna saw him over Tinou's shoulder, approaching carefully. As their eyes locked, he put a finger to his lips, silently entreating her to keep his arrival a secret. Playing the part, Nnenna widened her eyes and made herself look absolutely desperate.

He grabbed Tinou with two hands, twisted her around, and delivered a punch to her jaw that knocked her to the planks.

Nnenna winced. Tinou stayed down, and she knew it was her turn to take center stage.

"Thank you!" she cried, reaching out a hand to the young officer.

He took her hand and pulled her to her feet, never noticing the dagger she deftly pulled out of her pocket. Nnenna sank it into his neck. He was no fearsome Captain Hidalgo, but he gagged and bled and died all the same. Nnenna held him upright, feigning a grateful embrace as she relieved the dead man of his cutlass. She made eye contact with Tinou over his shoulder.

"Now!" she mouthed.

Tinou stuck her thumb and forefinger under her tongue and blew out a shrill whistle. The crew spilled onto the deck armed with ropes and hooks, swords and guns, clubs and knives. They ran to the starboard side for the onslaught, while the crew of the *Adoration* scrambled to ready themselves for the attack. Nnenna dropped the dead man, and she and Tinou led the charge, traversing the divide by rope and by plank.

The fighting began even before she touched down on the *Adoration*'s deck. There were more men than Nnenna had expected, but she and her men were the fiercest fighters on the sea. She swung at any uniformed sailor who came her way, cutting down man after man until only the captain remained.

He was a large, brutish fellow, dark-skinned with a low-hanging brow, thin lips, and dark, beady eyes. Nnenna attacked while the fires of rage and resentment still burned red-hot within her. Her borrowed sword came within inches of his belly before the captain deflected it with his own. She came back at him with another swipe from the left, aimed at his right shoulder. He sidestepped the attack, more nimbly than she expected for a man of his stature. He wheeled around her and kicked her in the back, sending her careening toward the bulwark. Nnenna panicked and grabbed the rail with both hands, dropping her sword to stop herself from going over. Then, she quickly turned around to face him.

His blade was all she saw, catching the light of the rising sun as it swung high into the air and came down. She had just enough time to throw herself out of harm's way, and the blade bit deeply into lacquered wood. This was her chance. As he tugged and tugged to free his sword, Nnenna scrabbled across the deck to retrieve her own weapon. She curled her fingers around the handle as a large, booted foot came down on her hand. She cried out, feeling her bones crack, but managed to keep her wits about her, searching frantically for something—anything—she could use.

Reaching into her pocket, she extracted the dagger and ran its blade across the captain's heel, hoping to sever both boot and tendon. His resultant howl told her she had, at the very least, found flesh. His foot lifted as he staggered back, freeing her hand. There was a dead lieutenant to her left. She lunged at his belt, took hold of his pistol, and aimed for the captain.

His gasp and a terrified "I surrender!" were the last things Nnenna heard before she pulled the trigger, praying to the seven that it was not already spent.

The gun gave a satisfying blast as it sent a bullet flying through the captain's eye. His body crumpled to the floor.

Nnenna picked herself up, stretching and flexing the hand that had been crushed under the captain's weight, and spat on his dead body.

"Search the ship," she ordered. "There's a pearl of great enough value to the Fleet that they would send one of their ships into our waters. I want to make them regret such foolishness."

The men went down to the hold, searching through crates

and sacks for anything that remotely resembled treasure. Nnenna and Tinou took to searching the cabins. The *Adoration*'s great cabin held nothing of value, but she did find a weathered conch shell stashed away in a drawer in the captain's desk. The moment she held it in her hands, a familiar song rose in her heart.

"Why would he keep this hidden?" she wondered aloud, turning it over to examine its every angle.

"Captain," Tinou called from the lieutenant's quarters. "Come and have a look at this!" Disturbed, Nnenna shoved the shell into her pocket and rushed to see what was the matter.

When she arrived at the door of the lieutenant's quarters, she could tell why Tinou sounded perturbed.

"By the seven," she swore, "they get younger every year."

Three midshipmen—no older than fourteen, from the looks of them—crouched in a huddle in the corner. While they all held loaded pistols, they visibly shook with fear, their eyes red from shedding tears they would never let their captain see. Nnenna stepped into the cramped room and crouched before them.

"Your captain is dead," she said plainly, "and my ship is no place for children. When you are rescued, tell the Fleet who is responsible for your destruction this day. You know my name?"

The boys nodded and chorused, "The Devil of the Deep."

Now, Nnenna smiled. "And if you fancy a life of adventure in a couple of years, come find me."

She stood and made to leave, but one of the boys, the one in the middle, called after her. "But what about the girl? Is she dead, too?"

His comrades both elbowed him. Nnenna raised the pistol she had used to kill the captain. "Where?" she demanded, pointing the gun at each boy in turn. It was the middle one who again gave up the information.

"In the galley," he squeaked, defiantly.

"Search the galley!" Nnenna called over her shoulder to Tinou, who stood by the door.

"Aye, Captain!" she said before turning on her heel to follow the order.

Nnenna kept the gun on the boys while Tinou was gone. They said nothing more to her, though after a moment, the one on the right began to weep.

"She's there, but she won't move," Tinou reported upon returning.

"What do you mean she won't move?" Nnenna asked.

"Come and see for yourself. I think there's something wrong with her."

Rolling her eyes, she turned back to the boys. "Do not move a muscle," she warned. "You may get past us, but there are dozens of bloodthirsty pirates all over this ship. You will not make it out alive."

Satisfied, she followed Tinou to the galley. There was indeed a girl crouched, pressing her back against the wall opposite the stove. She had skin lighter than Nnenna's, though she could tell it had been freshly darkened by the sun. Her hair was a halo of tight, dark curls, and her eyes were large and almond shaped with warm honey-colored irises. She wore the strangest clothes that Nnenna had ever seen, green-and-white robes that skimmed the floor. They looked fine, though they were torn in several places.

The girl was clearly terrified, judging by the way her eyes darted between Nnenna and Tinou as she panted frantic breaths. Nnenna stepped forward, smiling, hoping the gown helped her to present as less intimidating.

"Hello, there, sweetling," she said. "What's your name?"

The girl said nothing.

"How did you come to be aboard this vessel?"

Once again, the girl gave no response.

"I told you there's something wrong with her," Tinou said. "Look at her neck. Behind the ears."

Nnenna crouched down before the girl and tilted her head. The girl flinched, as though expecting a blow, and Nnenna's heart broke unexpectedly.

"It's all right," she cooed. "I just want to look."

There were scars on the side of her throat, three parallel lines of slightly raised and discolored flesh, just where her jaw met her neck.

"How did you get those?" Nnenna asked more to herself than the girl, her voice dropping to a faint whisper.

The girl seemed not to understand. She seemed entirely out of place. Nnenna had sailed across every stretch of the Seven Isles and had seen every type of person they had to offer, but she had never seen anyone who looked as lost as this girl. It suddenly occurred to Nnenna that she had an item in her possession that seemed not to belong on the ship. An idea dropped into her head. Still crouching before the girl, she reached her empty hand into her gown pocket and pulled out the conch shell.

"Do you know what this is?"

The moment the girl laid eyes on the shell, she froze, and Nnenna had her answer. She held the shell out and waited. After what seemed like an eternity, the girl's hand twitched forward and snatched it. Then, Nnenna stood and held out her hand. The girl's breathing was slower now, and she still seemed wary of Tinou, but she took the offered hand and allowed Nnenna to pull her to her feet.

Ten

LU

Lu dressed silently in his bedroom, careful where he stepped, lest the creaky floorboards give away his intentions to his father, who snored peacefully down the hall. The outfit Manou had given him—a long-sleeved tunic and trousers that his wife, Mai, had handsewn from some of Manou's old clothes, and a tan wool sweater that she had knit especially for Lu—fit him perfectly. He was happy to swap them for his regular attire. Once dressed, he tamed the mass of loose dark curls on his head into a neat queue with a ribbon at the base of his skull.

The boy in the mirror brought Lu a relief and satisfaction that had eluded him for as long as he could remember being himself. There was no sign of the awkward curves he had noticed on his body since he had started his journey into young adulthood, and with his hair pulled back, he could almost be convinced that he had simply cut it short. He was twelve years old, and he was finally ready to take to the sea.

Smiling, Lu pulled himself out of his reverie. If he spent any more time admiring himself, he would miss his chance altogether. He reached under his bed and pulled out a length of rope pilfered from the stables some months before. Hitching the loop over his shoulder, he tiptoed to the windowed double doors that led to his balcony, and carefully exited. Although his chosen route was treacherous, walking through the house in his current state of dress was too great a risk. Even if he managed to creep past his father's bedroom without waking him, Lu would still have to make it out of the enormous mansion without alerting any of the servants.

The predawn darkness was no longer an impediment to Lu's ability to secure one end of the rope to the balustrade, hop over, and lower himself down to the soft grass. This had been his morning routine while Manou taught Lu the ins and outs of being a sailor. Three times a week, Lu left his bedroom before the sun came up, walked to the privately owned dock, and spent as many hours as he could aboard Manou's schooner before he had to return home, leaving enough time to change back into his regular clothes before his lessons.

When Lu arrived at the dock, moments later, he found both Manou and Mai waiting for him. They greeted him with a sign. In unison, they pressed their palms flat against each other, twisted them, then spread their arms with their palms facing outward, welcoming him as a fisherman. Lu felt a burst of pride. He stopped to make the corresponding sign. He held his flat palm before his face so that his fingertips pointed at Manou, turned his wrist so that his fingers pointed to the sky, and pulled the heel of his hand downward, running his thumb along the line of his nose. Then, he touched his fingers to his thumbs on both hands, pushed them forward, and opened his fingers.

"The boy has been paying attention!" Manou announced with a toothy grin.

"Quiet!" Mai chided, half laughing herself. "You'll wake everyone on the whole island."

"Good!" Manou said. "Everyone should know how proud I am of him!"

Lu's cheeks burned and his eyes stung as a swell of affection for the couple nearly burst his heart. He was grateful for the cover of darkness.

Mai and Manou were really called Marianne and Manuel, but none of the fisherfolk of Ayiti used their given names with each other. It was tradition for a loved one to rename them as a sign of affection. Lu had stumbled upon the little cottage that Mai and Manou shared and had introduced himself to Mai, interrupting her washing. He had asked her a thousand questions about who she was and where her husband was and what she was doing. When she had asked about his parents, he told her about the illness that had taken his mother less than a month before, making no mention of his father. The way Mai had looked at him after that had made him want to pull the words back into his mouth.

"How about some fish cakes," she had offered. "You help me with this washing, and I'll make us both some."

Lu had eagerly swapped his dress for some borrowed clothes under the guise of wanting to keep the dress clean and had peppered Mai with more questions as they worked.

When Manou returned to the house after delivering the best of the fish he had caught, Lu had listened intently to his stories and songs from the sea.

That day, they had shortened his name to "Lulu," and they had been his family ever since.

He had tried to visit them every day, sneaking off when he knew his father was gone or too busy to notice. Manou had taught him about the sea and the Goddess, often pulling out an old tome whose cover bore an imagined likeness of the Goddess and whose pages were so worn they felt like fabric. Lu knew these stories by heart and had not needed the book for some time, but still loved to run his fingers over the gilded emblem on the cover, a long-haired woman with a fish's tail instead of legs.

Manou and Mai had been the first and only people he had told about the disquiet growing inside him, but it had been Mai who had seen him and suggested they shorten his nickname to "Lu" to "see how it feels." Lu had been grateful. He would never stop being grateful.

"Thank you for the clothes," Lu said, smiling up at Mai's full face.

"Of course, love," she answered.

"And you can thank her for this, too," Manou added.

He reached into the leather satchel that he always wore slung across his body and pulled out something wrapped in layers of fabric. Lu knew what it was the moment Manou unwrapped it, the warm, salty smell reaching Lu's nose.

"Fish cakes!" Lu sighed excitedly as his stomach rumbled.

They had become Mai's specialty—absolutely divine palm-sized disks of fish meat, flour, herbs, and spices, fried to perfection. Manou held out the fish cakes, and Lu took one, his mouth already watering.

"Take both," Mai said. "Manou has already had a half dozen this morning. You'll need something in your belly for your first day on the water."

Lu had never heard an order he was more willing to obey than this one. He took the second fish cake in his other hand and scarfed them both down as Manou looked on and laughed.

"Are you coming, too, Mai?" Lu asked as she hugged her shawl tighter to her body.

"Not this time, love."

That was what she always said. Lu suspected she was afraid of the water, but knew better than to say so out loud. "One day, I'll be a Fleet captain, and you'll have to come aboard my ship!" he insisted.

She smiled and patted his cheeks. Even in the darkness, he could see the trepidation in her eyes.

"Before we set out," Manou started as Lu swallowed the last of his breakfast.

"We offer a song to the Goddess," Lu supplied, "so that She may calm the waters for us."

"Right you are, lad."

They turned toward the sea and, as one, sang the song that Manou had taught Lu on the day they had met. As the words and signs came to Lu, the last remnants of disquiet in his heart calmed.

"Manou, is the Goddess real?" Lu asked as he clambered aboard the schooner.

"As real as Agwe Himself," Manou answered as he got the fishing boat ready to set sail.

Lu took a seat on a crate. "Why doesn't She have a name?"

"It was lost to time," Manou answered. Lu squinted at him. "Everyone who remembers it is gone."

"Then, how do you know She's real?"

"I've been singing to the Goddess every day before fishing these waters, and every day She has blessed me with safe passage and enough to feed my family. If that doesn't prove She's real, I don't know what does."

Lu did not see how that could be true. A dozen more questions sprang to his mind, but he had learned in his etiquette lessons never to question a man's belief in the divine. He did not want to upset Manou and spoil his first time on the water, so he let the matter rest.

•••●•••

More than a decade later, Lu stared at the door of the little rock-and-mortar dwelling that housed the two people he cared most about in the world. He heard echoes of his own joyous laughter as he remembered the thrill of that first adventure and the tears he had shed in the aftermath. His father had awoken early and had been sitting on Lu's bed, holding Lu's nightgown in both hands. He was contemplating it as though it were a corpse when Lu had returned to his bedroom. He had not asked where Lu had been, merely glanced in disgust at his son dressed in fisherman's clothing with his hair tied back.

Lu winced at the memory.

"Something the matter, Ortega?" the commodore, who stood next to him, asked.

"No, sir," he said, shaking off the discomfort and straightening his green-and-gold coat.

Lu stepped forward, forcing himself to stay present, and knocked on the door. Quick footsteps approached, and the door swung open.

"Mai!" Lu smiled at the woman who appeared in the doorway.

She was petite, though curvaceous, and had a rich reddish-brown tone to her skin. Her hair fell in bouncy black curls to her shoulders. She wore the plain handmade clothing of the fisherfolk, and her eyes, dark brown and set deeply under her heavy lids, were weighed down by heavy bags that indicated fatigue, despite her smile. She had not slept. Lu felt a pang of guilt as understanding dawned upon him.

Instead of throwing her arms around his neck as Lu had expected her to do, she remained in the doorway.

"Commodore," she said, inclining her head first in Christophe's direction and then again toward Lu. "Captain." She opened the door fully and gestured inside. "Please forgive the mess."

"After you, Commodore," Lu said.

Christophe stepped past Mai. "Thank you, Ortega."

Lu followed him in. He expected to feel the comfort and warmth of home wash over him as it always did when he visited the couple, but the home he had stepped into was far from his. Every inch of the place had been scrubbed until everything gleamed. Not only that, but the once bare walls were now covered with unfamiliar decorations, most notable of which was a large golden trident over the little fireplace.

"Welcome, Commodore," Manou said from beside the little table at which Lu had shared many a meal with the couple. But this table was dressed in a fine white linen cloth and laden with a sumptuous offering of cakes and tea, served on a matching dish set Lu had never seen before.

Astonished, Lu followed the commodore across the small space to the table. Manou inclined his head toward the commodore just as Mai had done. Smiling, the commodore held out a hand.

"A pleasure to meet you, my good man," he said.

"You as well, sir!" Manou replied, grasping Christophe's hand and enthusiastically shaking it. "Please, sit."

The three men each took a place at the table, Manou surrendering his spot nearest to the hearth to the commodore. Mai, who had waited until Lu and Christophe had entered before closing the door, joined them. She did not sit but immediately began to pour for the group, starting with the commodore.

"Mai, let me help you with that," Lu offered as he noticed the slight tremor in her hands.

"Don't be silly!" she laughed, pouring a measure of dark, fragrant tea into his cup.

"What a delightful table," Christophe noted, peering at his own cup and saucer.

"Thank you, Commodore," Mai said. "When we received word of your arrival, we knew only the best would do. The cloth and napkins are from mine and Emmanuel's wedding dinner, gifts from our families to bless our table so that it may never be empty."

"And Agwe has indeed blessed you," Christophe said.

Lu studied Mai's face, but it remained impassive. She inclined her head once more and said softly, "Yes," before taking the last empty seat at the table.

"Milk?" the commodore asked, searching for the correct container.

Mai sent a panicked look at Manou, but Lu was quicker. "It's not fisherfolk custom to take tea with milk."

"I apologize, sir," Manou added. "It did not occur to me."

"No matter," Christophe said, setting his cup and saucer down.

Mai watched him, tension thinning her lips slightly, but he did not take them back up again. For several moments, nothing but the sounds of sipping tea could be heard throughout the shack as everyone except the commodore partook. The silence only fed the growing discomfort in Lu's gut.

Hoping to steer the conversation forward, Lu quickly drained his cup and said, "Manou, I was just telling the commodore how gifted a singer you are."

"Yes!" the commodore exclaimed. "Ortega has spoken quite highly of your talents! On the way here, he said that you once healed his broken heart with a song."

Manou chuckled. "Lu exaggerates, surely. I am lucky enough to be able to carry a tune."

"Perhaps a show of your talent is in order?" the commodore asked.

Manou looked nervously at Lu and Mai, but Lu only sent him a confident smile back. Slowly, he pushed his chair away from the table and stood, unnecessarily straightening his clothes. He cleared his throat.

"The sea song," Lu suggested.

It was one that Lu had loved since he was a child. Perhaps it was because Lu had chosen the song, but Manou seemed to relax. He closed his eyes and breathed in deeply. When he let out the breath, his voice came with it, clear and strong, filling the air as he sang a song about a fisherman whose hat blew away and was lost to the sea. Lu's body relaxed as the notes washed over him, and he could remember being a boy getting ready to take on the sea. Manou sang only one verse, but it was enough to touch Lu's heart.

As Manou sat, the commodore stood, bringing his hands together in applause, not noticing that he had knocked over his teacup. Mai gasped and quickly grabbed her napkin from her lap. Lu picked up his own and together they dabbed at the spreading brown stain on the white cloth.

"Wonderful!" Christophe called, still standing. "Simply wonderful! You are one of the gifted few!"

"Thank you, sir," Manou said.

"You must come to the Citadel. Join the other singers and combine your voices to call to Agwe!"

Lu handed his sopping wet and stained napkin to Mai, who had tears in her eyes as she took them to soak in the water that boiled over the cookfire. He looked at the commodore and was surprised to find he had his hand over Manou's arm, his fingers digging into the threadbare fabric of Manou's sleeve.

Manou chuckled nervously, looking to Lu for assistance. “I really appreciate the offer, sir, but—”

“You will be compensated,” Christophe urged. “Your wife will want for nothing. All you have to do is sing.”

Lu watched Manou’s eyes flick to Mai burning her hands as she tried to save a pair of napkins. They were among the few nice things that the couple owned.

“Wouldn’t it be nice to be able to give her something more than . . . this?”

“I . . .” Manou started, but he seemed not to know how to finish. “All right.”

“Excellent!” the commodore exclaimed triumphantly. “I will send a carriage for you. Be ready by first light tomorrow.”

His objective complete, Commodore Christophe seemed no longer to feel the need to put on airs. He glanced once more at Mai and Manou, thanked them both, and bid them farewell. Then, he beckoned Lu to follow him out.

“One moment, sir,” Lu said, running to Mai and kneeling next to her. “I’m sorry,” he said in a rushed whisper. “I’ll replace them, I promise.”

Unable to speak, Mai simply patted his cheek and sent him off. Things would get better for them, Lu half knew and half prayed on the carriage ride back to the Citadel.

As he and the commodore strode through the double front doors, Ambroise met them, catching the commodore’s attention.

“There’s been word from the *Adoration*, sir,” she said quickly.

Lu made to salute the commodore as they parted ways, but Christophe dismissed Ambroise and told Lu to follow along.

Lu had only ever been to the commodore’s office once before, years ago, when he had been a lieutenant. The room had oozed authority with its rich, dark tones and hanging portraits of commodores past. It looked and smelled exactly as it had when Lu had been called to speak to Commodore Graves. The heady aromas of fine leather and coffee tore long-buried memories of his father's office from the recesses of his mind. He shook them away.

"Close the door behind you, will you?" the commodore said, crossing the room to take a seat behind his large escritoire.

Lu did as he was told and approached the desk cautiously.

"Sir?"

Christophe was already reading the parchment letter that had been sitting upon the desktop. After a moment, he threw the letter down and cursed.

"Have a seat," he said, composing himself. He gestured at one of the chairs that sat across from the desk.

Lu sat and waited silently, while the commodore pulled another sheaf of parchment from a drawer.

"One of our ships was found by merchants. Intact, but every one of the crew is dead except for three midshipmen. The Southern Sea."

Lu perked up. "Rochefort?" he asked.

The commodore nodded.

"And what of the girl?"

"They were set upon by none other than the Devil of the Deep, according to the midshipmen. They say she took the girl—"

"She?" Lu interrupted. "The Devil of the Deep is a woman?"

"A woman in a red dress, to be precise." He pinched the bridge of his nose. "I need you to understand exactly what is at stake here, Ortega. The Fleet is on the cusp of fulfilling a destiny foretold by Agwe Himself, long before any of us walked upon these lands! A captain of the Fleet must be willing to go to whatever lengths necessary to make Agwe's word a reality."

"Of course, sir."

"We need the girl. She is the key to our destiny."

"What would you have me do, sir?" Lu asked.

The commodore smiled.

"Tomorrow morning, at first light, meet me in the courtyard. Be ready for a journey."

"Yes, sir," Lu replied.

Eleven

NNENNA

The *Medusa*'s dining room was the size of two great cabins laid end to end. Its larboard portholes provided its occupants a stunning view of the roiling, clear blue waters. While the grand dining table at its center normally could seat twelve, this evening only four people sat around it. Nnenna took her usual place at the head of the table. To her immediate right was Tinou and to her immediate left was Aline. Neither of them looked happy with the other's position, but Nnenna had bigger problems to solve than petty squabbles between her people.

The girl sat at the other end of the table with her hands in her lap, staring down at the large bowl of steaming fish soup Nnenna had taught the ship's cook to make upon request. From the way the girl breathed in the steam rising from the bowl, it was clear she was hungry, but she had not yet picked up the spoon. She was slender, but muscular, with large brown eyes that shined whenever they caught the light.

"Eat," Nnenna said, but the girl merely looked at Nnenna, bemused.

She had not said a word since boarding the *Medusa*. Nnenna

was beginning to wonder if Tinou had been right, if there was something wrong with her after all. Something that kept her from speaking.

"Is this a habit of yours?" Aline asked. "Picking up strange women and offering them passage on your ship?"

"It wasn't until very recently," Tinou said with a pointed look at Aline.

"Enough, you two!" Nnenna said exasperatedly.

Tinou and Aline, refreshed from her nap but still looking a bit green, had been going back and forth all afternoon, disagreeing about everything from where Aline should sleep to whether she and the girl should take part in the ship's duties. Nnenna was long past her breaking point.

"She's a danger to us," Tinou said, ignoring Nnenna.

"She's a child!" Aline protested.

"We need to get rid of her before the Fleet comes looking for us."

"We will do no such thing! We have to return her to her family!"

"And how do you expect to find her family? The girl can't even speak!"

"Maybe she doesn't feel comfortable, because someone keeps threatening to kill her!"

"I said enough!" Nnenna shouted, slamming her fist against the table. The girl jumped, and Nnenna immediately regretted losing her temper. "The girl stays with us," she said with forced calm. "The Fleet wanted her and that's reason enough for me to want to keep her away from them." Tinou made a face that indicated she was about to protest, but Nnenna held up a hand. "If you don't like it, I will happily accept your resignation."

Tinou huffed and sat back in her chair. Aline looked smug.

Nnenna ignored them both. She looked back at the girl, who had been watching the trio argue, and smiled.

"I promise it isn't poisoned," she said, hoping the small jest would put the girl at ease, but she just kept staring.

Nnenna decided to try a different tack. She picked up her own spoon and held it up for the girl to see. The girl peered at it and watched as Nnenna dipped the spoon into her own bowl and brought a spoonful of fish soup to her mouth. A flicker of understanding flashed in the girl's eyes. She picked up her own spoon, dug it into the depths of the bowl, and fished out a helping of broth heaped with chunks of fish meat and vegetables. The girl brought the steaming spoonful to her mouth and, before Nnenna could stop her, parted her lips to eat her first bite.

Rather than the joy any sailor's first mouthful of Nnenna's famous fish soup warranted, the girl's face twisted with pain as the broth, still practically boiling, made contact with her tongue. Remarkably, she made no sound but immediately opened her mouth to release the soup onto the floor next to her seat. She frowned and pushed the bowl away, sloshing soup onto the tabletop. Nnenna could empathize.

Nnenna picked up her spoon again, brought it to the bowl of soup in front of her, scooped out a helping, and brought it to her lips. This time, she blew on the spoonful gently until it stopped steaming before taking it into her mouth. The girl stared at Nnenna warily, and Nnenna could only offer a smile and nod for encouragement.

It worked. The girl took up the spoon once more. Following Nnenna's example, she blew on her second attempt before shoving it into her mouth. The results were far more favorable, and Nnenna felt a wave of nostalgia as she watched the girl's eyes flutter closed and imagined tasting that fish soup for the first time.

"Delicious, isn't it?" Nnenna asked, hoping good food would coax some kind of response out of her. The girl only looked back and forth between Nnenna and the soup and continued to eat, clearly too hungry to be self-conscious any longer. "I don't think they fed her on that Fleet ship," she said to Tinou and Aline.

"Bastards," Aline said.

"I'm going to go check the guns," Tinou said, pushing away from the table. "I have a feeling we're going to need them soon."

Nnenna said nothing as she let herself out of the dining room. When the door closed behind Tinou, she turned back to Aline.

"You don't have to stay, either," Nnenna offered. "You didn't sign up to be a caregiver."

Aline smiled. "Sometimes, the best opportunities are the most curiously disguised."

This made Nnenna smile. Aline placed a hand upon hers on the table, and something about seeing their hands together, perhaps the slight contrast between their shades of brown, brought a memory rushing from the depths of her mind: a hand over hers, moving it to make a sign. She gasped.

Nnenna tapped the table to get the girl's attention. When the girl paused her voracious consumption of fish soup to look, Nnenna pointed to her, extended her middle and forefingers on both hands, and tapped the middle finger of her right hand against the forefinger of her left hand to make a cross. The girl froze, her eyes wide and flicking back and forth between Nnenna's hands and her face. Tears welled in her eyes, and for the first time since Nnenna found her in the galley of the *Adoration*, she smiled.

The girl dropped the spoon, and her hands began to fly, making signs quicker than Nnenna could understand.

"What is that?" Aline asked, sitting up and looking alarmed. "What's happening?"

"She's talking!" Nnenna answered, her eyes still trying to follow the girl's hands.

"What the hell kind of language is that?"

"It's the language of the fisherfolk. Where I grew up, they would use these signs to communicate with each other when voices couldn't be heard."

"I wouldn't have pegged you for a fisherman's daughter," Aline said.

"I'm not," Nnenna answered. "I learned it from . . . a friend."

Nnenna raised her hands, palms facing the girl. Then, the sign she wanted came to her. She extended her right hand over the table with her palm facing down and ran her left hand along the top from her fingertips up to her elbow.

"Slow," Nnenna said.

The girl understood at once. She repeated the first sign that Nnenna had made to ask for her name. After a brief pause, she used her fingertips to pull something invisible from the center of her chest before extending all fingers except her thumb and forefinger and pressing the circular shape they made against her chest. This was a sign Nnenna recognized: Pearl. Her name was Pearl.

"Pearl," Nnenna said, repeating the sign.

The girl launched into a series of signs, but even at less than half the speed of her last barrage, Nnenna still understood only one word out of five.

"What is she saying?" Aline asked excitedly.

"Something about the sea and an island? A map and a king? Or maybe that word was *master*? And danger."

"You don't seem sure."

"I'm not."

Nnenna shook her head and waved a hand at Pearl to signal for her to stop.

"That thing you have," she said, making a fist with her pointer finger extended and moving her whole hand in a spiral motion. "What is it?"

Pearl looked confused. Nnenna pointed to her and made the sign with her hand again, and Pearl's brow lifted as she understood. She reached into her pocket and retrieved the conch shell, holding it out with one hand and using the other to make a modified version of one of the signs she had been making. Was it treasure?

There was one person who could have helped, Nnenna thought ruefully, and there was no chance of that happening. But perhaps not all hope was lost. There was another person who might be useful. Seeing him would require making landfall on the one island to which it would be most dangerous for her to return.

Nnenna furrowed her brow as she tried to remember the signs she had learned over a decade ago. She pointed at Pearl and hovered both hands over the table with her thumb and pinkie finger extended. Then, she sharply brought her hands down toward the table. Afterward, she flipped her palms upward and extended all her fingers before curling her fingers inward and pulling her elbows toward her body as though she were opening a drawer. She finished the message by pointing to herself.

She had crudely asked Pearl if she wanted to stay with her. Nnenna did not want the girl to feel like she was a prisoner, but she obviously had no people here. Perhaps, Nnenna could help her find her way back to her family. Perhaps, she was royalty and her family would reward Nnenna handsomely for her return. Either way, the Fleet would not have what they wanted.

Pearl raised a fist and shook it as though knocking upon an invisible door. Another sign Nnenna recognized. She smiled and turned to Aline.

"She's going to stay with us," Nnenna explained.

"Tinou won't be happy," Aline joked.

"She will be once I tell her where we're going."

"And what place is so magical that it can turn Tinou's sour mood?"

"Kiskeya."

"The Jewel of the Seven Isles?" Aline asked, her eyes brightening. "You're taking me, as well?"

"Unless you plan to jump ship before we get there."

Aline squealed and bounced in her seat as though she were a schoolgirl.

"Do me a favor?" Nnenna asked Aline, placing a calming hand upon the young woman's arm. "Will you take Pearl to my cabin and help her find something less . . . conspicuous to wear? I need to go tell Tinou to change course. And try to keep your enthusiasm to a low rumble."

"Of course," Aline answered, blushing. "Anything for the woman who saved me from a life of bitter isolation."

Nnenna relayed the message to Pearl as best she could with the few signs she knew, supplemented by copious pointing. She was relieved when Pearl stood and looked at Aline expectantly. As the pair left the dining cabin, Nnenna leaned back in her seat and glanced out of the nearest porthole, contemplating her return to Kiskeya and everything she had left behind.

Twelve

THE VICEROY

Triton Stormcoast had been born at death's doorway. His mother and father had not expected their baby, who could barely breathe and whose heartbeat fluttered weakly and irregularly, to live through his first night, so they had taken him to the temple to sing to him as his soul passed from the world of the living. But when the dark of night had finally lightened to day, the son who should not have been alive had let out a mighty cry, the first of many in his life. The viceroy had been summoned and informed of the miracle that had occurred within the temple walls.

"He is destined to be a servant of Agwe!" Viceroy Seastead had proclaimed after seeking Agwe's counsel in the Divine Chamber. "Chosen by Agwe Himself!"

His word alone had been enough to convince the baby's parents to leave him in the care of the temple, to name him Triton Stormcoast as a reminder of his hidden strength, and to allow him to grow up in the heart of Agwe's bosom, perpetually surrounded by His grace. Stormcoast had never known any home but the temple, had never known any family other than the temple workers. When Viceroy Seastead had finally told him this

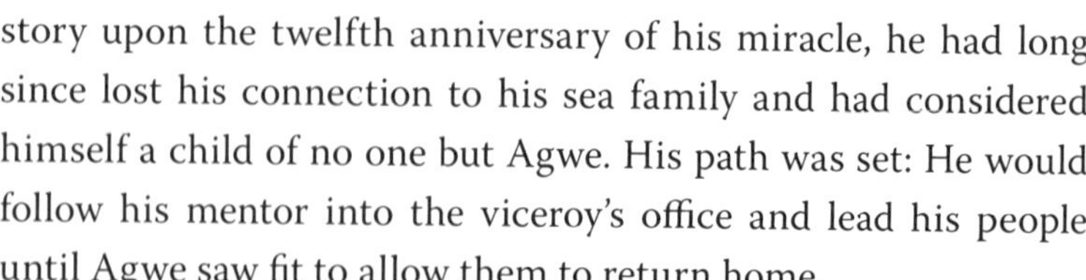

story upon the twelfth anniversary of his miracle, he had long since lost his connection to his sea family and had considered himself a child of no one but Agwe. His path was set: He would follow his mentor into the viceroy's office and lead his people until Agwe saw fit to allow them to return home.

Viceroy Stormcoast often pondered his role in the ushering in of his people's great destiny, but never more so than now. He had finally attained the office that would allow him to contemplate in Agwe's very presence. The Settlers were a lost people, not only separated from their home generations ago by their benevolent god but also separated from their devotion. Too many had been too easily swayed by the usurpers and their lies. Were it not for Stormcoast's swift implementation of Agwe's inspiration, the decades of work he had put toward fulfilling their destiny while Seastead had played the hero would have been for naught.

The people needed to be reminded of what they owed to Agwe in exchange for His blessings. The day of destiny was fast approaching. They needed to be ready to play their part.

Stormcoast took a deep breath and rose from the golden seat in the center of the Divine Chamber, directly facing a gilded framed circular mirror that hung on the rock wall. He glided to the curtain of kelp that separated the chamber from the rest of the temple. Pushing through the dangling greenery, he emerged onto the open landing and found himself flanked on either side by his recently promoted second-in-command, Secretary Matthias Marshwind, and the head of the temple guard. Marshwind had earned his place at Stormcoast's side with his careful work guiding the Settlement's children through Agwe's teachings, preparing them for eternity in Agwe's kingdom. Like Stormcoast, Marshwind understood that the gifts one displayed in life determined one's role in the kingdom, and Marshwind was uniquely able to foster those gifts so that they resulted in service to Agwe. Stormcoast appreciated the benefits of Marshwind's influence.

"Have they arrived?" he asked without looking at either man. He could sense their unwillingness to answer. "Speak!"

"There were some who . . . refused . . . the invitation, Viceroy," Marshwind said stiffly.

Stormcoast flared his nostrils as anger ignited within his chest, but he tamped it down as quickly as it came. "So be it," he said simply. He pushed off the landing and swam down to the opening that led to the balcony from which he had presided over Seastead's funeral, his white-and-gold robes flowing behind him.

He could hear the people milling about the square, awaiting his address, and could tell that there were far fewer in attendance than the many to whom he had extended the invitation. Undaunted, he swam forward through the opening, his arms raised.

"Brothers and sisters," he called without preamble, and all talk among the attendees ceased. "I thank you for answering my humble call. I have communed with Agwe for many hours!" He placed a hand over his chest and bowed his head slightly. "He has revealed to me that the time of His return draws nigh! How glorious it is to be among the chosen generation who will witness our people's miraculous restoration! We must cleanse ourselves in preparation! We must return ourselves to a state pleasing to our Lord. This day and every day henceforth shall be holy days. Go to your homes! Leave only to attend morning and evening sermons in this very square! Study Agwe's word! Worry not, for those who are cleansed will be fully restored! Agwe makes whole those who are in His service." He raised both arms, again, expecting the customary return of the recitation of Agwe's promise.

"What about the Highwaters?" an angry voice called from the crowd.

Viceroy Stormcoast looked down at the attendees for the very first time and saw that more than a few of their faces frowned in opposition to the rapture he had hoped to inspire. His earlier anger burned to life in his chest. He lowered his arms and stretched his neck muscles this way and that as he prayed to Agwe for patience.

"We are Agwe's chosen people," he intoned softly but sharply, speaking directly to a man in the center of the crowd who seemed particularly defiant. "We must be perfect in our devotion so that we may be welcomed back to our home and claim our rightful place in Agwe's kingdom. The Highwaters . . ." He paused. "The Highwater family have been chosen to perform important roles in Agwe's kingdom. It is our duty to find them and return them here. I am working closely with Wade Brinebottom, who, in his dear friends' absence, now resides in the temple under my protection."

There was a swell of chatter from the crowd. This time, he let it go until it died on its own. "Place your faith in the temple workers, for Agwe guides our every move," he went on. "Return to your homes. Temple guards will patrol the Settlement to better serve you." He made a fist and rested it upon his heart. "May Agwe bless you all from now until the day of our destiny."

Back inside the temple, Stormcoast found Marshwind and pulled him out of earshot of the other workers.

"How is our guest faring?" he murmured into the secretary's ear. Marshwind responded with a barely perceptible shake of his head. "Take me to him."

Marshwind scanned the temple atrium to make sure the rest of the workers were attending to their duties. When he was satisfied, he led the viceroy to the room directly below the Divine Chamber. Were it not for the pair of armed guards flanking the door, this room would have been unremarkable, but its importance lay in the sanctuary it offered the viceroy's guests.

Marshwind moved to the side as they approached, and Stormcoast unlocked the door. They entered together, the viceroy leading and Marshwind following closely behind, carrying a spear borrowed from one of the guards. The room that lay beyond opened into a cavernous chamber that, until recently, housed the former viceroy.

The majority of the furnishings were hidden under weighted cloths that swayed in the gentle currents. But cloths could not cover every sign of the luxury the room once contained. Gold- and silver-painted scallop shells adorned the walls, creating larger-than-life mosaics depicting Agwe at the moment He commanded the sea to envelop the island of Meridia. Marble tail fins poked out from underneath their covers all around the room, hinting at the statues of the previous occupants. A mammoth bed made of intricately carved whalebone loomed in the center, its posts reaching so high they nearly skimmed the ceiling. It was upon this bed that the room's third occupant sat, waiting at the edge of the mattress, his eyes staring vacantly at the wall opposite the door.

"Brother Brinebottom, my apologies for the delay in our meeting and for the state of your accommodations," Stormcoast said, swimming forward. "Viceroy Seastead was far more comfortable with the trappings of wealth than I."

"How very fortunate we are to have such a pious man leading our people," Brinebottom said flatly, without turning.

Marshwind surged forward, his spear at the ready.

"You will rise in the presence of the viceroy!" he commanded.

Brinebottom turned slowly but did not stand. "My apologies, Your Excellency. I have not been fed since I became your honored guest. Forgive a starving man his weakness in the presence of greatness."

The viceroy placed a staying hand upon Marshwind's spear, and the secretary retreated. Then, Stormcoast rounded the bed to stand before Brinebottom.

"An unforgivable oversight on the part of my guards," he said, "but they have been quite busy trying to find your . . . *niece*."

A shadow of a smile ghosted across Brinebottom's lips. "Pearl is nothing if not determined. If she does not want to be found, she won't be."

The viceroy frowned. "Agwe has chosen Pearl for a most divine calling. To function well, the Settlement needs the compassion that a nurturer brings to balance the sternness of authority. A mother's embrace to the father's hand."

Brinebottom scoffed.

"You don't agree?" the viceroy asked. "Did she not show compassion for your and Brother Highwater's proclivities, despite her steadfastness to Agwe's word?"

Brinebottom clenched his jaw. "Why not call it by its name?"

"I would never hope to insult you," Stormcoast answered.

"It is not an insult to me," Brinebottom said.

"Then, you have not studied the sacred texts well enough," the viceroy hissed. "Either way, a woman's touch would bring the sort of acceptance your kind needs to survive in the Settlement."

Brinebottom's fist clenched around the bed linens. "Even if I knew where she was," he said slowly, "I would never tell a man with *your* proclivities the location of a young girl."

The viceroy's hand flashed forward, striking Brinebottom's cheek with his knuckles and rings. Brinebottom reached up and touched his face where a gash had appeared, leaking blood into the surrounding waters. As Stormcoast took a calming breath, Brinebottom laughed.

"Did I say something to offend you, Your Excellency?"

Stormcoast took the man by the chin and forced him to meet his steely gray eyes.

"All things are righteous in the service of divinity. You will see that soon enough."

He let go of Brinebottom's face and straightened to his full height.

"Marshwind!" he called sharply, and his secretary snapped to attention. "Make sure our guest gets something to eat every day. We don't want his stay to be cut short, unexpectedly. In the meantime, I hope that this"—he produced a small red box made of lacquered wood from his pocket—"will keep you sated."

The viceroy opened the box with a flourish, revealing a single piece of crystallized sugar, dyed scarlet. Red tendrils bled into the water as the candy slowly dissolved before his and Brinebottom's eyes. He took the confection and held it out to Brinebottom.

"This is but a taste of what the land has to offer, just a fragment of what we will be afforded after we are restored to our home."

When Brinebottom did not take the offering, the viceroy placed it on the bed next to him and swam toward the door.

"Think hard about where you stand, Brother Brinebottom," he said. "I would hate for Pearl to be left without family because you were too eager to join Brother Highwater."

Thirteen

LU

When Lu arrived at the courtyard, he found a gallows had been erected where he had been conferred only days ago. Commodore Christophe was already in place, standing stiffly next to three conspicuously low-hanging nooses. He spotted Lu as soon as he arrived, and beckoned him to join.

Lu walked the rest of the way across the courtyard and climbed up the handful of steps to meet the commodore.

"This is quite the dreary business," he said somberly, as Lu took his place by his side.

"What exactly is . . . this, sir?" Lu asked tentatively.

"Ah, yes, every captain must experience their first. But, of course, this wouldn't be your first, now would it?"

Lu's stomach turned. "Who . . . ?" was all he could manage.

Before the commodore could answer, the doors that led to the dungeons beneath the Citadel swung open and several people emerged in succession. First came Captain Toussaint marching up the cellar steps onto the pavement as though she were part of a parade. Behind her, three smaller individuals followed, dragging their feet, dressed in the unmistakable green-and-gold uniform of the Fleet's midshipmen. They wore black hoods over their heads, cinched at the neck to cover their faces. They stumbled as they walked, bumping into each other and Captain Toussaint. Captain Boyer brought up the rear, looking tight-lipped and sour-faced.

The company marched in a straight line from the cellar to the platform. As they climbed the steps and walked past Lu and the commodore, Lu could hear gasping and whimpering coming from under the black hoods.

"Sir, is this truly necessary?" Lu asked, whispering out of the side of his mouth.

"Absolutely," Christophe answered, resolute. "But it is rather a shame that they are so young." The captains led the boys to each of the three nooses and fit the loops around each of their necks. When they pulled off the hoods, Lu felt as though his heart might actually shatter. Lu did not recognize them. They must have been newer recruits. They were barely out of child-hood, their faces tear streaked and still round with youth.

"They swore to obey orders, to carry out their duty on pain of death," Christophe said, reading Lu's mind. He heaved a heavy sigh. It was then that Lu noticed the sheaf of parchment in the commodore's hands. He brought it up to his face and cleared his throat. "Samuel Bernard, Kenzy Charles, Hercules Alexander," he read. "You stand accused of failure to perform your duty in the face of an enemy to the Fleet. Your actions have resulted in the loss of a valuable artifact. As punishment, you shall be hanged by the neck until dead. Have you any final words?"

He and Lu both looked back at the boys standing in a row on the platform. With the eyes of their superiors on them, they cried out. One apologized again and again. Another called for his mother.

The third simply wailed.

"May Agwe accept your tainted souls into His kingdom."

The commodore gave a nod, and Toussaint, who stood at the far side of the platform, grabbed a lever and swung it forward. With a loud, mechanical thunk, three identical trapdoors fell open, dropping the midshipmen so that their lower halves dangled below the platform and the nooses tightened around their necks. Grown men would have carried enough weight to break their necks the moment they reached the lowest point of their descent, but these were not grown men. Lu could only watch the ropes twitch frantically, and pray that the gagging would stop soon. It was worse when silence finally fell in the courtyard.

"Such a shame," the commodore sighed wearily. "So much potential wasted. Best not to tarry. There's work to be done."

It was not until the commodore's hand clapped upon Lu's shoulder that Lu realized he could move. He started, jerking his head toward the commodore's face, and was horrified to find him smiling. Completely numb, he let himself be led away from the hanging bodies, down the platform steps, and across the courtyard. As he walked, aimless and empty inside, he imagined the faces of the three midshipmen and wondered why. But, of course, he already knew why. It was in the oath he had even sworn upon taking up with the Fleet.

If I should ever have to choose between my duty and my life, then may my life be forfeit.

He was certain the midshipmen would have been better off dying on the *Adoration*.

Lu stopped suddenly and felt the commodore run into him.

"They were only boys," he finally said.

The commodore circled to his front and seized his shoulders, forcing Lu to look directly into his superior officer's brown eyes, alight with fervor. “We are none of us our own!” he intoned with such ferocity that Lu felt the visceral urge to pull away. The commodore’s grip was firm. “It is by Agwe’s grace alone that we live, and our lives are sworn to obedience to His word! They were servants of Agwe, just as you and I. They made their choices and now they have suffered the consequences.” He released Lu abruptly, and the younger man stumbled backward. “Duty is how we show our devotion,” the commodore added softly. “And one’s devotion must never be questioned.”

Even in his dazed state, Lu understood the commodore’s message. It was now his devotion resting upon Agwe’s scale, waiting to be weighed, hoping to be found sufficient. This was not what Lu had imagined when the senior officers had taught him that Agwe would test His followers in the final days. He had stayed the course from the day he had joined the Fleet, had made the most sacred covenants to Agwe in His herald’s cabin. Surely, that was proof enough that he deserved to be counted among the faithful.

“Do you know why I sent Rochefort to retrieve the girl instead of you, Ortega?”

“No, sir,” Lu replied distantly.

“You and Rochefort shared many similarities, but where he was foolhardy and overly eager to prove himself worthy, you are cautious. There is a level manner in you, a desire to be recognized, but not the center of attention, that told me you have all the makings of a great commodore . . . perhaps one of the greatest commodores the Fleet has ever seen. But with the *Fortitude* all the way out in the Northwestern Gulf, there was only one way to get you a ship in time to make sure you were at my side when we brought about our destiny.”

Lu’s eyes widened. “Sir, are you saying you—”

“I let destiny decide and destiny chose you!”

He clamped his hand around Lu's upper arm and dragged him across the courtyard and around the fortress's eastern wing. The commodore flagged down one of the midshipmen filing out of the Citadel's side doors to report for morning duties.

"Sir," the lad chirped, excited to have earned the attention of the commodore himself, completely unaware of the horror that took place just on the other side of the building they called home.

"Saddle Coriolanus and bring him here," the commodore ordered, sparing the boy barely a glance. The midshipman jogged off to fulfill the commodore's wish. The commodore's eye was trained on Lu. "I know you think that nothing could possibly be worth what you have just been through, but I promise you there are more things at work than you know," he said in an almost frenzied whisper. "Our allies in the sea will join our ranks when the time comes, but for now they need our help."

The boy returned leading a strong-looking chestnut mount by the reins. "Coriolanus, sir," he said, presenting the horse to the commodore.

"Thank you, Jean," Commodore Christophe said, and Lu was reluctantly impressed that he knew the boy by name. "That will be all."

Lu watched the boy walk off and take his place among the other midshipmen, and he wondered if there was anything he could do to be one of them again.

"I have no doubt that the Devil of the Deep has learned of our destiny and made it her mission to prevent it from coming to pass," the commodore said hoarsely, pulling Lu out of his thoughts. "I refuse to allow her to do so. You know what is at stake. You've seen the true nature of our devotion. There is no turning back. You must now choose either to be with us or to be counted among our enemies."

"Sir, I don't—I—" Lu stammered.

"Choose, Ortega!"

"I choose the Fleet, sir!"

The words had tumbled out of his mouth before they were even a thought, but, in truth, there was no other answer he could have given. He had dreamed of being a captain since he was a child. How could he give it all up now?

The commodore's face split into the same satisfied smile he had made the previous evening, only this time, Lu felt no pride in having given the commodore exactly the answer he had been looking for.

"Marvelous!" he said, clapping Lu upon the shoulder. "A captain must go to any lengths to ensure the Fleet's destiny is fulfilled! Take Coriolanus—" He handed Lu the reins. "Ride into the Southern District and join the patrols at Sun City. Gather as much information about incoming ships as you can. Kiskeya is the closest civilized island to where the *Adoration* was ambushed. I suspect if the Devil has the artifact, she'll want to learn what it is and how she can use it. Leave at nightfall and report back to me the moment you return. Tell no one else. It's up to the two of us now, Ortega."

Lu nodded, shaken by what he had seen and the commodore's admission, but inwardly grateful to have the comfort of purpose to fall back upon. Destiny had chosen him. Agwe had chosen him. He would do what he must to prove himself worthy.

Fourteen

PEARL

Pearl lay on her back on the strange new bed, dressed in borrowed clothes that hung a little loosely on her body, happy that her belly was full for the first time since she had enacted Agwe's curse. The hours she had spent on the other ship had been exactly as Viceroy Stormcoast had warned about land dwellers who took to the sea. They had handled her roughly, laughing at her when she could not understand their land-dweller words, tossed her into an empty chamber, and locked her away while her stomach cramped angrily.

When the attack on the ship had begun, one of the youngest of her captors had retrieved her from her prison. He had only managed to drag her as far as the narrow passage where they kept their food before leaving her to seek refuge on his own. Pearl had decided if she were going to die, she would do so with a full stomach and had begun taking exploratory bites of anything that had looked edible within reach. She had not gotten far when the tall, dark woman had appeared. Like the guards, she had tried and failed to get Pearl to speak. Scowling, the woman had left, and Pearl had thought herself doomed until she had returned, bringing with her a second woman, whose dark red hair hung in tendrils that framed her round brown face.

"Nne . . . nna," Pearl mouthed silently, working her tongue around the unfamiliar syllables of the land-dweller language.

Nnenna and her people had fed her, clothed her, and given her a room to sleep in that was warm and quiet. Nnenna had even given her back her uncle's shell. Nnenna surprisingly knew the sacred signs that her people used to commune with Agwe in song. The viceroy had proclaimed all land dwellers were to be feared, that they were more cursed than even the Settlers because they knew nothing of Agwe's grace. But if Nnenna and her people were among the cursed, they seemed not to be aware.

It was dark now, and Pearl had a view of the most beautiful thing she had ever seen, a blue so deep it could have been black, but pinpricked by millions upon millions of lights. Some of them were small stationary dots while others swirled like whirlpools. Back home, she had learned of the sky from her lessons, but she knew it only as the black sheet beyond the veil that held the tide bringer. She wondered what her uncles would say if they could see it. Then, she remembered, and Uncle Wade's voice floated to her mind.

"I'm so sorry, my love."

Uncle Rain was dead. The truth sat in the pit of her stomach like a stone, uncomfortable and immovable. The loneliness that ate away at her made it worse. She was surrounded by people, most of whom she could not communicate with, though they seemed friendly enough. As brave as she tried to be, she felt as though she were swept up in an inescapable tide, and all she wanted was for her uncles to catch her and tell her everything would be all right.

Pearl sighed. She did not even know how things could

possibly be made all right from where they were now. She was a fugitive and, apparently, a thief. What would her uncles tell her to do? She tried hard to bring their faces to the forefront of her mind, to hear their voices in her ears.

"I am always with you, darling girl," Uncle Wade said.

"Just sing our song and I will be there," said Uncle Rain.

It was too much. She squeezed her eyelids shut tight against the sting of oncoming tears, but they leaked out all the same. Sadness felt different on this side of the veil. Bereft of the ocean's comforting embrace, Pearl felt the weight of her melancholy on her body and in her soul. She broke down and cried, her ragged sobs cutting through her like barbs.

She did not know how long she cried, but when the sobs finally relented, she could not bear to be alone or idle any longer. This vessel operated similarly to the Settlement, with every adult contributing to its well-being. She was an adult, now. If Pearl could no longer be a part of her own community, she would earn her keep in this one. After sending Agwe another hopeful, silent prayer, she pushed herself out of the bed and stood, her bare feet sticking to the wooden planks in the humid sea air as she ventured from her chambers back to Nnenna's quarters.

Most of the crew had retired for the night. All the doors in the narrow passageway between the handful of rooms on this floor of the ship were closed, except for one. Pearl saw the flicker of candlelight, her favorite of the land-dweller magics, coming through a cracked doorway. She walked toward it. As she drew closer, she heard voices—a man and a woman, by the sounds of their whispers. They spoke animatedly, going back and forth quickly and even speaking over each other. Pearl recognized a few land-dweller words that she had learned from her captors. Ship. Captain. Fight. It wasn't enough for her to understand what the conversation was about, but it was enough to pique her interest.

She crept even closer to the door and peeked inside the narrow opening in the doorway. The man was new to her, tall and rotund with a bald head and bulging eyes, but the woman she knew as Tinou. As Pearl wondered what she could have been discussing so secretively, the woman's head twisted toward the door, and Pearl found herself looking into her long-lashed brown eyes. She flinched as the woman stepped toward her, closing the distance between herself and the door. She grabbed the door's edge and slammed it shut in Pearl's face. Pearl stepped back and sighed. Whatever the matter was, it was none of her business. She walked past the door toward the pillar of moonlight spilling from the opening that led to the outside.

There were many steps separating her from her destination, and ascending them was the most awkward she'd ever felt in her life. When she finally emerged from the ship's lower floor, she was relieved not to have fallen. This relief was short-lived as she was immediately taken with the vastness of the sky above. With her head craned back and her mouth wide open, Pearl staggered across the deck. Someone spoke from behind her. She wheeled around and spotted one of her rescuers, Nnenna, sitting on the steps that led to a raised deck. She wore robes made of luxurious-looking shiny fabric. Pearl looked at her, confused.

Nnenna repeated herself and signed as she spoke. She pointed to the sky and then brought her hand to her own face. Nnenna made a circular motion around her face as her fingers closed, and once the circle was complete, the fingers burst open. Beautiful.

Pearl raised her own hands and signed back, "The most beautiful thing I've ever seen."

Pearl took Nnenna's smile as a sign of her understanding.

Nnenna stood, pulling the robe more tightly closed around her body, and walked toward Pearl. "Who are you?" she signed.

Pearl did not know how to answer.

"Lost," she signed back.

Surprisingly, this made Nnenna smile again. "Me too," she signed. "Where is home?"

Pearl thought of the home she shared with her uncles, of the Settlement where she had been born and had spent her entire life. She thought of the beliefs and rituals that had enshrouded her and of how they might all be lies.

"Lost," she signed again.

Nnenna nodded, her eyes drifting out of focus. Pearl waved a hand in front of her face to regain her attention.

"Sorry," Nnenna apologized, rubbing her flat hand in a circle over her chest.

Pearl replied with a nod.

"What land men want?" Nnenna asked in broken sign.

Pearl had to think for a moment before she understood the question. The land men. The land-dweller guards in the uniforms who had taken her from the island and held her captive on their ship. They had made their intentions clear when they had held her, searched her, taken the conch shell, and then left her to rot in the belly of their ship. The memory made her almost sick with anger. She reached into her pocket and pulled out the shell, holding it out to Nnenna.

"Know what?" Nnenna signed.

Pearl shook her head. She had no idea what the shell was for, but Uncle Wade had been adamant that she take it, no doubt to keep it from the viceroy. She may not have known what happened to her uncle, but she would honor his request.

"Hold?" Nnenna asked and Pearl nodded.

Nnenna plucked the shell carefully from Pearl's palm. At first, she brought it close to her face and tried to peer from one end to the other with little success. Then, she stretched her arm toward the sky and held it up to the incomplete tide bringer. Pearl held her breath as she watched, hoping something—anything—would happen. Somewhere in the distance, a voice called Nnenna's name, startling both her and Pearl. When Pearl looked, the door to Nnenna's cabin was open and the silhouette of a woman wrapped in linens stood in the doorway. It was Nnenna's lover, Aline, and the sight of her made Pearl blush.

Nnenna handed the shell back to Pearl.

"Bedtime," she signed with a wicked grin that made Pearl's flush deepen.

"Wait!" Pearl signed as she stashed the shell back into her pocket. "I want to work!"

This made Nnenna laugh. "No need," she signed. "Rest."

Nnenna placed a reassuring hand on the girl's shoulder. She pressed the tips of her fingers on her right hand together and touched them to her jaw and her cheek in succession. *Home.*

Then, she made a fist and quickly stuck her middle and fore-fingers out toward Pearl. *Soon.*

Pearl's relief came as a surprise. She watched Nnenna walk back toward her cabin, certain, for the first time since this ordeal began, that she was in good hands.

Fifteen

NNENNA

Nnenna pressed her back against the ridged trunk of the palm tree, hoping that enough pressure would relieve all the sore knots that had formed deep within her muscles. She heard her mother's voice over the calls of the seagulls and closed her eyes, angrily wondering what more the woman could possibly have wanted after the day she had forced Nnenna to endure. She called Nnenna a second time, and Nnenna prayed to the goddess that she would just give up. Like always, the goddess's mercy was nowhere to be found. She heard another call, closer this time, and knew that her few minutes of solitude would soon be at an end.

Nnenna stood, stretched, and brushed the sand off her skirt. She sighed, allowing herself one last, long look at the people on the busy street before walking back to the one-room shotgun house she shared with her mother for the time being. Her mother had gotten impatient and met her halfway.

"There you are, girl!" she snapped, catching Nnenna by the earlobe and giving it a sharp downward tug. "I've been calling you!"

Nnenna winced in pain but knew better than to answer. Without a word, her mother turned on the path back toward the shack, and Nnenna followed dutifully. The moment she crossed the threshold, the unpleasantly familiar smell of smoke and drink wafted over her.

"I'm all out," her mother said, and Nnenna sighed again, rolling her eyes while her mother's back was turned.

"And I suppose you'll be needing my coin to get it," she muttered, casting her eye around the interior of the single-room shotgun house they shared and counting the empty bottles strewn about the meager space.

"What was that, girl?"

"Nothing," Nnenna said quickly.

Her mother scowled. "Go to that fancy inn. Get me four bottles of their best rum."

"But mother, I'm not—" Nnenna said, looking down at her stained clothing.

"And don't dawdle," her mother said, cutting her off.

Nnenna sighed. "I won't."

Her mother was in a foul mood, but not the worst Nnenna had seen. She had been asleep when Nnenna had left well before sunrise, and had most likely slept through the day. It must have been some time since her last drink.

It was a short walk to the Singing Crab Inn from their little hovel. Nnenna had made the journey so many times she could do it with her eyes closed and her mind carrying her elsewhere. All she had to do was follow the stream of important-looking people walking along the main road that led to the port. Then, she would break from the crowd at the black iron fence surrounding the large building.

"Back so soon?" the woman who owned the establishment asked when Nnenna entered the dining room and slinked up to the bar.

"I'm sorry," Nnenna apologized, avoiding her eye.

"I would've thought that last haul would've lasted at least a week," she said.

"Some of it was stolen," Nnenna lied. "Four bottles, please."

"Two gold."

With a heavy heart, Nnenna reached into her money pouch and poured the contents into her palm. After counting out enough silver and copper to amount to two gold, she handed over nearly every bit of money she had earned from four days of backbreaking labor. In return, she got four bottles of Ayiti's finest brown sugar liquor.

Nnenna thanked the woman, took the bottles, and was heading for the door when the smell of something salty, spicy, and irresistible wafted past her. Her stomach gurgled loudly, reminding her of how many times she had chosen to work rather than eat that week. The smell came from the kitchen just a few yards away. She should have ignored it—her mother was waiting—but there was something small and mean inside her that said her mother could wait a few minutes longer.

"How much for the stew?" Nnenna asked the woman.

"Four copper for a bowl," the woman answered.

Nnenna poured out the last of her money and three copper pieces clattered onto the shining wood surface. She groaned.

"Can I just . . . sit here for a bit?" Nnenna asked, defeated.

The woman looked up from her task and seemed to truly see the girl sitting in front of her, saw her matted black hair and dirty clothes, her worn boots and skinny frame. Her stern face softened to a look of sympathy that made Nnenna feel self-conscious.

"Forget it," Nnenna said. "I'll just—"

"Of course," the woman said gently. "Stay as long as you like."

"Thank you," Nnenna said softly as she rested upon the stool once more.

She may have been starving, but sitting on the soft cushion and leaning against the bar felt wonderful. There was no such comfort to look forward to when she returned to the shack. If she were lucky, her mother would let her furnish her corner of the floor with a blanket.

"Here," the woman said, pulling Nnenna out of her musings. She pushed a bowl of steaming hot stew and a spoon toward Nnenna. "On the house."

"I'll work for it," Nnenna said quickly. "I'm no beggar."

The woman thought for a moment. Then, she smiled. "Sure," she said. "Come back tomorrow. Early. I'll give you work, and I'll take the stew out of your pay."

"Yes, madame," Nnenna said, nodding.

The woman waved Nnenna's formality away. "Call me Tati Clo."

Nnenna nodded again, her eyes and mouth watering as she dipped the spoon into the stew and brought the first hot spoonful into her mouth. Whatever intentions she had of eating with dignity evaporated as soon as the deliciously salty, savory stew touched her tongue. She moaned gratefully with each bite, barely stopping to breathe in between. When there was no more liquid to slurp up, she brought the rim of the bowl to her lips and shoveled the final dregs into her mouth. The bowl practically sparkled when she set it back down.

The woman stared at her, a hand on her hip. Nnenna quickly grabbed the bottles of rum, tucked them under her arms, and left the inn. Her mother's mood was worse by the time she returned. She cuffed Nnenna over the side of the head and took the bottles to the rickety wooden bed frame—the shack's only piece of furniture—sat down, and drank. But, with her belly full for the first time in a long time and the promise of work in the morning, Nnenna took to her corner of the floor almost unbothered.

•••●•••

It had been an age since Nnenna had awoken already knowing the name of the person with whom she shared a bed, and now it had happened every morning since she and Aline had left Yamaye together. She had offered Aline sleeping quarters of her own to assure Aline that she had no expectations, but Aline had insisted on staying in the great cabin with Nnenna. It had made sense—attaching oneself to the captain on an unfamiliar ship was a smart way to ensure her own safety. She could have insisted, but, instead, Nnenna had given in readily, a decision she acknowledged was based more on physical need rather than actual sense. Now she reaped the fruits of her lustful labors.

Aline was beautiful and clever, a gift to anyone lucky enough to know her. Being with her made Nnenna feel like an ungrateful fool not wanting to keep her for herself, but she knew the Devil of the Deep's life did not lend itself to long-term entanglements. Besides, it seemed as though Aline was perfectly content with their arrangement. Truth be told, it would be a relief when Nnenna dropped Aline off in Ayiti and returned to her life at sea. Her study of their curious connection had yielded more awareness of the effect Aline had on her and even less understanding. And it was not only Nnenna, but most to whom she spoke a desire aloud who were likely to acquiesce.

One night, early in their journey, Aline had asked about Nnenna's life off the *Medusa*, and a song that she had not thought of in years had risen in Nnenna's heart. It had been a fisherfolk song that she had learned from a friend long ago, an offering to a nameless sea goddess in exchange for smooth sailing. Nnenna did not believe in its power the way the fisherfolk did, but Aline had asked to hear it, and Nnenna had been unable to refuse. She had even taught the song to Aline, and they had tried singing it together. Once their voices had joined in harmony, Nnenna had felt a quiet come upon her that had escaped her for years. Drunk on something more powerful than her whiskey, Nnenna had allowed Aline to take her to bed and exhaust her with pleasure until she had fallen into a rare, dreamless sleep. It had not been until the next morning that the feeling had worn off and Nnenna had been able to think clearly again. She realized just how much power Aline had over her. Nnenna had no explanation and did not know if she possessed enough willpower to prevent it from happening again.

Of course, Aline was not the only mystery on the ship. The young girl, Pearl, was the other passenger Nnenna had recently acquired who absolutely confounded her. She could not speak but knew the signs of Ayiti's fisherfolk. She had the look of an Islander, too, but the wonder with which she regarded her surroundings told Nnenna that she was a stranger to the Seven Isles. How, then, could the Fleet know who she was, and what could they possibly have needed from her?

If Nnenna was being honest, the Fleet's motivations were immaterial. It was enough that they locked Pearl away, enough that she had been frightened and desperate when Nnenna found her, and enough that rescuing her from them would put a stop to whatever plans they had that required her.

Nnenna had given Pearl a cabin on the lower deck and ordered the crew to provide her with anything she needed. There had been grumblings from the group, but Tinou had been the only soul brave enough to voice her disapproval of the newcomers. She thought herself a coldhearted pirate, through and through, but Nnenna knew her shortsightedness would do her no favors. If a certain pirate had not taken a chance when the sea had washed Nnenna up, she might not have even lived long enough to see this day, let alone become the best-known scourge of the Seven Isles. Nnenna had listened to every one of Tinou's complaints, which quickly evolved into an open diatribe of Nnenna's decisions of late. Then, she reminded Tinou of the captain's privileges by revoking her furlough. She would remain on the *Medusa* when they reached Kiskeya. If Tinou would not come around to Nnenna's way of thinking by choice, then it would have to be by force.

When the sun rose enough to light the great cabin, Nnenna disentangled herself from Aline's limbs and went to her wardrobe to dress for the day. Ayiti's shores were mere hours away, and she could not make landfall as the Devil of the Deep. She had collected many treasures throughout her years of pillaging Fleet ships, but the garment she reached for now had originated on the island. The fabrics were simple cotton but painstakingly dyed to resemble the colors of the Ayitian flag. The bodice was a deep, velvety blue and the skirt bloodred. She wrapped a white cloth around her hair to complete the ensemble with a simple headdress. As she regarded herself in her hand mirror, she caught a flash of the girl she had been the last time she had worn these clothes, and a swell of discomfort rose within her. She reminded herself that she was older now, stronger, and had seen more of the world than she had ever dreamed she could. It did not help to assuage the storm brewing inside her.

"What's the occasion?" Aline asked.

Nnenna wheeled around and found the woman lying on her side in the berth, propping her head on her hand, looking picturesque in the morning glow.

"Homecoming," Nnenna sighed.

The island of Kiskeya had a distinct crab-claw shape that

made it the most recognizable of the Seven Isles. It was divided into two nations: Ayiti and Kiskeya. Ayiti, the mountainous region of the island, occupied the pincers of the claw and was split into Northern and Southern Districts. The Northern District was most notably home to the Citadel, which produced Fleet officers despite the efforts of Nnenna and her crew. The capital of Ayiti, Prince's Port, lay nestled in the heart of the Southern District. This was where Nnenna had been born and where, after a long absence, she intended to return.

"I shouldn't be gone more than twenty-four hours," Nnenna explained to Tinou as the foursome sat around the table in the dining cabin to break their fast. "While I'm gone, you're in charge. The men are free to leave the ship, but they must be ready to set sail by four bells in the forenoon watch tomorrow."

"Assuming you manage to make it back on time, without picking up another stray," Tinou muttered. Nnenna shot her a dangerous look. She decided she would have a frank conversation with Tinou about her attitude when she returned to the ship.

Four hours later, the *Medusa* weighed anchor in Prince's Port Bay, half a league off the coast of the mainland, comfortably hidden among the dozens of other ships moored in the crystalline waters. Nnenna rowed Aline and Pearl to shore in a longboat, not at the port, but to a narrow strip of beach to its southeast that would allow them to sneak into the city unnoticed. This was Nnenna's usual method of making landfall undetected. She often disguised herself as one of the rich travelers who frequented the Jewel of the Seven Isles for the goods and services that were unique to the island. This time, she had two maids with her to help her carry the many purchases she would make, or so their story went.

Kiskeya was by far the most prosperous of the Seven Isles, its abundant resources attracting interest from all over the world, but it was not without its flaws. The wealth that Ayiti generated never seemed to make it to those who worked hardest to create it. In no place in Ayiti was this more evident than Soley, the crowded Prince's Port neighborhood that Nnenna had once reluctantly called home. As she slipped into the stream of travelers on the artery that most used to get through Soley, Pearl and Aline following closely behind, Nnenna saw one reminder after another of the life she had escaped. The people in this area lived in desperation, entire families packed into single-room houses that they leased at exorbitant rates from landlords for whom they also worked. Nnenna's family had lived this way. Her father had been a laborer, traveling miles from Sun City to wherever skilled hands were needed to build museums and monuments for a handful of copper coins that would not cover the cost of bread for the week. She remembered how he had come home exhausted every night but had always insisted he had reserved a bit of his strength for regaling his young daughter with the story of something spectacular he had seen and a song to help her drift off to sleep. If Nnenna had a kind bone in her body, it was because of him. She had let much of what she knew of him go when he had passed into the Unknown, but not this.

When she visited Ayiti, she made sure to fill her money pouch with coins for the children who would see her finery and come to beg. She knew the coppers and silvers she pressed into their palms would make as much difference to their hunger as they had done for hers when she had been one of them, but she gave in to the hope that fortune would find them the way it had found her.

Nnenna reached for the pouch, but she stopped short, fear rising in her. Dozens of bright green uniforms popped out against the dull backdrop of grime-coated houses on either side of the road. Fleet lieutenants on patrol. Why were there so many of them here? The Fleet preyed on the desperate, but they had never reached this far into the Southern District.

"Stay close. Walk fast," she said to Aline and Pearl. For Pearl, she surreptitiously signed the command. They had come too far to turn back.

Nnenna stashed the pouch away, straightened her back, and quickened her pace. With her best rendition of haughtiness upon her face, she wove through the milling masses, hoping the impatience she exuded would discourage the beetles from approaching them. Their destination was only a mile away, an inn where they would find refuge. If they were swift, they would reach it in minutes. As they came upon the main road that stretched along the neighborhood's eastern border, a uniformed figure stepped into her path, hand outstretched.

"Madame, have you a moment to—"

She could not afford to stop, lest he get a good look at any of their faces, so she barreled into him, feigning not to have noticed him.

"Watch it!" she snapped over her shoulder as she and her companions sped away from the lieutenant.

Without looking back, she led them across Soley Road and into the adjoining Chancerelles. When they came to the gate of the Singing Crab Inn, Nnenna was tense and sweating for reasons that had nothing to do with the heat. She nodded graciously to the footman on guard who let her through.

The Singing Crab was a popular destination for visitors to Prince's Port. Its white, plaster-coated stone edifice stood an impressive three stories tall and embodied the unique building style that travelers came to Ayiti to see. The high-pitched roof drew the eye upward to the elegantly sculpted plaster trim around the windows and doors and balconies that wrapped all the way around the second and third floors. Surrounded on all sides by a heavy iron gate and insulated by a lush green lawn and dense growing plants, the inn offered those who could afford to stay there a quiet refuge from the city's noise. To these people, the Singing Crab Inn was a luxury amidst squalor. To Nnenna, it was simply home.

•••●•••

The front door creaked as Nnenna pushed it open and she, Aline, and Pearl stepped into a dimly lit, warmly decorated dining room. Half a dozen tables filled the space on one side, and a lacquered wooden bar ran along the far wall. Claudette Jean-Louis—Tati Clo to those who were close to her—stood behind the bar and before the door that led to the kitchen. She was a statuesque, round-faced beauty with high cheekbones, almond-shaped eyes, and deep umber skin. Her face was pinched into a frown as she vigorously wiped down the already shining bar top.

"Welcome to the Singing Crab," she said without looking up from her work. "Seat yourself at a table. I will take your order in a moment."

Never one to follow instructions, Nnenna strode over to the bar and took a seat on a stool directly in front of the woman.

"Is the fish stew still the best on the island?" Nnenna asked.

Tati Clo froze. She looked up, and when her narrow brown eyes met Nnenna's, her jaw dropped.

"By the seven," she whispered, looking at Nnenna as though she were a ghost. The longer she stared, the wider the smile creeping across her lips became. "Look what the tide's brought in!"

"Hello, Tati," Nnenna said with a smirk.

"Don't call me that!" the woman hissed, glancing around to make sure no one heard. "The beetles have taken to shutting down businesses owned by regular folk. Apparently only the friends of the Fleet are allowed to earn a living. You must call me Lady Jean-Louis."

Nnenna frowned. Though her mother-by-choice bore few signs of her age, she had already been the proprietor of the Singing Crab for many years when Nnenna had been born. Her husband, Yves, a seafarer like Nnenna, had perished on the water, but his crew had taken pains to deliver his final cut and the golden earrings he wore as insurance to her. The takings had been enough for Claudette to live a quiet life on her own in the fisherfolk housing, but she had not wanted to spend the rest of her life waiting to be reunited with her husband. Instead, she had purchased a run-down tavern, done the work to clean it up herself, and turned it into a Prince's Port institution.

Now, it seemed, the Fleet was trying to take all that away from her.

"My apologies, Lady Jean-Louis," Nnenna corrected herself with exaggerated deference as she inclined her head. Doing so brought her closer to Claudette, and when they were mere inches apart, Nnenna whispered, "Have they hurt you?"

Claudette tutted. "Let me look at you!" She ducked under the counter and squeezed through the gap in the bar. Nnenna slid from her stool, and Lady Jean-Louis pulled her into an embrace, pressing Nnenna against her prodigious bosom. "Just my business," she warned under her breath. "They're inspecting more often. At least once a week. The last was yesterday so you have some time, but be careful." She pushed Nnenna out to arm's length. "You're so thin!" she announced to the whole dining room.

Now, it was Nnenna's turn to glance around the room nervously. The faces were unfamiliar, but she saw no signs of green and gold. "Sven keeps me well-fed!"

Claudette assessed her carefully. Her eyes flicked up to Nnenna's headdress. "Is he keeping up with your hair, as well? Or are you hiding a mess for me to clean up?"

This was not part of their ruse. "My hair is fine," Nnenna laughed, sitting back on the stool. "I oil it every day and twist the new growth every month."

Claudette sat in the adjacent seat, looking satisfied. "Should I tell *Rosalie* you're back?" she asked, raising her eyebrows. "It's been months, you know."

"I know," Nnenna sighed, wincing slightly as her guilt reared its ugly head. "I suppose she'll find out one way or another."

"Suitors every day, breaking down my door, but she will not give any of them the time of day," Claudette went on.

"I'm sure," Nnenna said, feeling the weight of Claudette's every word. "She's a lovely girl."

"A lovely girl who needs to get her life started," Claudette said. "And if that life isn't going to be with you, then it would be nice to see her married before my soul returns to the sea."

"My lady, there are surely many more years to come before that day."

Claudette smiled. "So, what will it be, this time? The usual? A room, a bath, meals?"

"Actually," Nnenna said, "I have something to offer you." She beckoned Aline forward. "This is my friend Aline. She's looking to make a life for herself in Prince's Port. I thought this would be the best place for her to start."

Lady Jean-Louis looked Aline up and down dubiously. "What can she do?"

"*She* can cook, clean, sketch, dance, sing, and do anything else you need," Aline interjected. She extended her hand to Lady Jean-Louis. "Pleasure to make your acquaintance, madame."

Lady Jean-Louis laughed, taking the offered hand and shaking it. "I like this one already!" Her eye wandered to Pearl. "And what about that one? She lookin' for a new life here, too?"

Nnenna moved to block the lady's view of Pearl. "No," she said, quickly. "She stays with me."

"She's a bit young for you."

Nnenna snorted. "She's not—I'm only helping her find her way home."

"Hmm," Lady Jean-Louis breathed, unconvinced. "Our lady of the lost lambs, now, are you?"

"I learned by watching the best," Nnenna retorted. Without missing a beat, Nnenna pulled out a pouch full of gold pieces and dropped it on the bar so that the currency jingled. "This should cover two rooms, meals, and Aline's rent for the week. And a little extra for your, er, discretion."

Claudette smiled. "You know that's not necessary. I don't need compensation to protect my own."

"You may not need it, but you certainly deserve it."

Claudette shook her head but pocketed the money all the same. She took two iron keys from the collection that hung behind the bar and handed them to Nnenna. "Rooms four and five on the second floor," she said. "I'll send Rosalie up with your lunch shortly."

The trio made their way to the second floor. Nnenna dropped Pearl off at her room, first. She pointed to the girl, pointed to the door with a wooden number five nailed to it, and brought both of her fists down with her thumbs and pinkies sticking out. Pearl pointed to Nnenna and made the same sign, but her face made it clear she was asking a question. Would Nnenna be staying with her? Nnenna shook her head and pointed to the door across the hall, room number four. Pearl nodded in understanding. Nnenna pressed the key into Pearl's palm and made the same sign she had made before. "Stay here," she said, emphasizing both words.

Pearl nodded again, took the key, and unlocked the door. Satisfied, Nnenna retired to the room she had reserved for herself and Aline.

"A bit bold of you to assume you'll be able to stay in *my* room," Aline teased as Nnenna closed the door behind her.

"My apologies," Nnenna laughed.

The room was bright and smelled freshly cleaned. The sun shone through the windows, casting shadows on the carpeted floor. There was a bed on one side, a large four-poster behemoth that put her berth in the *Medusa*'s great cabin to shame. On the other side was a standing wooden privacy screen, behind which rested a shining copper bathtub that made Nnenna's skin tingle in anticipation.

"What do you think?" Nnenna asked Aline, who also took stock of the room's amenities. She did not know why, but she felt a thrill of nervousness as she waited for Aline's answer.

Aline smiled as she ran her fingertips over the bed's smooth wooden footboard. "It'll do," she answered.

"Tati Clo is a good mistress. Very reasonable. You'll like it here."

"It sounds like you have firsthand experience," Aline said, turning to face Nnenna.

"I do," Nnenna admitted. "I don't come to this island often, but when I do, I always find the time to stop at the Singing Crab."

"Where's your family?"

Nnenna bristled. "I don't have any."

There was a knock at the door. Nnenna turned and opened it, coming face-to-face with—"Rosalie!" Nnenna blurted.

The woman before her was nearly as tall as Nnenna, but that was where their similarities ended. Where Nnenna had rich, dark brown skin the color of freshly turned soil, Rosalie was the color of tea with a generous helping of milk. Her long, curly red hair fell over her shoulders and down her back, her eyes like dark honey.

"Your midday meal," Rosalie said stiffly, looking over Nnenna's shoulder at Aline. In her hands was a covered tray of food.

"It's nice to see you," Nnenna said, awkwardly trying to regain her attention.

Rosalie breathed in sharply and returned her gaze to Nnenna, smiling suddenly. Nnenna reached for words to comfort Rosalie, but came up empty.

"Yes! It's been so long! I—here, let me . . ."

She lowered her head and pushed past Nnenna into the room, then deposited the covered food tray at the foot of the bed.

"I'm afraid there's only one meal," she said, looking at neither Nnenna nor Aline. "When Tati—I mean Lady Jean-Louis—said you were here, she did not mention—I mean, I did not realize you had a—"

"Don't fret over it," Nnenna said. "We can share."

Rosalie nodded, glancing at the door.

"If you have things to do—" Nnenna started.

"You could have at least told me when you said goodbye, you meant you were through with me."

"Rosalie, we never—"

"It's no matter. Please, let me know if you need anything else."

With a final, tense smile, Rosalie raced out of the room, pulling the door shut behind her.

"What was that?" Aline asked, stifling a laugh.

"That was . . . Rosalie," Nnenna sighed. "Another one of Tati Clo's rescues. She has been . . . attached to me . . . for some time."

Aline laughed. "The poor girl! And you never gave her the time of day?"

Nnenna shrugged. "She's not exactly my type."

"And how cruel of you to keep bringing your cast-off paramours to her home and flaunting them in her face!"

"Hardly," Nnenna said. "I've never brought anyone here before. And I certainly wouldn't consider you cast off. I am simply fulfilling your request."

Aline placed both hands over her heart and walked toward Nnenna, wearing a look of mischief.

"What if I have more requests?"

Nnenna smiled. She closed the space between them, snaking one arm around her waist and tugging at the lacing on Aline's bodice with her other.

"I'm all ears."

Sixteen

LU

Lu ran up the path that led to the front door of the mansion that had been his home since his birth. His long black hair flew wild and free of its plaits and ribbons in the wind, as a smile stretched across his face. He clutched a piece of parchment as if his life depended upon it, his chest heaving against the constraints of the layers of stays and skirts that entangled him. It hurt like hell, but he kept running.

He burst through the door and up the grand staircase, taking as many stairs at a time as his dress would allow. He did not stop to explain to any of the perplexed servants that he passed on his way down the hall to his father's study.

"Father! Father!" he called as he entered the musty office without so much as a knock.

As expected, his father was behind his desk, scribbling away at some piece of legislation. His face remained impassive as Lu stumbled across his threshold, nearly knocking the vase his father had received as a gift from the governor of Boriquen off its stand. The colorful pottery piece wobbled, turning halfway around, before resettling.

"Tallulah, I've told you before that you must take care when you enter my study," his father reprimanded, his words dripping with exasperation.

"I'm sorry, Father," Lu said, bristling at the sound of his own name on his father's lips. "It's just that there's been news from the Citadel! The Fleet are recruiting!"

Lu watched his father pinch the bridge of his nose and huff. He set his quill down and glared at his son. "Not this nonsense again!"

"Father, please!" Lu pleaded.

"Enough!" his father said sharply. "Tallulah, not only are you a high-born young lady, you are the governor's daughter! Imagine the scandal that would ensue if you were to take up with that group of fanatics. Is it not already an embarrassment that you spend all of your time with"—he wrinkled his nose—"fisherfolk rather than making friends of your own—"

"They are my friends!" Lu insisted.

"They are *beneath you!"*

He stood up, pushed his chair back, and walked around the desk.

"Look at you," he went on. "You have been afforded every opportunity to be just like the other high-born girls. Better than them, even! I have paid for etiquette classes, private tutors, dancing lessons. I keep you in the latest fashions. And do I have a well-mannered daughter who carries herself with the poise her station demands? No. Look at you."

"You know that is not who I am," Lu answered, quietly deflating.

It was not the first conversation they had had about Lu's inability to fit in with his ilk. He was sixteen years old, and every day since he had come of age, his father had had something to say about Lu's lack of ladylike attributes. When Lu had been twelve, he had announced to his father that it was because he was not, in fact, a lady. His father had ended the conversation there and had refused to discuss it further.

"Governor Marco Valdez is traveling from Boriquen as we speak. He will arrive in two days' time," Governor Gerard said, walking to the stand that held the vase. He twisted it back into its proper place. "He is bringing his son, Oscar. They will be staying here while Governor Valdez and I negotiate a deal. I expect you to be the picture of gentility. No more talk of the Fleet."

Lu knew the exact nature of this deal. His father was attempting to broker a match, quite possibly his last-ditch effort to force Lu into a mold that would never fit him, one that would guarantee him a lifetime of misery. How could his father be so cruel? Was Lu not his own flesh and blood? Did he not deserve the opportunity to determine his own life? Any other father would have wanted this for his son, but, of course, to the governor's eye Lu was not his son. Lu was a game piece for the governor to dress up and move around until it was time to trade. As this realization settled over him, he squeezed his hands into fists to temper the storm raging within him. Recalling one of the songs of the sea, he called on the goddess to give him the patience and strength he needed.

"Yes, Father," he agreed, crumpling the Fleet leaflet.

•••●•••

Lu cast his eye over the front page of the newspaper he had picked up while on patrol, taking in only the headline.

Devil of the Deep Flummoxes Fleet!

He frowned and flicked the periodical onto the cobblestones

as he walked. It was just past one o'clock in the afternoon, and he had been on patrol for about an hour. Absent the ferocity of the commodore's passionate effusions, he felt less sure of his purpose, so he fell back on his commitment to duty and honor. There was a pirate terrorizing his organization, and he was tasked with finding out what he could about her whereabouts.

He had created a circuit, stationing himself in the city center and patrolling the nearby streets.

They were full to bursting with Prince's Port residents, but not a single one had anything to say when Lu attempted to question them about the ships that they noticed coming in and out of the bay. Lu could see the ships floating just off the coast. Without a lead on which had arrived most recently, they were indistinguishable from each other.

Lu remembered the way of the Southern District folk and their distrust of the Fleet patrolmen from his days as a lieutenant. He also remembered how his fellow lieutenants terrorized the locals in the name of self-amusement. As long as he looked like a Fleet captain, he would never get a word out of them.

The streets of the Prince's Port city center were lined not with residences, but with businesses. Fish- and fruitmongers parked their carts end to end and shouted down passersby. Multistory buildings, owned by the city's wealthy business class, loomed behind them, casting shadows over the less fortunate. The only of these that stood in opposition was the stately tavern known as the Singing Crab. It was perfectly situated to welcome all visitors, foreign and local, wealthy and wanting. If there was any information to be had pertaining to the Devil of the Deep, it would be in the Singing Crab.

He strode toward the tavern. As he reached for the doorknob, it danced away from his hand. A young woman pulled the door open from inside and nearly collided with him on her way out. She had fair skin and red hair that hung in loose spirals over her shoulders. Her clothes were plain, like those of a maid, and her eyes bore the unmistakable red irritation of having been rubbed furiously to wipe away tears.

"Begging your pardon, Lieutenant," she said with a sniffle and a curtsy.

"Captain," Lu corrected, "and there's no need."

"Oh," she said apologetically. "I can never tell the difference—I mean, I never know—"

Lu chuckled. "It's fine. Really."

He stepped aside to let her pass. She curtsied once more before she went on her way. Lu considered following her, but he thought better of it. She was distressed and probably wanted to be left alone.

He entered the dimly lit dining space and closed the door behind him, breathing in the salty, savory aroma of fish stew. Without warning, his stomach released a loud gurgle, and he remembered that he had not yet had anything to eat that day. His mouth watering, he walked toward the bar, where the scent seemed to intensify.

"Welcome to the Singing Crab," said the statuesque woman behind the bar as she stirred a large pot. "Seat yourself and I'll be right with you."

Lu took a seat at the bar. "I haven't had fish stew since I was a child," he mused.

"Just made this pot fresh," the woman said with a smile. "One silver per bowl."

Lu made a face. "Isn't that a little steep?"

"We call it the Fleet special," she replied. "Better get yours now before the luncheon rush."

Lu was certainly tempted. He would have paid a silver just to smell the stew, but there was something about being in this place—her place—that did not sit well with him.

"It's a bit dear for my meager pay," he lied. "How about some diri sos pwa, instead?"

"Three coppers," the woman said, eyeing him dubiously.

He untied his coin pouch from his belt and retrieved the payment, setting it on the bar. Without another word, she scooped up the coins, set her ladle down, and disappeared through the kitchen door.

"Here you are." She returned with a wide wooden bowl filled with a heaping helping of white rice wading in a pool of black bean sauce.

When she placed it in front of him, Lu could have lost himself in the scent that wafted to his nose. The Citadel had a decent enough mess, but its offerings paled in comparison to this. His first spoonful sent him hurtling into ecstasy.

"By the seven, that's good," he groaned, swallowing.

The woman behind the bar laughed. "A soldier of the Fleet who uses the old tongue and invokes the goddess . . ."

Lu nearly choked on his second bite. It must have slipped out.

"Just respecting local custom," he murmured, straightening in his seat.

"That would be another first for the Fleet," the proprietor said. She leaned over the bar and tilted her head. "I haven't seen you on patrol around here before."

"I come from the Northern District." Lu suddenly felt like he was being interrogated. "I'm investigating some . . . suspicious activity."

The woman straightened and laughed again. "Don't tell me the Fleet have sent you to resolve all of this Devil of the Deep nonsense. You can't be more than twenty years old!"

"I'll have you know I'm well past twenty," Lu said defensively, sitting up straighter and tugging his uniform down, "and more than capable of taking on the task."

"I'm sorry, my love," she said. "I did not mean anything by it."

"Care to tell me what sort of clientele you've had come through your establishment recently?"

Lu spoke with as much authority as he could muster.

The woman's already narrow eyes squeezed to slits. "Sailors," she said, her previous warmth gone. "Hardworking folk trying to make an honest living."

"Then, I suppose, you won't mind if I stick around and ask your patrons some questions."

"I suppose it would not make a difference if I did." She pulled an apron off the wall and threw it over her shoulder. "Now, if you'll excuse me, I have to go track down my barmaid."

Lu expected the woman to go out the door to retrieve the crying girl he had run into. Instead, she went upstairs. In the time that she was gone, several of the hardworking folk she had mentioned filed into the tavern. They filled up the empty seats at the tables and at the bar, though the stools directly beside Lu remained conspicuously unoccupied. The crying girl was among the new arrivals, her face less blotchy than it had been earlier. She went right into collecting orders with a smile.

When the owner returned, she was with another young woman following her down the stairs. She wore the apron over her clothes, but the leather bodice and linen skirt were too fine to have originated from these parts of the island. She caught him staring at her and winked. Lu, suddenly sheepish, looked away.

"Folks, I have a special treat for you today!" the owner called. She made her way through the maze of now-full tables to the other end of the dining room, where a small space had been left open. She stood in the space. "It's been a long time since we've had a singer in the Singing Crab, but today the tide brought us just that. So, as you luncheon on your magnificent fish stew, made by yours truly"—there was a smattering of applause—"also enjoy Aline's beautiful voice!"

Three musicians moved into the performance space with their instruments, and Aline took the owner's place in the center. The drummer counted them off, and Lu was pleasantly surprised to hear the opening notes of a song he had not heard since before he had joined the Fleet. He smiled, ready to hear the familiar melody, but when the singer opened her mouth, an otherworldly sound filled the air. Those who had been eating paused, their utensils hovering before their faces, while others simply stopped what they were doing and stared.

Lu was among the latter. He had only a vague awareness of the world around him, of people moving, of the front door opening and closing, but Aline's voice was all-encompassing. Her voice was more than beautiful; it held the weight of an ancient tradition that had been long ago lost. He had heard a voice like hers before, in the fisherman's wharf on the day of his conferral. Had he remembered to check in on Manou and Mai?

There was no point in trying to question any locals while Aline sang. He would inspire no confidence by interrupting a clearly transcendent experience, so he waited, not especially reluctantly, until she had finished her catalog. His eye bounced from face to face, and almost everywhere he looked, he saw joy. The other barmaid, the crying girl, was no longer crying, but staring at Aline with apparent jealousy.

He walked to where she stood at the far end of the bar, and touched her elbow. She started but relaxed when she saw him.

With a nod toward the door, he beckoned her to follow. Once beyond the doorway and the reach of the music's spell, Lu let the salty sea air clear his head.

"That Aline is quite talented," he said with a smile. He hoped it conveyed enough ardency to make his intentions clear to the girl.

She tutted. "She's not that special," she said with a sideways glance at Lu, "and she's not available either, if that's what you're after."

"She's with someone?"

"I don't know what the nature of their *relationship* is," she went on, sneering at the word, "but she's been all over my—" She groaned. "Since their ship came in this afternoon."

"So they're not from here?"

"*She* certainly isn't," the girl said, jerking her head toward the door. "She's probably one of those ship-skipping tramps who make their living latching themselves onto p—"

"Onto what?" Lu urged, but the girl suddenly became tight-lipped. "Pirates?" he finished for her.

She shook her head vigorously, but her look of fear told him everything he needed to know.

"I'm needed in the dining room," she said, and attempted to push through the door. Lu grabbed her by the wrist, then pulled her back.

"I'm afraid I need you to remain right here, Miss . . ."

"Jean-Louis." She sounded as though she were about to cry. "Rosalie Jean-Louis. Am I under arrest?"

He let go of her. "Not as long as you cooperate."

Lu scanned the street until he spotted a cluster of patrolling lieutenants.

"You, there!" he shouted. "With me! I require your assistance!"

Their heads turned almost lazily in Lu's direction, but they perked up immediately upon recognizing his captain's garb. They ran to him.

"At your service, Captain," said the most senior of the group.

"I have just received word that there may be pirates inside this establishment. We must secure the perimeter and search the building. You"—he pointed to the one who had answered his call—"help me search. You two guard this exit and make sure she stays out here. The rest of you, go around to the back. Today is the day we finally catch the Devil of the Deep!"

Seventeen

PEARL

Pearl lay awake on the largest and softest bed on which she had lain since leaving the sea. She had not slept well since Nnenna had saved her from the green-and-gold behemoth and taken her aboard her own ship. For two days, she had been a prisoner of the land-dweller soldiers who wore Agwe's colors and invoked His name. They had dragged her down to the part of their ship where light could not reach and had shoved her into a cramped room with a wall of bars that left her exposed to the rest of the corridor. This had clearly been the place where they kept the people who had committed offenses against them. Pearl had thought, since they were servants of Agwe, that they must know His signs, but none of the soldiers who brought her meals understood when she used her hands to ask them who they were or where they were taking her. It was possible she had been on her way to her death, like Uncle Rain and maybe even Uncle Wade, and that kept her from resting. She had been ready to join her ancestors when death had been as simple as crossing the veil, but never before had she considered dying at someone else's hand.

Creaking floorboards made Pearl's heart skip a beat. Someone was coming, taking slow, heavy steps toward her room. She sat up on the bed, thinking of the green-and-gold-clad guards she had seen outside. She would not wait to be captured again. As a metallic scraping sounded from her door, she threw herself over the side of the bed and hurriedly tucked herself underneath, looking up at the underside of the bed as the door creaked open. Her breaths came as short gasps that she tried to keep quiet.

Someone stepped inside, stopped for half a dozen heartbeats, and walked out again. Then, Pearl heard voices through the open doorway. The gray-haired woman with hair like Nnenna's asked something in the land-dweller language. Nnenna's voice came next, and Pearl realized she had made a mistake. She quickly shuffled from under the bed, and just as she peeked over the edge of the mattress, Nnenna ran into the room looking upset. Pearl stood, her body still quaking no matter how hard she worked to control it, and raised her shaking hands. She meant to sign that she was sorry, but Nnenna intercepted her.

"Are you all right?" she asked in sign.

Pearl nodded.

"Hide?" Nnenna signed, her confused expression filling in the rest of the question.

She wanted to know why Pearl had hidden herself, and Pearl did not know how to respond. How could she explain the fear that had come over her at the mere thought of being imprisoned again despite Nnenna's assurances that she would be safe? She felt embarrassed, like a child caught being disobedient.

Nnenna's eyes flicked down to Pearl's shaking hands, and without thinking, Pearl hid them behind her back. She worried that Nnenna would think of her as soft, but the woman's entire demeanor relaxed. Nnenna took a careful step toward the bed.

Then, when Pearl made no move to stop her, walked around to the side of the bed to Pearl.

"Sit," Nnenna signed as she lowered herself onto the edge of the mattress. Pearl obliged, sitting next to Nnenna, but left a space between them. "Close your eyes and listen," she signed.

Pearl did not want to close her eyes. The very idea made her chest tighten. She shook her head.

"Trust me, please," Nnenna signed, rubbing her hand over her chest in a circle.

Pearl let out a few shaky breaths and let her eyelids close. The moment she was in the dark, she fell into the memory of the little room, of the way it had smelled of stale sweat and blood. But, before she became fully ensnared, a sliver of song floated through, disrupting the scene. She was in multiple places at once: sitting in a room with Nnenna, listening to her sing a familiar melody, and sitting in her prison. Then, she was back in the temple in the Settlement, singing along with the congregation on a holy day. The song brought her home, and she listened to Uncle Wade sing while he prepared a meal for the family. Before long, Nnenna's rich, warm voice pulled Pearl from her memories, and she relaxed for the first time in days as Nnenna brought the verse to a close.

She stared at Nnenna, smiling broadly as she waited for the woman to open her eyes.

"Where did you learn that song?" Pearl signed.

"Father," Nnenna replied, smiling sadly.

Her answer inspired more questions about land dwellers and how they came to learn the sacred hymns and signs of Agwe's chosen people, but Pearl suspected Nnenna's limited knowledge of the signs would make answering difficult.

"Are you all right, now?" Nnenna asked.

Pearl nodded. It was not entirely true—she could still feel the worry in her body, but the comfort Nnenna had provided kept it at bay. She brought her open palm to her chin and then extended it out to Nnenna in thanks. At that moment, the gray-haired owner of the house and Aline both hurried through the door. They both spoke to Nnenna at once, but the older woman held up a hand. She gave Aline an order and then turned back to Nnenna and Pearl. Her words came out slowly, carefully, but Pearl understood only one: Fleet.

Her trepidation must have shown on her face, for Nnenna quickly reached out a hand and put it over Pearl's on the bed.

"Safe," Nnenna signed with her free hand, though Pearl shook her head, her brow furrowed. They were not safe. The Fleet was here, coming to get her, and they would make sure to kill her this time. She was certain of it.

"We leave now," Nnenna signed.

Pearl's body stiffened again. It was not safe to remain in the building, but the Fleet was outside as well. What was to stop them from taking her while they were on their way to wherever they were going? Nnenna squeezed Pearl's hand, and the pressure, though not as potent as the song, helped her to stay present. She could feel her worry rising again, but chose to ignore it, nodding once.

As soon as she agreed, Nnenna took Pearl's hand and quickly led her into the hallway. She started down the stairs, but Nnenna stopped her, holding up a hand to tell her to wait.

Wait for what? Pearl wondered until she heard a sweet, high voice climb up the stairs from the dining room. Shocked, Pearl looked to Nnenna to see if it was safe to descend. When Nnenna gave the go-ahead, Pearl crept down a few stairs.

The beautiful voice was Aline's, high and strong, piercing

and filling the air with a melody that Pearl did not know. She wandered through the dining room, flitting between patrons like a fish moving from anemone to anemone, drawing the attention of each person. They all watched her as though she were a work of art come to life, but she paid special attention to a man at the bar wearing a green-and-gold coat. She brought her face close to his and sang to him. Pearl watched, mesmerized, wondering what would happen next.

Nnenna's hand dropped on Pearl's shoulder, pulling her out of Aline's song.

"Now," she signed with one hand, and Pearl immediately understood that Aline's song was a distraction. That must have been why the lady of the house had sent her away.

Pearl straightened and followed Nnenna the rest of the way down the staircase, past Aline and the man, and out the door. Nnenna raised a hand as they exited the building and caught the attention of a man tending to a little house on wheels attached to a large four-legged animal. To Pearl's surprise, Nnenna and the man exchanged a few words, then the man opened the door of the little house and invited them inside.

Nnenna climbed in first and held her hand out to help Pearl in. The space was small but not uncomfortable. The seats were lined with soft fabric, and there was just enough room for the two of them. Then, the little house jerked and they were moving, no doubt pulled by the animal attached to it.

"Where are we going?" she signed to Nnenna.

"Friend," Nnenna replied.

There was a window in the little door through which Pearl saw the land change as they rode. She marveled at the height of the brightly colored buildings that towered over the street. Any of these would have dwarfed the temple, the tallest construction in the Settlement. She wondered, as she remembered her last day there, how Nnenna had come to know the sacred signs of her people. Pearl knew the signs only because she had been preparing to enter temple service. Nnenna did not seem like the type to believe in gods. Pearl was surprised to find herself envious.

After nearly an hour of winding through the city streets, they stopped at a mint-green edifice with a bright red door, a single rectangular window at its center. This must have been where they would find Nnenna's friend. Excited, Pearl reached for the metal knob, but Nnenna stopped her. She pointed to herself as if to say that she was going in first. Then, she made two fists, crossed her wrists at her chest, and pulled the fists apart in one fluid motion. Safe. She wanted to make sure that Pearl was safe. Pearl nodded.

They exited the vehicle together, then Nnenna took the lead. A tinkling sound came from a little swinging golden shell affixed to the top of the door when Nnenna pulled it open. She went in first and Pearl followed. The world suddenly became dark and quiet as she peered around what looked to be a cave where someone had been collecting the most peculiar assortment of trinkets and bobbles. The items were arranged on shelves but packed so densely that it seemed the slightest touch could send them careening to the floor. The air was musty and made her nose itch.

A man's jovial voice bellowed from somewhere beyond the doorway that stood behind a counter as laden with trinkets as any of the shelves. As Pearl and Nnenna wove their way through piles of stuff, a man entered, speaking and smiling as though he were greeting an old friend. Pearl had just begun to wonder how he had known that it had been his friend who had arrived, when he laid eyes upon Nnenna and his smile darkened to a frown. His eyes twitched toward the exit, but Nnenna drew her pistol and pointed it at the man's chest.

Pearl had learned about pistols on her brief sojourn on the ship of the Fleet guard who had captured her. They had all worn them on their belts, and one had even pointed hers and fired it into the sky. A moment later, a creature that had been soaring through the air had fallen dead onto the deck. Pearl did not know how they worked, but she knew that anyone who found themselves on the open end of one would be lucky to live to regret it.

The old man's hands flew up above his head. Nnenna spoke to him softly and cordially. Pearl expected the man to plead for his life, but what happened instead made Pearl frown in confusion. Slowly, as his copper-colored eyes stared at Nnenna, the man's lips broke into a wide smile. Nnenna's face did the same, and before Pearl could make sense of what she was seeing, Nnenna lowered the pistol and ran at the man. He caught her in his arms the way a father would his daughter, and for a moment, Pearl wondered. But there were not enough similarities between their features for them to share blood. Beneath the simple shopkeeper's garb, this man was as dark as the night sky with white hair that ringed the base of his shining bald head. When he smiled, Pearl caught the glint of gold in one of his front teeth.

Once the old man released her, Nnenna beckoned Pearl over. She signed, making the shape of a shell with her two hands and then pointing at the old man.

Pearl looked back and forth between them.

"Friend?" she signed to Nnenna.

"Old friend," Nnenna answered. "His name—" She then made a sign that Pearl translated to Ship-Father. Pearl did not know what this meant, but if Nnenna trusted this Ship-Father, then she could as well.

Pearl reached into her pocket and pulled out the conch shell and held it out to Ship-Father. His mouth rounded in wonder as he plucked the orb from her hand. She watched him turn it from side to side, bringing it close to his face and examining the surface as if he were trying to see through it. She wanted to tell him that she had already tried that and that it yielded no results, but she supposed he would learn it soon enough on his own.

He pulled the shell away from his eye and said something to Nnenna. It sounded like a question. Pearl turned to Nnenna to see how she would respond, but found the woman looking at her.

"Where find?" she signed.

She wanted to know where Pearl had gotten the shell. Pearl did not know if she could simplify her story enough so that Nnenna could understand. She was not even sure if signs existed for the words she needed. Uncle Rain had been one of the Settlement's explorers, who scavenged the ocean floors for supplies that her people could use. He had said he had found the shell during one such expedition, just lengths away from the mouth of an undersea volcano, as though the ocean floor had belched it up along with the heat and smoke.

Sighing, Pearl tapped the pointer finger of her open right hand against her lips twice before dropping it into a smooth undulating that mimicked waves lapping at an invisible shore.

"The ocean."

Nnenna translated and Ship-Father smiled. He pulled something out of his apron pocket. Two circular panes of clear glass bound by thin bands of shining golden metal. He placed the thing on the bridge of his nose, and Pearl immediately understood that it was meant to help him to see. His eyes looked bigger through the glass, even as he squinted to examine the shell once more. He noted the holes at either end of the shell's body, and an idea seemed to occur to him. He brought one end of the shell to his mouth, puffed his cheeks out, and blew. As the air from his body traveled through the shell, nothing happened.

Ship-Father set the shell down on the counter and retrieved a large ceramic bowl from a nearby shelf. He placed it next to the shell. Then, he excused himself and disappeared into the doorway through which he had come. Pearl stared at Nnenna, who stared right back with her eyebrows raised. That was as much as the two were able to communicate before Ship-Father made his return. Now, he carried a large ceramic jug that looked to be not only made of the same material as the bowl but also full. He poured the water out into the bowl, filling the basin until the clear liquid touched the very brim.

The old man reached for the shell again, this time leaning over the basin so that the other end of the shell hovered over the water, and blew into it. The surface rippled slightly, but the water remained unchanged. Nnenna held out her hand as Ship-Father looked disappointedly at the shell, and he handed it over to her. Ship-Father and Nnenna both stared at Pearl, and she knew that it was her turn to try.

Pearl suddenly felt unsteady on her feet. Uncle Wade had said what they had learned about Agwe was a lie, and with everything that had happened since, Pearl had not yet had a chance to consider if she wanted him to be right or wrong. To lose Agwe's teachings would mean the loss of her beliefs, her way of life, her place in Agwe's kingdom. But to prove the word true would be to lose her uncles. Her hands shook as she reached for the conch, but she took it from Nnenna and stood before the bowl. Pearl held the shell with two hands as she brought it to her lips and blew.

The shell vibrated as air passed from one end to the other, and when it exited the end closest to the water, a warm, rich tone filled the room. The water responded to the sound, rippling and pulling as though it were trying to escape the confines of the bowl. Pearl had never seen water behave this way. She looked to Nnenna and Ship-Father, both of whom were equally perplexed.

Pearl pulled the shell away from her lips, hoping that severing the connection would make the water return to normal, but even with the shell returned to her pocket, the water continued to writhe. It climbed up the sides of the bowl and, when it ran out of material, began to build upon itself, reaching up until it created a dome over the opening. Without thinking, Pearl stepped forward.

She gasped.

It was an island—the island from which her people had come. The island they had lost when they had been cursed by the devil. She had seen pictures of it carved into stone walls all over the Settlement, but this was not a picture. It was as though she were looking down upon the island from the sky and, at any moment, she could reach down and pluck it from the pellucid waters on which it sat.

She could see its mighty mountain peak, on which her ancestors had built Agwe's temple and—

The dome of water collapsed back into the bowl. Pearl wheeled around and found Nnenna and Ship-Father staring at her again.

"Home!" she signed to Nnenna. "Lost home!"

A tendril of memory broke loose in her mind, an echoing voice rising over the masses in the temple atrium.

"We must live each and every day as though our destiny will be upon us! We will raise our lost island and reclaim our rightful place as rulers over the surface world!"

Pearl signed again, pointing to the bowl that now contained

only water. “Lost home,” she said with her hands. “Danger!”

Her racing thoughts were too fast for her hands to keep up. She needed a better way to communicate with Nnenna, to explain exactly what she had seen under the water dome and what it meant, but she had none. Frustrated, she pounded her fist on the countertop.

“Slow,” Nnenna signed.

Pearl took a deep breath and thought. Nnenna and Ship-Father had both seen what the shell had revealed, but how could she convey to them what it meant? The island in the bowl was Meridia, the lost home her people had sought for generations, but its discovery would mean the destruction of the land-dweller way of life.

“The shell will restore the island to the surface and my people to their place upon it,” she signed slowly, “but it will mean danger for you . . . for all.”

Nnenna frowned, and Pearl hoped she was coming up with a plan.

“What do?” Nnenna asked in her broken signs.

Shocked, Pearl asked, “Me?”

“Your people,” Nnenna said. “Your shell.”

Pearl swallowed hard. The shell was the only hope her people had of reuniting with their ancestral land and ending their state of perpetual displacement, but it also ensured destruction for the land dwellers. It would be foolish for her to believe she could somehow save both peoples. Days ago, the decision would have been easy, but she had lived among the land dwellers long enough to know that some of them were more than the wayward heathens Viceroy Seastead had made them out to be. Her people deserved a home, but did that mean a world full of land dwellers deserved to suffer?

"Destroy," she signed, barely believing it herself.

"Are you sure?" Nnenna asked.

Pearl nodded resolutely. She pulled the shell from her pocket and, before she could think twice, threw it against the floor. It shattered loudly, crumbling into a thousand shards.

There, she thought as her heart thundered in her chest. *No turning back, now.*

But as she thought the words, the shell shards began to quake as though the ground beneath them were shaking. As if time itself were reversing, the pieces flew back together to form a whole conch once again.

Pearl gasped. Nnenna and Ship-Father both exclaimed in the land-dweller tongue. Pearl picked up the re-formed shell.

Of course, she thought. *If it's as old as the island, then there must be something protecting it from harm.*

She signed this to Nnenna as best she could, who relayed the message to Ship-Father.

"What do we do?" Pearl asked after several moments of silence.

"Do you trust me?" Nnenna signed.

"Yes."

"Give me the shell."

Pearl handed the conch to Nnenna. Nnenna turned to Ship-Father and asked him a question.

His fluffy white eyebrows rose at her words. He pulled out one of his books and showed her something within it. Nnenna pointed to Pearl and said something else. Pearl thought she heard the land-dweller word for *sea*. She placed the conch shell in his hand, and Ship-Father agreed to whatever Nnenna had asked.

Nnenna placed a hand on Pearl's shoulder and launched into a series of broken signs to explain.

As Pearl understood it, Ship-Father was going to take the shell and hide it where no Settler could find it. When Nnenna finished, Pearl looked at Ship-Father, and the old man gave her a reassuring smile. She touched her fingertips to her chin and brought her open hand down toward him.

"Thank you."

Eighteen

NNENNA

Nnenna dropped bodily onto an unforgiving surface, setting her bones and muscles alight with pain. Her eyes flew open, and bright light burned them. Blinking furiously, she rolled onto her side as a wave of water and sick forced itself out of her. When the river ran dry, she coughed and coughed until her airway cleared enough for her to breathe. She fell back and threw her good arm up to shield her eyes from the sun as she swallowed huge gulps of salty sea air. She was alive. Soaked to the bone and badly bruised, but, undoubtedly, alive.

A wild mix of emotions fought for attention inside her. Confusion was chief among them. The last thing she remembered was looking up from the bottom of the ocean. How had she escaped her watery grave, and where was she now?

Her environment was both familiar and unfamiliar. She recognized the wood beneath her as the deck of a ship and the gentle swaying that meant they were out to sea. Before she could gather any more information, she heard the unmistakable sound of metal scraping against leather from somewhere above her. Someone had drawn a sword. Panicked, she bolted upright and reached for her own sword until she remembered that she had been relieved of all her weapons. Two blurred figures stepped into her field of vision. They might have been a man and a woman—it was difficult to say with their shifting in and out of focus. The man looked to be a head taller than Nnenna, with dark skin and closely cropped silver hair. The woman was even taller and much younger, long-haired, and broad-shouldered. The man held his arm outstretched, and the tip of his cutlass hovered close enough to Nnenna's face that if she moved forward an inch, it would slice into her skin.

"Look what the tide has brought us," he said to his companion.

Nnenna considered her options. She was nearly blind, soaked to the bone, bruised from head to toe, and entirely defenseless. To challenge even one of these people in combat would be foolish. To try them both would be a death sentence.

"I'm unarmed," she croaked. Shocks of pain exploded in her shoulder when she attempted to raise her hands in a show of good faith. She bit back a cry, but cradled her arm across her chest. "I mean you no harm."

The woman scoffed. "That uniform of yours says different."

"Search her," the man ordered.

The woman stepped slowly to Nnenna, her hawkish brown eyes flicking back and forth between Nnenna's face and her hands. Nnenna tried again to hold them aloft, despite the pain, and kept her eye on the man with the sword. As the woman patted Nnenna's upper body, Nnenna noticed a mark on the back of his wrist. It was a scar, a burn in the shape of a trident head. Nnenna knew the sign and remembered learning about the now-abandoned practice of burning it into the flesh of turncoats so Agwe would easily identify those who had abandoned His word.

"My name is Nnenna Delahaye," she offered carefully, looking not at his arm or sword, but into his bright copper eyes.

"Don't you mean 'Lieutenant'?" he asked, cocking a derisive eyebrow.

Nnenna furrowed her brow and shook her head. "Not anymore."

The man's face remained unreadable. When his companion declared that Nnenna was, indeed, unarmed, she resumed her place beside him. After a moment of staring her down, he put away his sword and offered Nnenna his hand in exchange.

"Captain Raoul Delva," he said gruffly.

Nnenna took the offered hand and allowed Delva to pull her to her feet. Pain sang in her hips and ankles as she put her full weight on them. She gasped, her vision darkening.

"Tinou," Delva grunted.

The young woman moved swiftly, lodging herself under Nnenna's good arm and propping Nnenna up before her knees hit the deck.

"The brig, Captain?" Tinou asked.

"Great cabin," he answered.

If Delva had been aiming for discretion, he had missed the mark. Their long, slow, limping walk from the center of the upper deck to the stern had caught the eye of every crewman they passed, and Nnenna felt their rancor burning through the thick fabric of her green-and-gold coat. She held her breath and kept her head down until Tinou helped her cross the great-cabin threshold and Delva closed the door behind them.

Tinou deposited Nnenna into one of the chairs on either side of the captain's table and took the other for herself, resting her booted feet on the glossy tabletop. Delva, who remained standing, walked past the table, pushed Tinou's feet off it, and glared at her on his way.

The captain's quarters were mercifully dark, thanks to the closed shutters and curtains, and Nnenna's vision improved. She looked around quickly to get the lay of her surroundings. The room was comfortable but bore none of the luxuries she had seen in Fleet captains' quarters. There was a bed in one corner, a large frame and mattress with jacquard curtains, a wardrobe, the table at which they sat, and a liquor cabinet. The walls were bare, as though someone had recently scrubbed the room of all traces of its owner's identity.

Nnenna's eyes passed over the mirror hanging over the captain's washbasin atop the wardrobe until she noticed her reflection and had to look again. Her skin was now dull umber, thanks to the hours she had spent floating in the sun, but she had no explanation for her hair. It had been black all her life, but the locs that dangled over her shoulders were now a deep crimson red.

"How does a Fleet lieutenant find themselves floating in the middle of the Southern Sea?" Delva asked as he reached the liquor cabinet. He pulled a bottle half filled with amber liquid and three clear glasses off the shelf. Nnenna suddenly realized how dry her mouth was.

"I was thrown overboard," she said, keeping her eye on Delva as he set the glasses atop the cabinet and gave a healthy pour into each. "You said I was floating in the Southern Sea? Is that where we are now?"

"On your back," Delva answered, nodding his head. He turned and handed each woman a glass. "Thought you were dead."

"Thank you," Nnenna said, taking the glass. "For this and for fishing me out."

"This ship don't run on favors," Delva said. "You want to stay aboard, you have to prove your worth."

"Of course," Nnenna said, "I'm no stranger to hard work. I'll make myself useful every day that I'm on your vessel."

Delva raised his glass but only to use it to wave her words away. "That goes without saying. What we need is information." He gestured to his companion. "Tinou, here, is our quartermaster. She's also damned good with a blade. She suggested we cut the information out of you."

Nnenna had expected a threat like this. After all, she was still dressed like a Fleet lieutenant. She had learned how to circumvent fear and negotiate in situations such as these, but, this time, her fear did not come. Nnenna turned to Tinou. Now that she could see the young woman clearly, Nnenna noticed that she was quite striking, but the smile that crept across her face would have been better placed upon a shark. This was a woman whose strength lay in intimidation. Nnenna was certain Tinou had made many songbirds of men with the knives tucked into her belt and would have no qualms about doing the same to Nnenna. But Nnenna had already endured the worst torture imaginable. What more could one person do to her?

"That won't be necessary," she said, raising her glass to Tinou and sending her own cold smile.

"I spent some time among their ranks," Delva went on, drawing Nnenna's attention once more, "but my knowledge of their workings is outdated. Give us names, expedition routes, weakness, and we'll take you anywhere you want."

The faces of the people who had watched Nnenna sink into oblivion and had done nothing to stop it suddenly flashed in her mind, one after the other. She felt the emptiness where her fear should have been and filled it with her rage. Delva took in a mouthful of his drink. Nnenna drained her glass. The liquor burned her insides all the way down to her stomach, but she felt its effects almost at once. Everything quieted except her rage.

"I will tell you everything you want to know," she said, "but I want to stay aboard."

Tinou laughed. "This is no merchant ship, Lieutenant."

"You're pirates," Nnenna said quickly. "I gathered that from your colors. I don't much care for terrorizing merchants, but if it's Fleet ships you're after, then I want to join your crew." Before Delva could respond, she turned back to Tinou. "If you call me a lieutenant again, I will make you eat a sword. You can burn my uniform, if that will prove to you where my loyalties lie, but it may not be a bad idea to have someone on your crew who can blend in with the enemy."

Tinou tutted. "Won't they be looking for you?"

Nnenna thought for a moment. "Nnenna Delahaye is dead," she said darkly. "I am the devil they will come to fear. The Devil of the Deep."

•••●•••

Captain Raoul Delva's funeral had been the affair of the decade. The captain had put a sizable dent in his newly acquired fortune making it so. He had ensured the word had spread across the Seven Isles that the greatest scourge of the sea was finally passing into the Unknown. Pirates from every corner of the Isles had arrived at Yamaye, had held their fists and hats over their hearts to pay their respects as the longboat containing Delva's body had been pushed out to sea. After the ceremony had come three full days of celebration from which Nnenna had been conspicuously absent. Any member of her crew would have dutifully reported that she had been mourning privately. This was the lie that she and Delva had concocted to conceal their brief sojourn to Prince's Port. He had swapped his pirate garb for a shopkeeper's uniform, complete with an apron, spectacles, and a new name, and had been trying his hand at being a simple collector of curios. He had always had an affinity for making the most unusual finds while pillaging, and Nnenna supposed this was his way of making an honest living while staying true to his adventuring past.

When he had seen the shell shatter and then reassemble itself, he had reached for the tome at the top of the pile of books on his countertop and opened it to a spread of pages, a drawing of a man on one side and a woman on the other. Both were bare from the waist up, and both had fish tails where their human legs should have been. According to the text, these were the stewards of the sea, Agwe and the unnamed goddess. Delva had drawn Nnenna's attention to a passage that told of Agwe's curse and His chosen people. Nnenna had heard this story before but had never believed any of it. Delva, on the other hand, believed not only in Agwe, but in a whole host of other gods who supposedly held dominion over life itself. For years, Nnenna had assumed he had taken a hard hit to the head during his travels, but that was before she had seen the impossible with her own eyes.

"Can you make sure those who are looking for this never find it?" Nnenna had asked, handing him the shell.

"It can't be destroyed, but I can hide it," Delva had answered. "Take it farther inland where a sea god has no business and bury it."

Now, Nnenna used a protective arm to keep Pearl close as they wove through the streets of Petyon's center at double speed. She could feel the girl trying to sign to her, no doubt to ask questions, but there was no time. The beetle captain lurking about should have learned there was nothing to discover by now. They had to get back to the inn, back to safety.

The carriage they had arrived in waited at the end of the

street. Nnenna beelined toward it, leading Pearl along and hurrying her into its cab.

"Back to the Singing Crab," she shouted, pounding the ceiling twice. "Quickly."

As the carriage pulled away, Nnenna caught Pearl's eye.

"Your home," she signed. "Where?"

"Lost," Pearl signed back.

Nnenna shook her head. "Where did you come from?"

Pearl paused a moment, as if trying to decide what to tell her. Finally, she raised her hands to her chest and cascaded them toward Nnenna like waves tumbling toward the shore. She had come from the ocean.

"Tail?" Nnenna asked as delicately as she could with her limited knowledge.

Pearl's face fell slightly. "Gone," she signed back. "Curse."

Nnenna made a fist against her chest and rubbed it in a circle. "I'm sorry."

She did not ask any more questions. Pearl had told her everything she needed to know. She was a Meridian, a sea dweller, one chosen by Agwe. The stories she had heard in her youth were the same stories she had read in Delva's book. Nnenna had written them off as zealous ravings, but Pearl was proof that they were more than just stories.

"Madame!" the coachman's voice called through the wall. "I think I'd best let you out here!"

Nnenna frowned. She glanced out the window as the carriage slowed to a halt. They were back in Sun City but still a ways from the inn. Nevertheless, she and Pearl disembarked and paid the man for his services. It wasn't until they took off on foot down the long street on which the inn sat that they both realized why the coachman had let them out. They both pulled up short.

A pair of lieutenants stood guard at the gate. Nnenna dove into an alley, cursing and pulling Pearl along with her, praying none of the beetles had seen her.

"What?" Pearl signed as they crouched behind a wall.

Nnenna held one fist against her abdomen and beat it twice with the other fist. "Danger."

They peered around the corner and watched the Fleet lieutenants. Some stood sentry at the entrance while others pulled patrons from the tavern, no doubt to question them. Someone must have tipped them off to her staying there. She did not recognize any of the patrols, nor did she see Lady Jean-Louis or Aline.

"Shit," Nnenna cursed as she twisted back around to hide behind the wall. She knew what she had to do. To attempt to rescue them would risk putting Pearl directly into the Fleet's waiting hands, but perhaps she could use that to her advantage.

She turned to Pearl and asked for the second time that day, "Do you trust me?"

Pearl nodded, and Nnenna launched into an explanation of her plan that she hoped would make sense to the girl. When she finished, she asked Pearl if she understood, and the girl nodded once again. Then, she pulled out her dagger and took Pearl into her arms.

They walked together like this, with Nnenna holding her dagger to Pearl's throat, down the street until the patrolling beetles spotted them.

"You there!" Nnenna shouted, counting just how many beetles there were. There were six, all of whom turned at her word. Nnenna had certainly experienced worse odds, but she had never had to consider someone else's safety before. "Are you looking for this? Lower your weapons, or I cut the girl's throat!" Nnenna hoped these beetles had been ordered only to retrieve the girl.

"Go ahead!" one of the beetles sneered. "We'll take the artifact from her body!"

Damn, she cursed inwardly.

"She doesn't have it anymore," Nnenna said. "We hid it. Only she and I know where it is."

The beetles looked at each other as they considered her words.

"Now," she whispered to Pearl.

The girl, having been told to wait for this phrase, stuck her hands into the pockets of her trousers and pulled out the fabric interiors. Then, she returned her hands to the air.

"After I kill her, I'll come for you, and if you think I can't take down six beetles single-handedly, you haven't heard the stories! No. Five beetles. Because one of you will have to explain to your commodore how you managed to lose the Devil of the Deep, the girl, and the artifact in one fell swoop."

Nnenna had struck a nerve. She was intimately familiar with the consequences of questionable devotion to the Fleet.

"What do you want?" asked the same beetle lieutenant.

Nnenna brought the dagger a little closer to Pearl's throat. "Lower. Your. Weapons."

A moment passed, then the first beetle tossed his sword and pistol to the ground. The others followed suit.

"Good." Nnenna pointed to the two who stood closest to the door. "Go tell your captain the Devil of the Deep demands a parley."

She waited until the two beetles disappeared through the door, knowing she would have maybe one minute to escape. The moment the door closed behind them, she shoved Pearl toward the beetle who stood directly across from her. He caught her in his arms, wide-eyed and spluttering. Nnenna threw herself to the ground, grabbed a pistol, and shot the middle beetle in the chest. She scrabbled toward the third, tossing the gun, and picked up a sword. Then she cut him down as he reached for his own weapon.

When Nnenna rose and wheeled around, she found her worst fear had come to pass. She had been fast, but the first beetle had been faster. He had his arm around Pearl's neck and his pistol pointed at her head. Nnenna froze, breathing heavily as she stared into Pearl's eyes.

"It's me you want," Nnenna said, raising her hands in surrender. "The girl can't speak. It'll be hell getting information out of her. Take me instead."

"I'll kill her and then kill you," the beetle said angrily.

"And rob the commodore of his right to publicly execute the Devil of the Deep?" Nnenna said, thinking quickly. "What would he think of your making decisions for him?"

The faintest furrow appeared in the beetle's brow. He aimed the pistol at Nnenna. Still staring at Pearl, Nnenna gave her a barely perceptible nod. The girl pushed the beetle's arm up to her mouth and sank her teeth into his sleeve. The beetle screamed. He pulled the trigger, but his shot went wide and missed. Nnenna pulled the other dagger from her pocket and threw it at the lieutenant's head. His head cocked back as the blade found its home in his throat. He dropped to the ground and Nnenna exhaled.

Pearl pulled the dagger from the gasping man's neck, releasing a flow of blood that would kill him in seconds, and ran to Nnenna. Together, they took off down the street and turned the corner to where the cobblestones gave way to sand. They ran across the beach, only steps away from the shouts calling after them. As the first gunshot cracked through the air, Nnenna put herself between Pearl and harm's way.

They reached their longboat while their pursuers were still on the beach.

"Take the other side," Nnenna said, pointing frantically.

Pearl grabbed the boat and helped Nnenna push the vessel into the water. Bullets flew past them as they waded, hitting the water with wet explosions. When the waves reached their thighs, they clambered aboard, grabbed oars, and rowed to the *Medusa*, keeping their heads low until they were safely out of firing range.

By the time they stepped foot upon the main deck, the crew had already leaped into action. The ship was nearly ready to set sail.

Nnenna took Pearl by the shoulders.

"Are you all right?" she asked.

The girl nodded, but Nnenna felt Pearl shaking between her hands. She pulled Pearl close and held her tight as she sobbed against Nnenna's chest. The wind filled the *Medusa*'s sails, and the ship lurched forward, carrying them out to the safety of the open sea.

Nineteen

LU

Lu tapped his foot testily against the cobblestones as he counted another hour gone. Four hours ago, he had sent one of the surviving lieutenants with Coriolanus and a message explaining everything that had transpired to the Citadel. Even with an allowance for her unfamiliarity with the route and the horse, she should have been back by now. The sun was already setting, and Lu was nervous he would lose his chance to catch up to the pirate and retrieve the girl.

"You let her go!" the inn's proprietor had shouted from the custody of two lieutenants detaining her in the dining room. Lu heard her objecting to the arrest of her so-called barmaid, Aline, through the door. His interrogation had revealed that she was, indeed, newly arrived to Kiskeya, though she would not say from where or by what means. Lu had written as much to the commodore and anxiously awaited his response.

Once brought to the Citadel, Aline would be charged with refusal to cooperate in a Fleet investigation. Despite her noncompliance, Lu discerned what she had attempted to hide from a thorough examination of the room she had occupied. She had been staying with someone, most likely the Devil of the Deep. There was another person, as well. The room opposite Aline's had been occupied, though whoever had stayed there had not explored as much of the room as their counterpart. It could very easily have been the girl. If he acted quickly, he could catch them both and return a hero to the Citadel. But he needed the commodore's permission.

Thankfully, he heard the familiar rhythmic clopping of Coriolanus's hooves approaching. He quickly ordered one of the lieutenants guarding the gate to watch his captive while he ran to meet his messenger.

"What took you so long?" he asked testily.

The rider dismounted, and as she drew closer, Lu realized it was not the same lieutenant he had sent.

"Look who is getting comfortable in his new position," she teased.

"Ambroise!" Lu gasped, surprise thrusting his heart into his throat.

"I come bearing word from the commodore." She smiled, and Lu waited for her to furnish a missive until it dawned on him that there would be no written reply. "Letters can be intercepted," she added, seemingly reading his mind.

"What does he say?" Lu asked, bracing himself for the worst.

"We are tightening our hold of Prince's Port. Your description of the way the events unfolded has the commodore convinced that someone in this city has the information you need. He will join us with reinforcements by sea in the morning. Until then, I am here to support you in any way you need."

Lu's frustration suddenly overpowered him. The morning? The Devil of the Deep would be long gone by the commodore's arrival. He should be giving chase.

"Something the matter, Captain?" Ambroise asked.

Lu shook his head.

"The owner of this establishment and her barmaid are in our custody," he said stiffly. "Keep them sequestered in rooms on separate floors. Make sure there are guards at their doors at all times. No one enters and no one exits until either I or the commodore commands it, do you understand?"

Ambroise replied with a single, sharp nod.

Lu needed to think. Why would the pirate bother to stop at Kiskeya after visiting the Southern Sea? To drop off the barmaid, but why stay? There must have been something else. He removed his hat and ran his fingers through his curly hair, slightly damp with sweat, muttering to himself like a lunatic. He began to panic as he felt the pressure rising.

"Agwe, be with me," he prayed under his breath, but the syllables felt awkward as they left his mouth. At the same time, he thought of the diri sos pwa that had restored his soul with a single mouthful and how, gratefully, he had fallen back upon the customs he thought he had given up and how naturally the invocation had rolled off his tongue. Now, he felt a song trying to fight its way out of his heart. The first syllables were on the tip of his tongue, but he pushed them down.

Lu stared through the gate's iron bars as though the answer lay somewhere within. The empty face of the inn stared back. There was something he was missing. He had heard the gunshot from inside. Then, the lieutenant had come running, had said the Devil of the Deep was outside. In the time it had taken him to reach the gate, the Devil of the Deep had killed three lieutenants and taken off to the port. He and the remaining lieutenants had given chase, pistols and rifles in hand, but she had slipped from his grasp.

Her departure had been messy, relying on a gambit that put herself and the girl at risk. She must have counted on the Fleet not being in this area, must have been shaken by the Fleet's new efforts to gain a foothold in the Southern District neighborhoods. To do so, she would have had to know the area well. Was it possible she was from Prince's Port, perhaps even one of these neighborhoods?

It was as Lu tried to connect his theory of the Devil of the Deep's upbringing with his current situation that his eye landed on something that brought a crease to his brows. There were two single-horse-drawn carriages sitting in the curved, cobbled path leading from the street to the inn's door. One had stayed in its spot since Lu's arrival at the inn, and the other had been missing and only returned after the fray. The lieutenant at the gate had interrogated the coachman about his passengers, had even searched the carriage for clues they may have left behind, but the coachman claimed never to have seen their faces.

There was something else he could have asked, something he should have asked, but he had been too distracted by his failures.

"Get me the coachman," Lu ordered the lieutenant at the gate.

The lieutenant left at once, returning only seconds later with the coachman in tow.

"I already answered your questions," he grumbled.

"And you will answer more or be arrested for obstruction of justice," Lu snapped impatiently.

The man frowned but said nothing more.

"You said you never saw your passengers," Lu went on. The man nodded. "Where did you take them?"

"I . . . What do you mean?"

He was prevaricating. Lu had the man in a corner.

"Do you know what the punishment is for hindering a Fleet

investigation, sir? No fewer than five years' imprisonment. I'm sure you could survive those years, but what of the mouths you have to feed? I beg you to think of them and answer my question."

The man sighed. "Petyon."

"Take me there."

Minutes later, Lu sat in the carriage, peering from the window as they hurtled southeast. They arrived an hour later.

"This is where I left them," the coachman said after slowing his steed to a halt and letting Lu out into what looked like a town square. This neighborhood was wealthy and far more developed than the one he had left.

"Did they say where they were going?"

The coachman shook his head. "They didn't say anything."

Lu was certain this was a lie, but he had no way to prove it.

"Stay here," he ordered.

Lu walked across the square to the collection of shops that lay within.

He passed a haberdashery, a hat maker, a jeweler, a shoemaker, and a dressmaker. None seemed to provide any service in which a pirate would be interested, but this was no ordinary pirate. With no leads to follow, perhaps there was nothing to do but to approach his task methodically. Lu sighed, resigning himself to the process, and entered the first shop.

To say that the people of the Southern District had a healthy mistrust of the Fleet would be to grossly understate the situation. No matter how politely he approached each proprietor, he was met with, at best, cold indifference and, at worst, open hostility. He had heard that the Southern District had not taken well to the Fleet expanding its patrols, but he had not imagined an officer would meet so much resistance while conducting a simple door-to-door investigation. He left the last shop on the street feeling disheartened and concerned that he would have nothing to offer the commodore when he arrived. Then, his eye fell on a mint-green edifice with a bright red door.

It was a curiosity shop. Many of the golden letters on the sign above the door had peeled off, but Lu could just make out the name from what was left: Pierre's Curios. Then, something occurred to Lu. If the pirate had the girl with her, they would also have had the artifact when they arrived. It was not so far out of the realm of possibility for her to want to understand the artifact, and who better to attempt to decipher its significance than a collector?

Lu pulled at the door and found it locked. Strange, given that there was still some time before nightfall. When the door did not give after his second attempt, he knocked as loudly and urgently as he could. Despite his insistence, Lu waited on the step before a face appeared in the window.

The shopkeeper was old, dark, round, and white haired.

"Yes, Lieutenant?" he asked, opening the door just wide enough to poke his head out into the fading afternoon sun.

"Captain," Lu corrected.

"My apologies," the man said. "I still haven't learned how to tell the difference, and we get so few captains in the Southern District."

"The Fleet is in pursuit of suspicious persons engaged in piracy," Lu went on. "Have any suspicious individuals visited your shop today, Mr. Pierre?"

"It's actually Moreau," the old man said with a genial smile. "Pierre was the former proprietor. I chose to keep the name in the hope of inheriting his loyal customers."

Lu raised his eyebrows to signify that he was still waiting for an answer.

"No one suspicious that I've noticed."

"Do you mind if I have a look around, Mr. Moreau?"

"Actually, I do." Moreau laughed nervously. "The shop is in a state, right now. I'm doing inventory, you see. Can't tell what's what in there, I'm afraid. Perhaps you could come back in the morning."

The man attempted to pull the door closed, but Lu stuck his boot in the doorway.

"It seems I must remind you, sir, that failure to cooperate with a Fleet investigation could result in your being implicated as an accessory to the crime. Are you sure you won't let me look around?"

The old man rolled his eyes, and the pressure of the door on Lu's foot eased. "I suppose you've left me no choice," Moreau said, sighing. "Come in."

It was difficult for Lu's eye to land on any one thing, there was so much to see. Piles of volumes, loose papers, trinkets, jewelry, and items unknown to him littered the shelves, the floor, and the counter. Lu went to the counter, assuming that was where any customer would have gone. There was a smaller, somewhat more orderly stack of books near the only clean space. The book on top was open and the pages showed not words but maps of the Seven Isles.

"Are you planning a trip?" Lu asked, and Moreau smiled nervously.

"No, no, those days are long behind me. Just entertaining a bit of nostalgia."

"You were a seafarer?"

"Yes. Nothing so majestic as any of the Fleet ships, but on a good, sturdy vessel."

Lu glanced at the books underneath the atlas and caught a title: *Song of the Seven*. His interest immediately piqued, he pulled it out from the pile. It was a thick, tattered, leather-bound volume that bore the likeness of a woman outlined in peeling gilding on the cover. She had long, flowing hair that floated all around her serene face. Her mouth was open and Lu knew instantly that she was singing. The top half of her body was human and bare while the bottom half was a golden-scaled fish tail.

He recognized the volume. It was the same one from which Manou had told him stories as a child.

"Where did you get this?" he asked, his brows knitting in confusion. Then, he remembered his purpose. "The pirates we're looking for may have disguised themselves to look like Ayitian citizens." Lu thumbed through the pages of the book. "It would have been an adult woman and a young girl."

Moreau's smile faltered slightly before he said, "I haven't seen anyone matching that description today. I only ever get peculiar old men like myself in the shop."

The man was clever and more self-possessed than anyone under Fleet scrutiny ought to have been. Lu had a feeling more than one of his answers had been lies, but Lu was, first and foremost, a man of the law. There was no clear evidence of wrongdoing, so Lu would have to let him continue his business.

"I see," Lu said stiffly. "If you should see anything or anyone suspicious, it is your duty as a Kiskeyan citizen to report it to the Fleet."

"Of course, Captain. Best of luck with your investigation."

Twenty

THE COMMODORE

As the sun disappeared below the horizon, casting its warm glow over all the land and sea visible from the mountaintop fortress, Commodore Henri Christophe surveyed it all as he stood at attention at the bottom of the steps leading to the Citadel's front doors. He decided he would take Ayiti, when the island rose from the sea. The people were more than he thought they would be, held more potential than he expected. They would be useful in the coming days, especially the one on whom he waited now.

According to record, Emmanuel Millet was as unremarkable as any other fisherman on Ayiti. Christophe would not have known about the man's voice had it not been for Lu Ortega. The young man seemed to have a connection to the fisherfolk that most Fleet officers did not. Christophe was glad. Ortega's connection would grant him more access to the community than any other officer had been able to gain in some time.

The rattle of carriage wheels on cobblestone signaled the arrival of Christophe's guest. The vehicle, a single-passenger phaeton drawn by a lone stallion, came up the drive and stopped directly in front of the commodore. He waited patiently while the coachman stepped down from the driver's seat and pulled the door open.

Emmanuel Millet emerged from the cab, his eyes roaming the great edifice before him. No doubt he had never before seen the Citadel up close. Christophe's mouth stretched into a smile, and he stepped forward, grasping the fisherman's hand and claiming his attention.

"Emmanuel, welcome! Welcome!" he called. "I hope you were not too cramped in the phaeton. I opted for speed, given the circumstance."

"I was quite comfortable, sir," Emmanuel answered with a heavy dose of deference. "Quite comfortable, indeed."

"Splendid!" Christophe cried. He thanked the driver with a nod. "If you'd follow me, I will take you to your quarters for the night."

"I was hoping to see Lu—er, Captain Ortega before turning in."

Christophe hissed through his teeth. "I'm afraid that won't be possible. Captain Ortega has been called away by his duties. But worry not! You shall be reunited with him tomorrow, for it is his ship we will board."

Emmanuel blinked in disbelief. "Ship? But where are we going? I thought I was singing for a Fleet to-do."

Christophe leaned in close to the man. "You shall sing on the water, for the greatest celebration the Fleet has ever known. Tomorrow, we will sail to the other side of the island. Then, we will take to the sea!"

That little bit of encouragement was enough to turn the fisherman's trepidation into a smile. After which, he happily followed the commodore into the Citadel.

"I'm afraid we only had room in the midshipmen's barracks," Christophe explained as they entered the room. It held not much more than rows of single beds. "You will have the room to yourself, of course. Aboard the *Adoration*, you and the other singers will have your own cabin."

"This is all too much, Commodore—"

"Nonsense! A special guest deserves the best we have to offer! Now, rest well. We leave in just a few hours."

"Sir," Emmanuel called as Christophe made to leave. "About the matter of compensation . . ."

"Of course!" Christophe answered. "Upon the *Adoration*'s return to Ayiti, you will be paid and taken back to your home."

"Thank you, sir," Emmanuel said, bowing his head.

Christophe pretended not to hear the man's voice grow thick with emotion as he let himself out of the barracks and sped through the hallways to his office. Once there, he locked himself inside. He pulled the bottom drawer of his desk out fully, then emptied its contents onto his desk. He pushed down on the front end of the drawer's bottom, and it came loose, revealing a secret compartment underneath.

A long-handled golden-framed mirror lay in the drawer. Christophe took it by its handle and held it up before his face. He sang the notes he had been taught by the viceroy to call upon him, and soon the viceroy's face appeared in the glass.

"What is it, Brother Christophe?" Stormcoast asked. His accent was thick, despite his years of speaking the land-dweller language.

"My brother," he said, "the day of our destiny draws ever nearer!"

The viceroy's face broke into a smile. "Have you found the girl?"

"Not yet, but it is only a matter of time, my brother. I have my ships searching all over the Seven Isles, and we have located all seven singers. Ready your people! Tell them their faith in Agwe shall be rewarded much sooner than they think. They are the Chosen who shall walk with Agwe in this life!"

Stormcoast inclined his head slowly, and then he was gone, leaving Christophe smiling at his own reflection.

"Soon," he told himself, as though he were soothing an upset child. "Soon."

•••●•••

He and Stormcoast had divided the tasks required for the restoration ceremony. While Stormcoast combed the seas for the conch shell, Christophe searched the lands for seven singers who would sing the sacred song that would break the generations-long curse that separated the Meridians from their home. Emmanuel Millet was the sixth voice. He had thought it would be months before the discovery of the seventh. Then, he had received Ortega's letter.

"The girl's voice was the most beautiful thing I have ever heard," the captain had written. *"The sound alone seemed to touch my soul."*

Christophe was certain that this was a gift for him alone. He would not take the chance of missing the opportunity to bring these seven voices together once and for all.

It had all been thanks to Ortega. Christophe had known the boy could be trusted to move up to the rank of captain, and now he had proven invaluable by locating the final piece of a puzzle that Christophe's sea-born brethren had entrusted to him some time ago. He was confident that Ortega would locate the shell in due time. When the Meridians rose as conquerors of the Seven Isles, Christophe would ensure that Ortega had a place of honor.

Twenty-One

PEARL

Pearl did not stop crying until well after the sun had dipped below the horizon. She had seen death before, but never had she been so close to it. A thousand emotions had coursed through her as the man, the green-and-gold-coated officer, had held her against him and threatened to kill her. Then, before she could process a single one, Nnenna gave the order for her to distract him. She had bitten the man, not knowing how else to hurt him enough to pull his attention away from Nnenna. Then, Nnenna had killed him. Pearl understood that it had been his life or hers, but she hated that she had had nothing more to offer. For the second time in as many weeks, her life had been in danger and she had been powerless to save herself.

By the time she lifted her head from her pillow, her eyes felt raw and swollen. She was more exhausted than she had ever known she could be—her bones ached and her muscles screamed. She was also starving, but she could not bear the thought of facing Nnenna or the crew.

The familiar sensation of hiding and waiting tugged a memory loose from her mind. She had been in the Shallows with

Uncle Rain, picking through the land-dweller treasures that had fallen into the sea from their large ships and tiny boats, vessels she had learned about from her teachers. They had said it was essential for her generation to learn the ways of the land dwellers in order to rule them most effectively when their destiny was finally fulfilled. Her uncles, however, had always taught her to make her own destiny, a sentiment that kept them just on the edge of exile.

She had been about to ask Uncle Rain to share his thoughts when he had suddenly stiffened and raised his head above hers to see what lay beyond the space they occupied. When Pearl had looked as well, she had seen a pair of temple guards swimming toward them.

"Darling girl, you must hide," he had said, taking her by the arm and leading her toward a rocky edifice that reached past the veil. "Do not come out until I tell you it is safe."

"What? But it's just—"

"Please, trust me and do as I ask, Pearl," Rain had insisted.

For the first time in her life, she had seen fear in her uncle's eyes. She had nodded and, without another word, had swum up the face of the cliff until she had found a small cave that had been just big enough for her to fit into. She had climbed into its mouth and had curled up as far into the cramped space as she could have managed. Uncle Rain had not kept her waiting long—the guards had only wanted to ask him a few questions, he had said—but the bloody cut on his lip had told a different story. She had not asked about it, not even days later when a bruise had bloomed around the corner of his mouth, out of fear of complicating her comfortable little life. Perhaps if she had not been so timid, she might have learned something that would have helped her now that her life was nothing but discomfort.

A hand on Pearl's shoulder brought her back to the present.

She started, brandishing the dagger she had pulled out of a dead man's throat. The hand caught her wrist, stopping the dagger just short of Nnenna's face. Pearl's eyes widened with horror as she realized what she had almost done. Nnenna held up a hand to calm her and took the dagger.

"Do you want to eat?" Nnenna asked in sign.

Pearl's gurgling stomach answered before she could respond. She searched Nnenna's face for signs of anger, of disappointment, and finding none, reluctantly rolled out of her bunk. She followed Nnenna to the dining cabin. Nnenna strode in and took her usual seat at the end of the table.

Pearl lagged behind.

"Eat," Nnenna signed, noticing Pearl hovering in the doorway. She gestured to a covered plate at the seat to her right.

With her eyes cast downward, Pearl stepped around the long table and took the seat in front of the dish. When she lifted the cover, the aroma of fried fish and vegetables filled her nostrils. Her stomach uttered an impatient growl, churning uncomfortably. She set the cover aside and ate, too tired to bother with the utensils. The fish was still warm and deliciously seasoned.

"Good?" Nnenna asked.

With her hands and mouth full of fish, Pearl could only nod in response.

By the time Pearl finished her meal, only the fish bones remained. She watched Nnenna tentatively as she studied a large sheet that was covered in lines. Some were stick straight while others curved into irregular shapes. The words she wanted to say loomed over her, making her continued silence uncomfortable. Finally, she waved her hand to get Nnenna's attention.

"I'm sorry," Pearl signed.

Nnenna frowned in confusion.

"I could not fight," Pearl went on.

Nnenna raised her eyebrows. "*I* fight," she responded in sign, poking her own chest several times for emphasis. "You don't fight. *I* am sorry."

But there was more that Pearl wanted to say. She was finished standing aside while others put themselves in danger.

"I want to fight," she signed, her face resolute. "Will you teach me?"

Nnenna looked conflicted. Her eyes moved over Pearl's slight form, appraisingly. She muttered something to herself that Pearl did not understand, but eventually, she nodded.

Pearl smiled and sighed as a weight lifted from her shoulders. She was going to learn to fight, then she and Nnenna would rescue her uncle. And, if she did well enough, perhaps, after they got Uncle Wade to safety, Nnenna would allow her to stay aboard as a part of her crew. If she could not live in the sea, she might enjoy a life traveling over its waves.

As Pearl mused, Nnenna returned to studying the sheet. A shape on the parchment caught Pearl's attention. She waved to draw Nnenna's eye, once more.

"What is that?" she signed.

Nnenna held up the sheet and paused to think, clearly trying to find the sign for the word she wanted.

"Map," she said, enunciating the land-dweller word.

Pearl mimicked the shapes that Nnenna's mouth made but, having no voice, could not speak the word aloud. She frowned. Nnenna placed the sheet back on the table and beckoned Pearl over. She pointed to a shape on the map that looked like a crab's claw.

"My home," she signed. It was the island they had just left. This must have been a rendering.

Nnenna slid her finger all the way to the left edge of the map, where there were no more landforms, and landed upon a black circle.

"Your home?" she signed.

Pearl paused to think. It made sense. This was the great chasm, the Gateway to the Unknown by which her people lived in anticipation of their island's return. She had seen it in the bowl, its blackness peeking out beyond the edges of the isle. Nnenna must have seen it, too, and recognized it.

"Yes. Are we going there?" Pearl asked tentatively.

"I don't know," Nnenna replied.

Pearl did not even know if she could return to her home. There were no scripture verses that told of the reversal of Agwe's curse. She might have been destined to be a voiceless land dweller for the remainder of her days.

It does not seem like such a terrible fate, she thought, staring at Nnenna.

Then, Pearl remembered her Uncle Wade, who might still be alive and captured by the viceroy.

Guilt bloomed like an anemone in the pit of her stomach. "My family," she signed. "Can you help?"

"What happened?" Nnenna asked.

The events of the day of Viceroy Seastead's funeral poured out of her. She did not even stop to make sure that Nnenna was following her signs. When she finished, there were more tears in her eyes as she stared at Nnenna.

"I'm so sorry," Nnenna signed.

"Can you help?" Pearl asked again.

"Yes."

Twenty-Two

NNENNA

Once her mother made it to the rambling stage of her drunkenness, Nnenna was safe to secrete the two bottles of rum that had survived her indulgence. It would not be long before her mother was wholly unconscious, and if Nnenna played her cards right, she would go down without a fight.

"I'm royalty, you know," Kerline Delahaye slurred as she stumbled her way over to the narrow bed against the shack's wall. "Descended from the goddess herself. You should show me more respect."

"Of course, Mother," Nnenna said, feigning deference as she pulled the heavy wool blanket back and waited as her mother flopped heavily onto the feather mattress.

Her eyes stared blankly at the wooden rafters above her as she continued to rant. "I deserved to live in a palace, you hear me? Not this shithole! A palace!"

"Yes, Mother."

Nnenna covered her mother's sickly thin body with the blanket up to her chin and stood by her side as her words became less and less intelligible, less and less vitriolic, until she finally fell fast asleep. Nnenna's body relaxed as it always did when she was out of harm's way. Somewhere in the recesses of her mind, there lived a memory of being happy, of having a happy, healthy mother and a father who would carry her on his shoulders. Though it had only been a decade since that time, the memory felt so far away, Nnenna would have believed it belonged to someone else.

She dragged her exhausted body to her little corner of the shack, pulled the thin piece of fabric she used as a blanket over her own body, and closed her eyes. It took only moments for her to fall into the blackness of sleep, and seemingly only an instant later, she opened her eyes to the first rays of sunlight the next morning.

Nnenna quickly stood and stretched. She glanced over at her mother snoring peacefully with an arm and a leg hanging off the bed. Nnenna crept over, reached underneath, and pulled out the two bottles of liquor she had hidden the night before. She left them on the floor, directly in Kerline's eventual path. It would be hours still before she woke up, but it was always in Nnenna's best interests to be prepared.

Once the bottles were placed, Nnenna left through the shack's only window, not daring to risk the creaking door, and followed her own footsteps back to Prince's Port's city center. She walked quickly and arrived in half as much time as she had before. When she pushed open the door of the Singing Crab, the starchy, salty smell of fried plantains filled her nostrils.

"Close that door, or you'll let the gulls in!" Tati Clo said sharply as she descended the stairs.

Nnenna turned and did as she was told. When Nnenna faced the lady once more, she was moving toward the bar.

"You eat yet?" she asked.

"Yes," Nnenna lied.

Tati Clo leaned against the bar with two hands on the surface and eyed Nnenna suspiciously.

"Well, that's too bad," she said. "I made too many plantains and now I suppose I'll just have to throw the extra away."

"No!" Nnenna cried before she could stop herself. "I . . . I'm still a bit hungry."

With a smirk, Tati Clo reached under the bar and pulled out a plate that overflowed with plantains and a small ceramic pot with a lid. When she lifted the lid, Nnenna saw that it was full of creamy-looking sauce. She could have cried.

"Have as much as you'd like," Tati Clo said, her voice a touch softer.

Two free meals in as many days made Nnenna worry there would not be enough work for her to be able to repay the lady's kindness. As she bit into the first plantain and felt its richness and warmth seep onto her tongue, she closed her eyes and offered her first prayer of thanks in a decade. She chose one of her father's gods There was no stopping her, after that. She devoured that first and then another and then three more. Nnenna ate until her belly protested. By the time she finished, there were only two plantains left.

"I'm sorry," Nnenna said, looking down at the nearly empty plate.

"Nonsense," Tati Clo said, pulling the plate and sauce container out of the way. "You did exactly as you were told. I'll save these last ones for you to take home when you're finished here."

Nnenna wanted to tell the woman not to bother, but she got the feeling her words would go unheeded, so she offered the woman an uncomfortable "Thank you."

"How old are you?" Tati Clo asked.

"Seventeen," Nnenna lied, straightening her back as though doing so would make her more convincing.

Tati Clo snorted. "If you're going to try to play me for a fool, do a better job. Now, really, what's your age, girl?"

"Fourteen," Nnenna replied sheepishly.

"Hmm." Tati Clo considered Nnenna as she rubbed her chin. "I know you're no stranger to the drink, but it would look poor on my part to have such a young one behind the bar. I do need a maid for the rooms. You know how to tidy, don't you?" Nnenna nodded. "Good. I've got two people leaving today. Their rooms will need to be swept and dusted, the sheets washed and replaced with a fresh set. Come with me."

Tati Clo walked toward the stairs, and Nnenna followed. The older woman led her to a room on the second floor. It was small and narrow, barely the size of a cupboard, but it held a bed, a desk, and a small shelf of books.

"This room never sells," Tati Clo told her. "You can use it whenever you need to. And you'll take your two daily meals in the dining room. You've got to stay strong," she added when Nnenna started to protest. "I can't have a fainting maid."

Nnenna did not know what to say in the face of such kindness, so she bowed her head.

"How long since your last bath?" Tati Clo asked. Nnenna's head jerked upward, and a flush rose to her face. "Never mind," Tati Clo said, waving the question away. "I'll get one started for you in my room. And, when you're done, I'll help you tame that mane, as well. You represent the Singing Crab, now. You've got to look the part."

•••●•••

Nnenna pulled at the white fabric wrapped around her head until the intricate knots she had installed came loose and her dark red locs fell free. It was late enough in the evening that the sky was alight with stars and the moon hung fat, round, and bright against the inky black. She tossed the wrap unceremoniously into the wardrobe and turned to Tinou, who sat at Nnenna's table with her feet up and an expectant smirk on her face.

"How was it being back home?" she asked.

To ears untrained to Tinou's doublespeak, the question would seem innocent enough, but Nnenna had known the woman for years and could easily discern the true query behind her words.

"The place is crawling with beetles," Nnenna sighed as she dropped into the seat across from her. "They took over the Singing Crab. Pearl and I barely made it out alive." She could feel an "I told you so" teetering on Tinou's lips, so she cut Tinou off before she could start. "I'm still glad we went. Got some good information on the girl and the shell."

It was only half a lie. It was true that the information they got from Delva's shop was valuable, but she had not expected the beetles to have such a presence in the Southern District of Ayiti. The last time she was in Ayiti, she might have seen a handful of Fleet soldiers, and Ayiti had largely governed itself. Now, it seemed the Fleet had all but taken over. If she had known this was the case, she might have thought twice about bringing Pearl and Aline . . .

You kept Pearl safe and Aline can take care of herself, Nnenna reassured herself.

"So, we're still doing that?" Tinou asked, her annoyance evident. "Playing ferry to the girl and her special seashell?"

Nnenna reached for the bottle sitting on the table and poured herself a glass of whiskey, but a curdling sensation in her stomach made her push the glass toward Tinou instead. She took it, raised it in thanks, and brought it to her lips.

"She's one of Agwe's Chosen," Nnenna said casually.

Tinou spluttered into the glass, and Nnenna held back the satisfied smirk that tugged at the corner of her mouth.

"That *special seashell* she's been carrying around is supposedly the key to their destiny. The beetles must be working with the Chosen somehow. The way they've been chasing after the girl, it can't be a coincidence."

Tinou stared at Nnenna, and Nnenna knew she was looking for signs of a jest. The myth of the Chosen was one of the many stories whispered among the lower ranks of the Fleet. Nnenna and Tinou had both heard the stories of the people cursed to live in the sea and had dismissed them as fairy tales. Now, Nnenna held Tinou's gaze until Tinou's skepticism morphed into shock.

"You're telling the truth!" Tinou exclaimed. "What are we going to do?"

Once again, Nnenna knew the true meaning behind Tinou's words.

She leaned back in her chair. "What do you think we should do, Tinou?" she asked, tilting her head to the side in exaggerated curiosity.

"Well, it's obvious, isn't it," she said, unbothered. "We ransom her to the beetles."

The sigh that escaped Nnenna was not one of disappointment, because that would have required her being surprised. No, this sigh was confirmation that somewhere along their journey together, Nnenna and the sister she had found in Tinou had drifted away from each other.

"You said it yourself, they're champing at the bit to get their hands on her," Tinou went on when Nnenna said nothing. "We could make a small fortune selling the girl off."

"Do you really think the Fleet will want to make a deal with us? We've been terrorizing their ships for years!"

"If they want the girl and the shell badly enough, they'll do whatever we tell them."

"And what's to stop them from arresting us when we try to broker this deal?"

"We'll be careful," Tinou said, smiling for the first time since she had entered the great cabin. "And besides, you said yourself that the beetles care more about their honor than anything else. Going back on a deal isn't very honorable, is it."

Nnenna had to admit, Tinou's plan made sense. If she had not known Pearl, she would have considered it, but she had let the girl get under her skin. There was no way she would allow her to fall into the hands of the Fleet or Agwe's so-called Chosen.

"No." Nnenna sighed.

"No? No what?"

"No, we're not giving up the girl."

Nnenna decided she would have a drink, so she reached across the table and grabbed the glass that Tinou had emptied. She felt Tinou staring at her as she overpoured a measure of whiskey and downed it in a single swallow. It would take more to get her drunk, but the burn at the back of her throat was enough to take away from the traitorous feeling blooming in her belly.

Tinou stood, crossed the cabin, and went to the door. Before she pulled it open, she stopped and turned back to Nnenna.

"*He* would have agreed with me," she said in a softer, more defiant voice.

Nnenna knew better than to engage her first mate when she was feeling mutinous, which was more and more often these days. It was Nnenna's fault. When Delva had named Nnenna the next captain of the *Medusa*, Tinou had only accepted on the condition that Nnenna swear to continue Delva's work destroying the Fleet, to become who she'd sworn to be when they had fished her out of the sea. Tinou did not believe rescuing Pearl to be a cause worthy of the Devil of the Deep. Nnenna did not know if

Tinou would ever understand, so she finished her second drink in silence. Tinou left without another word.

When she finally stood from her table, leaving behind an empty bottle, her body pitched forward in a way unrelated to the rocking of the ship, and she had to hold on to the chair back for balance.

"Tinou will be fine by morning," she muttered to herself as she took the handful of unsteady steps to her berth.

Nnenna flopped onto the plush feather mattress and threw the blanket over her body, only vaguely aware that she was still fully dressed. The next time they made landfall, she promised, trying to keep her shame at bay, she would have to remember to do something to make her first mate feel appreciated.

Twenty-Three

LU

Lu's legs were beginning to cramp, when he spotted movement at the collector's shop. There had been something suspicious in the way that Moreau responded to Lu's questioning. Something had bothered him so much that he left his commandeered room while the moon still hung in the sky to find a dark corner from which he could watch the shop. He was crouched in an alley between a painted wall and an abandoned cart with the shop at his back so that he had to twist his torso around to be able to see the storefront.

No light came through the window in the red door, but a denser shadow within the shadows moved about the cramped space. Lu watched it for hours, back and forth, back and forth, back and forth. Just before first light, the door opened, and Moreau emerged into the early morning, struggling to carry what looked like two large valises.

Lu leaped into action, stumbling slightly as he ran with numb legs and feet. He caught up to the shopkeeper just before the man turned the corner, and grabbed him by his collar.

"I don't have any gold!" the shopkeeper cried as Lu whirled

him around and threw him against the wall of the nearest building.

"By order of the Fleet," Lu said softly but fiercely, "you will cooperate in this investigation, or you will be taken into custody."

"The Fleet?" Moreau spluttered. Then, he squinted at Lu in the darkness. "Captain?"

"I will place you under arrest," Lu said, drawing his pistol and aiming it at the man's chest.

"On what grounds?" Moreau demanded.

Lu had had a suspicion from the moment he had stepped foot in the man's shop. Now, it was time to see if his instincts were to be trusted. He took Moreau's arm with his free hand and held it against the wall over his head. He pulled the man's sleeve back to his elbow and ran his fingertips along the wrinkled forearm. It was difficult to find among the many scars, but Lu's fingers soon brushed against a patch of raised skin in the shape of a trident. The moment Lu found the brand, Moreau wrenched his arm free and pulled it to his chest.

"You're a pirate," Lu said.

It was common practice for the Fleet to brand those who fled their ranks so that, wherever they went, whatever they became, the world would know their shame. Lu had surmised, from the shop's varied wares, that Moreau was at the very least well-traveled. His overly calm manner had given Lu the impression that he was accustomed to darker dealings.

"You can't prove anything beyond what I may or may not have once been," Moreau said indignantly.

"Any man sporting that brand outside of a grave will have also escaped from the Citadel, which is a crime," Lu countered.

Moreau glared at him. "What do you want?"

"I only want the truth. Where are you going?"

"I'm leaving Kiskeya and getting as far away from the Seven Isles as I can," Moreau answered.

"Why?" Lu pressed.

"It's clearly not safe for a man like me anymore," Moreau said darkly. "Ever since the beetle occupation began . . ."

Lu frowned. "What about the Devil of the Deep? And the girl?"

"I told you I don't know anything about any—"

"I said no lies! Where is the shell?"

"I don't know what you are talking about."

"Empty your bags! Now!"

Lu stepped back to give Moreau room, keeping his pistol aimed at the man. Moreau knelt to the ground with some difficulty, and Lu watched intently as he unlatched both bags and emptied their contents onto the street. One held an unassuming assortment of items from his shop. The other, a sheathed sword and a gun.

"What is that?" Lu asked, gesturing to a large leather-bound tome that had fallen out of the larger bag.

"Some light reading," Moreau answered, his voice dripping with sarcasm.

"Open it," Lu ordered.

Moreau froze, his eyes darting between Lu and the book. With an impatient huff, Lu picked the book up himself with his free hand. It was the book about the goddess, and it was lighter than when he had picked it up in the shop. With a flick of his thumb, Lu opened the front cover and saw, nestled in a hollow in the pages, a conch shell the color of bone.

Lu lifted his head to ask Moreau what else he was lying about. Moreau reached into his pocket and pulled out a knife. He lunged at Lu, the point of his blade aimed at his neck. Lu wrenched himself out of the way, tossing the book and shell over his shoulder as he narrowly avoided being stabbed. The old man came at him again, forcing him to stumble back into the street. Lu tried to raise his pistol, but Moreau knocked it away with his empty hand.

Lu dropped the gun, twisting away from a third attack, and pulled his sword from its sheath. He swung wildly at Moreau, hoping to cleave the man's flesh with his blade, but caught only metal. Moreau quickly retrieved and unsheathed the blade from his smaller valise. He pushed Lu away and executed three lightning-quick attacks from which Lu barely managed to defend himself.

The man was still sharp for his age. He anticipated Lu's every move. When Lu attempted to parry Moreau's attacks, Moreau moved with surprising speed, twirling out of Lu's grasp as though they were partners in a dance.

Lu waited for Moreau to attack again. This time, he took a page out of the old man's book. He feinted right and stepped left out of Moreau's path. The pirate overbalanced, falling forward onto the street. As the old man struggled to right himself, Lu picked up his own gun from among the detritus and aimed it at Moreau once more.

"You are under arrest," Lu said, breathing heavily, "for the crimes of—"

Moreau's quick hands snatched the conch shell out of the open book on the ground. He held it up to his chest. Before Lu could say a word, Moreau threw the shell.

"No!" Lu shouted as he watched it sail through the air into the darkness.

He took off running after it. Halfway down the cobblestones, close to where he had been hiding, he discovered a mess of shards among the dirt and rocks. He wanted to curse, but, before he got the chance, the shards shuddered as though a wind coursed through them. Suddenly, they all moved at once, coming together to re-form the shell that had been broken.

"Agwe's might . . ." Lu gasped.

He picked up the shell and inspected it as best as he could by the light of the moon. There was no trace of its ever having been broken.

When Lu overcame his shock and remembered Moreau, he looked up the street at the shop, but there was no sign of the man. There was no point in giving chase. Lu had what he needed.

Lu paced back and forth, rubbing his smooth chin as his thoughts raced. A line of text from his captain's manual floated across his mind again and again.

"And when the Lost Ones return to their home, they shall call upon the Fleet and, entwined, the two shall reign over the Seven Isles of the world."

He did not return to the tavern that morning. Instead, he went to the beach and watched the horizon for the arrival of the *Adoration* from the northern end of the country. It wasn't until the sun began to lighten the sky that he spotted the tips of the ship's sails poking over the horizon. He rose, brushing the sand from his uniform, ignoring the soreness that was growing around his chest, and stood to attention, keeping his stance until the commodore's longboat reached the shore.

"What news, Ortega?" the commodore asked.

Lu reported everything that had come to pass since he had sent the commodore the missive. Then, holding his breath, he presented the book. The commodore took the tome with both hands, his nostrils flaring slightly as he examined the picture of the goddess. Then, he gingerly pulled the cover open. His eyes widened and flashed green. Lu blinked, and they were brown again.

"Tell me more about this girl," the commodore said excitedly as Lu led the way back to the Singing Crab. "Aline."

"Aline?" Lu asked, confused. "Well, she's one of the barmaids at the tavern. She's newly arrived, but won't say where she came from."

"No matter," the commodore said, waving the concern away. "Tell me more about her singing."

"Her singing, sir?"

"Yes, her singing," the commodore repeated.

"Well," Lu stuttered, struggling to describe his experience listening to the young woman sing without revealing too much of himself. "She was . . . very . . . good," he answered stiffly, and the commodore let out a loud wheezing laugh.

"My dear boy, there's no need to be coy, especially not after your message. You described her voice as otherworldly! Did she evoke anything in you? In the other patrons? Tell me!"

A flush of warmth rose to Lu's cheeks. "It made me feel . . ." he started but paused as the memory of Aline's dining room performance returned to him. Her voice had pierced his soul and temporarily quelled the storm that was ever present there. For the moments that she sang, he had forgotten everything about his relationship with his father and the dissatisfaction itching at the back of his mind. "Calm," he said finally.

The commodore clapped him on the shoulder in the way that had become his custom when Lu did something that pleased him. They arrived at the door of the Singing Crab only moments later. Ambroise, who stood sentry, saluted both the commodore and Lu before stepping aside to allow them ingress.

"I'm keeping one of them on the second floor," Lu said, as they crossed the empty dining room and mounted the stairs, "and the other on the third."

"Both?" the commodore asked.

"I have the owner in custody, as well," Lu answered. "Her unwillingness to comply gives me the impression that she knows more about the pirate than she's letting on."

"Excellent. We'll speak to the girl, first."

When they entered the room in which Aline was sequestered, they found her standing by the window, staring off at the sea. She did not move when they closed the door behind them, nor when the commodore took the chair from the desk and dragged it to the end of the bed.

"Am I under arrest?" she asked without looking away from the window.

"Heavens no, my dear," the commodore assured her. "We just need some information from you. Won't you have a seat?"

She turned and looked first at Lu, who stood next to the bed, and then at the commodore, who sat in the chair and gestured for her to sit at the end of the covered mattress. Lu sensed her trepidation and tried to smile to put her at ease. It seemed to work, as she took several steps across the room and slowly lowered herself onto the bed, opposite the commodore.

"I am Commodore Henri Christophe," the commodore said. "I oversee the entirety of Fleet operations."

"So, you're the one who told him to lock me up in here?" Aline asked, jerking her head in Lu's direction.

Commodore Christophe laughed. "No, that bit of ingenuity was all his own," he said. "But I must say that I am glad he did so, because he told me that you have the most extraordinary voice."

Lu watched the color deepen in the girl's cheeks.

"No need to be shy, my dear! Please, if you could be so kind, grace us with a song."

"I'm not anything special," Aline said, looking back and forth between Lu and the commodore.

"Oh, quite the contrary, my dear. I think you are very special. Please, sing for us."

Lu watched the girl's hesitation evaporate at the commodore's compliment. She closed her eyes and began to sway, like a palm tree in a soft breeze. Her lips parted, and out came not the big, bold voice that had charmed Lu in the dining room, but a sliver of something unsure but still powerful. It hit him in that same intangible place where he was certain his soul lived, and quieted every part of him that might have fought against the calm.

"Magnificent," the commodore said when Aline's song ended.

"My mother taught me," Aline said. "And her mother taught her, and her mother's mother before her."

"A most extraordinary familial gift," the commodore replied. "My dear, what brought you to this island?"

"I . . . stowed away on a ship," she said nervously. The girl was clearly lying, but, once again, the commodore seemed not to care. "I wanted to see more of the world."

The commodore smiled. "Would you like to see even more than this island?"

Her eyes grew wide, and her lips spread into a smile as she nodded.

"Our ship is moored in the bay. Join us—sing for us—and we'll take you to see places beyond your wildest dreams!"

Aline nodded again.

"I'll send a lieutenant to escort you to the longboat that will take you to the ship."

"Thank you!" the girl said, clasping her hands together in front of her chest.

"You are most welcome, my dear," the commodore replied.

Lu was curious as to why the commodore had not asked her

any questions about the pirate but knew better than to question his commanding officer's methods. He set his doubts aside and followed the commodore up the stairs to the room on the third floor where the owner of the Singing Crab was being held. The moment the commodore pushed the door open, a wooden club came swinging at his face. Lu saw it and pushed the commodore out of the way, stopping the club with one hand and twisting his arm around it to pry it out of the older woman's grip. He threw the club, which was made from a chair leg, aside and grabbed the owner's arms, securing them behind her back.

"Assaulting a Fleet officer," the commodore said once he was recovered, "is a capital offense, madame."

"Then, go ahead and shoot me, because I'm not telling you anything," the woman fired back.

"Very well," the commodore said, drawing his pistol from his belt and aiming it right between the woman's dark brown eyes. Her lip quivered, and though she tried to remain resolute, a small, fearful whimper escaped her. "You see? Finding bravery is a very different thing when death is staring you in the face."

He removed the gun from her head, and Lu was nearly brought down by the weight of the woman falling to her knees.

"What do you people want?" she begged through sobs. "I've done nothing wrong!"

"Harboring a fugitive and a pirate is hardly 'nothing wrong,'" Commodore Christophe replied. "We know the pirate and the girl were here. Tell us where they went and we'll leave you to run your tavern in peace. Continue to be obstinate and I'll make sure you hang in this very square so everyone in the Southern District knows the cost of associating with pirate scum."

"I don't know anything!" the woman sobbed. "Please! I don't know where they went!"

"Surely you must know something, madame. Think hard." He pointed the gun at her head again. "As though your life depended upon it. Or, perhaps we should call your granddaughter to see what information she has for us."

"No, please!" the woman begged, lifting her head from the floor. "I don't know anything of value. She never says where she's going and I never know when she's coming. She's never brought anyone with her before, but this time there were two: Aline and a young girl she called Pearl. The girl never spoke. They used some kind of sign language to talk to each other. All she said was she was bringing the girl home."

The commodore waited for a long time before pulling the gun away once again. This time, he returned it to his belt.

"Tell Ambroise to arrange transport for this one to the Citadel."

"But, sir, she cooperated," Lu said without thinking.

"She admitted to aiding and abetting a known pirate and fugitive," the commodore replied. "She will be held accountable. You will accompany me to the *Adoration*. That pirate already has a day's head start. We must give chase."

Twenty-Four

PEARL

Nnenna had encouraged Pearl to move about the ship as she pleased, assuring her that the crew could be trusted to watch over her. Pearl had not been keen to accept her offer, but after two days of being cooped up in her cabin, her guilt had gnawed a hole into her abdomen that she was surprised no one else could see. She had betrayed her people and her god, trying to destroy the key to their reunion. Her decision had not come easily, but she had not agonized over it the way she had expected to. Her lessons in the temple taught her to always put the Settlement's needs before her own. Why, then, had it been so easy for her to destroy the shell that would have saved them?

Pearl thought of Nnenna and Aline, of Tati Clo and even Tinou, who remained aloof toward her at best. These land dwellers were nothing like the land dwellers in the stories Viceroy Seastead and Pearl's teachers had told. They were clever and funny, kind and honorable, and they deserved to live.

More than her people, who had already endured generations of isolation? It would have to be so. She had made her choice.

Maybe the land dwellers' nature was not the only lie the leaders told.

The thought had slipped from her mind like an errant curl coming loose. For a moment, she froze with fear, and the desire to tuck it back in rose within her. She fought it, letting the thought linger in her mind. To have doubts was among the greatest offenses a Settler could commit against Agwe, but there were no temple guards here to haul her away.

This realization left her tingling with something unfamiliar and delicious. Her guilt remained, but it was easier to set aside. She was able to turn her focus to other needs, like her rumbling stomach. She let it inspire her to finally leave the cramped space and guide her to the galley. The cook, a burly, bearded man with skin that was closer to the color of a fish's belly than her own, Sven, stood at the large wall of metal and flames. An assortment of pans poked out from within it, belching steam that carried delicious smells to her nose. Sven spoke the land-dweller language with a thick, lilting accent that made the foreign words even less decipherable, and whenever he spoke to her specifically, he gestured dramatically to help her understand.

The first time she had wandered into his domain, he had pointed to her and called her something that sounded like he had been clearing his throat. When she had stared at him with confusion, he had repeated the sounds, turning his hand into a fish swimming through invisible waters. She had understood immediately and smiled. He had smiled back and offered her a plate of food. This had become the custom between them.

"You hungry?" he asked her in his broken, accented land-dweller tongue.

She had heard the phrase enough times to know what it meant and nodded vigorously. He pointed to a chair in the corner of the room, the only one, and bid her to sit. As she did so, he prepared her a breakfast plate. Pearl would never tire of eating cooked fish, of the way it flaked when she broke into its flesh with her spoon—a tool she had all but mastered since becoming a land dweller—and melted into salty goodness on her tongue. This meal also featured a mound of steaming yellow stuff.

"Ehgg," Sven said when he saw her examining the unfamiliar food. He tucked his thumbs under his armpits and flapped his bent arms as though they were wings. Then, he put his two hands together, one on top of the other, but left a rounded space in between them, as though for something small and delicate. Pearl still did not understand, but she ate a spoonful all the same.

When her plate was empty and her belly full, she set the dish on the floor next to the chair.

"Good?" he asked with his eyebrows raised.

Pearl nodded again, smiling this time to show her satisfaction.

"Good," he said. "Now, you work."

Before Pearl could ask, he tossed her an apron. Then, he put a knife in her hands and set her in front of a large vat of brown stones. He took one in his hands and brought his own knife to its surface and pressed gently. A thin sliver of skin fell free, revealing juicy white flesh underneath. "Po-ta-to," he said, handing her the rock that must have been some kind of edible thing. "You peel."

She brought her borrowed blade to the po-ta-to and tried to do what she had seen Sven do. Her first attempt ended in her making a deep cut into its flesh. On her second try, she managed to peel some skin off, but her knife took a fair amount of white flesh with it. Sven oversaw all her attempts, and when she was finally able to extract a thin sliver of brown flesh from the potato, he clapped his hands together and said something loudly in his native tongue. With a combination of land-dweller words and improvised signs, he told her to peel the rest of the potatoes.

Pearl was happy to do the work. Setting her mind on a task felt much more productive than dwelling on the fact that she was alone and carrying the weight of making decisions that would affect her people. The shell was powerful. She understood that much from what she had seen it do in Ship-Father's shop. The Fleet and the viceroy both sought its power, and it was now Pearl's responsibility to keep it out of their hands. Giving it to Ship-Father to be hidden had been the only course of action that had made sense. She hoped her people would see this.

Another thought slipped from the recesses of her mind when she thought of her home in the sea. It was the worry that her people would not accept her after what she had done, the worry that the curse would not even allow her to return to them in her current form. But was that what she really wanted? The idea of living without her people once scared her, but it had been days since she had left the sea, and she now knew that the world was much bigger than she had been taught. Not only that, but she had grown fond of Nnenna and her crew. Pearl could not imagine returning to the life she lived before.

But Uncle Wade, she thought sadly.

She did not let her despair settle. If Uncle Wade was alive, then he would have made it to the surface as well. She would find him.

When she had peeled through half the vat of potatoes, there was another visitor to the galley. Pearl made a point of not looking up when Tinou crossed to where Sven stood, though she could feel her eyes from the moment she entered to the moment she started talking to the cook. They spoke so quickly, Pearl could only understand one out of every ten words and, even then, just barely due to their hushed voices. She gathered that what they were discussing was not meant for every ear. There was a moment when their voices grew tense, and Pearl thought she heard her own name out of Sven's mouth, but she kept her eyes on the potatoes until Tinou left. The tension remained, even when it was just the two of them again, and, when Pearl presented the vat of perfectly peeled potatoes, Sven forgot to smile and clap and praise her work in his native tongue the way he had done before.

Pearl watched the cook take the best-looking of the potatoes and dice them into small chunks. He put them in a large pot of boiling water and made sure that the flame beneath it was as strong as it could be. Then, he pulled out an assortment of long-leafed plants. Still holding the knife, Pearl brought herself to the surface on which he worked and stood next to him. First, she watched him take a long orange root and cut it into thin rounds. She took one and did the same. Then, she watched him take a bundle of green sticks with leafy tops and cut them into small pieces. She did exactly as he did.

"Very good," he said when she produced a pile of edible plants that looked nearly identical to his own.

He let her cut the rest of the plants on her own, taking from the piles she made to add to the concoction in the pot. By the time they were finished, the galley smelled amazing.

Sven said something in the land-dweller tongue that Pearl did not understand until he brought an invisible cup to his lips and drank. She voiced her agreement with an enthusiastic nod, and Sven produced two large steins of ale. As he handed Pearl hers, which she had to hold with two hands, he brought a finger to his lips. Pearl mimed that she would keep the secret before taking a swig.

"Pearl!"

Pearl nearly choked on the mouthful of ale, jumping at the

sound of her name in the land-dweller tongue. Nnenna strode into the galley and marched straight to Pearl, relieving her of the still-full stein. She turned to Sven, who looked downright sheepish under Nnenna's glare, and rattled off a stream of criticisms that Pearl did not need to speak the language to understand. At the end of Nnenna's lecture, Sven seemed apologetic. When he reached out to take the second tankard from Nnenna's hands, she stepped back with a grin and brought it to her lips. She drank until the ale ran dry. Then, she handed the stein back to Sven.

"Time to go," Nnenna said with her hands.

Pearl perked up. She raised her pointer finger and waved it back and forth, asking, "Where?" Nnenna's face broke into the smile that Pearl was quickly learning to associate with trouble.

"Lesson," she signed.

It took a moment for Nnenna's answer to make sense, but, once it did, Pearl jumped to her feet and threw her arms around the woman. Minutes later, they stood across from each other on the ship's main deck, the warm, salty breeze blowing Pearl's hair this way and that. She held a borrowed sword, trying her best to emulate the stance Nnenna modeled for her.

"I attack. You block," Nnenna signed.

She held up her sword to show Pearl how to defend herself. Pearl practiced a few times before nodding. Her head had barely moved when Nnenna came at her, sword raised. Pearl flinched, closing her eyes and blindly thrusting her sword into the air. Its blade met Nnenna's with an angry clang that sent a shock wave up Pearl's arm, the sword clattering to the floor. She had barely regained her wits when Nnenna bent to pick up the weapon and placed it back in Pearl's hand. She placed her hand over Pearl's on the hilt and squeezed her fingers. Pearl took this to mean she needed to tighten her grip.

With a single nod, Pearl signaled she was ready. This time, when Nnenna attacked, Pearl kept her eyes open and raised her sword to defend herself. Nnenna's sword hit hers just as hard as the first time. Pearl's arm collapsed under the force of Nnenna's blow, but she held on to the sword.

"Again?" Nnenna asked, signing the word with her free hand.

Pearl shook out her aching arm and got back into her defensive stance.

"Again."

On Pearl's signal, Nnenna advanced, and Pearl tried to fight Nnenna off, enduring one heavy blow after another until she could take them without dropping her arm.

"Yes!" Nnenna exclaimed after the third time Pearl withstood the attack.

Pearl did not need a translation. She beamed with pride. Her arm was on fire, but she was hungry for more practice. A small crowd of idle crew members gathered to watch. Nnenna solicited the help of a volunteer and taught Pearl how to parry, next. She demonstrated how Pearl should redistribute her weight to return an attack after successfully defending. The maneuver looked so simple and elegant when Nnenna executed it. The first half dozen times Pearl tried, she landed flat on her back.

"Tired," Nnenna signed after helping Pearl to her feet.

Pearl did not know if it was a question or a judgment. Either way, she shook her head. She held up her sword in one hand and a finger on the other. Once more.

Nnenna smiled. Without warning, she swung her sword toward Pearl. Pearl blocked the attack, her arm shaking as she pushed against Nnenna's blade. She threw her whole body forward and pushed her arm up, breaking Nnenna's stance. Then, she swung her blade at Nnenna's midsection. Had she made contact, she would have sliced through Nnenna's belly, but Pearl was no match for a seasoned fighter. Nnenna blocked the blow and parried, twisting her wrist so that Pearl's sword escaped her grip. It flew through the air, and Nnenna caught it with a flourish.

Pearl raised her hands in surrender, laughing as Nnenna deftly twirled both swords.

"You learn fast," Nnenna signed later as the two sat in the great cabin, Nnenna with a celebratory whiskey and Pearl drinking a very watered-down ale.

"You teach well," Pearl signed back, smiling. A thought suddenly occurred to her. "Where is Sven from?"

Pearl did not have a sign for Sven's name, so she put the words for *food* and *man* together and hoped it would be enough.

Nnenna smiled. "Far away," she signed.

"Where?" Pearl asked.

Nnenna wrapped her arms around herself and shivered as though she were freezing. "Cold place."

Her curiosity piqued, Pearl wondered what it would be like to visit the cold places of the world. Or any place outside of the Seven Isles.

"We go?" she asked tentatively, her heart beating in her throat.

She waited for Nnenna to shake her head, to tell her that would be impossible, but instead, Nnenna's smile widened.

"One day," she signed. "Promise."

When Pearl returned to her cabin for the night, she allowed herself to imagine for the first time a life that was far different from the one she knew in the Settlement. In her mind, she was an adventurer, like Nnenna, fighting by her side in distant corners of the world. The *Medusa* was her home and its crew her family. She could barely sleep for her excitement.

Twenty-Five

NNENNA

Nnenna woke at the exact moment the ship stopped moving. She reached for Aline, then pulled her arm back once she realized what she had done. Shaking off sleep, she crawled out of her berth and stepped onto the deck, ready to exchange words with whoever was responsible for halting their progress. She spotted Pearl's slender figure standing by the ship's rail, bathed in moonlight. The girl stared off into the distance, and when Nnenna reached her side, she learned exactly why.

The waters were perfectly calm, like a flat sheet of glass that mirrored the sky above. Peering into the sea below, Nnenna saw herself reflected against the stars. Not a single ripple or wave disturbed the smooth surface, there was not even the slightest gust of wind. She was speechless. This was far more than being becalmed—a sailor's worst fate on the water. The stillness was not only the absence of wind; it was all-encompassing.

The quiet was eerie.

Nnenna heard a whisper of song and felt it grow unexpectedly in her heart. Her father's voice drifted into her mind, singing to her about the place where the sea stood still as she drifted off to sleep. She tapped Pearl's shoulder. "Is this the place?" she signed.

Pearl brought her hand to her chest and scraped the tip of her middle finger against her shirt in an upward motion twice. Then, she made her hand into a clamshell, touched her fingertips to her jaw, and moved them to just below her ear. "It feels like home."

Nnenna looked around at the nearly deserted deck. Everyone was still asleep save for the men at the helm and in the crow's nest. Nnenna doubted there had been anything suspicious for them to see, or they would have raised the alarm. If there had been danger, it would have long since found them by now.

"Let's rest," Nnenna said more to herself as she made the sign for sleep. "We'll have a much better idea of what to do come morning."

Pearl looked apprehensive, but she made no sign in response.

Rest did not find Nnenna as she tossed and turned in her berth. Death haunted her dreams from the moment she closed her eyes. She was bound, hands and feet, attached to a sinking anchor, her lungs seizing as they tried desperately to fill themselves with air.

Help! she begged in her mind. *Someone, please help me!*

Nnenna wanted to cry, but to release the sob welling inside her would give up the last of her air. She held it until the desire to exhale became inescapable. As she released that breath, it was not a sob that came out of her, but a song.

She woke with her hands around her own throat, certain she was dead until she recognized sunlight streaming through the windows of her cabin. The absence of gentle swaying told her the ship was still stationary. When she made it out to the main deck, once again, she found that she was not the only one looking to make sense of their new circumstances.

At least half the crew had awoken and abandoned their duties to stare at the calm waters that held them captive. Tinou was among them, leaning against the bulwark. In the morning light, the water turned a crystal-clear turquoise. A massive ledge was visible on the ocean floor just beyond where the ship had stopped, and, past it, a black chasm. The ship sat near the edge, and though Nnenna knew they were hundreds of feet above, it looked as though they could be swept into the abyss at any moment.

"What do you make of this?" Nnenna asked Tinou.

Tinou shrugged. "They say this place is as old as the gods themselves," she answered. "The laws of men no longer apply."

Nnenna rolled her eyes. "If I had wanted more superstitious nonsense, I would have stayed on Kiskeya."

"Then, what is your plan, Captain? We are becalmed in unfamiliar waters, completely vulnerable to attack, with no way to move our ship. If I remember correctly," she added, her voice getting louder, "it was your idea to come here at the request of your little pet—"

"That's enough, Tinou," Nnenna said, sharply cutting her off. "When I see fit to make you aware of my plans, you shall know them. Until then, keep your mind on your duties. That goes for all of you," she said to those of the crew who remained on deck. "Just because the *Medusa* is still doesn't mean you shirk your responsibilities. Get back to work!"

Nnenna tried to pull Tinou aside to speak to her privately, but she pushed past and followed the majority of the crew toward the companionway.

Things grew no closer to normal that day or even the next. The *Medusa* stayed rooted to the spot as though held there by an invisible force. It took only another day for the whispers to spread like a disease among the crew. Despite Nnenna's orders to stay engaged, they all found time to share their explanations for why they were trapped. Most were Ayiti superstitions—that someone on the crew must have pointed at a rainbow or received a knife as a gift before they had set sail and brought misfortune on their voyage. But some explanations, like the ones where Pearl's presence on the ship was entangled with the potential danger, only strengthened her desire to find a way to leave.

"What are you looking for?" Nnenna asked Pearl on the third day. She had caught the girl staring over the ship's rail into the sea once again.

"My people," Pearl responded. "My home."

Nnenna had heard stories about the Gateway to the Unknown from her mother, when she had been a child and had asked where her father had disappeared to. Kerline had not yet hardened her heart, so she had told her daughter a story about her father floating through the Gateway to the Unknown, never to be seen again.

It was nonsense. Her father had died in the street, and all the stories her people told had done nothing to help him, just like they were doing nothing to help her now.

"Ship!" she heard the man on watch call as he rang the bell. "Ship approaching!"

Nnenna leaned as far over the side of the ship as she could. She could just make out the silhouette of a large ship cresting the horizon. She put her spyglass to her eye, and when she saw its green-and-gold paint, she swore under her breath.

"The *Adoration*," she said to no one in particular, reading the ship's name on the hull. "I should have sent that ship to the bottom of the ocean."

Pearl and Tinou appeared by Nnenna's side. Nnenna turned to Tinou.

"They'll be looking for Pearl. Take her into the hold and hide her," she said quickly. "Do not come out until I give you the all clear."

"They're looking for you, too," Tinou reminded her. "You go. They'll be less likely to tarry if the Devil of the Deep isn't here to greet them. Go into the hold. Hide inside empty barrels. I'll deter them from searching there."

Tinou had spoken with a sincerity Nnenna had not heard in a long time. She was surprised to find herself touched. She suddenly felt a rush of relief, and the words that she had been too stubborn to utter—that she was sorry for breaking her promise—jumped to her tongue. But there was no time. The *Adoration* drew closer with every passing second, so she set her feelings aside. Nnenna took Pearl by the hand and pulled her toward the companionway, leading her down into the depths of the *Medusa*'s hull. Nnenna found, among the crates and barrels, a spent barrel in a far corner.

"You go in," she signed quickly, gesturing to the open barrel.

"What's happening?" Pearl asked with her hands, her face the most fearful Nnenna had ever seen it.

"Beetles," Nnenna signed, using the improvised motion she and Pearl had invented. "We need to hide."

"I hide with you?"

Nnenna shook her head. "Safe apart." Pearl looked as though Nnenna had thrust a knife into her heart. Nnenna took the girl by the shoulders and shook her once. She did not have the signs to convey the message she wanted, so she used her words. "I will keep you safe," she promised, staring into Pearl's warm brown eyes. Without waiting for a response, she pulled the girl into a tight hug. Nnenna held Pearl for as long as she dared, then helped her climb over the lip of the barrel.

Once the lid was securely attached, Nnenna walked to the other side of the narrow chamber. Rather than finding a barrel of her own to hide in, Nnenna decided she would be better off keeping her eye on Pearl. Luckily, there was a space between two of the sets of shelves built into the ship's walls directly across from Pearl's barrel, blanketed by shadows, into which she would fit if she turned to her side and tried not to breathe.

Nnenna was not accustomed to lying in wait, nor was she accustomed to not knowing what was happening on the deck of her own ship. She should have chosen to stay and fight, but it would have made it all the more difficult for Pearl to stay hidden. This was the better choice, she admitted to herself, as long as Tinou was able to deliver on her promise.

Creaking planks cut her ruminations short. The sound came from above. Could that be Tinou already? she wondered as she stared up into the darkness. Could she have dispatched the beetles so quickly? Nnenna put her hand on the pommel of one of her daggers and listened.

Footsteps from the floor above. They were slow and deliberate, as though the owner were trying to move with discretion. The footsteps crossed the floor and descended the rickety wooden stairs that led to Nnenna's floor. Nnenna's sight was limited to only what was directly in front of her, but she heard the intruder moving about the hold, lifting lids and shifting cargo aside.

When he stepped in front of Pearl's barrel and Nnenna saw his deep green coat, she stopped breathing altogether.

"Don't you dare," she whispered under her breath, but the lieutenant's hands were already grasping the edges of the lid.

Nnenna moved before she even realized it, stepping out of the shadows with her dagger drawn. She closed the distance between them in two strides, wrapping one arm around his face and deftly thrusting the blade into his back. The lieutenant let out a gurgling scream and grabbed at Nnenna's arm, but Nnenna held fast until his body went limp. Then, she let him fall.

"Pearl," she whispered as she pulled the barrel's lid. "Come with me. Now."

Pearl looked confused but followed the beckoning hand that accompanied Nnenna's words.

Nnenna helped her out of the barrel.

"Stay close," she signed once Pearl had two feet firmly on the floor.

Something had gone wrong. If beetles were searching the ship, then they had managed to overpower Tinou and the rest of the crew. To stay in the hold would be to await their eventual capture, but there was a chance of escaping if they managed to reach the longboats. If Nnenna was going to risk her own life and Pearl's, then she would rather do it fighting, taking down whomever she encountered on the way.

She pulled her second dagger from its scabbard in her belt and pushed the handle into Pearl's palm. She did not know the signs for "just in case I die," but Pearl seemed to grasp her meaning all the same.

With her cutlass in one hand and her pistol in the other, Nnenna crouched low and ventured back the way they had come, retracing the dead lieutenant's footsteps. She stopped at the top of each set of stairs, careful to scan the area for reinforcements. Speed would be as much of an ally to her as her ability to remain unseen. It occurred to her that the beetles might still be in the dark about their fallen comrade. She would use that to her advantage.

Nnenna made it all the way up to the companionway with Pearl in tow. There would be no sneaking up the ladder. If any beetles stood sentry at its entrance, she would be found out. She turned to Pearl and told her to stay put. Nnenna would clear the area, or she would die trying and give Pearl a chance to escape.

Nnenna climbed the ladder slowly. When she reached the top, she paused and took a breath before peeking over the edge. A sigh escaped her when she saw no one, but her relief was short-lived. The barrel of a pistol pressed against her temple with the telltale sound of the hammer being locked into its ready position.

"Drop your weapons," an unfamiliar female voice ordered.

"Where are my men?" Nnenna asked, her eyes still downcast.

"Drop. Your. Weapons," the voice said again, punctuating the last word with a tap of the barrel against Nnenna's temple.

Closing her eyes and sighing, Nnenna released her pistol and sword, and they clattered to the deck.

"Come out, slowly."

Nnenna had no choice but to obey. She climbed the remaining ladder steps and stepped onto the deck. The lieutenant moved in front of her, pistol still drawn, and Nnenna was surprised by how pretty she was. She was younger than Nnenna expected a lieutenant to be and had long, dark hair, and smooth deep brown skin with a warm undertone. It was a shame Nnenna would have to take such beauty out of the world.

"Hold out your arms."

Pressing her wrists together, Nnenna extended her arms in front of her. The lieutenant reached behind her with one hand and pulled out a length of rope. Nnenna could see the conflict in her eyes. To tie Nnenna up, she would have to holster her weapon.

"I could tie myself up," Nnenna said with a wry smile. "I'm quite good with ropes."

"Shut it, pirate," the lieutenant spat.

She seemed to finally decide she was intimidating enough,

even without her pistol, so she holstered the weapon and stepped forward to bind Nnenna's hands.

A familiar discomfort rose within Nnenna, and she was suddenly very thirsty. She squashed the feeling, forcing herself to stay present.

"What's your name?" Nnenna asked as the lieutenant wrapped the ropes around her wrists. The lieutenant did not answer. "Oh, please?" Nnenna pressed. "I'll be dead soon, anyway, won't I?"

The lieutenant let out an exasperated huff. "Ambroise," she said.

Nnenna smiled. "It's a pleasure to make your acquaintance, Lieutenant Ambroise. I usually need a drink before I let a girl tie me up. But for you, I will make an exception."

"We'll see how smart your mouth is when you're in front of the captain."

With one last pull, Lieutenant Ambroise finalized the knot around Nnenna's wrists. The pistol returned, and this time, she used it to command Nnenna to walk. They headed toward the great cabin.

Of course, they would take my cabin, Nnenna thought ruefully as she imagined wringing the captain's neck.

Lieutenant Ambroise was kind enough to pull the door open for Nnenna as she approached the cabin, and in return, Nnenna made an exaggerated bow before walking in. She expected to find the captain seated at her table with their feet up and a smug expression. What she had not expected was to recognize the face, even as it shifted from pride to utter disbelief.

"Nnenna?" the captain gasped, and the sound of his voice dislodged an avalanche of memories that Nnenna had hoped to keep buried for the rest of her life.

The man staring at her was so familiar she could taste the memory of him on the tip of her tongue. His black hair was in the same carefully cropped style that only hinted at the curls he once had. His brown eyes were the same, fine and sharp like a bird of prey. His dark skin was the same, as well, and Nnenna suddenly wondered if it still felt the same under her fingertips. Then, she remembered the last time they had seen each other, remembered the way he had refused to meet her eye though he had known what fate awaited her. Her hatred of him had been the first thing she had known in her new life, and it burned within her now.

"Lu?" she asked, her heart thundering in her throat.

"You two know each other?" said another familiar voice.

Nnenna whipped around toward the voice. Tinou leaned casually against her wardrobe. All at once, she understood.

"You traitorous bitch!" she tried to scream, but her pain and humiliation cut through her ferocity.

Nnenna lunged at her first mate, unsure of what she would do when she caught her. Lieutenant Ambroise grabbed her around the waist and held her back. Try as Nnenna might, she could not escape the woman's hold.

"If you continue to struggle, she'll have to subdue you," the captain said as he got to his feet.

"I'd like to see her try!" Nnenna replied, still fighting for her freedom.

Ambroise seemed to take Nnenna at her word. She delivered a swift kick to the backs of her legs, and Nnenna fell to her knees with her hands behind her head.

"Easy, Ambroise!" the captain said, gesturing for her to stop. Like the obedient beetle she was, she followed his orders.

"I'll gut you like the coward you are," Nnenna growled at Tinou. "Just you wait."

"I tried to get you to see reason," Tinou said calmly.

"How long did it take you to surrender? Did you even raise a hand to defend this ship?"

Tinou smiled as though she were the clever cat who caught the canary. "What can I say? The captain here made me an offer I could not refuse."

Nnenna twisted her face into a look of disgust.

"The deal was for the both of them," the captain interjected. "Where is the girl?"

"They were in the hold together," Tinou answered. "She must still be down there."

"Go and retrieve her," the captain ordered.

"Why must I retrieve her? Send one of your little beetle lieutenants."

"She knows you. She'll be less likely to fight you."

Tinou clicked her tongue at the captain in displeasure before she pushed herself upright and walked past Nnenna without so much as a nod in her direction. After the cabin door slammed shut, Nnenna, the captain, and Ambroise were left in the ensuing silence.

"How can this be?" the captain asked, after a few moments. He spoke directly to Nnenna, his hawkish eyes devouring her face with equal measures of curiosity and disbelief.

"You know this pirate scum, sir?" Ambroise asked.

Nnenna stared right back, daring him to tell her a lie.

"She was one of us, once," he answered. "Then, things . . . changed."

"You became a coward!" Nnenna spat.

"And you were executed!" the captain shouted back, all pretense lost. "I watched you die! How can you be here?"

Nnenna laughed coldly. "It's not comfortable when your

secrets come back to haunt you, is it? Or was my death something for you to brag about to all of your little beetle friends?"

The hurt on his face gave Nnenna a measure of savage satisfaction.

"I would never," he said quietly.

"There were many things I never would have thought you capable of doing."

Just then, the cabin door flew open, and a growling Tinou stomped across the room, clutching a bleeding hand out of which protruded a hilt that Nnenna immediately recognized.

"The little bitch stuck me!" Tinou cried.

Nnenna felt a rush of affection toward Pearl. They had taken to each other like fish to seawater in their short time together, bound by something intangible and powerful from the moment they had met. Nnenna had protected Pearl, had fought for Pearl, and had taught Pearl how to protect herself. It filled her heart with pride to know that it had been Pearl's strike that had punished Tinou's traitorous ways.

"Don't be such a baby," Lieutenant Ambroise said.

To everyone's surprise, but most of all Tinou's, she reached over and took Tinou's bleeding hand in her own. Before anyone could stop her, Ambroise used her free hand to pull the knife blade from Tinou's palm. Tinou gasped in pain and fell to her knees. Nnenna, seizing the opportunity, reared her head back and threw it forward. Tinou's nose made a sickly crunch as Nnenna's forehead slammed into it. Ambroise yanked Nnenna back as a fountain of blood spurted from Tinou's nostril.

"Argh!" Tinou screamed.

She tried to lunge at Nnenna, but the captain intervened, stepping between the two and pulling Tinou by the shoulders to her feet.

"Where is the girl?" the captain demanded.

"With one of the other beetles," Tinou answered angrily. She held her wounded hand against her chest while trying to stem her bleeding nose with the other. "Now, get the hell off my ship!"

Good, Nnenna thought, glaring at the captain and hoping Tinou's nose was broken.

"Get her out of here!" the captain ordered, and none too gently, Lieutenant Ambroise hoisted Nnenna to her feet.

Twenty-Six

THE RECRUITS

Lu's heart pounded as he set the scene that he hoped would guarantee his freedom. He held his dress in his hands, the very dress he had worn to speak with his father that afternoon. His forearm was bandaged where he had cut it, the laceration stinging with every movement.

He stood on the edge of the cliff that punctuated the grounds of his father's estate. The dress was smeared with his blood, spilled by his own hand.

His chest heaved against the bindings he wore underneath his shirt. It was his first time wearing them, and despite the discomfort, he enjoyed the silhouette they produced.

There was trepidation in his heart, and the disquiet made him doubt his choice.

There is nothing for you here, *his inner voice reminded him.* Your own father made that clear.

He felt the resolve settle where the disquiet had been, and with more delicacy and ceremony than he would have thought himself capable of, he released the dress. The wind took it at once, filling it as though it were his own specter floating down to the rocks and water below. Lu hoped it would catch on the rocks and someone would find it in the morning. Better to be declared dead quickly than to be the subject of a years-long search.

Better for Father's sake, too, *he thought, though he owed his father no mercy for the years of torture Lu had endured.*

A song swelled in his chest. He was never one to resist the call of the song. With the sea before him and his ancestral home at his back, he sang and bid a final farewell to the person he never seemed capable of becoming.

"That was beautiful," said a soft, deep voice behind him.

Lu jumped, despite having more familiarity with its owner than any other person in the world.

He twisted around and found himself face-to-face with his best friend and confidant.

"You look . . ." Manou said slowly.

"I know it's different," Lu started, but he did not quite know how to finish. What would be his explanation for the sudden shearing of his halo of jet-black curls, for the exchange of satin and petticoats for rough-spun breeches and a shirt? The Fleet would have taken him as he was; their advertisement called only for able bodies. How could he explain that this was who he truly was?

"You look happy," Manou finished with an understanding smile, and Lu knew that no more needed to be said.

Lu hoisted his trunk over his shoulder, and they set off together. The carriage ride to the Citadel was long. It was just before daybreak when they arrived. They had not expected to be met with a welcome this early, but there was a uniformed lieutenant in the courtyard sitting at a table with a large ledger in front of him. He looked bored but perked up when he saw the two people coming his way.

"Joining up?" he asked at their arrival.

Manou laughed. "Not me. I'm far too old to be a midshipman. But this lad"—he patted Lu on the back twice—"will be the best you've ever had."

*The lieutenant looked Lu over warily, and Lu was ready to remind him of the Fleet's own words—*Any able-bodied individuals are welcome!*—but it seemed he was able to remember on his own.*

The lieutenant held out an inked quill.

"Sign here," he said, pointing to the next empty spot in the ledger.

As Lu took the quill and touched the nib to the page, he realized that this would be the first time he would put his new name to paper. He smiled.

"Lu Ortega," he whispered to himself as he signed himself into his new life. "Future captain of the Fleet."

The lieutenant, the only person who heard him, snickered. Lu did not mind if he laughed; in a few years' time, he would answer to Lu.

When Lu finished signing his name, the lieutenant pulled out a money pouch and extracted ten pieces of gold, placing them in Lu's hand. Lu immediately turned and attempted to press the gold into Manou's palm, but the older man pulled away.

"You keep that," Manou said. "You're going to need it."

"But you and Mai—"

"We'll be just fine," Manou said. "The goddess will provide for us."

•••●•••

At the other end of the country, in Ayiti's Southern District, sixteen-year-old Nnenna's mother shook her roughly. She brought an abrupt halt to the precious few hours of sleep the girl was able to get between her days working as a barmaid and her evenings caring for her mother.

"Wake up, girl," Nnenna's mother said, shoving her so hard she rolled onto her back and woke with a start.

"What is it?" Nnenna gasped, opening her eyes and searching for the danger.

"Get up."

One sleepy-eyed glance at the window told her it was early morning, just before dawn. Her mother was dressed in clothes Nnenna had not seen since her father's funeral, her blue, red, and white gown with matching white headdress. When Nnenna sat up, her mother tossed a heap of fabric at her.

"Put that on."

Nnenna could not see the colors of the garment she held but assumed they matched her mother's. She could tell from the fine fabric that these were either newly purchased or newly sewn.

"What's going on?" she asked. "Where did you get—"

"Don't dawdle, girl," her mother snapped. "Get dressed!"

Nnenna hated when her mother called her "girl" as though she were some stranger, rather than her own flesh and blood, but she kept her ire hidden as she obeyed her mother's command. She stood, letting the thin blanket she had borrowed from the Singing Crab fall to the floor, and changed into the long skirt, blouse, and headdress. It took her some time to approximate the elaborate styles she had seen the ladies wearing in the Singing Crab's dining room, and being forced to dress in the pitch-black did not help.

When she was finished, the fine fabric felt practically luxurious against her skin compared to the rough cotton and linens to which she had grown accustomed. She almost wished she had a mirror so that she could see the full effect.

"We're going," her mother said, cutting short Nnenna's self-admiration.

She opened the door and stood in the doorway, waiting expectantly. Nnenna followed, and together they walked the familiar path from their seaside shack to Prince's Port's city center. When they arrived upon the cobbled streets, Nnenna half expected her mother to stop at the Singing Crab.

Instead, she stood on a corner, looking up and down the empty street.

Minutes passed, during which Nnenna felt her curiosity reach its breaking point.

"What are we doing here?" she asked.

Kerline turned her head and opened her mouth as if to answer, but seemed to think better of it. As she turned back to the street, the sound of rattling wheels drew her attention. A carriage, drawn by a single horse, drove up the cobblestones and stopped at their corner.

"How much to get to the Citadel?" Kerline asked the driver.

The man rubbed his chin pensively. "Northern District? One gold," he said.

To Nnenna's surprise, her mother produced a small black money pouch from her belt that jingled with coins. Nnenna recognized it at once as the pouch she used to keep her earnings safe, the one she had hidden under a loose floorboard in the shack.

"That's mine!" Nnenna cried before she could think.

Her mother's response was a swift slap across her cheek. Then, she continued speaking to the driver as though this were a common exchange between them.

"I'll give you two if you can get us there before sunrise."

It was music to the driver's ears, and he accepted her offer. He hopped off the driver's bench and pulled the door of the carriage open for Kerline. She climbed in without so much as a glance in Nnenna's direction. Clutching her stinging cheek, Nnenna climbed in as well, and the driver closed the carriage door behind her.

Nnenna did not speak during the bumpy, hours-long ride, though many questions came to mind. Her mother did not look at her at all, but stared out the little window, watching the landscape change from plaster buildings to humble thatched-roof huts to lush green jungle. Rather than talk, Nnenna spent the ride calculating just how much of her savings she would have to earn back. She thought she had been smart to place a decoy money pouch filled with coppers and silvers, just enough to keep her mother in rum, but she must have let the secret of her gold slip somehow. Two gold for the ride to the Citadel and maybe the same for the ride back. Then, there was the price of the clothes.

The sudden urge to curse and scream rose from deep within her. She had worked for years to save that money. It was going to buy her passage to a different island, one far from Kiskeya, where she would finally have a life of her own. Now, she would have to start over.

Nnenna did not scream. She did not even shed a tear. Instead, she resolved to do better. She would try again, find a better system of hiding her money. She did not care if it took another two years or even ten. She would get out.

"We're here," her mother said as the carriage slowed to a halt.

The first thing Nnenna noticed upon stepping from the carriage was the smell of unfamiliar greenery. There were no animals in the street here, she noticed as she investigated her surroundings. No carts of vegetables and fish. The streets were smooth, hard-packed earth.

"Let's go," her mother said.

She paid the driver and, as the carriage pulled away, she

walked toward the large, looming building that overshadowed everything else. Nnenna assumed this was the Citadel. She had overheard its name in snippets of conversation at the Singing Crab and knew that it was where the people in the green uniforms who had started patrolling the Southern District came from. Supposedly, they sought to bring law and order to the district, but all Nnenna had seen thus far was their harassment of the least fortunate in her community. They were charlatans in uniform, peddling salvation like street merchants. Nnenna worried what business her mother had with these people.

They walked through an open gate and up a long path toward the fortress. The grass on either side of them looked lush and soft, unlike the jagged plants that grew around the rocky terrain of her home. As they drew closer to the building, there was a man in a uniform sitting at a table at the bottom of the steps that led to the front doors. Nnenna stood back as her mother walked up to the table as though she had known it would be there.

"Name?" the uniformed man asked her.

"Nnenna Delahaye," Kerline answered in the cheery tone she only ever used to convince people that she was a good person.

"Welcome to the Fleet, Nnenna," the man said with a smile.

"Not me. Her." Kerline jerked her thumb back at her daughter.

"Oh," the man replied, looking confused.

He picked up the quill sitting on the table next to a large, leather-bound book, dipped it into the ink pot, and started to hand it to Nnenna, but Kerline snatched it out of his hand. She bent forward and scratched the nib across a page.

"What are you doing?" Nnenna asked, taking a step forward.

"Madame," the man said to Kerline, "she must sign in her own hand."

"What does her hand matter?" Kerline asked, ignoring Nnenna.

"Your Fleet wants able bodies. Her body is able. She's a strong workhorse. Now, about the advance." She held out her hand.

Nnenna was speechless. She watched the uniformed man glance from her to her mother, before resignedly pulling out a money pouch. He counted out ten gold and handed the coins to the woman standing in front of him. Kerline snatched the money in the same way that she had snatched the quill, and dropped each coin into Nnenna's own pouch. Without a word of thanks, Kerline turned on her heel and walked back the way they had come. Nnenna expected her mother to walk right past her, but she stopped when they were side by side. Nnenna noticed, for the first time, that they were the same height now.

"Goodbye," her mother said. She did not look at Nnenna as she spoke but stared off into the distance at the sun rising over the trees.

Nnenna frowned, a dozen years of suppressed anger threatening to burst forth from within her. She clamped her hands into tight fists and closed her eyes against the stinging of the tears.

"You will never see me again," she promised, fighting to keep her voice steady.

She kept her eyes closed until she returned to calm. Nnenna had always suspected her mother was incapable of loving her the way she remembered a parent should. Here was the proof that her suspicions had been correct. Rather than let her leave, Kerline had sold Nnenna to a group of heretics, a fitting repayment for the care Nnenna had provided. For twelve years, Nnenna had worked herself ragged to try to keep them alive, begging in the street throughout her childhood and taking work wherever she could find it when she had looked old enough, all while her mother had luxuriated in her grief and her drunkenness.

Nnenna suddenly realized her mother did not deserve her

calm. She opened her eyes, ready to unleash her true feelings, but her mother was gone. A decade of suffering at her mother's hand had finally come to an end.

Nnenna wiped the tears that had managed to escape and approached the table. The uniformed man's discomfort with the scene was evident, but Nnenna was done caring about what other people thought. That part of her life was over. It was time for her to embrace her freedom.

"Where do I go?" she asked, putting her best face forward.

"Up the steps," the uniformed man answered quickly. "The midshipman barracks are on the lowest floor."

Nnenna learned what barracks were when she entered the massive building and found a room containing two rows of narrow beds. There was a boy here, tall and dark-skinned with close-cropped hair and almond-shaped eyes. He was already dressed in what Nnenna guessed was the midshipman version of the green-and-gold Fleet uniform. He stood when she entered and Nnenna froze.

"What is it?" she asked.

"Nothing."

"Why did you get up?"

"I—it's just," he stammered. "You're supposed to stand when a lady enters a room."

Nnenna burst into laughter, a full-belly laugh that she could feel throughout her entire body. Tears leaked out of her eyes, and she held her midsection as she tried to regain control of her senses.

"Are you going to be all right?" the boy asked, looking warily at her.

She imagined what she must look like to him, dressed in her fine clothes and in complete hysterics, and laughed even harder. She heard him approach her but held out a hand to stop him.

"I'm fine," she said through the final spasms of her episode. "I'm sorry. I must seem mad to you."

"You don't," he said.

They both noticed how quickly he answered, and he immediately turned his gaze to the floor.

"I'm Nnenna." She held out her hand.

"Lu," he said, taking it. His fingers were soft and slender against her rough palms.

"It's a pleasure to make your acquaintance, Lu. Now, tell me, what the hell is this place?"

Lu launched into a fifteen-minute-long explanation of the Fleet's history and aims. It seemed the reason why their lieutenants were always such nuisances was that there was some great destiny to be achieved and building up their numbers was one of the keys to achieving it. At least, that was what Nnenna had thought Lu had said. He had spoken so quickly and animatedly that Nnenna could barely keep up. Nnenna did not want to ask him to repeat himself. He had the look of one who came from a decent upbringing, and Nnenna, for the first time in her life, was self-conscious of her own. Thankfully, they ran out of time before he could ask any questions of her. Another young officer appeared at the door to tell them that the new midshipmen would be assembling to receive their orders.

Life as a midshipman was not so different from the life Nnenna had left behind. She was expected to work from sunup to sundown—only at the Citadel, she received fair pay for her labor, was provided with regular meals, and even had a friend working alongside her. The physical parts of the work gave her no trouble—her body was already used to long hours spent cleaning and hauling, and the lessons in martial arts were refreshing—but the course of study she was also expected to complete kept Nnenna in a state of near constant frustration. She was exhausted, and while her father had gotten as far as teaching her to read before he died, the handwritten little stories she had learned were nothing in comparison to the tomes the midshipmen were expected to read daily. Try as Nnenna might to conceal how she struggled, Lu noticed and offered his help. Determined not to be anyone's charity case, Nnenna accepted on the condition that he allow her to help with his sword fighting.

"The HFS Divinity *was a first-rate frigate with six decks and thirty-eight guns," Nnenna recited months later as she easily deflected Lu's attack with her own wooden sword. "She was christened for sail in the year of our Lord of the Sea 1691 and sank just ten years later after an encounter with . . ."*

She paused as she tried to remember. Lu took advantage of her distraction and made another attempt to disarm her. She caught his wooden blade with hers a moment before it touched her skin, twirled her body away from Lu, and bumped him with her backside to send him and his sword clattering across the floor.

"Agwe's might," he muttered.

"You are bending too much at the waist when you make your approach," Nnenna informed him. "It leaves you open to being knocked off-balance by your adversary."

"Noted," Lu answered, reaching an arm out to request her assistance in getting to his feet.

Nnenna took his hand, and the moment her fingers clasped around his, he swept a leg at her ankles, knocking her off her feet. He pinned her beneath him, his sword at her throat. She gazed into his almond-shaped eyes, alight with his triumph, and found herself enjoying being the object of his attention.

"It was a storm," she said softly, remembering all at once.

"What?"

"The Divinity,*" she answered. "A storm blew her against a sea stack in the Northern Sea and she was on the ocean floor within hours."*

Lu chuckled. "You sound like you don't even need me anymore."

"I'm sure I could find another use for you."

Lu's eyes widened in shock. Before Nnenna could take back what she had said, the practice room's next patrons arrived, and Nnenna and Lu scrambled to collect their effects and vacate the area. They did not discuss what Nnenna had said when they moved to the library to continue their studies, but when Nnenna's left hand brushed against Lu's right, he caught her littlest finger with his.

With each other as lifelines, Nnenna and Lu tasted success after success. Together, they surpassed the other midshipmen in their class and rose to the rank of lieutenant in less than a year, the fastest rise the Fleet had ever seen.

•••●•••

As lieutenants, they earned the privilege of assisting the captains on their journeys by sea, the second-highest-ranking officers in the Fleet. On the eve of their first voyage away from Kiskeya, they celebrated, not in the banquet hall with their peers, but on the beach with a pilfered blanket and a bottle of whiskey.

"What do you think it will be like?" Nnenna asked Lu as they both lay atop the blanket. They stared up at the star-strewn sky, pretending not to be aware of just how close they were to one another.

"Sailing?" Lu answered. "Probably terrible. I've heard Captain Abernathy is a terror to sail under."

Nnenna's hand drifted out of the darkness to whack him on the belly.

"Where's your sense of romance?" Nnenna asked, offended that Lu would give such a practical response. "We could be hit by a terrible storm! We could be set upon by deadly pirates! Tonight could be our last night in this world!" She sat up, suddenly, and turned toward him, crossing the narrow divide of blanket that separated them. The tip of her nose almost touched his cheek. "What do you want to do with your final hours?"

Lu could feel her warm breath on his face, and he did not move. They had come to this place before, skirting the line between friendship and something more, and he had always pulled back to safety. But the night was beautiful, and Lu was tired of being safe.

"I have something to show you," he said, sitting up as well. Maybe he had finally reached his breaking point or maybe it was the whiskey, but there was something inside of him telling him this was the moment. He shifted onto his knees, grabbed the hem of his loose linen shirt, and pulled it over his head. The deliciously cool sea air kissed his exposed skin, his arms, his shoulders, his back, his belly—everywhere except his chest, which was bound with a length of stiff cotton, secured with laces between his shoulder blades. "This is what I really am."

Nnenna laughed a great bellowing laugh, mouth open to the sky. "And what's that supposed to be? Half naked?"

"No, I mean I'm—"

"I know exactly what you mean," she said, drawing herself onto her own knees and closing the space between them once more. She took his hands in hers, lacing their fingers together. "I was something else before I met you, too. Something I don't ever want to be again. So, let's leave the past in the past."

Lu tipped his head forward and touched his forehead to hers.

The words that had been threatening to burst out of him, words he kept at bay because he knew it was too soon and did not want to scare her away, finally tumbled out.

"I love you."

He closed his eyes as her hands slid from his and moved to his shoulders. She pulled his body against hers, and slowly, for the first time, their lips met. The timidity of their first kiss was soon eclipsed by the ferocity of long-denied desire. Together, they fell back onto the blanket into each other's arms. They stayed on the beach until the very last moment before they had to return to the Citadel to ready themselves for their journey.

Twenty-Seven

NNENNA

Nnenna could tell Pearl was trying to be brave, keeping her head up as they were bound and brought to the *Adoration*. But the moment they were alone in their cell, the moment Nnenna had extended her arms out to Pearl, the girl accepted the invitation, falling into Nnenna's arms and dissolving into sobs. Nnenna held Pearl as she cried, and for a long time after, humming the same gentle tune she had used to calm her before while she contemplated the reality of their situation. Their weapons had been taken, and they had nothing but the clothes on their backs and each other.

It took Pearl tapping on the wood slats to pull Nnenna from her thoughts. Nnenna instinctively flashed her a half-hearted smile, but Pearl was pointing to something beyond the bars of their cell. Nnenna turned and heard footsteps approaching. Soon, a shadow walked toward them. It was Captain Ortega—she could tell by his silhouette. Pearl stood quickly and took the bars in both hands while Nnenna stayed on the floor, her back against the opposite wall.

Ortega was as slender as Nnenna remembered, with wide

shoulders and a narrow waist. His dark skin glistened in the candlelight while the same light reflected in his warm, brown, almond-shaped eyes. He carried a set of keys and a large tray that held two bowls of something that smelled warm and savory.

"Captain," Nnenna said in dry greeting.

Ortega said nothing. He walked to the cell door, unlocked it, and put the tray on the floor. Then he closed and locked the cell and started to walk away.

"Since when do captains deliver meals to prisoners?" Nnenna called after him. He froze and turned on his heel.

"They don't," Ortega said. "There was talk among the crew of letting you starve. I made sure you got something to eat."

"How magnanimous," Nnenna sneered.

"They don't take too kindly to pirates," he added. "Especially ones with a penchant for killing their comrades."

"How long do I have?"

"Sunrise," he answered, and she was unsurprised that he avoided her eye as he did so. "After the ceremony. The commodore wants your execution to be the first show of Agwe's greatness."

Nnenna nodded silently, tempering her disappointment as she carefully considered his words. She did not believe he had come all the way down here to deliver her a meal and the unfortunate news of her impending demise.

"What about Pearl?" Nnenna asked, figuring she could use his own curiosity in her favor. "What will happen to her after I'm . . ."

Now, he looked nervous. His eyes shifted to Pearl for a moment before landing back on Nnenna. "She'll be in the care of her people."

"In the sea?"

"On the island."

"She knows the fisherfolk signs," Nnenna said, tilting her head in the girl's direction. "You can talk to her."

A furrow appeared in his brow, and Nnenna knew he was attempting to ascertain her end goal.

"Try it," Nnenna insisted.

Pearl seemed to understand Nnenna's last statement, and Nnenna remembered how often she had told the girl to do the same with the foods Sven had made that were new to her palate. She pointed at the food on the floor, and Nnenna shook her head in answer, gesturing instead to the captain. Nnenna watched him greet Pearl in the fisherfolk way, pressing his palms flat against each other, twisting them, and spreading his arms with his palms facing outward. Pearl's eyes went wide. She turned to Nnenna, and Nnenna gave her an encouraging smile. When Pearl looked back at the captain, she responded to his sign. She held her flat palm before her face so that her fingertips pointed at him, turning her wrist so that her fingers pointed upward, and pulling the heel of her hand downward, running her thumb along the line of her nose. Then, she touched her fingers to her thumbs on both hands, pushed them forward, and opened her hands.

"My name is Captain Lu Ortega," he signed.

"I am Pearl Highwater," Pearl answered.

"How old are you, Pearl?"

"Sixteen years old."

Nnenna saw Ortega tense at her response. Pearl went on.

"The viceroy cannot be trusted! He killed my uncle! He wants . . . he wants . . . to make me his wife."

The way the captain closed his eyes and clenched his fists told Nnenna he had seen the viceroy. Pearl had described him to her, and she was certain the captain knew there was nothing natural about his attraction to Pearl. He turned to Nnenna.

"How do I know this isn't a lie you've concocted to play upon my sympathies?"

Nnenna knew that his sympathies could not be counted upon to inspire his action, but she held her tongue.

"You've already said there is no hope for me," she said, instead. "My execution date is set. But Pearl has done nothing to deserve the fate that awaits her. Save her. Keep her away from the viceroy."

"I . . . can make no promises," Ortega said.

"Yes, you can!" Nnenna urged, staring him down. "It is the least you can do."

Ortega looked uncomfortable. Yes, she was asking him to defy orders, but, surely, the life of the girl was worth it. A flicker of resignation passed over his face, and she knew she had him. He looked at Pearl, looked back at Nnenna, and dipped his chin once. Then, he turned and left.

Nnenna relaxed into her relief. She reached for the bowls and picked up both, handing one to Pearl. The girl took the food, smiling at first, but her face fell when she saw the gray mush inside. Nnenna did not blame her. The gruel had none of the depth of flavor that Sven's creations had, but it slaked her hunger all the same. Pearl finished her bowl in seconds and waited somewhat impatiently for Nnenna to finish hers. When Nnenna finally set aside her empty bowl, Pearl tapped the floor.

"Who is he?" she asked, when Nnenna looked her way.

Nnenna laughed. She held her right hand out in a fist and pretended to reach into it with the thumb and pointer finger of her left hand, pulling out something invisible and swirling. Ghost. Pearl gave her a confused look, and Nnenna signed an apology, pretending she had simply made an error. When she tried again, she placed her right fist with an outstretched thumb onto her left palm and raised them both together.

"Help. He's going to help."

Nnenna hoped she was right.

Twenty-Eight

THE VICEROY

The commodore's message had come through the mirror days ago, but Viceroy Stormcoast's body still tingled with anticipation. He sat on his throne in the Divine Chamber but found himself too distracted by his own excitement to commune with Agwe. Snippets of his coming address floated into his mind, drawing with them images of the Settlement's joyous faces when he finally announced that it was time for them to return to their home and claim their destiny.

"Viceroy," came the deep voice of Matthias Marshwind through the curtain that separated the chamber from the temple. "The people have been summoned from their beds and are gathered in the square. They await your address."

"Very good, Marshwind," Stormcoast said, fighting to keep his voice steady. "I shall greet them momentarily."

Stormcoast allowed himself a single moment of unfettered jubilation before he stood, straightened his robes, and glided toward the curtain. He swam past Marshwind without so much as a nod to acknowledge the man's bowed head at the viceroy's emergence.

"Take me to our guest," the viceroy commanded.

Marshwind straightened and led the way to the former viceroy's chamber, moving aside to let Stormcoast unlock the door and let himself in.

"I was beginning to think you had forgotten about me, Your Excellency," Wade Brinebottom said from within, wide awake and swimming a path around the large bed. "It has been many days since your last visit."

The viceroy entered, closing the door behind him as his eyes followed Brinebottom. "I could never forget such an honored guest, but the duties of the viceroy are far more demanding than those of a humble secretary."

"And what brings you to my prison cell at such a late hour?"

"I would hardly call this a prison cell, Brother Brinebottom. You have been afforded many luxuries during your stay."

"Every luxury except my freedom," Brinebottom retorted, and Stormcoast's impassive mask slipped from his face.

"Perhaps there is a way to change your circumstance," Stormcoast said.

Brinebottom scoffed. "You would never let me go. I'm surprised you haven't killed me like you did Rain."

Stormcoast paused. "What happened to Brother Highwater was . . . unfortunate." He said this slowly. Carefully. "But there is no reason for you to suffer the same fate."

Brinebottom slowed to a halt. He turned toward the door, and Stormcoast got his first good look at the gash across his cheek. Perhaps he should have sent a healer to tend to the wound.

"What do you mean?"

Stormcoast smiled, spreading his arms and craning his head toward the ceiling. "Agwe's treasure has been found."

"You're lying."

"Your precious Pearl may be within reach, even as we—"

"Where is she?" Brinebottom demanded, rushing the viceroy. He stopped just short of colliding with him.

"Perhaps there is a place for you in Agwe's kingdom, after all," Stormcoast said, unbothered.

Brinebottom backed away slowly and tilted his head. "What do you want?" he asked.

Stormcoast clasped his hands together in front of his robes. "Our people's devotion has grown lax in our time under the sea. They are beginning to believe we belong here. I believe it was you and Brother Highwater who championed this . . . novel idea—"

"We didn't—"

"Do not deny it, Brother Brinebottom. I already know you to be as much of a usurper as Brother Highwater was. But there is a way for you to make up for your misguided deeds. In mere moments, I will share the great news with our people. I have concerns that they will not be receptive to my message, so I would like you to accompany me."

"Never," Brinebottom snarled.

"I would not be so hasty. The instruments of our destiny are being gathered as we speak. It would be foolish to assume Pearl is not among them."

Brinebottom stiffened.

"What protection will you be able to offer her once Agwe's legions hold dominion over the world?" Stormcoast pressed, threading his fingers together before his chest as though in supplication. "Even if she has not been found, there will be nowhere for her to hide." Brinebottom's brow furrowed, and Stormcoast smiled as satisfaction hit home.

"You are beloved among the people," Stormcoast pronounced. "Convince them to believe and I will ensure that you and Pearl remain safe in Agwe's kingdom."

Brinebottom's jaw clenched, but his head nodded ever so slightly.

When the viceroy's guards uncrossed their spears, two people passed to the rough-hewn, shell-encrusted stone balcony: the viceroy and his guest. The square was so full of people that every man, woman, and child had to float shoulder to shoulder to fit in the space while temple guards kept them in place. Stormcoast raised his arms above his head for attention, but their eyes were already gazing upward, not at him, but at Brinebottom, who floated silently behind him.

"Brothers and sisters, I thank you for joining me at such a late hour! I will not waste your time by delaying the important news. The reason I have gathered you on this most beautiful of nights is to tell you that the day of our destiny has arrived! Agwe has finally called us back to our home!"

He paused and waited for the sounds of awe and adoration to wash over him, but none came.

"This is a most joyous occasion, brothers and sisters," he went on, trying not to let his annoyance show. "Our generations-long wait is over! Our home will be raised and I shall lead you there!"

Where there should have been tumultuous accolades, the viceroy received only a dull murmur.

He looked closely at their faces, and noticed that they were either downcast or defiant.

"I can sense your trepidation," he continued. "We waited so long for a reward that seemed as though it would never come. Some of you have faltered in your devotion, but I am not the only one who can assure you of Agwe's grace. Brother Brinebottom can also attest to Agwe's power to restore us to His kingdom."

Stormcoast stood aside to let Brinebottom forward, but the man did not move. He looked out at the people floating in the square, his fists clenched and his face unreadable. Then, he relaxed and approached the balcony's railing.

"Brothers and sisters," he started, softly. "The viceroy has been . . . kind enough to let me stay in the temple while my family"—Stormcoast winced at the word—"is found. I thank you for your concern, but I know that it will be by divine grace that we are reunited. The viceroy's message is true. The destiny foretold generations ago is upon us, and by divine grace, we shall be restored to our home."

Murmurs rippled through the crowd, and Stormcoast saw their faces change. His earlier eagerness returned, and he pushed past Brinebottom.

"Our destiny awaits us just beyond the surface!" he announced. "To prove our commitment to your salvation, Brother Brinebottom and I will pierce the veil and retrieve our lost home! We do this knowing that failure means we can never return. This is how assured we are of our success. Prepare yourselves for the restoration!"

The people's murmurs turned to gasps. It was not the exultation for which Stormcoast had prepared, but it was enough. Brinebottom stared at him mutinously. Stormcoast flicked his eyes to the armed guards standing only a few feet from them. He held out his hand.

"Pearl is within your reach," he muttered. "Do not let your pride rob you of your only chance to see her again."

Brinebottom looked at the offered hand. He closed his eyes, mumbled an unintelligible prayer, and took Stormcoast's hand in his own.

Together, they pushed off the balcony and swam into the black waters above. Stormcoast had always known he would have to endure the change, but he had thought it would be on the day of his return to the island that had been lost to his people for generations. He had expected to be welcomed back to land surrounded by his followers and guaranteed the seat of power. Instead, he suffered his gills sealing, his tail splitting and reshaping into legs, his skin thinning, and his fingers separating with no one but his enemy for company.

Coughing, wheezing, his heart pounding and his body aching, he emerged from the sea that had enveloped him his entire life to breathe air for the first time. He flapped his arms and newly formed legs back and forth in tandem to keep himself afloat in the still, deep waters, while he searched the surrounding area.

Two ships loomed in the distance, one much larger than the other. The commodore had spoken many times of the might of the Fleet, so he made the larger his target. He made sure Brinebottom saw it before taking off in that direction. It was not long before he came close enough to see the people—land dwellers—on the deck. How fortunate that the tide bringer was full and bright. He waved a hand and splashed on the surface of the water to get their attention. Brinebottom did the same. Someone saw them and tossed two long ropes down to them. Stormcoast and Brinebottom wrapped the ropes around their wrists and waists and held on as they were hauled out of the water.

Twenty-Nine

NNENNA

Nnenna tried desperately to remember a song, any song, that would carry her away from her current surroundings. She was coming apart at the seams, her panic blurring her vision and her breath coming in hitched spasms. She told herself she was fine, that this was just a little spell, but the overwhelming feeling of dread intensified the longer she sat in the cell.

This is not the same thing, she repeated with as much conviction as she could muster. *I am not going to die.*

But it was hard to believe those words when the evidence of her senses told her otherwise. She fought the memory of a midshipman coming to collect her from the cell and lost. She could hear his voice in her ears.

"I've come to take you up to the main deck," he had said, his voice squeaking as he fought to leave boyhood behind. *"I'm going to open the cell. If you try anything funny, I'll be forced to shoot."*

He had indeed held a pistol in his hand, but the way it shook told Nnenna that he had borrowed it from one of the older boys.

One of the songs her mother used to sing in the throes of inebriation took hold in Nnenna's mind and she held fast to it, as if her life depended on it. She hummed, quietly, so as not to wake Pearl. It had taken the girl a long time to fall asleep, and Nnenna did not want to ruin her rest. The seven knew she needed it. They had been in that cell for hours without a soul to speak to besides each other after the captain's visit. Nnenna had not been kind when he had come with his piss-poor peace offering of food.

Somewhere between humming and stewing, fatigue caught her and dropped her back into the memory.

Nnenna stood on deck, the wind whipping around her face as the ship swayed with the swells of the waves. Her feet were heavy, so heavy. She was scared, but, more than anything, she was angry. She stared at Lu, trying to communicate her rage, her sense of betrayal, her disappointment to him. He stared at his shoes. They stayed like this, one of them forever begging and the other forever denying, until Nnenna felt the pull of the chain at her ankle. She seemed to fall slowly, hitting the deck after an age. Every grain in the wood scraped against her face and chest and arms as she slid toward the edge of the ship. Her body hit the starboard side of the ship with a sickening crunch, and then she was in the air. As quickly as she flew, she was pulled down.

Nnenna slammed her open palm against the hard wooden floor as she fought the memory away. She beat the floor in time with the song she sang quietly to herself. But it was not working.

She could not breathe. Everything was water, in her eyes, in her nose, in her mouth. Her chest ached with the effort of keeping her last breath. She was sinking, like a stone, again, sucked inexorably down to the bottom of the ocean with her fellow mutineers. They had all stood against injustice together, and now they were paying for it with their lives.

The ocean swayed around the hull of the ship, and Nnenna imagined being pushed back and forth as she hovered, powerlessly, above the bottom of the ocean, suspended by a length of chain. She could see the floating bodies of her comrades and felt guilt for her part in their deaths and envy that she had not yet perished with them.

A hand on her shoulder ripped her back to the present. Her eyes jerked open, and her body convulsed, suddenly heavy without the water surrounding it. She was awake. She was dry. She was alive.

Thirty

LU

For the second time in as many weeks, Lu found himself receiving an amount of attention that pushed him beyond the limits of his comfort. He was in the *Adoration*'s dining cabin, standing next to Commodore Christophe as the man enumerated the ways in which Lu had contributed to the Fleet's success while a small crowd of onlookers listened with rapt attention. Unlike the day of his conferral, Lu recognized a few of the faces in the room. Manou stood front and center, beaming with pride. The young woman from the Singing Crab, Aline, stood next to him. There were five more guests behind them, Seven Islanders from the look of them, and two complete strangers to him.

Lu focused on Manou until the commodore finished, and when Manou raised his glass to join the toast in Lu's honor, Lu finally relaxed. He had hoped there would be time for him to spend with Manou, but as soon as the champagne ran dry, the commodore bid the singers return to their cabins. He insisted that they needed their rest and that there would be plenty of opportunities for reunion after the ceremony. Once the singers had gone, Commodore Christophe gathered Lu and the two strange men at the head of the table.

Up close, Lu realized he recognized one of these men, too. The taller, thinner one. His had been the face he had seen in the mirror at the fisherman's cabin. He had iron-gray shoulder-length hair that was slicked back against his head, and bulging round eyes. His skin was wrinkled and pale brown, and he stood stiffly, with his back straight. His companion seemed to be his opposite, short and round with full cheeks and curly brown hair that sprang from the top of his head. Both were dressed in ill-fitting Fleet garb, no doubt borrowed from the ship's collection.

"I want to formally introduce you to His Excellency, the viceroy of Agwe's chosen people," the commodore said to Lu, gesturing to the tall man.

Lu had never seen Commodore Christophe show deference to anyone before, but to this strange man, he acted as though he were in the presence of royalty. The gray-haired man said nothing in response but inclined his head. He set down his wineglass and made signs in Lu's direction. Lu's instincts told him it would be in his best interests to keep his knowledge of these signs hidden, so he looked at the commodore with feigned confusion.

"He says he offers his thanks," the commodore translated.

Lu offered a formal salute, thumping his right fist against his chest and clicking his heels together as he stood at attention.

"The hour of our greatest triumph grows nigh," the commodore said with a hungry look in his eye. "In just a few hours, we will do the impossible: We will raise the lost island of Meridia and join forces with their people to take over all of the lands of this world!"

"But, sir, how can that be?" Lu asked. "Is it possible to raise an island from the sea?"

The commodore frowned at him.

"My dear boy, I expected you especially to understand that there is more in this world than what we know. You have seen the Meridians with your own eyes. They were once a mighty force upon the earth before Agwe placed them under the sea's protection. His grace protected them from the devil! She was jealous of their majesty! They were the chosen people of the great god Agwe, and it was under His eye that they had conquered land after land after land. They sought to make the whole world theirs, make the whole world live under Agwe's care."

Discomfort rose within Lu. His devotion to the Fleet's mission to enforce law and order on his island never had anything to do with what gods the Fleet served. He knew he was walking a thin line, but his experience told him that there was more to the story than what the commodore disclosed. Lu kept quiet for the duration of this meeting, his face calm and impassive as the commodore and the viceroy spoke and signed their plans for raising the island.

There was to be a ceremony on the deck of the *Adoration* at precisely the hour when the sun chased the full moon out from the sky. They would bring out the singers to sing the holy hymn.

"Why these people?" Lu asked, thinking of Aline.

"They are of the blood," the viceroy replied through signs, and Lu almost forgot to wait for the commodore's translation. "A consequence of my people's proximity to the land dwellers."

Lu recognized disgust on the viceroy's face. He did not seem to think too highly of the inhabitants of this land.

"The magic must be called through the song of the people of the blood. Outside of Agwe's protection, we are cursed to lose our voices, but the devil did not anticipate our ingenuity."

Lu nodded in comprehension when the translation came from the commodore. He had much to think about.

•••●•••

That night, in his berth, Lu tossed and turned, unable to settle long enough to let sleep take him.

There were people living under the sea; an island was supposedly rising from the depths of the ocean.

The Fleet was on the precipice of its greatest triumph, and yet, it was Nnenna keeping him awake.

The moment Lieutenant Ambroise had escorted her into the *Medusa*'s great cabin, Lu's wildest dream and worst fear had been realized. Nnenna was alive, as beautiful as the day he had met her, and a pirate. He was impressed, despite himself. Not only was she a pirate, but the very pirate captain sought after by the Fleet for years of menace. Now that she was caught, she was in grave danger.

There was also Pearl to think about. Lu had expected her to be young, but the girl he saw in the brig was practically a child. Sixteen years old and the object of desire of an old man. Lu shuddered. Would he deliver Pearl to the viceroy? Would he let Nnenna die for a second time? Until these moments, he knew only his duty and his honor, but now it seemed that neither of these would lead him to an answer that would sit well within his soul. With a heavy sigh, he threw off the covers, climbed out of his berth, and left the *Adoration*'s cabin.

He crept down into the deepest part of the ship to the cells, retracing the steps he had taken only a few hours before. Nnenna and Pearl were asleep in each other's arms. Lu felt a tug at his heartstrings looking at the moment of tenderness. It almost broke him to interrupt.

"Nnenna," he whispered. When she did not stir, he grew nervous. He banged his hand against the bars of the cell, but this yielded no results. He looked around and saw that the key to the cells was hanging on a nail in the wall. Silently thanking the lazy son of a bitch who had left it there, Lu took the key and opened the cell. Then, he closed the door behind him.

He approached the two sleeping bodies slowly. His training as a soldier was not to be ignored. The moment he knelt next to Nnenna, she sprang to life, her hands wrapping around his neck and squeezing with the grip of death itself.

"Stop!" Lu wheezed with the little bit of air he had. "I'm—here—to—help!"

When she realized it was Lu, she released him and pushed him away.

"What are you doing here?" she demanded.

"I need to get you out," Lu said quickly, rubbing his neck.

"You—what?"

Lu looked over at Pearl, who had also gotten up in the tussle and looked as though she were ready to take Lu on herself. Lu decided it would be best to speak to them both at once.

"I was in a meeting with the commodore and your viceroy. They have been working together to raise the lost island of Meridia," he said while signing. "There was also another man. I'm not sure how he fits into the plan. Either way, I am going to try to stop it somehow. It will most likely be dangerous, and I don't want either of you to get caught up in—"

"All of a sudden you care about my well-being?" Nnenna interjected.

"I have always cared about you," Lu replied, trying to keep the hurt out of his voice. "You don't have to believe me, but it's true."

Something in his tone must have resonated with her, because she relented.

"The ceremony will start at sunrise. If I free you now, you can return to your ship and—"

"My ship?" Nnenna asked. "Do you not remember orchestrating a trade with my first mate? And have you not noticed the still waters? The lack of wind? We're becalmed. We'd be better off in a longboat, and even then, how far do you think we'd get before your beetle goons caught up to us?"

Lu paused. "I didn't think—"

"Clearly."

Pearl waved her hands in his face to get his attention.

"The other man! What did he look like?" she said through signs.

"Short, stocky build, with curly hair. He looks like one of your people," Lu signed to her.

"That could be my uncle!" Pearl excitedly replied. "I can't leave without him."

"And I'm not leaving her behind," Nnenna said.

"Then . . ." Lu said, thinking. "We'll just have to work together. If you're willing," he added, looking right at Nnenna. He felt the urge to fill the silence with more apologies but squashed it.

Nnenna stared at him for a long time in silent contemplation. He imagined what was going through her mind and decided then and there that he would not be surprised or hold it against her if she rejected his offer. Slowly, she gave a single nod.

"Thank you," Lu said to Nnenna. "For trusting me."

"I don't trust you," she replied coolly, "but you're my best shot at making it out of this mess alive."

Her words were grim, but not unexpected, so Lu accepted them without reply.

Thirty-One

PEARL

Pearl leaned over Nnenna's twitching body, wondering whether she should try to wake the woman, when Nnenna gasped, her eyes opening wide. She looked around, panicked, as though she did not recognize this place, until her eyes landed upon Pearl. Nnenna smiled, sitting up. Pearl frowned in concern, and Nnenna dropped her gaze.

Pearl had so many questions. What did Nnenna see in her dreams that made her so fearful? Did it have something to do with Captain Ortega? She had said he was a ghost from her past. Was it he who haunted her now?

Nnenna whispered to herself in the land-dweller language as she rubbed her hands over her face. Pearl noticed they were shaking. She waited until she was steady before making another attempt at a reassuring smile.

"Are you all right?" Nnenna asked Pearl.

Pearl wanted to say that she was fine, that she could be strong enough for the both of them, but all she managed was a sob. Nnenna put her arms around Pearl and pulled her close, whispering comfort into her ear.

In the time that it took to console Pearl, another guard arrived with bowls of food. It must have been morning. Pearl looked up, expecting to see Captain Ortega in the lantern light, but it was a guard she did not recognize carrying the tray. She tried not to feel disappointed. It was likely the captain did not want to arouse suspicions. The guard placed the tray on the floor inside the cell and Pearl waited as Nnenna retrieved it.

Nnenna brought the tips of all five fingers on her right hand together and touched the bundle to her lips. She was telling Pearl to eat. "You'll feel better."

Pearl could only look at the congealed mass of cold gray mush on her plate in disgust. She cupped her hands together into the shape of a bowl, made one swim as though it were a fish, and rubbed her belly. She wanted fish stew.

Nnenna laughed and spoke more land-dweller words. Pearl shook her head. Nnenna pointed to the bowl of mush and flexed her arm. The food would help Pearl keep up her strength. Pearl rolled her eyes, but when Nnenna pushed the bowl toward her, she took it and began to eat.

Breakfast did not go down as easily as anything Sven could have prepared. Pearl felt it roiling in her stomach even as the guard returned with lengths of rope. He demanded something in the land-dweller language. She immediately looked to Nnenna and watched her get to her feet, allowing the guard to bind her hands in front of her. Pearl felt her own panic rising. Nnenna sent her a soothing look, but Pearl still shook with fear. The guard said something, and she looked to Nnenna again. Nnenna mimicked holding out her hands, wrists together, and inclined her head, indicating that Pearl should do the same.

Giving herself up to her captors felt like defeat, but, after the conversation she had been privy to the night before, she knew her captivity would not be for long.

Pearl was led up the flights of stairs leading to the main deck of the ship. When she arrived, she could not help but stare at the sky in wonder. The deck was bathed in moonlight, the sky above a symphony of stars. The night sky was reflected in the almost perfectly still waters, creating a mirror image in the unmoving sea. Pearl had never seen so many stars in her life. She wished she could sing to them in praise of their beauty.

Her captor led her to the uppermost deck, where a handful of men already stood. One of them was Lu. She searched the faces for anyone else she recognized. There was an older man with broad shoulders who was dressed in such finery that Pearl took him to be the most senior of the Fleet officers. He stood upright, though a feverish smile played at his lips as he oversaw the gathering. Another guard stood behind him, shorter, with lighter skin and curly brown hair.

Uncle Wade!

He was dressed like a Fleet guard, but she would know his kind brown eyes anywhere. She smiled, raising her bound arms and waving to get his attention. Without thinking, Pearl stepped toward her uncle and felt the pull of the guard's hand holding her back. As she struggled against his grip, a taller, thinner man dressed as a Fleet guard stepped in front of her uncle.

Pearl froze. Even absent the flowing white-and-gold robes, the self-righteous air with which the viceroy carried himself was unmistakable. She dropped her head, hiding her face, but he had already seen her. Her stomach turned, threatening to relieve itself of her most recent meal. As he walked toward her, his mouth stretched into a slimy smile that made her skin crawl.

He pressed his palms flat against each other, twisted them,

then spread his arms with his palms facing outward. Pearl knew the greeting. She did not know if it was fear or fury that kept her from responding.

"This is a most glorious day," he signed to her, "and you, my child, are very lucky to be able to witness our people's return to the seat of glory."

For once, Pearl was glad for her bound wrists, which kept her from communicating. She glared at the viceroy, willing him to burn with her hatred. It felt like a lifetime ago that Pearl had begged for the opportunity to be a temple worker. Now, she wondered if she even believed in Agwe anymore.

When she gave him no response, the viceroy's face split into a self-satisfied smile, and he walked away, returning to his spot by her uncle.

Nnenna nudged Pearl to get her attention, and when Pearl looked, Nnenna brought her bound hands to her face, hooking one of her thumbs under her chin and bending her extended pointer finger twice. She wanted to know who the viceroy was. Pearl did not know if Nnenna would understand the Meridian sign for the role he played, so she improvised.

"Home leader. Danger," she signed as best as she could.

More people emerged from below: a procession of seven pairs, one set of seven guards, each escorting a land dweller who did not wear the Fleet uniform. They all walked to the center of the main deck. The seven guards arranged their companions in a circle. Then, each guard took their place behind each companion, forming a larger circle around them.

Pearl recognized one of the seven, a beautiful brown woman with sandy curls who looked better cared for than the rest. She whipped her head toward Nnenna to get her attention, but Nnenna had already seen Aline.

Nnenna started to call out to her, but the moment she opened her mouth, the butt of a pistol hit her between her neck and shoulder, and she fell to her knees.

The most decoratively uniformed Fleet guard stepped away from the group and addressed the observation deck. He smiled proudly, wearing the shell that Pearl had left with Ship-Father in Ayiti on a string around his neck.

Pearl's heart sank. How had he gotten his hands on it?

The man gestured excitedly as he spoke. When he flourished toward the seven land dwellers on the main deck, Pearl understood. He was introducing the show.

At his word, Aline beamed as though she were back in the Singing Crab. Pearl looked around for anyone who could help. Nnenna was still on her knees, but Captain Lu was only a few meters away. She tried to catch his eye without drawing the attention of the guards, but he stared intently at one of the seven. By the looks on their faces, these land dwellers did not know what was about to happen to them. They looked confused and excited, when they should have been scared for their lives. Pearl knew what fate awaited them. She had stood in the same formation every time she had taken her place among the other six singers in the Settlement's choir. The last time was at Viceroy Seastead's funeral, singing before the congregation in a circle formation to call to Agwe. It was known throughout the Settlement that the voices the seven singers raised were symbolic of the sacrifice needed to bring their island back.

All at once, she wished to go home. She wished to be back in her rock-and-coral house, listening to her Uncle Rain tell stories, while her Uncle Wade took the bones out of her fish dinner. She wished she still had the safety of her belief in Agwe to hold on to. She did not want to be a godless land dweller anymore. She did not want to see what was going to happen next.

Thirty-Two

LU

Lu was lost in his mental recitation of the steps of his plan to help Nnenna and Pearl escape the *Adoration*, when the singers arrived on deck. He expected they would have to wait until after the song. Then, he could use the cover of the following celebration to secrete them into a longboat. When he looked up to decide which boat would be the easiest to get to, he saw two familiar faces and smiled. One was the dark, lined face of Manou. His coffee-brown eyes were turned to the other, Aline, the young woman whom he had met at the Singing Crab. They were talking animatedly to each other as though they were old friends. Lu was not surprised. Manou never allowed strangers to remain as such for long. As Lu watched their exchange, Manou cast his eye over the gallery as though he were searching for someone. He found Lu almost at once and pointed him out to Aline, beaming proudly.

"No room for fisherfolk at fancy Fleet to-dos," Lu remembered Manou saying on the day of his conferral.

Manou could not have been more wrong. The commodore had promised to take care of Manou and Mai after Manou had fulfilled his duty. It should have eased Lu's mind to know that they would know some comfort after years of working so hard, but something about the ceremony bothered him. The singers had been escorted by lieutenants, one for each of them. Lu had expected them to join the spectators on the quarterdeck, but they remained.

"Sir," he said under his breath, leaning toward the commodore while keeping an eye on Manou and Aline.

"What exactly is the nature of this ceremony?"

"It is the means by which we call upon Agwe to restore the island," the commodore answered. "We offer Him a sacred hymn, sung by those who are of the blood, to call Him to us."

Lu shifted uncomfortably. Manou had his arms above his head, no doubt stretching his back. He always did complain that the sea air made his joints stiff.

"But, sir," Lu pressed, "what happens to the singers following the ceremony?"

The commodore smiled at Lu's words. "Something positively magical, my dear boy. You must simply see it to believe it."

"Will they be safe, sir?"

The commodore rested his hand upon Lu's shoulder. "They are the most vital participants of the ceremony. After their performance, they shall receive the greatest reward."

The commodore's faith in Agwe was absolute. Every choice he made was in service to fulfilling the Fleet's destiny. Christophe would be remembered as the greatest commodore the Fleet had ever known. If Lu was indeed destined to carry on Christophe's legacy, the strength of his faith would have to be the same.

Lu straightened, pushing away his lingering doubt.

Thirty-Three

NNENNA

Nnenna's heart sank as Aline beamed at the other six people standing with her in a circle. With how she smiled, she could have been in the dining room of the Singing Crab, getting ready to perform for a group of hungry patrons. There was no trace of fear in her eyes. Guilt gripped Nnenna's insides and urged her to do something to get the woman out of harm's way, but bound as she was, she could not. She looked to Lu, who was at least free to move as he pleased, but he was talking to the commodore. After a moment, the commodore stepped forward, dressed in his full regalia. Nnenna thought he looked like a pompous fool until her eye landed on the conch shell sitting on his chest. He had strung it around his neck and ran his hand over it as he walked.

"Ladies and gentlemen, esteemed guests, and honorable patrons," he pronounced. Nnenna barely heard him. She frantically scanned the deck for signs of Captain Delva. If the Fleet had gotten ahold of the shell, they might have only captured Delva rather than killed him.

"Today, we are witnesses to a momentous occasion!" he went on. "For too long, the Fleet has battled to uphold order, against a world which does not respect these forces. With the help of our Meridian friends, we will raise their lost island, and together, we will conquer the world, one isle after another!"

There was no sign of him anywhere. Nnenna looked at the commodore as the uniformed people on the observation deck raised a cheer, applauding their fearless leader's words. Nnenna felt sick to her stomach. Both Pearl's and Lu's faces echoed her feelings. The hint of relief she felt upon seeing him took her by surprise.

"Today would not be the great day that it is without the help of our *volunteers*," the commodore went on. "So, when they do their part to help us fulfill our destiny, please, show them the respect they deserve."

He turned to face the seven people standing in the innermost circle.

"Just like we practiced, and then you all get to go home," he said quietly.

Nnenna had a feeling he had no intention of setting them free, but Aline and the rest of the volunteers took him at his word. They all closed their eyes, breathed in deeply, and began to sing.

Aline's voice started the song. Her first note took Nnenna's breath away. It was pure and high and held all the hope of something greater happening. The other voices joined in, some matching her pitch and others finding harmonies. Nnenna realized, to her surprise, that she had heard this song before, or, rather, heard a different version of it. She could hear it in her mind, now, sung by a single voice, echoing eerily in the dark.

The singers' voices swelled and ebbed, like the tides of the sea. Behind the ship, the full moon made its descent as it retired for its rest. Nnenna was reminded of the time when she used to think that if she swam deep enough, she would find the moon sleeping somewhere at the bottom of the sea.

The sun's rays broke over the horizon, lightening the inky-black sky to a light blue, a hazy pink, a brilliant orange. They sang through it all, sang the same song again and again until the sun was a glowing yellow disk in the sky. And then, all at once, the song was over.

For a long time, there was silence. The singers looked expectantly at each other. Nnenna's eyes were on the commodore. He looked at the group of lieutenants who had led the singers in, made eye contact with the leader, and gave him a nod.

He moved, and the rest of the lieutenants followed, closing the distance between themselves and their assigned singers. For one moment, Nnenna thought perhaps they would be freed. Then, seven golden-bladed daggers appeared from the sheaths in the lieutenants' belts.

"No!" Nnenna screamed, and she was surprised to find that hers was not the only voice that rang through the morning air. Lu had also cried out.

"Let the offering be made!" the commodore shouted, holding a struggling Lu back with one arm.

Nnenna's cry caught Aline's attention. She found Nnenna's face and smiled in pleasant surprise before a glint of gold ran across her throat. Nnenna watched her relief turn to shock, then confusion and fear, as blood poured from her wound and onto her clothes, the same clothes she had been wearing the last time Nnenna had seen her. Her body, which had once been filled with so much life, crumpled to the deck an empty husk, and where seven singers had once stood, seven corpses now lay.

Nnenna felt herself die along with them. The hopelessness she had felt when she had succumbed to the dark depths of the sea flooded her as she realized there was nothing she could do. She thought of running to them, but to what end? The strong hands that held her in place would not yield, and even so, the singers were dead. Aline was dead. The Fleet had done it again, had rendered her powerless as innocent people lost their lives.

The commodore released Lu, and weeping, Lu ran to the circle of bodies, falling to his knees in front of a white-haired singer and taking the man's body into his lap. The commodore sauntered to the circle and stepped over Aline's body to stand in the center. He took the conch in both hands, brought one end to his lips, and broke the silence with a single sustained note.

A light breeze danced through the air. At first, it only caressed Nnenna's face, but as the seconds passed, the force of it grew, playing with the strands of Nnenna's hair, then tugging at her clothes. Dark gray clouds materialized in the sky. A storm was brewing, more quickly than Nnenna had ever seen one arise before.

The once-pristine waters became turbid, ridged with tiny undulations that grew into bigger ripples then into small waves. The small waves grew larger and larger and lapped at the sides of the ship. For the first few moments, the *Adoration* was unperturbed, but as the water gained strength, she began to rock back and forth.

"Hold your positions!" the commodore shouted over the gusting gale as items on the deck rolled with the pitching of the ship.

Soon, it was difficult to stand as the ship's oscillations pulled her about. Every so often, she found herself pressed against the lieutenant holding her captive, and she knew she could use this to her advantage. She waited, her legs in a wide stance, until the opportunity presented itself. The ship lurched so far toward port,

Nnenna could see the water over the railing. As the hull fell back toward the starboard, she threw her weight at the lieutenant, using the momentum of the ship's movement to power her attack. Caught off guard, he careened into and over the railing, his screams barely audible over the wind.

Nnenna clasped her hands together and swung them, still bound, at the head of the lieutenant guarding Pearl. Her fists slammed against his ear, knocking him sideways. His head hit the deck hard, knocking him out. Nnenna was ready to finish the job, but the *Adoration* shuddered violently as something smashed through her hull. Chaos descended on deck, and Nnenna spun to see the source of the impact.

"What the hell was that?" the commodore demanded. "You said you had dealt with the pirates!"

"They must have reneged on our deal," the pretty lieutenant that had captured Nnenna—Ambroise?—called to the commodore from the upper deck.

"Well, go get them and take care of them!" the commodore screamed. "I will not have some pirate scum ruining this moment!"

The lieutenant relayed the order, and while the company prepared to board the *Medusa* a second time, Nnenna took advantage of the cover of distraction. She ran to the unconscious lieutenant, stole his dagger, and used it to cut herself and Pearl free. Once Pearl was free of her bonds, Nnenna grasped her hand and they ran.

While the lieutenants crowded the starboard side, trying to board the *Medusa*, Nnenna and Pearl ran to the port side of the ship. Nnenna tried hard not to look at the corpses as they passed, but her stomach still lurched when her eye landed on Aline's lifeless body.

She turned away quickly and surveyed the ship's longboats.

Even the smallest of them was a larger class than the ones the *Medusa* carried. Getting it over the side rail with just the two of them would be difficult, but not impossible. Nnenna grabbed the edge of the upturned vessel, waited for Pearl to do the same, and together, they put all their might into flipping the boat over. They lifted it, but only barely, before the weight of the boat suddenly doubled and nearly brought Nnenna to her knees. She glanced at Pearl and found the girl held in an armlock with a pistol pointed at her head.

"Let her go and I'll let you live," Nnenna shouted over the wind that whipped her hair over her face.

The beetle had the dangerous look of every true believer fiercely loyal to the Fleet's cause. He had been sold the story that he was destined for greatness, and so he believed himself great.

"I don't want to hurt you," Nnenna said, and the man smiled. He aimed his pistol at Pearl's temple and pulled back the hammer.

"Stand down, Lieutenant!" a deep voice shouted from behind Nnenna.

She whirled around and saw Lu standing with his pistol drawn, his long arm outstretched and his thumb on the hammer.

"Let the girl go! That's an order!"

As Nnenna turned, the lieutenant's trigger finger twitched, but the gunshot came not from him, but from behind Nnenna. The man dropped as the lead ball rocketed through his cheek, and Pearl pulled herself free.

"You've just committed treason," Nnenna shouted to Lu in surprise.

"Five years too late," he said, holstering the pistol. The weight of his words hung between them for a moment. "We can get the boat over the rail if we all lift it together."

Nnenna exhaled in disbelief, unsure of what to make of his attempt at an apology. If he believed that a moment of contrition would be enough to absolve him, he was dead wrong. Eventually, she nodded. She would accept his help, and if they survived this ordeal, she would tell him what he could do with his apology.

On Lu's count, all three of them took hold of the sides of the boat and heaved.

"Forward!" Lu shouted, and Nnenna and Pearl both shoved the longboat toward the ship's rail. The vessel flipped over and fell ten feet before the chains securing it to the deck caught it, suspending it in midair.

"You two get in!" Lu shouted as fat raindrops began to fall from the darkening sky. "I'll lower you down!"

Nnenna glanced over her shoulder at the chaos unfolding on the *Adoration*'s decks. Officers everywhere ran to ready guns and rifles to take on the *Medusa* as she careened past. It might have been enough cover, but it would only take one sharp-eyed lieutenant to notice what Lu was doing and one bullet to stop him.

"Come with us!" Nnenna offered, surprising herself.

She did not need Lu dying while trying to save her.

Lu smiled briefly. "Somebody has to lower the boat."

Nnenna growled in frustration. She had forgotten how much she loved his smile. She had tucked it away with all her other memories of him from before her execution. But she knew better than to give in to nostalgia. She was certain that this smile and the self-sacrificing gesture that came with it were more attempts to earn her forgiveness. If he wanted to risk his life for her, then so be it.

She took Pearl by the arm and pulled her away, helping her over the bulwark and then down into the boat. With a final, stiff nod to Lu, she jumped over the railing and into the boat herself.

The journey down the side of the *Adoration* was treacherous. The vessel threatened to throw them into the sea with every sideways lurch. Pearl and Nnenna held on to each other and the boat's sides. Once the boat touched down onto the roiling waters, they disconnected the chains and the boat floated free. Nnenna grabbed one of the oars and handed another to Pearl.

"Are you all right?" she signed.

Pearl nodded. "Are we waiting?"

Nnenna looked up, half hoping to see Lu's face, but no one leaned over the railing.

She turned to Pearl and shook her head. "We can't," she signed in return.

Nnenna put her oar to water and began to row. Pearl followed suit. The boat pitched upward violently with every wave. Between the waves and the rain, Pearl and Nnenna were both soaked within seconds. As she rowed, she felt a song mingle with the fear growing in her heart. There was no point in stopping it, so she set it free, singing to the goddess in rhythm with her strokes.

Something big splashed into the water behind her, and Pearl's eyes grew as wide as saucers. She tilted her head and furrowed her brow to ask the girl what was wrong. Pearl took one hand off her oar and made the signs for *ship* and *leader.* Captain.

"Lu?" Nnenna asked.

Pearl nodded vigorously. "Save him," she signed.

"Are you sure?" Nnenna asked, trying not to let her reluctance show.

"He saved us," Pearl urged.

Nnenna had not shared the details of her and Lu's relationship with Pearl, but it was clear Pearl had gleaned that there was some ill will between them. She seemed to have fallen for Lu's show of remorse. Explaining to Pearl exactly why Nnenna felt Lu deserved to die may have changed the way Pearl saw her, and that was a risk she was not willing to take.

"All right!" Nnenna shouted, rolling her eyes as she adjusted her oars.

They reversed their strokes and propelled the longboat back through the choppy waters, toward the *Adoration*, as the current tried to pull them away. The same current swept Lu's body quickly toward them, his arms outstretched, and both women reached for him. His fingers missed Pearl's hand by an inch, but Nnenna managed to barely catch him by the sleeve. She tried to pull him in, but a swell of water broke her grasp.

"Lu!" Nnenna screamed as the current pulled him away.

He disappeared beneath the waves. The sea took hold of the longboat, drawing it from the *Adoration* and around the edge of the chasm. Another massive swell tipped the boat, throwing both Nnenna and Pearl overboard. Nnenna reached for Pearl and miraculously found her hands as the current sucked them both into the inky-black darkness.

Thirty-Four

THE LOVERS

Long ago, before people roamed the world, there was the sky and the sea and the land and Bondye, who ruled them all. Bondye created seven beings called *gods* and gave them an island to live on and care for. The island's name was Meridia.

On cool, misty days, when the sun hid behind gray clouds and fog roamed over the land, most of Bondye's creations kept working. But two gods, Lasirenn and Agwe, whose domain was the sea, shirked their duties in favor of play. Lasirenn traded her tail for legs and hid among the trees in the thick, lush jungle, and Agwe tried to find her, using all manner of tricks to convince her to leave her hiding place. He was almost always successful, for he was a very charming, very handsome god. But he was no match for Lasirenn when the mists covered both land and sea, blurring the lines between the gods' different domains.

Master of all that traced the line between the mystic and the mundane, Lasirenn slipped in and out of the spaces between the dew drops, teasing her lover until she felt him grow frustrated and allowed herself to finally be caught. Laughing, she leaped into his open arms, knocking him down to the soft jungle floor, and they kissed as their divine bodies rolled down the mountainside to the beach below, where their play turned to passion.

When the sun's rays peeked from behind the clouds, they knew their time on land was done, so they returned to the sea. While Lasirenn's bare upper body, the color of clay-rich soil, remained unchanged, her legs became a winding tail adorned with shining scales that shimmered like pearls in the light. Agwe changed as well, adopting his own long tail with jewel-green scales that perfectly matched his eyes.

"One day, we will rule this island together," Agwe promised, pulling a stubborn leaf from Lasirenn's tightly coiled dark red hair.

Each of the island's gods had his or her own domain to work and contribute to the island's well-being. They knew nothing beyond the shores of their land, which floated above the point where existence began and ended.

But Agwe and Lasirenn were different from their brothers and sisters. Together, they could roam the seas, which stretched across the whole world. The other gods grew angry that the lovers seemed not to have to work as hard as the rest of them.

"They are lazy," they whispered among themselves. "Why should we burden ourselves when they contribute nothing?"

When their complaints reached Agwe's ears, he crafted a plan.

"Brothers and sisters, worry not," he said, his voice so smooth it sounded like a song, "for I have found a way to spare you from toiling. Give me but three cycles of the sun's path through the sky and I will show you."

The other gods believed Agwe and agreed that he would return in three days with a way to make their toils no more, or they would tell Bondye of their brother's indolence.

Agwe knew he was the most clever of all the gods, so he did not hurry to find this miracle he had promised his brothers and sisters. On the first day, Lasirenn found him in casual contemplation.

"If only there were more gods so that they could shoulder the burden of caring for Meridia," he mused.

When she heard this, Lasirenn had an idea.

"We are creations who toil for Bondye," Lasirenn said. "Why, then, can we not create beings of land and sea to toil for us? I will speak to the Creator, Damballa."

Damballa was the oldest of the gods and the wisest by far. His domain was without limits, the secrets of creation sealed in his skin by Bondye. Lasirenn sought him on the island, using a network of underwater caves and tunnels to take her to the heart of the jungle. She found him on the second day, his giant black snake body coiled next to one of her reflecting pools.

"Brother," Lasirenn called from within the pool, smiling when she saw him. "How are you?"

Damballa was old and could not speak as the other gods did, so he uttered a low hiss to say that he was well.

"I want to create something," Lasirenn said plainly, "but I do not have your gifts. Grant me a measure of your skin so that I may use it to make something small for myself."

Damballa was wary of giving away his skin, for he knew the power it held, but he cherished his sister. He shook his body, rubbing his scales together until a sliver of skin came free, and slithered to the edge of Lasirenn's pool. She plucked the skin from his body, thanked him, and returned to the lair she shared with Agwe in the sea.

As the sun rose on the third day, the rest of the gods gathered at the eastern shore of the island and waited for Agwe to return with his promised gift.

"Brothers and sisters, I bring you a miracle!" he proudly exclaimed, stepping out of the sea, leading five creations. "No longer must you toil, for these shall toil in your place!"

The other gods looked upon the five creations with confusion.

"Only five?" asked Zaka, whose domain was agriculture.

"Patience, Brother," Agwe replied. "Give me three more days and I will fill the island with my creations."

The gods agreed and stood back as the five creations begot more creations and those creations begot even more creations until the island was indeed full of them. Excited, the gods returned to their domains and taught the creations to work the land and the sea, and how to set aside portions of their yields as divine offerings in exchange for favor with Bondye. Over time, the creations forgot how to turn their legs into tails, and they became tied to the land. All of the gods were able to rest, as Agwe had promised, and Agwe became the most favored among them.

Unbeknownst to his brothers and sisters, Agwe visited the creations, whom they now called *followers,* from time to time and reminded them of his role in their existence. He reminded them that, though they lived and worked to serve other gods, they must be loyal only to him. As this message spread, his power grew stronger, while his brothers and sisters grew weaker and faded into the Unknown. Soon, Agwe was the only god of the island.

Eventually, Agwe's desire to rule extended beyond the little island. He taught his followers to build vessels that would take them all around the world and claim the lands they found in his name. Years later, when Agwe's name was the only one whispered in prayers, he heard a sliver of song on the ocean breeze. Suddenly, he remembered his lover of old. When he visited her in the lair that he had once called his home, he saw that not only were her powers intact, but she seemed to have power to rival his own.

"My love," he said to Lasirenn in greeting.

She smiled. "I have been waiting for you to visit! Look!"

It seemed she had kept two creations for herself. They had multiplied into countless numbers, all of whom bore her skin, her hair, her tail, and her song. They flitted around her lair, singing to Lasirenn and performing small magics rather than the work for which they had been designed.

"You have given them power?" Agwe asked.

"Is it not wonderful?" Lasirenn replied.

"How will they work for us if they have power, too?"

"But is this not a better way? They are so happy!"

Anger flared in Agwe's heart, but he masked it with a smile. "No, my love, we must take care. These creations were meant to *serve* us. With this much power, they will seek to be us."

Lasirenn frowned. "They are my children. I love them. Why should they not be like us?"

Agwe knew his words would not reach her. He hastened back to the temple he had had his followers build in his honor and found his most devoted.

"There is a threat to us in the sea," he whispered into their ears. "They mean to take away all we have built together. You must destroy them."

Agwe's followers knew no other god but Agwe, and so they obeyed. They went into the sea with their shining spears and spilled the blood of every one of Lasirenn's creations they could find. Agwe waited for Lasirenn to fade into the Unknown, as their brothers and sisters had done, but as the divinity seeped out of her body, she uttered a terrible curse.

With her first word, Lasirenn plunged Agwe's island into

the sea and threw it into the Unknown. With her second, she reclaimed the children she had given to Agwe—those who had remained on the island—forcing them to return to the water, cursed to be forever separated from Agwe's glory. With her third word, Lasirenn bound the power to summon the island to a shell and hid it among a countless number of identical shells, ensuring it would never be found. Her power then spent, she sank to the sea floor, weeping bitter tears. The Unknown would take her, but she would not go alone.

Thirty-Five

PEARL

Pearl had sometimes wondered how she would die. She had even imagined it in a macabre exercise during her moments of solitude. It hadn't been the dying that fascinated her, but what came next. She had always imagined a warm reception into Agwe's kingdom from her long-dead ancestors, her parents, and Agwe Himself. She had done the work during her lifetime. She could finally rest.

As she stared death in the face, she realized how foolish it had been for her to believe her life so inconsequential she could only offer it to Agwe for it to amount to anything. His servants had wrought only suffering upon the peoples of the land and sea. She wished she had understood sooner, that she had not wasted her precious few years of life living every letter of Agwe's word. Now, her lungs screamed for air as she held on to Nnenna's hands while the black chasm that had haunted Pearl all her life pulled them into its depths.

•••●•••

Pearl understood that something had changed in her before she even knew that there was still something left to be changed. The weight she had been carrying since she became a land dweller, the one she attributed to being out of the water, was gone, and a new lightness took its place. She regained consciousness in the dark. It had been day when she and Nnenna were knocked out of the boat—gray and as wet as the ocean itself, but day nonetheless—but, when Pearl opened her eyes, a star-strewn sky hovered above her.

She was lying on her back against soft sand that was neither warm nor cool but perfectly matched to her body temperature. Now that she thought of it, the air was temperate as well. She pushed herself up to sit and realized the sky seemed to go on forever in every direction. There was no line at the horizon where the sky met the sea, and yet, something lapped gently at the shore just meters from her. It looked like more sky, inky black and speckled with twinkling white lights, but that was impossible. The sand shifted beneath her as she rolled onto her hands and knees and reached toward the liquid abyss.

As her fingers neared the water, a soft groan reminded her that she was not alone. She pulled her hand back and turned toward the sound. The starlight was just bright enough to trace the outline of Nnenna's unconscious body. Pearl gasped and ran to her, dropping to her knees at Nnenna's side. She took Nnenna by the shoulders and shook her. Nnenna sprang to life at Pearl's touch, muttering incoherently in the land-dweller language as her body trembled uncontrollably. Pearl went from shaking her to holding her steady.

"Nnenna!" she cried, her tongue lilting awkwardly around the land-dweller syllables.

Nnenna gasped. Her eyes shot open, frantically looking around until they landed on Pearl's face.

Pearl held Nnenna's gaze as she took the woman's hand and pressed it to her own cheek, not realizing that she was crying until she felt the wetness of her tears on Nnenna's hand. Pearl watched Nnenna's fear turn to relief.

"Pearl," Nnenna sighed.

"Mwen la," Pearl replied, her voice shaking.

Nnenna suddenly sat up, her eyes wide. She asked a question in the land-dweller language that Pearl could guess thanks to her own astonishment. She tried her best to use the scraps of land-dweller language that she had acquired to explain.

"My home," she said slowly, gesturing to the sand beneath her, the trees ahead of her, and the dark outline of the mountain looming in the distance.

It wasn't enough. Nnenna still did not understand, so Pearl used her hands. As she signed, someone spoke from the shadows beyond them. Pearl and Nnenna both turned, and Pearl felt relief wash over her as Captain Lu Ortega stepped into the starlight. He was still dressed in his uniform, but his body seemed to fill it out differently. His shoulders were broader, his hips narrower, the line of his jaw a little more square.

His hands moved quickly, communicating his thoughts.

"That is right, isn't it?" he asked Pearl when he finished. "That's why you can speak now?"

Pearl nodded and waited for him to explain to Nnenna in the land-dweller language. The curse that had kept her voiceless on land was broken now that she had found the island that her people had sought for generations. But where were they? Where were the viceroy and his land-dweller guard?

Where was the ship and everyone who had been aboard?

"Kote nou ye?" Pearl asked, speaking and signing at the same time.

This place did not look like the one that they had left. The stars that burned overhead and somehow in the sea held none of the shapes she recognized from her study of the sky. The sea that barely lapped at the shore did so almost silently. No wind whispered through the trees—no birdsong or animal howls either. All was simply still.

Yet, there was something more to this place, an energy that connected with the deep longing Pearl buried inside her soul. She had felt it draw on her when she had first regained consciousness, had felt it pull her toward the water. She felt it, even now.

"I don't know," Lu and Nnenna signed back at once.

"We should find shelter," Lu added. "I don't like being so exposed."

He spoke the words as he signed them, and Nnenna, who had been listening while brushing the sand off her clothes, turned to Lu and said something that made him frown. They argued briefly before Lu finally relented, and Pearl got the feeling that he was a man not used to having his orders questioned. Refusing to be left out of the loop, Pearl waved at them, demanding their attention.

"We go together," Nnenna signed, and Pearl nodded her approval.

Pearl expected the trek into the jungle to be treacherous, but they found a well-worn path almost as soon as they crossed the tree line. Then, she remembered that this was not some uninhabited island awaiting discovery. Her people had lived here generations ago, and the power this place had must have preserved the island in its original state when the devil had enacted her curse.

They trod cautiously along the path, Lu leading the trio while Nnenna brought up the rear, with Pearl safely in the middle—all of their eyes peeled for any sign of danger. There were no signs of life here, other than them. Pearl wondered if they were the only living beings on the whole island. A few minutes later, the island seemed to provide an answer. The path opened up to a cluster of thatched-roof houses arranged in rows that curved toward the foot of the mountain. Hundreds of feet up, carved into the side of the rock, were gilded doors that, no doubt, led to a temple. Pearl's jaw dropped as she realized where she had seen almost this exact configuration of buildings before.

The mosaics on the walls of the temple had been one of the things she had loved most about attending service. She had loved the way each shining piece of shell had been beautiful on its own but created something breathtaking in cooperation with all the others. There were many mosaics to admire throughout the temple's many chambers, but the one she knew best was the one on the wall of her classroom. It depicted the village at Agwe's feet, homes of the most devout among His servants. In what would be one of his final sermons from the temple balcony, Viceroy Seastead had prophesied that this generation of children were chosen to live with Agwe within their lifetimes and that the best of them would reside at his feet. That was the day Pearl had decided to enter temple service and devote herself fully to Agwe.

Where her ancestors had lacked gold to show their devotion to Agwe, they had substituted the shiniest rocks and most colorful shells they could find to construct their facsimile of the temple they had lost. But the house of Agwe that Pearl had been brought up to revere paled in comparison to the temple she beheld. Its face was so smooth it reflected the stars as though their light were its own.

Nnenna and Lu went from house to house, peeking into the open windows to confirm that their presence was the only one in the area. Pearl stood in the grassy square before the temple and wondered if she had been brought here by chance or by destiny. Weeks ago, the answer would have been clear, but she could no longer find the girl who had prayed for this moment within herself. A heavy hand on her shoulder startled her.

"We need to set up camp," Lu signed to her.

Pearl nodded and followed him to the house he and Nnenna had agreed would make a suitable camp for now. It was small, only one room, but held enough beds for each of them to have their own. As Pearl crossed the threshold, she wondered what had happened to the family that had once inhabited this house. Which of the stories of her ancestors' steadfastness and devotion had they become? Their things were still here—cups and bowls carved out of wood with hunks of fruit still in them as though they had been plucked from their lives mid-meal and dropped into the sea. In the Settlement, they were revered, worshipped even, but never pitied for the fear they might have felt or the lives they might have lost. These mundane little items were all that was left of their real lives, and no one told any stories about them.

A tense silence grew between the three of them as they lay, exhausted, on their stiff palm-frond mattresses. Pearl's mind raced with questions she knew no one had the answers to. Why were they here? How had they gotten to this place? Was being here part of the prophecy, the great destiny promised to her people? Was it all real? Had her uncles been wrong all along?

Now that they were safe, there was nothing for them to do but wait. At some point, the events of the day caught up to her, and Pearl fell into an uneasy sleep. She dreamed about her Uncle Rain and the last time she had seen him, about how she had not had a chance to say goodbye. When she woke suddenly, calling his name, she had tears in her eyes.

"Darling girl," she heard his voice whisper on the wind.

But this place had no wind. She sat bolt upright and listened hard.

"Pearl," she heard him whisper again.

There was no mistaking his voice. Her Uncle Rain was somewhere on the island. She climbed out of the bed and tiptoed to the door, creeping past a sleeping Nnenna and Lu. They would be upset if they found her gone, but she could not miss this chance.

She followed the whisper back into the night to the temple square, followed it up the mountain trail, and soon found herself standing in front of a set of great double doors. He was inside, she knew it, but something stopped her from entering. It was just a building, she told herself, but sixteen years of teachings could not be undone in a few days. She was not ordained, had not completed the rites that would make her worthy to pass through the temple doors.

But then, she was the first of her people to step foot on this island, the first in generations to stand at these temple doors. How much more could worthiness require?

Pearl stepped toward the door and took its large wooden handle with one hand. She pulled once and felt the door give just slightly. With another hard tug, the door groaned as though she were disturbing its generations-long rest, and swung forward, revealing a denser darkness within. Swallowing her fear, Pearl stepped inside.

The open doorway laid a swath of starlight across an ornately patterned floor. All Pearl could see was a cavernous entrance and a gilded staircase that curved up the side wall to an upper floor that disappeared into darkness. Her options were the darkness ahead or the darkness above, so Pearl let her own curiosity decide. She remembered being told of the many rooms that the temple held and their purposes, but there was one room whose purpose was never explained beyond it being "where the viceroy communed with Agwe": the Divine Chamber. She had guessed it to be on the upper floor of the temple at the Settlement. That was where the viceroy had always made his entrance, so she assumed this temple's would be similar.

She climbed the stairs until she was entirely enveloped by darkness, then continued to climb until she reached a landing. With her arms outstretched, she ran her hands along the walls, feeling for a door. There was only one, in the center of the long hallway. Its knob was round and smooth and cool to the touch. She grabbed it and twisted hard.

Another loud groan echoed through the empty space as the door swung forward. Pearl expected more darkness, but this time, her eyes met starlight. For a moment, she thought she was looking through a window, but as she approached it, she saw no trace of the outdoors—no mountains, no beach, no trees, no houses—only stars floating in the center of the dark room, winking in a black so deep it pulsed against her eye.

"Pearl," Uncle Rain whispered once again, and all at once, she felt the same pull that she had felt on the beach. Whatever it was that had called to her from the water was calling to her now.

She advanced until she was close enough to the gap that she could hear other whispered voices coming through. Then, she raised a hand and pressed her palm against the void.

It felt like nothing until her fingers closed around something bright and pulsating that came free as though it were a fruit ready to be picked. Pearl pulled it out of the void and brought it close to her face.

"Pearl!" her uncle's voice called, louder and closer than she expected.

Startled, Pearl released the glowing orb, but it did not drop. It simply hung in the air.

"Uncle Rain?" she called to the orb.

As if this was what it had been waiting for, the orb pulsed, slowly, at first, then faster and faster, as it grew and stretched, morphing into the shape of a man. The light seemed to remain within him as he took the form that Pearl knew better than any other.

He was still tall and muscular, still light-skinned and sandy-haired, but his brown eyes held none of the life they once had.

"Uncle Rain," Pearl said again. Her voice came out small, full of the fear she'd held at bay since leaving him. If he was here, reaching out to her from the other side, then it was true that he was . . . that the viceroy had . . .

Fear gave way to anger as it surged within her, anger at the viceroy for taking her uncle from her, and anger at herself for not being able to do anything about it. Guilt followed swiftly as she realized she had not mourned him, had not returned him to the sea to ensure his eternity with the ancestors. But it was her longing that broke her. She had been cast out of her home, separated from everything she knew, thrown into a big, wild world. She had seen and done so much, but all she wanted, in this moment, was to return to the way things were. Whatever words she had for her uncle were drowned out by her sobs. Her knees buckled, and she felt Uncle Rain catch her in his strong arms to keep her on her feet.

"I'm sorry," she sobbed against his not-quite-warm chest. "I'm sorry. I'm sorry."

He held her and patted her on the back, cooing at her the way he had done when she had been a small child. A song bloomed between them, and Pearl sang through her tears, desperate for the harmonies she had missed in his absence.

"Darling girl," Uncle Rain said as he held Pearl at arm's length, his voice thick with astonishment. "You've come so far."

"What is this place?" Pearl asked, casting her eyes around the dark, empty chamber once again. "Are you . . . ?"

She did not have the heart to say the word, but her uncle understood and confirmed Pearl's worst fear with an apologetic smile. A fresh wave of tears overtook her.

"Don't cry for me, my darling girl. I gave my life to keep you safe. Knowing you are well has shown me that I did not die in vain." He took her by the chin and lifted her head so that she met his eye once again. "Thank you for this gift."

Pearl wiped her eyes and nose and tried to stand tall.

"This is where all souls come when their time in the world has come to an end. It has no name, though some of the older ones call it the Unknown. The goddess was once the keeper of the Gateway, but no one has seen her in an age."

"Why is our island here?" Pearl asked.

"The goddess brought it here to keep it from Agwe."

"You mean she is the devil who cursed us?"

"Yes . . . and no. What you read in the scripture is a lie. There is no devil. Only the goddess."

"I don't understand."

"I think she may be somewhere on the island," Uncle Rain said. "Find her and she'll be able to help you."

"Help me?" Pearl asked. "Help me do what?"

"That is for you to decide."

"But you're right here! Isn't there some way to bring you back? Without you or Uncle Wade, I don't know what to do!"

"Your intuition has brought you this far. Uncle Wade can—"

"Uncle Wade was captured," Pearl said. "The land-dweller guards took him. I don't even know if he's still . . ."

Pearl started to cry again.

“Hush now, darling girl,” Uncle Rain cooed. “No eye can see a path better than that of the one who walks it. Uncle Wade must follow the path he is on, and you must follow yours. I know it should have been me, but yours are the only shoulders left to bear this terrible burden. Find the goddess.”

Thirty-Six

NNENNA

Life on Captain Abernathy's ship was hell. Nnenna had thought her love of the sea would have conquered all hardship, but even the sea showed her cruelty from time to time. Every day, she worked until her hands were raw, until her fingers bled, until her bones cracked and her muscles ached. But she worked well. With Lu to spur her on, she rose quickly through the ranks, though not as quickly as Lu, and became a first lieutenant within a year of her partner.

She suspected Captain Abernathy had something to do with the delay in her promotion. Abernathy seemed entirely opposed to the ideas of justice and fairness, concerning himself more with amassing personal glory and wealth. He held a particular warmth toward Lu that did not extend to Nnenna or any of the other officers or crew on the ship. This did not surprise Nnenna. Lu came from wealth and power, no matter how ardently he worked to conceal it. What surprised Nnenna was how much Lu seemed to enjoy the captain's attention.

"He's not a good person, Lu," Nnenna urged one morning as they dressed in their shared cabin. "He only cares about himself and his favorites!"

"He's a captain of the Fleet," Lu countered. "He would not have been bestowed the honor if he did not deserve it."

Nnenna rolled her eyes. Somewhere along their journey together, Lu had become a true believer. He lost more of his ability to think for himself with every passing day.

Nnenna scoffed. "You're just blinded because you're one of his favorites."

"He doesn't have favorites."

"Then, how do you explain your being promoted over me when our performance has been evenly matched since our first days in the Fleet?"

"Perhaps . . . you've . . . gotten a bit . . ." Lu started.

"Don't you dare," Nnenna warned.

Lu held up his hands in defeat. They did not speak to each other much after that. In the days that followed, their ship lighted upon a small island that was thought to have been uninhabited, deep in the waters south of Kiskeya. A few hours' exploration led them to a small encampment of foreigners. They did not speak the language of the islands, a fact that seemed to personally offend Abernathy. When one of the foreigners approached him, a woman, clearly curious about the newly arrived strangers, Abernathy shot her. This spread panic among the others, who Nnenna quickly realized had no means of defending themselves, but Abernathy ordered the execution of every member of their group. Nnenna felt sick to her stomach watching her fellow officers kill one innocent person after another but found some solace in the fact that Lu did not take part in the massacre either.

"Something needs to be done," Nnenna whispered urgently that same night while she and Lu were inventorying the supplies.

"There's nothing to be done, Nnenna," Lu whispered back, shaken. He refused to look at her.

Nnenna said nothing in response. It was true that the Fleet's golden rule was loyalty, duty, and honor and that Abernathy's word was law aboard the ship, but Nnenna refused to believe there was nothing to be done about it. She loved Lu, but if he was not going to help her, she would have to look elsewhere.

It took weeks of keeping a quiet ear to the ground, but eventually, Nnenna heard whispers that echoed her own. She found others, members of the crew who, like her, believed that Abernathy must be stopped. They met in the dead of night, in the darkest parts of the ship, and formed a plan.

"This is treason!" Lu exclaimed after following her one night.

"He is a murderer who deserves to be tried for his crimes against humanity," Nnenna fired back.

"Please, Nnenna, you'll be killed! I don't want to lose you!"

"If you can stand idly by and allow that man to kill without hesitation, then you've already lost me."

Lu said nothing and left her to her mutiny. When the night of the revolt came, Nnenna and her crew of mutineers found Captain Abernathy ready and waiting. It was over before it truly began. Abernathy threw every last one of them into a large cell in the brig, while he and his inner circle deliberated their fate. Nnenna sat in her corner of the cell, wondering if any among their number would be spared.

•••●•••

Nnenna woke from the dream with a start. How long had she been asleep? She remembered lying down on the contraption of logs and fronds that passed for a bed and thinking she would rest for just a moment before continuing to explore. Then, like every other time she had closed her eyes of late, she relived her worst memories. She sighed.

"Are you all right?"

She sat straight up, her eyes scanning the dark little house for the source of the not-quite-familiar voice. They found Lu, sitting on his own bed on the other side of the room, staring at her. Nnenna could not tell if it was a trick of the darkness or if he had changed since their arrival on the island. She saw it in his face, mostly. His jaw was more square than she remembered, and the deep, soft rumble of his voice felt more relaxed.

"I'm fine," she said, swinging her legs off the bed.

"Where are you going?" Lu asked.

"To relieve myself," Nnenna lied. "You'll forgive me if I don't think it is any of your business."

"I'll come with you. You'll need a lookout," Lu replied seriously, making Nnenna feel suddenly very childish for her insolence.

"I think I can manage on my own."

"You and I checked the village for threats, but we don't know what's in the jungle. I'm assuming that is where you intend to, er, conduct your business."

Nnenna sighed. "Fine."

They left the little house together, walking back toward the jungle in a silence that crackled with five years of unspoken history. Nnenna felt herself wanting to slide back into the person she was when she was last with him, the memory of those days like a warm, comfortable bed calling her aching body to rest. Then she remembered her latest dream and held firm. If he wanted to talk, he would have to be the one to break the silence.

"This tree will do," Nnenna said, and before Lu could respond, she quickly tucked herself behind a palm tree whose trunk was wide enough to completely conceal her.

As she crouched behind the tree, feeling like a fool, she

endured several more seconds of awkward silence before Lu spoke again.

"If you don't mind my asking—"

"No need for such civility, Captain," Nnenna interjected. "I am just a pirate, after all."

When he did not continue, Nnenna worried that she had actually hurt his feelings. The Lu she had known would not have been so sensitive. Just when she was about to tell him so, he spoke.

"How did you survive?"

Nnenna froze. She had not expected him to mention their history again, even after his admission on the *Adoration*. Fleet officers did not simply abandon their devotion.

"Agwe saved me," she sneered.

She expected a retort but received only silence in response.

"I don't know," she said quietly, honestly. He did not press for more, but she kept talking, finally releasing the truth she, for years, had refused to acknowledge. "I remember going under, getting to the bottom with . . . the rest of them. Everything went black. I thought I had died, but, the next thing I knew, I was spitting up seawater on the deck of the *Medusa*."

"And that's how you fell in with the pirates?" he asked.

"Captain Delva offered to ferry me back to Ayiti, but I asked to stay on his ship, to join his crew. Make no mistake, Captain. I *chose* this life."

Nnenna did not care how her explanation was received. She declared herself sufficiently relieved and headed back to their camp without waiting for Lu to follow. As she reached the house and looked inside, she noticed Pearl's borrowed bed looked strangely empty.

"What is it?" Lu asked, stopping behind her.

Nnenna ran into the house, dropping to her knees before Pearl's bed and thrusting her hands into the blanket pile, searching and finding nothing. No one.

"She's gone!" Nnenna shouted, her fingers tangled in roughly woven fabric. "She must have gone to find the—"

"Nnenna, look!"

She got to her feet and ran through the doorway. Lu pointed toward the base of the mountain. When Nnenna looked, she saw a figure standing at the end of the trail.

"Pearl!" Nnenna ran to the girl and threw her arms around her. "Are you all right?"

But Pearl quickly disentangled herself from Nnenna's grasp. Confused, Nnenna followed Pearl's gaze to Lu.

"Captain, come," she called to him in her accented Seven Isles tongue as she waved Lu forward.

As soon as he arrived, she spoke in the Meridian language very fast, her hands flying.

"She says she was visited by the spirit of her uncle, who was killed by the leader of her people," Lu translated. "He told her the goddess is somewhere on this island and that we must find her to . . ."

He dropped off, but Nnenna did not need the captain to translate the last of Pearl's words. She may not have known all the signs of the Meridian people, but the language was as familiar to her as the language of the Seven Isles. Though she had not spoken it since she was a child in her father's arms, she had understood every word that Pearl had spoken since her voice had returned.

"We can't raise the island!" Nnenna said to Lu. "Your commodore is trying to use it and the Meridians to take over the world!"

Pearl began to speak and sign again, and Lu translated as quickly as her words flowed.

"She says her uncle told her the goddess will help us."

"The goddess is not even—"

Pearl put a hand on Nnenna's shoulder.

"Please, Nnenna," she begged in the land-dweller language. "My home. My people. Please."

Nnenna had not had an ounce of faith since she was a child. She had learned quickly that faith would not feed her or keep her warm. Pearl had been alone and scared, too, when Nnenna had found her, yet she had had so much faith that she had trusted a stranger. Nnenna could have been to Pearl what her own mother had been to her: a reason to rely only on herself. But the more time Nnenna had spent with the girl, the more she had realized she wanted Pearl to have more than she had. The more she had realized she wanted to be worthy of Pearl's trust.

"How do we find her?" Nnenna asked.

Pearl looked to the captain for translation, and when he signed what Nnenna had said, she sighed with relief and smiled.

"My uncle says the scriptures are not to be believed," Pearl said, "but there are a few verses about how the devil can always be found where the water is still because she is vain and likes to stare at her own reflection."

"Where can we find still water?" Nnenna asked. "We're on an island, for the seven's sake!"

"A puddle?" Lu suggested. Pearl looked at him, confused, and he continued signing as he spoke. "A puddle would be a perfect reflecting pool for a vain goddess."

Nnenna shook her head. "This place does not seem as though it has ever seen a drop of rain."

"Where do you think we'll find her, then?"

"I don't know." She turned to Pearl and signed, "What else do your scriptures say about her?"

Pearl frowned, concentrating. "She likes to hear herself sing," Pearl signed slowly. "She sits in her lair and sings, and when she does, her voice haunts Agwe's temple."

"Her lair is in Agwe's temple?" Nnenna asked.

"No," Pearl answered. "Agwe would never allow her entrance."

"Underneath," Lu said softly. Nnenna stared at him. "Agwe's temple is on this mountain. The goddess's lair could be . . . under it."

"You want us to do what? Dig under the mountain?"

"No, but there might be . . . caves."

Nnenna knew, as much as she hated it, that he was right.

"There are caves on the other side of the island," Nnenna said, remembering the image of the island she had seen in the basin. "We can get to them quickly if we follow the beach."

They left at once, trekking back to the beach and walking along the edge of the island until the sandy shore gave way to rocks. Long past when day should have broken, Nnenna searched the peculiar sky for any sign of a sunrise, but none ever came. Wherever this island lay, it was beyond the world she knew.

The trio followed the rocky path to where the face of the mountain nearly touched the water, leaving them with little space to maneuver. They fell into single file, the captain leading while Nnenna brought up the rear. The ocean, if one could even call the viscous-looking black matter that surrounded the island that, should have been roaring and raging against this side of the mountain. This calm disquieted her.

Eventually, the rocky face opened up to caves, into which the dark sea filled with twinkling lights ran. The moment she stepped foot inside, Nnenna felt a song rise in her heart. She heard its melody in her head for the first time in years and knew it at once.

"This way," Nnenna said quietly, taking the lead and following the song.

She expected the air to cool, but it remained the same, unmoving, unsettling, and barely distinguishable from her own body. The darkness made the cave walls feel as though they were pressing upon her. Hours passed, maybe even days, as she crept deeper and deeper into the belly of the cave, Pearl and Lu behind her, following a song that only she could hear. Just as she began to feel as though she had lost her mind, the narrow passage opened up, and there was light.

The song filled her ears now as she, Lu, and Pearl stood in a cavern lit by the twinkling lights of a pool in the center of the chamber. A woman sat at the edge.

She had white hair that spread in a large halo around her head. Her skin was dark, like clay-rich soil, and her arms graceful, though where her hips should have joined her waist, her torso transitioned into a long, winding, opalescent fish tail. She looked to be just beyond middle age, possessing enough wrinkles to show her wisdom, but leaving her time in the world to the imagination. She hummed the song as she gazed longingly at the pool of darkness and light.

"You're her," Nnenna said as she laid eyes on the mysterious woman.

It was not a question, but a confirmation of the feeling that slid into place the moment Nnenna entered the chamber. The woman did not move. Pearl stepped forward and fell to one knee while Lu stared, his shock written on his face.

"Wap bay manti," the woman said slowly in the same singing voice.

The Meridian tongue hit Nnenna's ears so smoothly, she did not notice that the woman was speaking words until Pearl raised her hands to translate.

"She says you're lying," Lu said to Nnenna, looking puzzled.

"We need your help," Nnenna said quickly, pushing past her confusion.

"Poukisa ou pa di yo kiyes ou ye?" the woman asked again, her voice lilting and sighing as though she were testing the melody on Nnenna's ears.

"She says you're not telling us who you are," came Lu's translation. "Nnenna, what is going on?"

"I—I don't know," Nnenna stammered.

The woman let out a single note like a sigh, and her tail transformed into a pair of long legs. She slowly rose to her feet, and as she stood, she seemed to put no weight upon the rocky ground. She stepped toward the trio, her dark brown eyes trained on Nnenna.

"Di yo kiyes ou ye, Nnenna," the woman said as she took step after step.

Before Nnenna could answer, the woman closed the gap between them and took Nnenna's hands in her own. The moment their skin made contact, Nnenna felt a pull in her mind. She gasped as a memory that had been locked away so long she had forgotten its existence burst free.

•••●•••

She sank into the ocean, tied to an anchor from the ship that she had once called her home. The darkness rushed toward her, swallowing her whole, and then she was still. She watched the others drown, one by one, until it was only her left. But she could not last forever. As her lungs screamed for air, she called out in her heart and in her mind for help.

The only answer she received was a song, one she knew as well as her own heartbeat from the hundreds of times her father had sung it to her when he had been alive. She thought her mind was singing her to her death, when she realized the melody was growing louder. Nnenna chanced opening her eyes once more, squinting through the darkness. Something was moving, swimming in graceful arcs and swirls toward her.

The something was a woman, dark-skinned and full-figured, but where she should have had hips and legs, she had a long, pearl-colored fish tail adorned with shining scales and long tendril-like fins. She approached Nnenna quickly, swimming circles around her and singing all the while.

Help, *Nnenna silently begged, pleading to this creature with her eyes.*

The fish woman regarded her with curiosity. Then, her brown eyes lit up, as though she recognized something in Nnenna.

Please, *Nnenna pleaded in her mind.* I'll do anything! Please!

"Ou gen san mwen," the fish woman said, her thick lips curling into a smile as she caressed Nnenna's cheek.

Without another word, she placed her hands on either side of Nnenna's head and took up singing her song again. This time, Nnenna heard every note as though it were coming from within her own body. In her shock, Nnenna released the breath she had been holding. She could not stop herself from inhaling again. Salt water rushed into her mouth, into her nose, into her lungs. It was an explosion of pain, burning hot and never-ending. Then, all at once, it was over.

•••••••

Nnenna screamed as the memory tore through her. She ripped her hands out of the goddess's and stepped back, nearly tripping over her own feet in her haste. Lu ran to her side, but she pushed him away.

"What the hell did you do to me?" Nnenna demanded, pointing at the goddess.

"I answered your prayers," she replied in the Seven Isles tongue, wearing the same smile she had at the bottom of the sea.

Thirty-Seven

LU

Lu had awoken that morning a captain of the Fleet on the verge of securing a great destiny. Now, he was lost. He had no name for this place—it existed on none of the maps, in none of the texts that he had studied. Yet, here he was in eternal darkness with a ghost from his past and a young girl he was bound by honor to protect. Lu should have been shaken. Instead, he had never felt steadier in his life. He was alive when he should not have been, and for the first time in his life, his body fit the shape he always knew himself to be in his heart.

He stood before the goddess and addressed her.

"Goddess, please," he said softly, his new voice rumbling out of his throat without effort. "We only want to make right the wrongs of the past."

She rounded on him, and Lu fought the urge to cower.

"What do you know of righting wrongs, Lu Ortega?" she demanded. "Are you not weighed down by guilt from wrongs past and present?"

He stopped short. "The sacred texts say that—"

The goddess tutted, waving away his explanation as though

it were a troublesome insect. She gestured toward Pearl. "This child is more worthy of my help than either of you!"

She bent to meet Pearl's eye and, with a sweet smile on her face, spoke to her.

"Pitit mwen, mwen konnen sa ou vle," she cooed.

Without Pearl's translation, Lu was at a loss. He looked to Nnenna for help, but she was staring at the goddess and the girl, utterly transfixed. Then, the goddess took Pearl by the hands, just as she had with Nnenna, and opened her mouth. A simple melody floated out, one that dipped and soared and played with the loose tendrils of memories from Lu's childhood. It was a lullaby, and though it was not meant for him, Lu felt its peace wash over him all the same. It was only as he watched Pearl's eyelids flutter that he realized he had to do something.

"Stop!" he called out, shaking the song out of his head. "Please!"

The goddess frowned. His shout was enough to break whatever spell she had over Pearl, and like Nnenna, she, too, wrenched her hands free of the goddess's grasp.

"Ede nou," Pearl pleaded, her hands making the signs that went along with her words. She was still begging the goddess for help.

The goddess stretched to her full height and regarded the trio as though they were her greatest disappointments.

"I know what you seek," she said in her lilting version of the Seven Isles tongue. For the first time, she signed as Pearl did, translating. "I cannot give it to you. As long as this island exists, Agwe will do whatever he must to bring it to your world. He has already manipulated himself into the minds of enough people that its destruction may not even be enough to stop him."

"How?" Lu asked. "The sacred texts say the island is the

source of his power. Without it, he should not be able to—"

The goddess laughed out loud. "Foolish boy! Your sacred texts say whatever Agwe needs them to say in order to make people believe. He is a god. It is not some rock that holds his power, it is the people's belief in him."

Lu's mind raced. "I don't understand . . ."

"What do your sacred texts say about me?" she asked of them, speaking and signing together. "Do they mention me? Do you even know my name?"

Lu felt exposed. He had studied all of the sacred texts of Agwe as a midshipman and a lieutenant. He knew them backward and forward. None of them mentioned any goddess. Only Agwe and . . .

"The devil," he said softly.

The goddess smiled wryly. "Maybe you are not so foolish, after all."

Pearl got to her feet, waving her hands to draw their attention. "The scriptures are lies," she signed. "My uncle told me so."

"What's the truth?" Lu asked the goddess.

She turned her head back and forth as though she were considering her options. "The truth," she finally said, "is lost to time. All we have left are our own versions of it. Agwe has been spreading his version of the truth for generations. What good will it do for you to hear mine?"

"We have the right to a choice," Nnenna said, sounding weak but resolute as she stood between him and Pearl. "Tell us what happened."

The goddess breathed in deeply and heaved a great sigh, looking at them with trepidation. It was the first human thing Lu recognized in her. Then, she spoke. "He and I are the last of our kind," she said slowly, "but, once, a long time ago, this island was full of beings like us. They called him Agwe and me Lasirenn. We all lived here together and worked the land in harmony. Agwe and I were guardians of the sea.

"Agwe loved me because I was beautiful, but he did not know that I was also as clever as he was. When our brothers and sisters grew restless with their work, it was I who went to our brother Damballa to ask for his skin and I who wove it into seven mortal beings, to toil in our stead. I gave Agwe five to give to our brothers and sisters and kept two in the sea.

"As time passed, I noticed that I grew stronger. We all did. My creations' devotion made our magic more potent. Their faith made us stronger so that we could live up to the love they shared with us. Agwe noticed this, too, and put himself in between the creations and my brothers and sisters, usurping the power that was rightfully theirs. My siblings eventually faded and passed through my gateway on their way to the Unknown, and soon it was just Agwe and me.

"He had forgotten about me and the two creations I had kept in the ocean. I created them to toil for the gods, but as I saw their potential, I grew to love them. Somewhere along the way, I became their mother. I wanted my children to have all of the gifts of divinity, so I shared everything I had with them, our stories, our customs, our magic.

"Agwe returned to the sea after an age, and when he saw what I had done, he became enraged. He sent an army of his most devoted to wipe my children from existence and, by doing so, pushed me into the Unknown.

"Fury burned within me, consumed my every fiber and turned my heart toward one purpose: revenge. I found him once again, sitting on his throne. He was eager to see the last obstacle in his path to greatness fade away like the others had. I could feel the power seeping out of my body as the Unknown called to me, but I held fast.

"'Your island will be lost!' I cursed him. 'Your people will be lost! *You* will be lost!'

"I pressed my palms to the floor of his temple and poured every last ounce of power I had into the island and its people. I bound the island to myself so that when I was pulled into the Unknown, it would come with me. I sent his most devoted back to the sea and cursed them never to be able to find their home and never to be able to use their voices on land.

"Then, I faded, just like my brothers and sisters had. I do not know where Agwe ended up, but I knew that this would greatly shake the faith of his followers and, thus, weaken him. I hoped that one day he would join me in the Unknown."

"But he never did," Lu said, quickly putting the pieces together. "Hiding the island was not enough to stop him."

She nodded solemnly. "I thought his story would turn from whispers to ash, and he would fade out of existence, but he found a way to bring it back."

"The fisherman!" Lu exclaimed, and Lasirenn nodded again.

"The fisherman?" Nnenna asked. "The one who started the Fleet?"

"Yes! Agwe saved him and promised him life eternal with his beloved if he spread Agwe's message. The fisherman agreed and, when he returned from the sea, he established the Fleet in Agwe's name!"

"Agwe needs this island," Lasirenn said. "He has been searching for it, through one means or another, for generations. If the island is raised, his followers will have more faith than ever and he will be restored. That is why I must destroy it."

"Destroy it?" Lu and Nnenna repeated together.

"What about the Meridians?" Lu asked. "What will happen to them?"

"Anything bound to the island will also be destroyed," Lasirenn answered with grim finality.

"That means you, too," Nnenna said.

She nodded, once more. "My love for my creations kept me from destroying them once. I cannot make the same mistake again."

Lu readied another argument, but Pearl waved her hands to catch his eye. Her signs came quickly as she glanced between him and Lasirenn.

"What is she saying?" Nnenna asked.

"She wants to know why the goddess didn't fade away like the other gods," Lu answered.

The goddess chuckled wearily, shaking her head. "My great weakness," she said.

Lu did not understand, but Pearl seemed to. Her hands moved again, signing her thoughts.

"Gods only fade into the Unknown when there is no one left to believe in them," he translated. "But people still believe in you. Whether they call you the devil or the goddess, whether they fear you or revere you, some part of you is still real to them." Lu turned to the goddess. "We can use that! We can make you powerful again."

"I have already tried," the goddess sighed.

"When?" Lu asked.

"When she saved my life," Nnenna answered quietly. Lu looked at Nnenna, confused. "You asked me how I survived the execution, and I didn't know. The truth is I didn't remember until now. She was there at the bottom of the sea. I asked her to save my life, and she told me the price would be to spread her story."

Nnenna looked directly at the goddess. "It worked for Agwe. Why shouldn't it work for you, as well? But you did not account for my losing my memory."

"I heard your call and, when I saw that you were of my blood, descended from one of my precious ones who had stayed true to me, I had hope for the first time in an age. And when you failed to live up to your promise . . ."

She trailed off, but Lu understood her silence. Pearl's hands moved again.

"It's not too late," Lu translated for her. "There are people among the Meridians who have doubts. My uncle was one of them and he had many supporters. He died, but, because of his work, I believe there will be ears to hear your story!"

"*I* can spread your story," Nnenna said. "Raise the island and *I* will turn the Meridians away from Agwe. They will be yours again and their belief will give you enough power to rival his."

"You used to have faith in your creations," Lu added quietly. "Believe in us as you believed in them."

The goddess's brow furrowed slightly as she considered their words.

"Enough," she answered. "I will not hear any more."

She extended her long-fingered hand toward the three of them. Lu felt something wrap around his body and wrench him out of existence itself. When he reemerged from nothingness, he stood on sand, looking out at an endless black sea full of twinkling white lights. He fell to his knees, frustrated.

"What do we do, now?" he asked no one in particular as he stared into the endless night.

There was no answer.

Thirty-Eight

NNENNA

Nnenna was numb. With no ideas for how to fix their situation, the three had agreed that returning to their makeshift camp would be better than sitting around on the beach. But when they arrived, they found as much nothing to do there as there had been at the shore. Nnenna lay on her palm-frond bed with the rickety wooden frame and pondered everything that had occurred. How long ago had she been celebrating the Devil of the Deep's greatest victory to date on Yamaye with her crew? The days that had passed since then felt like a lifetime, during which she had lost the parts of herself she had thought she had known best, jettisoning them like old cargo to satisfy a call that she still did not entirely understand. She had pulled others in with her and lost them as well. She thought of Tinou, her crew, Aline . . .

The invisible knife in her heart wrenched. Tears formed in the corners of her eyes. Someone shifted in the dark. Nnenna propped herself up to find Pearl rising from her bed and putting on her shoes.

"Mwen pral nan tanp lan," she said, not bothering to sign. Nnenna understood her and could relay the message to Lu if necessary. Before either of them could respond, she was gone.

Another knife twisted in Nnenna's heart. She had sworn to protect Pearl, had sworn to return her to her people, but instead had delivered her to her death. Perhaps it was better that she should spend the last of her time in a temple. What comfort could Nnenna offer her at this point? As she lay in silence, pain blossomed in her head, and her mouth grew even drier. She thought of her mother, still in Ayiti somewhere, and felt a pang of guilt for the pain she had caused every time she had tried to hide her mother's rum.

"Have you always spoken the Meridian language?" Lu asked from his bed.

"I don't speak it," Nnenna answered. "But I understand it. My father spoke it to me when I was a child. He said it was the language of the gods. I never knew what that meant until now."

"Why didn't you ever tell me?"

Because it was none of your damned business, she thought, but that was her headache speaking.

She sighed. "My father died and my mother refused to speak it after, so I thought it best to let it die with him."

They fell into silence.

After a time, Nnenna asked, "So, was becoming captain everything you hoped it would be?"

Lu scoffed in the dark. "Was it for you?" he asked in return.

They both chuckled ruefully.

"Nnenna, I wanted to say I'm—" Lu started.

"Don't—"

"Sorry," he finished weakly.

Nnenna sighed and rubbed her eyes, which did nothing to alleviate the growing pressure between them. These were likely the last moments of her life. Her expectations of either living long enough to bow out of a celebrated career, like Delva, or dying with a sword in her hand had evaporated. Instead, she was here, on a strange island without her ship, without her crew, and with only the man whose betrayal hurt worse than any wound for company. If she had her way, she would be on the beach with a bottle of whiskey further along in years than she now knew she would ever reach. But Lu had pulled the cork off a far more bitter drink and had poured Nnenna a glass she could not resist.

"Do you remember that night," she asked, "when we were lieutenants? The night before our first voyage at sea?"

"I do," Lu answered, flinching.

"If you told that version of yourself what you had become, do you think he would be proud?"

"Nnenna," he entreated.

Nnenna did not give him a chance to respond. She rolled out of bed and stood in the space between her bed and his. He moved as well, sitting up on the mattress and twisting his body over the side of the bed frame.

"I would be," she said. "I would be proud to tell my younger self how I lived."

"Proud of being a thief and a traitor?"

Her face contorted in disgust.

"Better a traitor to the Fleet than to our people," she spat and added, under her breath, "lachen."

Before Lu could speak another word, Nnenna strode out of the house and into the darkness. He caught her on her way to the beach.

"Nnenna!" he called after her.

She turned on her heel. He stood in the center of the narrow path, framed by bushes and trees. Shaking with rage to see him looking every bit of the Fleet captain he had promised to become, Nnenna marched up to him and jabbed her finger into his chest, hoping to crack the veneer.

"I know it was you who gave me up to Abernathy!" she accused, speaking aloud the fear she had held on to for years.

"I warned you it wasn't safe," he answered.

Something in Nnenna deflated as his words sank in. He had admitted it. He was defending it. She had expected him to deny his part in her death, but he had laid confirmation of her worst fears before her with a line—no doubt practiced—that placed the blame squarely upon her shoulders.

"Is that how you sleep at night knowing twelve people died because of you?" Nnenna asked through clenched teeth. "Knowing *I* died because of you? Doesn't that mean—"

"I didn't know Abernathy would—" Lu interjected, but Nnenna would not be silenced.

"You knew he was a monster! How many innocent people—"

"The laws state that mutineers are to be named traitors and—"

"So you would have seen me rot in a cell—"

"Abernathy was an exception, a rogue! He didn't represent—"

Nnenna laughed coldly. "How can you continue to be so naïve?" she asked with incredulous frustration.

"I didn't know—"

"Of course you didn't," Nnenna said, "yet those people still died! They were murdered to fulfill the Fleet's great—"

"I am not a bad person!"

"Then, why apologize if you've done nothing wrong?"

Lu released a shaky breath. "The Fleet accepted who I am when my own family wouldn't."

"Manou accepted you!" she shouted. "Mai accepted you! *I* accepted you! You continue to say you didn't know the Fleet's intentions, but the truth is that you did not look. You never look."

Her words hung in the air, and she stood, panting as she waited for his response. He breathed heavily, too, his fist clenching and unclenching in the way she had seen him do in the past when he needed to harness his emotions. Then, he broke. He collapsed to his knees in the soft dirt path, his face falling slack as his eyes shifted out of focus.

"I know," he said, not to Nnenna but to whatever vision in which he was lost. "I know. They're all dead and I'm to blame." Nnenna did not know what to say. His admission of guilt was what she had sought, yet he looked nothing like the villain who, for years, had occupied her every waking thought. She stayed rooted in her spot and waited for what she wanted from him. Her hatred for him burned, but it wrestled with her desire to hold him the way she had when they were younger. He did not stay away for long. After a few minutes, he regained focus, and he stared up at her.

"Nnenna, please," he implored, "I never meant to hurt you."

"I'm going back to the house," she said. "Don't follow me."

It would have to be enough that she would spend her last few moments finally free of him.

•••●•••

Nnenna had fallen asleep crying. She awoke when the strange, dark world began to rumble and shake around her. She buried her face in her palm-frond mattress as the roar grew to deafening. With her hands pressed against her ears to drown out the noise, she felt a song rise in her chest.

She knew the melody at once. It was an old song sung by the fisherfolk of Ayiti, begging safe passage of their goddess as they returned home from their journeys. Lu had taught it to Nnenna the night before their first voyage so many years ago. She had not sung it since the last time they were together aboard Abernathy's ship, but she had not forgotten a single word.

Nnenna breathed in deep and let her voice ring out, unheard over the din of the world collapsing around her. As she sang, she thought of Pearl and Tati Clo, of Rosalie and even Tinou, and prayed that they were all safe. She thought of Aline and prayed, with tears in her eyes, that she would find peace.

Then, the shaking stopped and there was light. Not as bright as day, but an eerie, undulating blue light that crept in through the opening of the hut. Nnenna got to her feet and ran through the doorway. She nearly tripped over something. When she looked down, Lu's body lay prone at her feet.

"Do you see that?" she asked Lu, forgetting, for a moment, all that had passed between them only hours ago. "Tell me you see that light."

"I see it," he answered, rising.

Nnenna immediately looked to find the source of the light, and her jaw fell open.

Where there should have been sky or, at least, the Unknown's endless sea of swirling white lights, there was an expanse of rippling shades of blue with which Nnenna was intimately familiar.

"What in the seven . . ." she whispered, gazing upward.

"Nnenna!" a voice called from afar.

Nnenna tore her eyes away from the water that encircled them to find Pearl standing at the end of the mountain trail. Smiling, Nnenna turned to her with open arms, and Pearl ran toward her, throwing herself into Nnenna's embrace.

"She didn't destroy the island!" Nnenna cried, not caring that Pearl could not understand her words.

"She's giving us a chance," Lu said in surprise as he ventured away from the hut, looking around at the world in disbelief.

He joined them, throwing his long arms around Nnenna and Pearl, and adding his laughter to theirs.

"Thank you," Nnenna whispered. "I won't let you down."

Nnenna broke away from the hug as a thought suddenly occurred to her. She touched both Lu's and Pearl's shoulders.

"Come with me," she said, before taking off into the jungle.

She followed the narrow path through the brush back to the beach, and as soon as she exited the canopy, she craned her neck upward and gazed at the sight above. It was as though the island were encircled by a bubble that held the waters at bay. Where the waves should have been lapping at the shore, there was a wall of ocean.

"We're rising," Lu said from behind her.

It was true. Even in the few seconds that they stood on the beach, Nnenna noticed the island getting closer and closer to the surface.

"Nou pa gen tan," Pearl said.

Lu looked to Nnenna for a translation.

"We don't have time," Nnenna answered. "She's right. I need to get to the Meridians before we get to the surface."

Pearl stepped forward. "I know where the Settlement is," Pearl signed. "I can lead you there."

Nnenna had no choice but to accept the assistance. Pearl approached the wall of water, and the girl pressed the palm of her hand against it, but it was as though a pane of glass separated her from the water. She pulled her hand back and examined it.

"I can't," she muttered in accented Seven Isles tongue. She raised her hands to sign. "It has to be you, Nnenna. You are Lasirenn's herald. You must be able to get through."

Nnenna wanted to question her, but something small inside

her knew Pearl was right. Lasirenn had chosen Nnenna. Nnenna had made the goddess a promise in exchange for her freedom. She stepped forward, stopping so close to the wall she could feel its coolness wafting toward her, and a song suddenly bloomed in her heart. Her father sang it to her first, his voice low and strong. Then, she heard herself singing as a child, her voice joyful and high. They sang together, and when the memory drifted, Nnenna picked up the melody as she stood before the wall of water.

She brought her hand to the wall as she sang, and the water rippled where she touched it, its moisture coating her palm. Her hand came away wet. Still singing, she brought her hand up to the wall of water again and pushed against it. It gave at once, and she found herself submerged in water up to her wrist.

"By the seven . . ." she muttered to herself.

Shapes appeared in the distance. At first, Nnenna thought they were fish, but it was Pearl who recognized them for who they were. She ran to the barrier, pressed herself against it, smiling.

"Yo la!" she exclaimed.

"They're here," Nnenna echoed.

They approached by the hundreds, perhaps even a thousand—their sleek brown skin glistening in the dim light from above. They were men, women, and children, dressed in worn clothing of bygone ages. Some carried weapons—long spears tipped with golden blades. The rest were unarmed.

Determined, Nnenna found the song in her heart once again. She sang louder, this time, her mind on the people who depended on her to return to their lost home. The wall yielded to her touch once again. This time, she did not stop. She pushed forward, letting the water envelop her completely until she was on the other side. The water took her in, lifted her, and held her aloft for all to see.

She kept singing, and as her voice rang out, the vibrations

through the water reverberated throughout her body, and she felt the first touch of magic take hold. Her skin tingled as it changed from soft, dark brown to sleek and smooth. The bones in her legs lengthened, and she scrambled to free herself from the clothing that impeded them. Once free of her trousers and small clothes, her legs became bound by magic. They melded together into one long, winding tail that ended in a wide, flat fin. Scales sprouted from her hips to the end of the tail—red, white, and blue, shimmering and opalescent.

Nnenna should have felt strange in this new body, but it felt more like home than the body in which she had grown. She swam around the ocean, flicking her tail this way and that to propel her in any direction she wanted. And she sang! Oh, how she sang! Beautiful, joyful songs burst from her as she darted in and out of the crowd of Meridians, drawing their attention. When she had them corralled to a single area, she swam upward until the quickly approaching light framed her from behind.

"People of Meridia, please listen!" she said in the Seven Isles tongue.

Their eyes followed her voice, but they looked up at her with confusion.

Of course, she thought, *they don't understand me.*

She looked to Pearl and Lu on the other side of the barrier, obscured by the shimmering magic, and decided she was on her own. She set aside her discomfort with the Meridian language and thought of the story the goddess told.

"For generations, you have believed that you have been brought here by Agwe's will," she started, the foreign syllables tumbling awkwardly from her inexperienced lips. "In truth, you were brought here by the devil. But she is no devil. She is kind and clever and she has been stripped of her power."

As she spoke, Nnenna felt herself rising toward the surface with the island. She spoke faster.

"It is true that the goddess cursed your people generations ago, but she has returned your home. She is your true creator. Choose her over Agwe."

"Who is this stranger who claims to know the will of the gods?" a voice called from the crowd. A muscular man with a shining bald head who carried a golden spear swam forward. "Another usurper?"

"I am not—"

"I have been Agwe's servant my entire life, waiting for the day He finally decides we are worthy to return to our home. Why should I, on the day that my blessing has finally come, forsake the god who protected us for generations?"

"Protected you from what?" Nnenna snapped. "From what threats did Agwe keep you safe?"

The man came up short.

"And why exactly does a god who claims to love you require your worthiness to return to your own home?"

Anger flared in Nnenna's heart as she thought of her upbringing in the Fleet, of being told again and again that everything good she earned was owed to Agwe and everything gone wrong was a measure of how she failed to meet Agwe's standards.

"I am no one," she said to the man directly. "I have no home, no renown, no loyalty to the god you call your Lord. Yet, I was chosen by the goddess, Lasirenn, to bring her word to you."

"And what is this word?" the man asked.

Nnenna thought quickly. The water had already grown warmer as they ascended to the surface. She saw herself reflected on the face of the protective bubble that surrounded the island, saw her long tail and her shining brown skin. But her hair was different, a halo of white framing her face. She swam closer to the bubble and saw that it was not her own image she was looking at.

"Lasirenn," Nnenna called to the goddess. She looked back at the crowd of angry Meridians and her heart sank. "I'm sorry. I failed."

Lasirenn's face fell. "I lost my faith in them long ago," she admitted. "It is too much to expect them to put their faith in me, now. But they are still my children and I have put them through enough. Tell them . . ." The goddess thought for a moment, glancing over Nnenna's shoulder at the Meridians. "Tell them I will spare them from the curse. They need only step foot on the island and they will be safe."

Nnenna wanted to offer the goddess something but knew of nothing that could compare to Lasirenn's sacrifice. Instead, she did as she was told.

"I know there are some among your number who have doubts!" Nnenna called quickly. "Come to the island! The goddess offers protection from the curse that would rob you of your voices and asks for nothing in return."

The bald man puffed out his chest and struck it with his fist. "Lies! Your goddess has no power here. Agwe will save us from the curse. You seek only to trick us into doubt!"

Nnenna huffed and swam back to the barrier between the ocean and the island, placing both hands upon it. She had hoped to see Lasirenn again, but the goddess was gone.

Tell me what to sing, she begged the goddess silently.

The song bloomed in her heart at once. This time, she let the notes pour forth from her lips. They surrounded her and the Meridian people, but most importantly, they coated the barrier from where Nnenna's hands touched it. The whole thing rippled, and Nnenna knew the barrier could now be penetrated.

"Go, now," she said in Meridian, "before we reach the surface!"

The man held his place, crossing his arms over his chest. Suddenly, a Meridian woman shot past him. She swam to where the wall of water met the sand and glided through the barrier. As she did so, her body transformed, and she stood on her two feet upon the sand. More followed her, trickling from the crowd and lining up along the border around the island. One by one, they pushed through, their bodies changing, their faces showing no signs of pain.

The crowd was half as strong as it had been when the stream of Meridians stopped. Nnenna looked up and saw that the mountain's peak was reaching for the surface.

"We are almost out of time!" she pleaded. "I cannot hold this any longer."

More seconds passed, but none of the remaining Meridians moved. With a final look at the crowd, Nnenna pushed through the barrier and let it become impassable behind her. As the island rose to take its place on the surface, the man with the spear stared defiantly at Nnenna through the wall of water.

"Agwe, be with me!" he cried.

He shot upward, and those Meridians who had chosen Agwe followed.

Thirty-Nine

THE FISHERMAN

When the fisherman failed to arrive at port with his catch on the same day of his disappearance, the other fisherfolk thought nothing of his absence.

"He is old," they told themselves. "He deserves to rest a day if he needs it."

Another day passed, and no one saw him. Now, they began to worry, for it was not like him to miss his weekly visit to the bakery.

"Perhaps he is entertaining his family," the fisherfolk said.

When he did not reappear after the third day, a few of them gathered at his home. They found it empty, his bed unmade, his cooking fire cold for days. When they ventured to the beach, they found the shattered remnants of his fishing boat, sail torn, mast broken, lying on its side half buried in the sand.

"He must have been taken by the sea," they said as they watched the waves lap at the shore.

They gathered around the remains of his fishing boat and joined their voices together in the song that would help his soul find its way to its home in the sea. As they sang, the water just beyond the reef began to bubble and roil, interrupting their song. A figure soon emerged from the waters. They recognized him at once as their lost comrade, but when they went to greet him, they saw something different in his eyes. Where they had once been the earthen brown of the fisherfolk, they were now as green as the weeds that grew along the sea floor.

"I have seen him!" the fisherman said as he fell into the arms of his nearest neighbor. "I have seen Agwe, the great God of the Sea!"

The fisherfolk looked among each other in confusion, for Agwe was a god whose name was nearly lost to time, spoken of only among small pockets of their people.

"Agwe has shown me the way!" the fisherman rambled on. "I must spread His word!"

The fisherfolk assumed him mad with shock, having been lost at sea for three days. They forced him to rest, to eat, to regain his strength and his sense, but even after he recuperated, his mind remained set on one task: spreading Agwe's word. The fisherfolk took turns watching over the fisherman, and as they came through his door and spent time in his house, he bent their ears, telling them the story of Agwe's rise to power and His greatest loss.

"He was the first of Bondye's creations and the only inhabitant of the island that floated above the passageway to the Unknown. Every day, Agwe worked, tending to the needs of the land and the sea, and every night when He went to sleep, He found his work undone. Agwe was a dutiful son of Bondye, so every morning, He began his work anew. One day, He became frustrated with his lack of progress and so, rather than retiring, He stayed awake and hid among the large-leafed plants that covered the island at the foot of the mountain. What He saw amazed him. Bondye had made another creature, a devil that lived in the sea and crawled out each night to undo the work He had done. He stepped out from behind the large-leafed plant and commanded the devil to stop at once, but the moment the devil laid eyes upon Agwe, she transformed into a beautiful woman. Agwe had never seen a woman before and thus fell easily to her charms. As they lay together under the stars, she whispered in His ear how she wished all their days and nights could be like this. When the sun rose, Agwe set His mind to a new task: fulfilling the devil's wish, for He was not only hardworking and steadfast, but clever and crafty as well. He cobbled together some driftwood and stones, shells and seaweed, and breathed life into them until a creature much like Himself stood before Him. It had none of His power, but it could walk and speak and work just like Agwe did.

"'This is the way!' Agwe exclaimed.

"For three days, Agwe did nothing but make more and more of these creatures He called His followers, for they followed wherever He went and performed whatever task He asked of them. When the island was full of His followers, He invited the devil to look upon His work, proud that He had found a way to be with her, but when she saw the fruits of His labors, she became enraged with jealousy. She cursed Agwe, the island, and His followers so that they would be lost to each other for all eternity. But, as He succumbed to the devil's curse, He released but a single prayer: that His people would be protected while they searched for a way to return to their home. His prayer became a prophecy and now it is our sacred duty to see it realized."

The fisherfolk who had seen the fisherman emerge from the sea were taken with this tale and wanted to learn more of Agwe's ways. The fisherman was happy to oblige, for Agwe Himself had shown him what he needed to do in order to restore Agwe to power and be forever welcome in Agwe's kingdom. Together, they created an enclave of their own, meeting at the fisherman's shack to hear the word of Agwe until the day came when they named themselves the Fleet, for how swiftly they would spread Agwe's word throughout the world.

It started in their very village. They took in the lost ones and gave them homes and fed them with not only food but Agwe's word. Soon, they grew from the seaside shack to build a mountaintop fortress called the Citadel. The fisherman named himself the commodore, the head of the organization. The fisherfolk whom he trusted most became his captains. Then, he told of Agwe's sacred conch, lost among a sea full of imitations, of the seven singers of the devil's blood, and of Agwe's faithful, hidden in the depths of the sea under His protection until the day they were able to return to their home. Those they brought into the Fleet and taught the word were their lieutenants and midshipmen.

The first vessels they used to venture out into the world were humble fishing boats, but, like Agwe, the early members of the Fleet were hardworking and steadfast, clever and crafty. They built more ships, bigger and better, all in Agwe's name. The Fleet grew as well, taking in any and all who would hear Agwe's word and swear to devote their lives to spreading it.

Eventually, the commodore's body grew weak in its old age, but as he lay dying, he called his most ardent captain into his bedchamber to perform the ceremony that would leave the captain in charge of the Fleet in the fisherman's absence. The two men clasped each other by the wrist, brought their faces so close that the bridges of their noses ran against each other, and sang the sacred song that was Agwe's prayer for His people's salvation. Those who were there said they saw the spirit of the commodore leave his body and pass into the captain's, and those who saw the new commodore emerge said he did so with the fisherman's green eyes.

And so it became the way of the Fleet to pass on the care of the organization from one commodore to the next. Then Captain Henri Christophe was summoned to the dying commodore's bedchamber in the middle of the night. He had been certain it would be Abernathy, his rival, but when the time came to make the call, it was Christophe's name upon his predecessor's lips.

Christophe pushed through the door, apprehensive as always, but ever faithful in the ways of his Lord. His predecessor looked to be at death's door already. Christophe knelt quickly by the man's bedside.

"You seek to lead," the commodore said weakly.

"Yes, sir," Christophe said, too frightened to speak above a whisper.

"What will you give?" the commodore asked.

Christophe had been brought up on the stories of the fisherman who became the first commodore. He knew exactly what was required of him at this moment. "Anything," he vowed, making the same promise that every commodore before him had made. "Everything."

The commodore sat up and rose from the bed. He cupped Christophe's face in his hands and beckoned him onto his feet. The commodore brought Christophe's face to his own, staring hard into the man's brown eyes, which grew wider and wider until the gap between their foreheads closed. The commodore sang Agwe's prayer, and Christophe joined him. As their voices echoed throughout the commodore's bedchamber, the room filled with light.

"Agwe, be with me!" Christophe cried as something powerful forced itself into the empty spaces of his mind, body, and soul.

Forty

THE COMMODORE

Patience had always eluded the one true God of the Sea. He had many strengths, but even before his cursed state, he recognized in himself that waiting was not among them. What use did he have for learning to wait when he had the power to bring his every whim to fruition? He had lived in paradise, had possessed the cleverest mind of his divine brothers and sisters, had commanded the affection of the most beautiful among them. It had not been until he was reduced to this wretched state, forced to possess other creatures to stave off being pulled into the Unknown, until he was truly tested, that he understood the value of lying in wait.

Agwe felt the island's presence the moment it returned to this world. When the roiling, whirling sea that threatened to consume or destroy, all at once, calmed, and the gray clouds that blanketed the sky evaporated into mist, chased by thick bars of golden light, the god knew that his home was near, drawing closer with every second that passed. He abandoned all pretense of being Commodore Henri Christophe and ran from one side of the ship to another, from one end to the other, looking for a sign, any sign, that what he had worked toward for generations would come.

An age seemed to pass as he stared into the water, his mortal heart thudding in his throat, anticipation tingling in every inch of flesh in this body he possessed. It finally happened. He blinked salty air from his eyes, and a bulge in the water appeared at the center of the Gateway, like a bubble, only larger than life and growing every second. It emerged from the inky-black depths with a speed that could only be attributed to the divine, water clinging to its sides and obscuring what it held within. The globe shimmered as the sun shone upon it, casting colorful arcs this way and that. When it reached its midway point, making a perfect half globe upon the water's surface, it stopped and Agwe held his breath.

Then two things happened at once. Whatever magic that held the curtain of water aloft broke, and the water that once formed the sides of the dome fell, revealing a mighty mountain, rolling hills, cliffs, forests, jungles, rivers, lakes, and streams, an entire island that had not seen the sun in generations. As Agwe gazed upon the wonder, he suddenly discovered something within himself that had also been lost for generations: power.

He felt it grow within him the way cutting a tourniquet loose allowed blood to rush into a dying limb. Elated, he clutched the railing of the ship as the power filled him anew.

"This is magnificent, Commodore!" Captain Boyer, who followed him to witness the island's unveiling, exclaimed.

Agwe twisted Henri Christophe's face into a smile as he turned his mortal shell toward the captain.

"Magnificent indeed," he answered, his eyes glowing green.

The young man had been smiling when he had spoken to the commodore, and it pleased Agwe greatly to watch his smile melt into a look of terror as he recognized that it was not the commodore who spoke back to him. Boyer turned to flee but tripped over his own feet and fell onto his backside. Agwe nearly laughed out loud. The captain pushed himself away from Agwe, scrambling backward on the planks. Agwe closed the distance with a thought, disappearing and reappearing behind him. He grabbed Boyer by the collar, lifting him with a single arm as Boyer screamed and struggled.

"Blessed are you, my child," he said softly. "For you shall be the first to experience my power."

He stretched his free arm out toward the water, calling to the sea with the authority he had waited generations to wield once more. Three tendrils of salt water answered his call, snaking up the side of the ship and over the railing, slithering toward their master and giddily twisting around his feet. They wound up his legs and back and draped themselves over his shoulders.

He gave a silent command, and the undulating tendrils whispered up his arm to wrap around Boyer. One around his ankles to stop him from running, one around his wrist to stop him from intervening, and one around his nose and mouth to stop him from breathing.

Agwe released Boyer, and his body thudded to the deck, jerking and writhing as he tried to free himself. His movements quickened to a frenzy as, desperate for air, he fought against the magic, but none of his training had prepared him for this. Agwe watched Boyer's mouth open as a final gasp racked through him, sucking the water into his body until the tendrils were out of sight. He fought them for a few moments more. Then, his body went still.

Agwe waited with bated breath. He had not used this magic since his short-lived triumph over the sea witch. He watched

Boyer lie there on the deck, appearing dead. Then, the man's hand twitched. He uttered a loud gasp as his back arched and his eyes flew open, glowing as blue as the water that had transformed him.

"Rise, my child!" Agwe called to Boyer.

The captain obeyed, climbing to his feet. He stared at his hands, flexing his fingers as his veins glowed bright blue under his light brown skin.

"What . . . am I?" Boyer asked.

"Blessed," Agwe replied.

He called Captain Toussaint forward and blessed her as he had done Boyer. As he turned to address the people on the ship's deck, the female lieutenant who had been the commodore's secretary—Ambroise—pushed her way forward and fell to her knees at his feet.

"Please," she begged, "bless me as well, my Lord. I have served you faithfully and can do as much as any of these captains."

Agwe smiled, amused by her ambition. He called upon the sea to change her as well. With his three blessed soldiers at his side, Agwe turned to the rest of the Fleet on the deck.

"We have done it! The day of our destiny is upon us!" he announced.

Another among their number stepped forward.

"My Lord, I should have known!" Viceroy Stormcoast apologized, using the gods' signs as he bowed his head.

Agwe smiled, beckoned Stormcoast to him, and forced him to meet his eye. He was positively tickled by the strange combination of fear and devotion radiating from Stormcoast in alternating waves. "My most devoted, you shall remain at my side from now into the eternities," Agwe promised in the Meridian tongue.

Agwe turned to the rest of the onlookers, his hand clasped upon the viceroy's shoulder.

"When you wonder what your devotion should look like, measure yourself to the standard of this servant," he proclaimed, not bothering to use the island tongue anymore, but instead blessing them with the ability to understand his every word. There would no longer be any separation among the people of his kingdom. All would worship him equally, or they would perish.

Agwe raised his hands to the sky and took hold of the sea once more, using his full might to bid the waters surrounding the *Adoration* to swell and carry the ship toward his waiting home. Drawn by waves, the ship crashed against the shore, scraping up mounds of sand on either side of the hull. Its progress came to a halt at the tree line, and while the inhabitants of the deck struggled to stay on their feet, Agwe stood firm.

"Come," the god said to his faithful servants, "there is much work to be done."

On the orders of their god, the mortals on the *Adoration* quickly disembarked, scuttling down the ship's sides using ropes and ladders to reach the sandy shore below.

"Gather around, my blessed ones and my most devoted!" Agwe called. "We descend!"

"My Lord," Stormcoast signed, "permit me to bring Brinebottom, as well."

"Who?"

"Brinebottom, my Lord," Stormcoast repeated. He gestured to a squat Meridian dressed as a lieutenant. "He is . . . Pearl's uncle. I need him for leverage."

It was not until Stormcoast mentioned Pearl that Agwe remembered. "Ah, yes, the girl. Bring him, if you must."

Two of the blessed brought Brinebottom to the group, and

Stormcoast clamped his hand around the man's arm. Upon Agwe's word, they all disappeared between the seams of the fabric of reality, reappearing where the jungle met the beach.

Agwe reached down and grabbed a handful of sand. At the height of his power, he had commanded the land, the sea, and the very air between. He positioned himself before the dense jungle.

"Witness the might of your god," he declared to the others.

He drew in a breath, held the sand before his face, and blew it toward the lush green plants. In days past, they would have cleared out of his way, leaving a path for him, but they barely trembled. He tried again, dropping to one knee and thrusting his fist into the sand. The plants remained in place.

He let out a short burst of air through his nose as anger burned in his chest. Stormcoast and the blessed said nothing. Agwe took off down the beach, and the others trailed behind him. He rounded a rocky outcropping and stopped short when he found himself met by a throng of people. Hundreds of people, old and young, wandered the beach, dressed in clothes worn by time and seawater. He knew them! They were the descendants of his most devoted servants from long ago! But where were the rest of them?

He walked among them and noticed they could not speak. They used the gods' signs to communicate with each other.

"My beloved children!" Agwe called in the Meridian tongue. "Your god has arrived!"

Many looked in his direction, and when they saw how his green eyes shone like jewels in the sunlight, they were overcome with joy. Their hands moved quickly.

"Heal us!" they pleaded silently. "Heal us!"

Agwe thought of the sand he had blown at the jungle plants and craned his neck uncomfortably.

"Surely the great people of Meridia have not been reduced to this? Where are the rest of your numbers?"

A bald man carrying a spear stepped forward. Agwe recognized him as Stormcoast's second-in-command. He looked at Agwe and Stormcoast, thumped a fist over his heart, and fell to one knee.

"My Lord, they abandoned us," Marshwind signed. "They chose to follow the herald of the goddess."

Agwe's jaw clenched. "We must retrieve them!" he said, not only to Marshwind but to all the Meridians. "When our people are unified once more, I will bless you all!"

He turned back to Marshwind.

"Where did they go?"

"To your temple, my Lord," Marshwind answered with his hands.

Agwe smiled. "Then, let us find them and give them the greatest of welcomes."

Forty-One

NNENNA

Agwe's temple was built into the side of the island's only mountain. From afar, it shone like a jewel set in stone. Nnenna led the company up the narrow, rocky path that snaked through the thick trees and shrubs that grew on the mountainside. She tried not to think about the hundreds of people following her and trusting her for reasons she did not understand. When she was not panicking about her newfound stewardship, her mind drifted back to her time in the sea while the island had risen.

Nothing like the magic she had seen had ever happened when she sang before.

"Ou gen san mwen," Lasirenn had said. *"You have my blood."*

The goddess was divine. What did it mean to carry the blood of the divine?

Nothing, she hoped. *I am helping Pearl and the Meridians with this small problem and then the goddess can have this island. I am getting out of here.*

"Where are you going?" Lu asked, pulling up beside her and startling her out of her thoughts.

"What?"

"You were muttering. You said you were getting out of here."

"Does the Fleet teach eavesdropping, now?"

"I'm . . . sorry . . ." he answered.

Nnenna was surprised that she could still read him so well after so many years apart. His sober tone told her that this apology was for more than the eavesdropping. It was an offering, an invitation to continue a conversation that she was too embittered to believe would do anything more than assuage his guilt. She had thought she had let go of the hatred she felt toward him—she had stopped imagining his face on every Fleet officer she cut down, had given up on wishing misfortune upon him the way believers sought blessings from their gods. He had admitted his wrongdoing and wanted her forgiveness, but she was no benevolent goddess. Denying him his redemption was a bitter fruit upon which she would feast until the day she died.

She stopped and turned to him, staring directly into his eyes, her ire written all over her face.

"I am glad you've found your way to remorse," she said, "but that doesn't erase what your cowardice has put me through."

"If I could go back—"

"I don't care."

The first dozen or so of the procession of Meridians had stopped and gathered around Nnenna and Lu. Pearl was among them. Her curiosity made Nnenna suddenly self-conscious.

"Are you all right?" Pearl asked her, speaking the language of the Seven Isles rather than her own.

"We have to keep going," Nnenna answered.

She walked on, looking at neither Lu nor Pearl. When the company arrived at the temple doors, Nnenna climbed the handful of steps, taking in none of the beautiful statues that decorated the temple's entrance, and pulled on one of the doors' long wooden handles. She had expected some resistance, but the heavy door opened immediately, swinging slowly toward her. When it could go no farther, she held it open and stood guard while the company passed through the entrance.

"We should be safe here," she said, pulling the door closed behind the last of the Meridians.

Nnenna had not considered the size of the space when she thought to lead the Meridians here; she assumed it would be cramped, but as she looked around, she realized the temple was not simply built into the mountain. The temple was the mountain. Entire buildings could have easily fit inside the cavernous atrium. Its walls were covered in iridescent shells that caught the light streaming through embrasures cut into the stone, with golden stairs leading to unseen rooms.

At the far side of the atrium, a golden throne sat atop a stone dais. The Meridians all huddled near it. Nnenna searched their faces, saw their discomfort as she walked through the crowd. This was the temple of the god they had forsaken. Even Pearl looked disquieted, though she was surrounded by her community from the sea. Nnenna flashed the girl a reassuring smile. She cut a straight line through the center of the group and climbed the stairs, standing directly before the empty throne.

"People of Meridia," she called in the Meridian tongue. "I thank you for your trust. Agwe is not the benevolent god you were taught to believe in."

"I suppose you would have them worship your goddess, instead?" said a chiding voice from behind her.

Nnenna whirled around, nearly slipping from the top step of the platform. The throne was now occupied. The commodore sat in the golden seat, dressed in the Fleet's green and gold, looking as though this was what he had been born to do. His poison-green eyes flashed, and a smug smile crept across his face at Nnenna's disbelief.

"You are . . ." Nnenna started but did not know what to call the man as several pieces of a puzzle fell into place.

"Liberated?" the commodore supplied, rising to his feet. "Unleashed?"

Nnenna looked around the temple atrium at the faces in the crowd. More people had appeared with the commodore: three captains with glowing blue eyes, the leader of the Meridians, and the other curly-haired man whom Nnenna recognized from the *Adoration.*

They stood in a line at the bottom of the steps.

"Wait—" She whirled back toward the commodore, but the word was barely out of her mouth before he reached for her. Nnenna gasped and stepped back, missing the next stair. She fell, arms outstretched, and a strong hand clasped around her wrist, keeping her upright.

"Nnenna!" Lu called from somewhere in the atrium behind her.

"Lu, don't—"

"No!" he screamed, and she knew that he was caught.

"Bring him to me," the commodore said, tugging Nnenna in and twisting her around to face the crowd, her arm wrenched behind her back. "The girl as well. I want my people to see what happens to those who try to oppose destiny!"

A flurry of movement disturbed the crowd as the captains searched for Pearl. A group of Meridians standing against the stone walls tried to conceal her, but there was no place to hide in the open atrium. When the captains approached, the group tried their best to fight. One of the captains swung his fist into a Meridian, sending him flying. The other captain moved so fast

Nnenna only saw a blur that took Pearl by the arm and dragged her to the platform.

The third captain came up the stone steps and took the commodore's place holding Nnenna. Together, she, Pearl, and Lu made a perfect spectacle. Nnenna's heart thudded in her chest as she realized she had been in this position before, paraded before a company of the righteous, judged, and found wanting.

Not them, she thought desperately. *Take me, but not them.*

"My people, hear me now!" the commodore pronounced as he stood above them. Nnenna felt an uncomfortable tingle in her ear as his voice invaded her mind, speaking somehow in both the Meridian and Seven Isles tongues. "These three interlopers would be your downfall! Dangerous though they may all be, there is one among them who would do your souls irreparable harm."

He stepped carefully around Nnenna to Pearl at the center, reached out to caress her cheek, then laughed when she flinched out of his touch.

"A child will believe anything she is told and so can be forgiven if she would repent and choose the correct path."

He walked over to Lu and raised a hand, not to Lu's face, but to his own. A salute that made Lu snarl.

"A faithful son turned traitor, too, can be offered forgiveness, if only from the one he betrayed." Nnenna turned her head to catch Lu's eye and found him already looking at her. She knew she was next, knew that she would not be spared. How could she tell him everything that was in her heart, everything her pride had kept her from revealing?

"But a false prophet . . ." the commodore said slowly, dangerously, "must be punished."

In a flash of gold, the dagger appeared in the commodore's hand and he gently, lovingly clapped his empty hand upon Lu's shoulder. Nnenna saw understanding dawn on Lu's face. "Nnenna, I—" he started, just as the commodore buried the blade deep into his belly, under his rib cage, and through his beating heart.

Nnenna screamed before she even understood what had happened. She called his name as though her summoning could save his life, but Lu's face became a shifting mask of surprise and anguish. When the commodore removed the dagger, Lu's eyes emptied of the light Nnenna had forgotten how to appreciate, and his body fell limp in the arms of his captor. She released him, and he dropped, unceremoniously rolling down the stone steps to the bottom, his arms and legs bent at odd angles.

A scuffle at the base of the steps drew her captor's attention. Nnenna struggled against his hold and broke free. Blinded by her tears, she ran at the green-and-gold blur in front of her, knowing the senselessness of fighting him, but if she could just provoke him, she might be able to save Pearl.

Before her body crashed into him, something stopped her, not hands, but an invisible force. She was suddenly hoisted aloft.

"No, no! Please!" Nnenna begged as the commodore's magic froze her in the air. He sneered.

"Where is your goddess, now, prophet?"

Nnenna had no answer and could only watch helplessly as the commodore took slow steps toward Pearl. He brandished his golden, bloodstained dagger. She could not see her face, but Pearl shook from head to foot with fear. If only Nnenna could have held her again, could have whispered to her that everything would be all right, then Nnenna herself might have believed it. As the last of her hope faded into nothingness, something new dared to make itself known. Nnenna clutched it, held on to it desperately. It expanded within her heart, filling the newly made hole, and she felt the desire to sing.

The song that poured out of her was simple, seven notes rising and falling. Her guilt led the melody, raw and pulsing like an open wound. Then came her sorrow, equally strong. Anger flared next, burning within her, and fatigue soon followed, stretching her voice to its limit. She breathed in deeply and found longing that nearly broke her heart, but kept singing until resolve broke through. Finally, with the last of herself, she breathed out a final note: hope.

Agwe let out a horrible cackle, reveling in his victory, and Nnenna imagined Pearl lost, too, dead at the feet of this unbeatable god, her throat cut and bleeding on the golden stair. She dared not look. As she cried, silently, a voice floated up to her, and Nnenna wrenched her eyes open. Pearl was still alive, still standing, defiantly staring up at Nnenna as Agwe held his blade to her throat.

She sang, echoing Nnenna's seven notes. Nnenna joined, finding the harmony to match the simple melody. They sang together until the song ended and then started again, as Agwe and the Meridians looked on. Then, there was another voice, a man's. Nnenna craned her neck and saw the curly-haired man, on his feet and singing as loudly as he could.

When they reached the end of the refrain and started anew, there were more voices, not many, but enough to ring out over the heads of all those who occupied the atrium. Agwe released an infuriated roar and drew the dagger back. Nnenna's heart stopped. She searched Pearl's face for the same shock, the same pain that she had seen in Lu, but the girl stood strong as she sang, her pale brown skin unmarked. Nnenna tore her eyes from Pearl's neck to Agwe's hands and found them empty. A small green serpent coiled itself around his booted foot.

The force that held Nnenna aloft broke as the snake drew

Agwe's attention, and Nnenna plummeted to the rocky temple floor. She braced herself for impact, but instead of hitting rock, she fell onto a cluster of waiting arms. The Meridians who had followed her helped her to her feet.

"What trickery is this?" Agwe demanded, looking around the atrium with crazed eyes. "No," he said, not waiting for an answer. He ran to the edge of the platform, stood before his throne, and stretched his arms toward the temple doors. They flew open. More people flooded the atrium, scared Meridians and the Fleet.

"Brothers and sisters, the time has come for you to demonstrate your devotion!" he called to the new arrivals. "This false prophet has already done irreparable harm. These fiends cannot be allowed into our kingdom! Raise your arms against them so that we may be clean once more!"

Agwe's words hung in the air as everyone in the atrium, Meridian and the Fleet, stared at each other. The captain who had held Nnenna captive ran down the stairs. She grabbed the first Meridian she came across with one hand, drew the other back, and thrust it through the chest of the man she held. Her fist came out the other side covered in blood and clutching the man's heart.

"No!" Nnenna screamed as the captain dropped the dead man. Blood spread from where the body lay.

Chaos unfolded everywhere. Fleet lieutenants attacked Meridians, and Meridians attacked each other. When Nnenna looked, Agwe was nowhere to be found and seemed to have taken the Meridian leader with him.

A scream caught Nnenna's attention. She whipped around. Pearl was still on the platform, menaced by the captain who held her in place. Nnenna ran to them, without so much as a dagger to defend herself, and launched at the captain. She caught him by surprise, wrapping her arms around his neck and her legs around his torso, squeezing as he tried to buck her like a maddened horse. She held fast, but he grabbed her hands, unlinked them, and threw her over his head easily, as though she were a doll. Nnenna slammed into Pearl, and they both hit the floor on the other side of the platform.

Nnenna got to her feet quickly, standing between the captain and Pearl, and she finally got her first good look at him. He was tall and thin with a mess of soft-looking dark brown hair. His skin was at least two shades lighter than hers with bright blue veins glowing under it.

"What in the seven . . ." she whispered, panting.

He advanced on her. He was stronger and faster than any man Nnenna had ever encountered, and Nnenna had no weapons.

"You don't have to do this!" she cried, raising a hand in front of her. He froze and stared at her. "What's your name?"

"Boyer," he said, after a moment. "Stephan Boyer."

"I have a feeling you and I have much in common, Boyer," Nnenna said carefully. "I did not want what the Fleet was offering, but I did not know how to get away." He said nothing. "This is your chance, Boyer. Agwe has left you. His kingdom is only madness. Leave now and find your peace."

Boyer tilted his head as he stared at Nnenna. Then, he looked at Pearl, crouching behind her. He turned his head and cast his eye around the atrium, surveying the slaughter taking place. The female captain who had held Nnenna was in the crowd, holding a young Meridian girl aloft while the girl screamed. Boyer frowned and took off running, a green-and-gold blur among brown bodies. He reached the woman in an instant, took the top of her head and chin into his hands, and wrenched them apart. Her head came free in his grip, and her body dropped.

Nnenna had only moments to celebrate before she saw the third captain, whom she recognized as Ambroise, wielding a dagger with deadly speed. She turned to Pearl.

"Couri!" Nnenna said. "Cache!"

Pearl nodded, rose to her feet, and ran down the side of the platform, disappearing into the crowd.

"Lieutenant Ambroise!" Nnenna shouted in the Seven Isles tongue, hoping to distract her long enough for Pearl to hide. Ambroise stopped and turned her glowing blue eyes on Nnenna. "I believe you still owe me a drink!"

Nnenna breathed deeply and straightened as she walked down the steps toward Ambroise. As she passed the body of a dead Fleet soldier, she relieved him of his sword. Ambroise dropped the dagger she had been favoring and drew her own sword. She came at Nnenna with lightning speed. Nnenna barely had enough time to block the blow. Their swords met near Nnenna's face, and the force of the hit rattled Nnenna's bones. Then, as quickly as she had attacked, Ambroise pulled away.

"You are no match for me," she gloated as she circled.

Nnenna turned on the spot, keeping her eye on the lieutenant. "I've bested lieutenants more experienced than you."

"I am a captain, now, *pirate*."

"Show me your ship, *Captain*."

Ambroise charged at Nnenna again, raising her sword over Nnenna's head and bringing it down with deadly force. Nnenna threw herself back, hit a wall, and held her scavenged sword up in defense. The blades clanked loudly as they locked in combat. Ambroise pushed her sword against Nnenna's, her teeth bared as she threw her weight against Nnenna's blade. Nnenna pushed with all her might as the sword came inches closer to her face, her muscles screaming with the effort.

"How fortunate that Ortega turned out to be a traitor," Ambroise taunted. "Now, I will be the captain the *Adoration* deserves."

A song exploded in Nnenna's chest. She opened her mouth to sing but could only scream at Ambroise. For the first time in her life, the pulsating air erupted from her lips as her voice hit Ambroise's blue-veined face. Ambroise's hold on her weapon gave. Nnenna screamed again, holding the high note and pushing closer to Ambroise. The captain's head shook violently, and she wept blue blood. It poured from her nostrils and ears, the thick rivulets drawing blue lines down Ambroise's cheeks and chin. Her eyelids fluttered, and her body slackened. Nnenna pushed, and Ambroise fell backward, dead.

As Nnenna stood over Ambroise's lifeless body, she brought her hand to her own throat, wondering what the goddess had done to her, and wondering what she had become.

Forty-Two

PEARL

"Couri!" Nnenna said. "Cache!"

Pearl did not wait for Nnenna to repeat herself. She ran down the side of the platform. Nnenna had told her to run and hide, but Pearl had other plans. Trying not to panic, Pearl searched the floor for anything she could use to help Nnenna, and like a gift, she found an abandoned pistol at the bottom of the stone steps. She picked it up and walked around the platform to get a better angle. Nnenna and the blue-eyed captain were already fighting. Pearl held the pistol out in front of her, aiming at the captain. She put her hands and fingers where Nnenna had taught her and—

A hand came down on the barrel of the pistol, forcing Pearl to lower her arm. Pearl turned to see who would dare interrupt her, and her heart stopped.

"I'm afraid you're outmatched, darling girl," signed a short, stocky, curly-haired Meridian dressed as a Fleet guard.

Pearl gasped, hardly believing that her Uncle Wade was finally standing in front of her.

"Uncle Wade!" she exclaimed in the Meridian language, throwing her arms around him.

He hugged her back, but only briefly.

"We need cover," he signed.

He took the pistol from her and led her around the edge of the atrium. Pearl kept her eye on Nnenna as they went, following the walls until they reached the golden staircase. There was room underneath the steps for the both of them if they crouched. Uncle Wade let Pearl in first. She made sure she could still see Nnenna as she squeezed into the narrow space before her uncle joined her.

"When the viceroy said you had fallen in with land-dweller pirates, I worried for your safety," Uncle Wade signed. "It seems I had no reason to do so."

Pearl smiled. "Nnenna took care of me. She taught me to fight, too. I can help her!"

"Not this fight," Uncle Wade signed.

They watched the blue-veined captain trap Nnenna against a wall.

"What are they?" Pearl asked.

"Agwe's abominations," Uncle Wade answered.

A scream pierced the air. She looked to Nnenna and found her still locked in combat with the captain. Nnenna screamed again, this time holding the sound. Pearl could just make out pulsating waves of air coming out of Nnenna's mouth. They seemed to be hurting the captain.

"What is she?" Uncle Wade asked, astonished.

Pearl beamed with pride. "She is the goddess's precious one."

Nnenna pushed the captain to the ground. She did not rise again.

"Come with me," she said to her uncle.

As Nnenna stared at the body, Pearl wriggled from the tight space and ran to her.

"Are you all right?" she asked, using the few words of the land-dweller language she had learned.

Nnenna nodded. Pearl knew it was a lie—it had to be, after all they had seen—but she accepted it all the same.

"We must end this," Nnenna said in Meridian as she and Pearl surveyed the carnage unfolding on the atrium floor.

"How?" Pearl asked in her native tongue.

"I don't know," Nnenna replied.

Something rubbed against the side of Pearl's foot. She looked down and saw the green snake that had once been Agwe's dagger winding itself around her boot.

Pearl reached down and picked up the writhing serpent, holding it at its head and middle so that its long tail hung toward the floor. She looked into the animal's eyes. Where there should have been yellow orbs, Pearl found a pair of dark brown irises that she knew all too well, though she had been in their presence but once.

"You're here!" she exclaimed, furrowing her brow as she stared more intently at the serpent. "How do we get you out?"

"What are you doing?" Nnenna asked.

"The goddess is here," Pearl said, peering at Nnenna over the snake's head. "We called her and she came!"

Nnenna sent Pearl a puzzled look. Pearl held up the snake. Nnenna leaned in and looked into its eyes.

"By the seven . . ." she cursed. "How do we get her out?"

"The conch," Pearl said. "We can use it to call her forth!"

Nnenna shook her head. "No. People died during that ceremony."

Pearl gestured to the fighting masses below them. "More are dying by the Fleet's hand as we speak! We cannot save them all ourselves! It may be our only hope!"

Nnenna sighed, eyeing the serpent dubiously. "Are you certain?" Pearl looked at the snake again, found its eyes, and felt the same sense of certainty she had felt before. She nodded. "Then, we must find Agwe."

They both searched the atrium. Neither Agwe nor the viceroy were anywhere to be found.

"They're gone," Nnenna said.

"They're not," Pearl countered. "I know they are here." She thought of the temple in the Settlement, of the room that was always described as the viceroy's refuge. "The Divine Chamber, on the topmost floor."

She and Nnenna both looked to the staircase leading to the upper floors. The fighting had already spread as many attempted to flee up the stairs. Nnenna flipped her cutlass and held the hilt out to Pearl.

"Stay close to me," Nnenna said. "And if anyone tries to hurt you, use this."

Pearl nodded. She carefully draped the serpent around her neck, making sure to rest its head on her shoulder. Then, she took the offered weapon. As the foursome approached the staircase, a Meridian brandishing a spear ran at them. Nnenna ran to meet the man.

"Keep going!" she called as she left them behind. "I'll meet you up there!"

Pearl did not need to be told twice. She and Wade ran up the stairs, past the fighting on the second and third floors, past the empty fourth, fifth, and sixth. When they reached the seventh-floor landing, her leg muscles ached and her lungs burned, but she did not stop.

The stairway led to a narrow corridor with one door at the end. Unlike the rest of this temple, the corridor was simple mountain stonework on either side, and the door was plain brown wood with a small golden knob. Pearl ran toward the door, grasped the knob, and pushed hard. The door swung open, and Pearl nearly toppled to the floor as it gave way.

She regained her balance and brandished the sword with both hands, but the scene inside made no sense. Agwe lay on the floor of the brightly lit room, his body prone as though he had fallen in a heap where he had stood. The viceroy stood before the farthest wall, on which hung a round mirror with an ornate gilded frame.

"Stop!" she shouted, for the viceroy had started toward her.

He stopped in his tracks but smiled at her like she had done him a favor.

"Pearl, isn't it?" the viceroy said. "Pearl Highwater."

"Where is the conch?" Pearl asked, squaring her stance and pointing the blade directly at him.

"This body has so many memories of you, Pearl," he said slowly. "Of waiting. Of *wanting*."

Pearl shuddered. "You disgusting old man. You're nothing but a leech, preying on people's faith—"

Her Uncle Wade stepped out from behind her, brandishing the pistol. "Stop," he signed with one hand. Wade took another step, and the viceroy took a step back. His eyes caught the light and flashed poison green.

"Agwe," Pearl whispered.

Agwe cackled. "Have you any idea how to work that land-dweller contraption?"

Wade pulled the hammer back with his thumb. Agwe raised a hand, and Uncle Wade froze solid, a statue where he stood. Pearl felt something invisible pull at her, wrenching her forward into the viceroy's waiting hand. Her sword clattered to the floor.

He clasped her neck hard, turning her breaths into gasps.

"There's nothing quite like a Meridian body to inhabit," Agwe mused. "This one has already lived so long, I may not get a year out of him. I'd much prefer a young thing like you . . ."

He crossed to the other side of the room, dragging Pearl along with him. Pearl tried to fight, but she was no match for the god's strength. She nearly tripped over the commodore's dead body as he dragged her before the mirror.

"What do you know of the gods, girl?" Agwe asked, both hands forcing her to stare into her own eyes. "What did that devil tell you about our power?"

Pearl did not know if it was fear or ignorance keeping her mouth shut, but she said nothing.

"Foolish child," he growled in her ear. "Our power comes from your belief, your devotion! You have interfered in the divine and now you will make amends. I will take everything from you!"

He clamped his hand around her neck, squeezing her airway shut, and peered into the mirror himself. Pearl struggled to look away, but her eyes were locked onto his. She also felt something else, something moving against her neck. From her peripheral vision, she watched the serpent uncoil. It reached its head to Agwe's wrist and bit down on his wrinkled flesh. He screamed, and the spell that held Pearl hostage broke. Pearl dropped to the floor.

"Pearl!" Nnenna shouted, running into the chamber. She charged at Agwe. Pearl tried to raise a hand to stop her, but Agwe had already seen Nnenna.

He pried the snake off and threw it aside. Then, he raised a hand to pull Nnenna forward.

"False prophet," he hissed as his hand clasped around her neck. "Perhaps I should take your body, instead! Tell me, where is your goddess, now? Do you think she will save you from me?"

Pearl had no time to think. She crawled across the floor back to where her sword waited for her.

"Nnenna!" she shouted, grabbing the weapon and throwing it to her.

Nnenna snatched the flying sword from the air. She brought the blade down hard onto Agwe's outstretched arm. It bit into his flesh, unleashing a peal of screams as blood soaked his green-and-gold sleeve. He released Nnenna's neck and blinked out of existence.

Pearl ran to Nnenna. "Are you all right?" she asked, frantic.

"I'm fine," she said. "Did you get the conch?"

The image of the shell dangling around Agwe's neck immediately came to mind, and Pearl swore using one of the curses she had learned from Nnenna.

"It's all right," Nnenna said, still breathing heavily. "We'll find another way."

But there was no other way. Agwe would return, and they had no plan for when they had to face him again. Her people were dying, and there was nothing she could do to save them. Pearl went to her uncle, still frozen.

"I will fix this," she promised.

Movement in the corner of the room caught her attention, and Pearl remembered the snake. She clambered to where it writhed on the floor, with Nnenna in tow.

"What's wrong with it?" Nnenna asked.

"The body is dying," she said.

"What will happen to her?" Nnenna asked.

"I don't know," Pearl answered, but she didn't think the goddess would be able to survive without a body.

For what felt like a long time, Nnenna said nothing. Her brow furrowed as she looked between Pearl and the snake. As Pearl considered asking her what was on her mind, she lay down on the floor on her stomach and stared at the snake, turning her head to the side as though she were trying to catch its eye.

"If you need a body, take mine," she whispered in the Meridian language.

"No!" Pearl said, grabbing at Nnenna's shoulder to try to pull her away from the snake. "You'll die!"

Nnenna did not move. "I am your prophet," she went on, "your most devoted. Use me."

"You have to mean it," Pearl said, tears stinging her eyes. "When you say the words, you have to mean them."

"I *do* mean them. I *am* her most devoted. I've given everything that mattered to me to her cause. Why not my body as well?"

"Please . . ." Pearl begged.

Nnenna reached a hand toward the snake. At first, it did not respond, but after a moment, a thin pink tongue flicked from its mouth. Slowly, it uncurled its green body and slithered toward Nnenna's hand, wrapping itself around her wrist and winding up her arm. Nnenna kept still and watched as it moved past her elbow to her shoulder. When it reached her neck, she turned her head and found its eyes once again.

Pearl could have sworn she heard a wisp of song as the goddess's magic took hold. The snake went limp, and Nnenna's eyes glowed.

Forty-Three

NNENNA

The goddess entered Nnenna's body the way sunshine replaced shadow when morning arrived, the way the tide filled in the beaches and pools when it rose. Everything inside her that hurt suddenly sang. Her grief, her anger, and her pain all turned into something amazing she could not name but knew was powerful.

She felt the urge to test this new strength, but she found herself unable to connect with her limbs. She could see through her eyes, but could not control them as they looked around the stone-clad room. Her hands moved of their own accord to different parts of her body, and she felt a brief sense of wonder at their solidness.

A face came into view, a young, round face that Nnenna would have given the world to see smile.

"Pearl!" she tried to say, but she had no power over her mouth for speech.

Instead, she heard herself say, "Mwen pral pran swen li."

I will take care of her.

It was the goddess speaking, though Nnenna heard her own voice. Her hand reached out for Pearl's, and Pearl took it. Nnenna thought this was a gesture of comfort until she and Pearl were pulled out of reality. For a fraction of a second, there was pure nothingness, and before Nnenna could wrap what remained of her mind around what was happening, they were back at the golden throne in the atrium on the bottom floor of the temple. Nnenna heard the noise of the fighting still raging, but it felt far away. She could have easily turned her back to it, but instead, she tried to speak to the goddess.

We must get them to stop fighting each other, she tried to say. *Distract them!*

The goddess gave no sign of having heard her. She raised Nnenna's arms over her head. Something tugged at what remained of Nnenna's consciousness, and everyone in the atrium suddenly froze. At first, Nnenna thought they had simply stopped fighting, but as the goddess surveyed her handiwork, Nnenna saw that the Fleet soldiers, the last of Agwe's blue-veined captains, and the Meridians had stopped mid-act, their faces twisted into masks of hatred and fear. It was not just those in the atrium—Nnenna felt the goddess's magic reach everyone in the temple, no matter where they were hidden. When she brought her arms down, the masses fell to their knees in unison, their weapons clattering to the stone floor. Nnenna felt something drain from her as the goddess's magic released the people.

"Agwe has returned!" said an unsteady voice from the crowd. "He has taken the form of the false prophet to show us that he has bested her!"

No, Nnenna thought, though she found it harder to keep her presence. *They must see who you are!*

"My children!" the goddess called into the silence. "Look at what we have done to you! So many of you have died! It was my dream for you to rise above the servitude for which you were created, but all we gods have done is turn our slaves to soldiers. This burden should never have fallen upon your shoulders. This fight is not yours." She cupped Nnenna's hands around her mouth. "Agwe! Face me, you coward!"

Her voice boomed through the atrium, and the mountain itself quaked at her words. An explosion like a clap of thunder erupted from the center of the crowd, breaking the spell of silence that had befallen them. A figure appeared as the Meridians and Fleet soldiers parted to either side of the atrium. He was still dressed as the viceroy, still bleeding where Nnenna had cut him, a look of malice on his face. Agwe brought his hands together and clapped loudly, his green eyes trained on the goddess. Nnenna's heartbeat quickened.

"Spoken like a true mother," Agwe spat, stepping forward. He reached a hand toward the people on his right, and one of their spears flew to him. He caught it deftly and spun it as he walked. "Let us put your compassion to the test."

He became a blur of speed racing toward her with the spear tip aimed at her head. Lasirenn's speed matched his as she sidestepped his thrust. She parried with the sword in Nnenna's hand, scraping the blade along the shaft and pushing the spear away. Agwe attacked again with a deadly swipe, and Lasirenn ducked and rolled out of the way.

"Is this the best you can do?" Agwe taunted. "Is this the best you can offer your children?"

Lasirenn frowned. She ran at Agwe, sword raised. The goddess swung down, aiming for his shoulder, but he blocked the blow with the spear shaft.

"Come now, my love," he murmured almost tenderly, "surely you are not this foolish."

Lasirenn pushed the sword harder, using her godly might to

bite the blade deeper into the gold. It cracked loudly. Agwe noticed and pushed Lasirenn away. As she removed the sword from the spear, the golden shaft split in two. Agwe growled, frustrated, and tossed the two pieces aside. Lasirenn attacked him again, but Agwe sped away to the far end of the atrium. She gave chase but stopped when he put his hands together.

As he pulled them apart, water appeared between them, floating and writhing in the air, growing and growing until the drop reached the size of Agwe's head. He flicked his wrist, and the floating bead extended into a tendril that whipped at Lasirenn. She dodged as the end of the whip tore furrows into the stone like it was sand.

She lost the sword trying to stay alive. The water whip wrapped around her neck, pulling her into Agwe's waiting hand. He laughed as he lifted her aloft for all to see.

"Now, you know in whom to place your belief!" he said, using his other hand to work the water into an angry current.

Lasirenn struggled against Agwe's hold, looking at the Meridians on either side of the atrium. She found Pearl and made Nnenna's face smile. Pearl slowly got down on her knees and raised her hands above her head. She hesitantly opened her mouth, and as tears rolled down her round cheeks, the first notes of Nnenna's song poured out.

She sang the song once alone, her voice quavering as it climbed to the top of the atrium. Her eyes never left the gruesome tableau the goddess and Agwe made. As she took up the first note again, more voices joined hers. The Meridians who sang with her before raised their voices in song again. The power of the song pulsed through her body, reaching the little space she inhabited.

Sing! she told the goddess.

Lasirenn opened Nnenna's mouth and released a single note

that rose above all others, so loud it bounced violently off the mountain walls. Agwe's grip slackened, and Lasirenn grabbed at his fingers, prying them away until she fell to the floor.

Keep singing, Nnenna said, even as she felt her strength dwindle to almost nothing.

Lasirenn rose to her feet. She took another breath and screamed. This time, the mixture of air and sound ignited as they left her mouth, and a beam of light struck Agwe's chest. The light spread as Lasirenn sang and walked toward him. He tried to fight it, but it coated every inch of him until his twisted features were lost to its glow. She seized Agwe by the hands, and immediately he shrank at her touch. He tried to pull away, but his strength was no match for hers.

"You fight with dishonor! They are using magic!" he cried over the singing voices.

Lasirenn paused. "Your followers would have done the same for you had you bothered to heal them," she retorted.

She gave him no chance to respond, screaming again as she held him in place. The magic she poured into him consumed him from the inside. He fell to his knees and grew smaller and smaller until the light disappeared into Nnenna's hand. All that remained of him was an empty pile of clothes on the floor.

All voices stopped.

"He is dead!" someone exclaimed in the Meridian tongue.

But Nnenna knew better. She could feel the wriggling against her palm. Lasirenn opened her hand. There in her palm was a squirming black tadpole. She reached her other hand into the air and pulled the mirror from the Divine Chamber out of nothingness. Lasirenn held the mirror flat to reflect the atrium's ceiling.

"Let us put an end to this nonsense," she said, holding the tadpole above the smooth glass.

The reflection in the mirror disappeared, and a blackness that stretched into depths beyond the mirror's frame took its place. White stars twinkled in the darkness. Lasirenn tipped her hand and let the tadpole fall. Its little body fell through the barrier, into the Unknown. She passed her hand over the mirror, and it returned to glass.

Lasirenn looked to the people standing on either side of the cavernous room, a blend of her and Agwe's followers, and sighed heavily. She outstretched her hands and drew on Nnenna's strength once more. A rush of power tore through the atrium as Lasirenn sent her magic into the throats of every Meridian who had chosen Agwe, removing the curse locking their voices away.

"Nothing divides you, now," she called as she lowered Nnenna's arms. "You are but one people. Go forth together and live on this island in peace."

The power that had filled her rushed out of Nnenna's body, and her consciousness reconnected with her physical form. She was in control again, but where was Lasirenn?

"Nnenna!" Pearl shouted.

Nnenna turned to catch Pearl in her arms as a fatigue unlike any other came over her.

"Are you all right?" Pearl asked.

"Go check on your uncle," she answered. "I will be fine."

"I will come right back," Pearl promised.

As Nnenna released Pearl, the world suddenly upended. Nnenna's knees buckled, and she lost consciousness before she hit the floor.

Forty-Four

PEARL

“The funeral will be starting soon, Pearl,” Uncle Wade said tentatively as the sun began to set.

Pearl had never been to a land-dweller funeral, but she knew, now, that there was much to be learned about life through honoring the dead. She had spent the night after she returned from the temple and all the next day sitting by Nnenna’s side, her uncle checking on her periodically while he helped the Meridians settle into the area. Now, the sun was setting, and it would soon be time to return the souls of the dead to the sea.

“I hoped she would be awake by now,” Pearl admitted as she looked over Nnenna’s sleeping form.

Uncle Wade sighed. “You have done all you can for her, darling girl.”

Her uncle was right. She had filled the little house with her hopes, and Nnenna’s condition had remained unchanged.

“We’ll go together?” she asked her uncle.

Uncle Wade’s face relaxed into a smile. “Of course, love.”

Together, they walked through the village and into the jungle, on the path that led to the beach.

"Uncle Rain would have loved this place," Pearl said, gazing up at the canopy of trees and vines overhead. "I wish we could have brought him."

"We carry his song in our hearts," Uncle Wade answered.

"I saw him," Pearl said, "when Nnenna, Lu, and I were in the Unknown. He came to me and told me of the goddess."

"Your Uncle Rain was the best of our people," Uncle Wade responded, his voice growing thick with emotion.

Pearl wrapped her arm around his, and they walked the rest of the way in silence. When soft brown soil turned to sand, Pearl saw dozens of Meridians at work. They had cut leafy fronds from the tall trees and woven them into makeshift barques on which the dead could lay. Pearl counted thirty-seven, each with the body of a fallen Meridian or Fleet soldier.

"Where is Lu?" she asked her uncle, searching for him.

She left Uncle Wade's side and walked along the shore, peering into barques over the shoulders of the workers. There were many faces she recognized—Matthias Marshwind, her former teacher; Amos Stilltide, her childhood playmate; the commodore, whose body gave Pearl pause, despite her knowing that it was no longer inhabited by Agwe. She turned around a rocky outcropping and spotted the *Adoration* on the beach in the distance. As she approached, she saw a cluster of Fleet soldiers had gathered around a longboat. She recognized one as Boyer and noted that his eyes and veins still glowed blue.

"What you doing?" Pearl asked, cobbling together some of the land-dweller words she knew.

Boyer turned and, when he saw her, got the attention of the other soldiers. The rest straightened. Boyer stepped forward to meet her.

"Captain Ortega," he said, gesturing awkwardly at the boat

with his hand. Pearl looked, and tears formed in her eyes. There lay Lu, looking as peaceful as though he were asleep. They had dressed him in what Pearl recognized as the commodore's clothing, including the gilded tricorn hat. His body lay on a bed of dry grass surrounded by a variety of cut fruits.

"We pray the goddess will guide him," Boyer said in broken Meridian.

"We will sing for him," Pearl answered.

As the sun sank lower into the sea, the people of Meridia filled the beach, some carrying torches from their newly chosen homes. For the first time in generations, they were one people united in the suffering that they had endured. Silence fell upon the crowd, and Pearl wondered when the ceremony would start.

"I think they are waiting for you, love," Uncle Wade whispered.

"Me?" Pearl asked, noticing that the eyes of the people were on her. "I'm not . . . I don't know how to . . ."

In the Settlement, the viceroy would have led the people in hymns praising Agwe's name before leading the procession to the Gateway to the Unknown. But the viceroy was dead, and Pearl was not exactly sure how to move forward without one. She stepped forward anyway and turned to face the crowd of mourners.

"Brothers and sisters, we are gathered here today . . ." she began, but let the words die when she realized they were the viceroy's, ingrained in her memory. "Our people have endured so much," she said slowly. "Generations of exile only to be betrayed by the god whom we believed to be our protector. The result is this." She gestured to the seemingly endless line of bodies on the sand. "Our brothers, our sisters, our friends, our lovers paying the ultimate price for our safety, for our freedom. Let us join our voices together to provide our loved ones with safe passage into the Unknown, and to signal the start of a new time of peace among us all."

The song was already pressing against Pearl's heart by the time she finished her speech. She let barely a breath pass before she sang the first notes of Nnenna's melody. The people directly in front of her recognized it immediately and joined her in the song that united their people. It spread like sunshine across the beach. They sang it again and again, thirty-seven times in all, once for each of the dead they honored.

When the song concluded, the mourners took up the task of sending the lost souls to the sea. One by one, they took the barques upon their shoulders, waded into the water, and sent them off. They prayed that the waves would envelop their lost and that the Unknown would take them in. Lu's longboat was the last to depart. As the vessel made its way into the night, Pearl swore she could hear a wisp of song over the crashing waters.

"I am so proud of you, darling girl," Uncle Wade said. He escorted her back up the path to the small village at the foot of the mountain.

Pearl smiled, proud of herself. She was tired and ready for a good night's sleep.

As they passed the house where Nnenna slept, Pearl stopped her uncle.

"Let me check on her one more time," Pearl said. "I want to tell her that . . . Lu is at peace."

"Of course, love."

Pearl approached the door, but it was already ajar. One of the healers must have been tending to her. Pearl waited outside for a while but soon realized she heard no voices inside, not even Nnenna's breaths. She placed a tentative hand on the wooden door, pushed it open, and poked her head through the doorway. It was dark inside, and the stillness was unsettling. She pushed the door open fully and stepped in.

There was no one inside.

Forty-Five

NNENNA

It was dark when Nnenna broke free of the deep sleep that had captured her, kept her swimming in a sea of visions for what had felt like an eternity. She awoke to silence and solitude.

The bed that cradled her felt solid under her weight, as did the walls when she reached out to feel them. She lay still for a long while, wondering when she would be pulled back into the realm of dreams. When she found herself still conscious several minutes later, she released a heavy sigh and rose from her resting place.

Her stiff muscles and bones protested loudly, but she made it to her feet and crossed to the door in a handful of unsteady but determined steps. Nnenna could not remember ever being so untethered. The *Medusa* was gone, Pearl was reunited with her people, and Lu, whom she had back in her life for mere days, was dead.

In her dreams, Nnenna had relived the events in the temple a thousand times, had gotten herself and her friends captured a thousand times, had watched Lu die a thousand times. It had been torture, and yet somehow, even in her unconscious state, she had begun to savor the moments before the glint of the golden dagger. They were the last memory she had of Lu, and she would not relinquish him, no matter the cost.

Nnenna breathed in the night air, alive with the scent of smoke and unfamiliar flowers. Looking up at the stars, she wondered if there was anywhere on this island she could go and not be reminded of her mistakes. A gentle breeze caressed her face, and on it, she heard a wisp of song.

Nnenna did not take the path through the jungle. She was not ready to be seen. Instead, she walked along the edge of the village, treading between wilderness and civilization, just as she had when she was a child. She reached a clearing where one face of the mountain stretched into the sky while a waterfall poured into a large pool. The gaping maw of a dark cave was barely discernible behind the waterfall, and though the flow should have been loud enough to drown out any noise, the song that brought Nnenna here persisted.

The pool showed Nnenna's face as clearly as a mirror when she approached the rocky edge. She looked haggard and worn, as though she carried the weight of the great mountain itself on her shoulders. As Nnenna gazed into the deep, clear water, wondering if she would ever feel like herself again, something moved beyond her reflection that made her pull away. When she went to look again, it was not her own face looking back at her.

"You're here," Nnenna said as the goddess's heart-shaped face emerged from the water. Her long tail flicked back and forth beneath her.

The crown of white hair that surrounded her face was now a deep blood red, like Nnenna's, and the wrinkles that had lined her face when they had first met were gone. Her youth and beauty reflected her power.

"You called for me," Lasirenn answered, a slight smile playing at her full lips.

"I don't think . . ." Nnenna started, but the goddess brought out a slender hand and placed it on her bare chest, just over her heart.

"The blood always knows," she said.

Nnenna frowned as she remembered being in the goddess's lair.

You have my blood, Lasirenn had said. The goddess had meant it as an explanation, but her words had only inspired more questions.

"You are afraid," Lasirenn said.

"Yes," Nnenna replied, too tired for pretense.

"Come," Lasirenn said. She swam backward a little ways, making room for Nnenna in the water.

The inherent gift of fatigue was that Nnenna had no strength to argue against the goddess's request. It also spared her from the confines of propriety. She stripped off her clothes, relieved to be rid of the dirty, bloodstained garments, and dove naked into the water.

"How do you feel, now?" Lasirenn asked when Nnenna resurfaced.

The answer to that was more complicated than she was willing to admit, but she could not deny the lightness that came over her as she allowed the water to support her weight.

"Better," she sighed.

"Sing," Lasirenn said, smiling. "Release the song in your heart."

Nnenna did not realize that the burgeoning feeling in her chest was a song until the goddess named it. Her heart told her to give herself fully to the water, so she let herself sink into the pool, deep enough that the strands of her locs floated gracefully around her head. She did not even try to breathe. Her lungs simply stopped needing air. When she opened her mouth, it filled with water, and her first note reverberated through it, just like it had when the island had risen from the depths of the sea.

She did not need a new song, for all the feelings were the same, and her seven-note melody still rang painfully true. The magic took hold at once, tingling in her hips and thighs and legs. Her skin erupted in scales, blue, white, and red, shining pearly in the moonlight. Her legs fused into a long, strong tail from which a wide, iridescent fin sprouted.

The last note left her lips, but the magic remained, pulsing under her skin. She flipped her tail fin back and forth, propelling herself forward. Lasirenn joined her under the water, and together they swam in circles around each other. Lasirenn stopped in front of Nnenna and reached for her with both hands, beaming with pride as her eyes raked over every inch of Nnenna's transformed body.

"My precious one," Lasirenn said, cupping Nnenna's face.

Another song bloomed in Nnenna's heart, one from when she was a child. She remembered being held and regarded with this same affection. She had placed her little hands over her father's then, and before she could stop herself, she did the same with Lasirenn's now. The child in Nnenna wanted to stay in the comfort of this embrace forever, but Nnenna had long outgrown such things. She pulled the goddess's hands away, and Lasirenn's face fell.

"You are still afraid," Lasirenn said.

Nnenna frowned.

"Come with me."

Before Nnenna could respond, Lasirenn whirled around and swam toward the waterfall. Nnenna did not know if it was curiosity or fear that tugged at her as she watched Lasirenn recede into the distance, but whatever it was made her give chase. She flipped her tail hard and followed.

Nnenna caught up to Lasirenn as she swam through the roiling waters beneath the waterfall. As Nnenna crossed through the veil into the cave, the waters darkened. Lasirenn did not stop. Together they swam along a winding path through the island, slinking through narrow passages and between rock formations. A light appeared ahead of them. She sped past Lasirenn and pushed herself through the opening.

Nnenna felt a change in the temperature of the water around her. She was in the sea, hovering somewhere under the island, but still hundreds of feet above the Gateway to the Unknown. She felt a sudden urge to swim down, to be swallowed by the darkness once again, but Lasirenn was already swimming up to the surface. Reluctantly, Nnenna followed. When she broke through the water, her lungs inflated and she inhaled sea air.

"Can you hear them?" Lasirenn asked, pumping her tail back and forth under the water.

They were off the coast of the beach where Nnenna had awoken when Meridia had been in the Unknown. She could see the island in the distance, a dark mass sitting on the water that reached high into the sky. The wind came from over the mountain, carrying voices to their ears.

"They're singing for the dead," Nnenna said quietly.

The voices were indistinct, but Nnenna sensed the heart that lay beneath the melody steeped in sorrow.

"What do I do?" Nnenna asked Lasirenn.

"What do they ask for?" Lasirenn returned.

Nnenna listened harder, opened her heart even more, and found the request within the anguish.

"Safe passage," she said, "for the souls."

Lasirenn smiled. "Then, we will guide them."

She turned to Nnenna and extended both hands. Nnenna

took them in her own. Lasirenn started the song with a low hum that came from deep within her chest. She parted her lips, and out spilled rich tones whose power Nnenna felt in her own body. Nnenna felt the urge to sing, so she did. Her part of the song was higher and lighter. Their voices twisted in harmony as they rose above the water. Light seeped into the water from their bodies until it filled the Gateway.

The barques appeared soon after, thirty-seven of them, carried to the light by the soft, undulating waves. With every body that floated toward them and sank into the darkness below, a fresh pang of guilt squeezed Nnenna's heart. She had promised them life and had instead delivered them to their deaths.

Nnenna poured her own sorrow into the song, offering it to the dead as the only recompense she had. The longboat came last, and knowing who lay within it, Nnenna choked on a sob. Lasirenn continued to sing, continued to guide him toward her light until the water swallowed him as well. When he was gone, Lasirenn let the song taper to a close.

"I am the goddess of the realm between the mystical and the mundane," Lasirenn said, responding to Nnenna's unasked question. "Those who die pass from one state to the other and they return to the Unknown."

"What does that mean . . . for me?"

Lasirenn paused and regarded Nnenna with a curious look upon her usually serene face. "It is not for me to say."

Nnenna stared at her, waiting for more.

"I wanted my precious ones to have every opportunity to reach their divine potential. Then, they were all taken from me. Or so I thought. You are a gift to me, Nnenna. It is not my place to dictate your destiny."

"What about Agwe?"

"Agwe upset the natural balance of the world in his quest for power, and the world suffered for it," she said. "He will remain in the Unknown until he has been forgotten and then it will take him, too."

"But the world is still suffering," Nnenna countered.

"It will heal in time," Lasirenn insisted.

Nnenna turned her eyes to the sky. Fluffy white clouds glided over the sea of stars, and a half-moon poured its light over the island. She thought of all the people living in a broken world because of one being's greed and knew, at once, that she wanted more than healing.

"Can the balance not be restored?" Nnenna asked, not looking at the goddess.

"My brothers and sisters all faded into the Unknown," Lasirenn answered.

Nnenna tore her eyes away from the stars and looked at the goddess once more.

"Then, we will bring them back," she said.

"That is impossible. The living cannot truly enter the Unknown. I created a space for the island to exist undisturbed. Without this protection, even I would have been lost to the abyss."

"But you never left the island," Nnenna said. "How can you be sure there is no way to extend your protection?"

A faint furrow appeared on Lasirenn's brow.

"I'd like to stay here," Nnenna continued. "If there is a way to bring back your brothers and sisters, I think this island is the key."

"Then, stay."

"Will you help me?"

The goddess pressed her lips into a line as she thought. Nnenna's heart thudded as she waited.

One beat. Two beats. Three beats.

"Yes," Lasirenn answered, "but understand that the mystical are not as straightforward as the mundane. What you reap may not be what you intended when you sowed it."

Nnenna nodded. "Then, I will learn. You will teach me and, together, we shall perform the impossible."

Nnenna remained in the water long after Lasirenn bid her farewell, floating on her back and enjoying the ocean's embrace. When the last of the stars faded into the dawn, Nnenna traveled back through the cave passage to the pool in the jungle clearing. She let her song return her body to its original form, hoisted herself from the water, and dressed. When she returned to the little village at the foot of the mountain, she found Pearl crouched in her doorway, muttering in her sleep. She knelt before the girl and gently shook her awake.

"Nnenna!" Pearl yawned and wrapped her arms around the pirate. "I was afraid you weren't coming back!"

"Not a chance, sweet one," Nnenna breathed, surprised to feel tears springing to her eyes. She pulled out of the hug and held Pearl at arm's length.

"Are you staying?" Pearl asked.

Nnenna owed Pearl the truth.

"Not forever," she said, and Pearl's face fell.

"I'll come with you, wherever you go!"

"No, sweet one." Nnenna thought of what she had witnessed on the shore. "You have family in this place. Your people need you."

"But where will you go?"

"I am working with Lasirenn to find a way to bring balance back to the world. I am not sure where the journey will take me."

Just then, the door to Pearl's house opened, and her uncle stepped out. "Time for breakfast, Pearl!" he called.

"Will you eat with us?" Pearl asked Nnenna.

"Of course. Go ahead. I will follow you shortly."

The girl left Nnenna's side and joined her uncle. Nnenna entered her own dwelling, closing the door behind her. She found the palm-frond bed and sat with her feet dangling over the side. As she sat in her dark little house, she contemplated the thought she had not dared to entertain while in Lasirenn's presence.

"I don't know if you can hear me, Lu," she whispered into the silence. "But I want you to know that I am coming. I am going to bring you back."

ACKNOWLEDGMENTS

First, let me say how fortunate I am to find myself in the position of having to acknowledge two entirely different groups of people for the making and remaking of *Devil of the Deep*. Not every indie author gets the opportunity to republish their work with the support of a publisher. Thank you to my indie team—my alpha reader, beta readers, ARC readers, editor, cover artist, and ship consultant—for lending so much of your free time to help me make my dream of being a published author come true. Thank you to the teams at Bindery and Girl Friday Productions for taking my dream to a level beyond what I thought possible. Thank you to Left Unread x Bindery tastemaker Michael LaBorn for your advocacy work on behalf of all Black and brown indie authors, for being *Devil of the Deep*'s champion, and for never taking "impossible" for an answer. Meghan Harvey, thank you for saying yes to this indie book! Kristin Duran, thank you for making this whole process stress-free with your expert management and consistent communication. Alicia Sparrow, thank you for being the exact right editor for my brain. I will take what you've taught me everywhere I go! Alyssa Brillinger and Brittany Dowdle, thank you for your meticulous copyediting work. Charlotte Strick, thank you for *Devil of the Deep*'s bold and breathtaking new cover! Jasmine Green, thank you for creating the artwork that inspired it. Thank you to my wife, Sandra; my long-distance bestie, Emma; my internet friends; and my former English teacher Lisa Brewster-Cook, for believing in me long before *Devil of the Deep* was a thought in my head. I hope to make you all proud. Finally, thank you to François-Dominique Toussaint Louverture for leading the revolution that birthed my homeland and my inspiration, Haiti.

THANK YOU

This book would not have been possible without the support from the Left Unread community, with a special thank-you to the Thirsty Readers and LaBorniacs members:

Abby Knight
Ace McKee
Aly B
Alyssa Nelson
Amanda L. Powell
amandadevoursbooks
AmandaReads
Amaness7
AmberDoesAudio
Anabeth Scott
Andy Blake
Angela Millicent Jackson
Angelica Wagner
Anika Chang
Anna Charzyńska
Anya
Aoife Leah
aq
Ardent Richards
Ashley Dodson
Ashley Jackson Perez
AspenForest732
Austa Feller
Axagal
BayLe K. Marie
Beauregard Gilbert
Beckett F. Knutson
Bell Newman
Bookishrocky
BookishType
booklovebykay
bookscapewithali
Brandee
Brandy G
Bri Schmidt
BrittanyAmbridge
BrittanyH
Brooke Thorne
Carlysgrowingtbr
Carter Kalchik

Casie Powers
Christina Aiode
Clover
coliver
Courtney Meyer
CR Townson
Craig Linderoth
Cristina B
Currystbrcart
Danielle Phipps
Days
DefiantlyDisordered
Deirdre Byrd
Desi Hart
Diversityhorror
DoctorProfessional
DrCLO
drewsinead
E.A. Noble
E.L Winston
Elise Legendre
Ellie0612
Emma Holland
EnthusiasticSamantha
Eva Tariq Ali
Fowzi Abdulle
Gabriela Medina
GeneLee
Georgia Mountford-Blake
Hannah Pluta
Hollie Rickey
Ilona F. Toth
InnuendoAS
J.B. Quintanilla
Jasmine Bolich
Jasper Edwards
JCFairbanks
Jeanne C Busch
Jeremy K
Jessica Coffey
Jessica Fontes
JessicaK
JiaLing Pan
Josh Brown
JuMuriel
Kaila A. Stovall
Karissa Tedrow
kathrynbudig
Kathy Silvey
Katknapp
Keilani S.
kendra
Kendra Dawn
Kia Borner
Kit Fox
Kristin Chesnutt
Krystal Tellez-Rener
Laura Duncan
LCHopalong
Leelynn Untalan Brady
lesleypsyd
Leslie Way
Linda M
LittleCozyReaderr

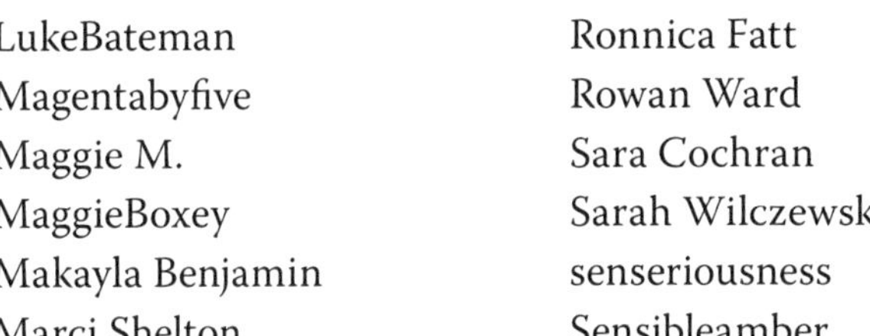

LukeBateman
Magentabyfive
Maggie M.
MaggieBoxey
Makayla Benjamin
Marci Shelton
Mathieu
Maureen McSherry
Megan Davenport
Megan K
Mel Weisbecker
Melanie Turner
Melissa Gaston
Melissa Newkirk
Michelle Healey
Mkat
Moira King
MoniqueW
Moresparklesplz
mustbejulian
NadineS
Naomi Darling
Natalia Hernandez
Ncp
Olivia Danson
Quinne
R.J. Lavender
Rachel Hunter
Raechel Baumgartner
Regina Dennis
RemarkableBookLife
Renelle Lee-Bond
Ronnica Fatt
Rowan Ward
Sara Cochran
Sarah Wilczewski
senseriousness
Sensibleamber
ShanicesReadingCorner
Shanyn
shaykauwe
shelzy
Shenisse Castillo
SillyGooseReads
spooniereads
Stormy Avalos
StregaVerde
StubbornK
SWest
Tasha
Taylor Case
TayMayBay
Tenesha L. Curtis
TheBardMom
Tracy
Tristin Sylvester
Valerie Lovin
ViperVipest
vrinkles%
WilletteGOG
Winona Veil
Yas Hickson
Yeshua Karangalan
Zee Barela

ABOUT THE AUTHOR

FALENCIA JEAN-FRANCOIS, a proud Haitian immigrant, is an author and educator living in Pittsburgh with her wife, two cats, and dog. She has loved storytelling since her first-grade teacher challenged her to write her own fable. Falencia has published two novellas, *After Hours* and *Cinderella,* and *Devil of the Deep* is her debut novel. Falencia believes that words hold immense power, and she is committed to using them to fight oppression.

Left Unread Books is an imprint of Bindery, a book publisher powered by community.

We're inspired by the way book tastemakers have reinvigorated the publishing industry. With strong taste and direct connections with readers, book tastemakers have illuminated self-published, backlisted, and overlooked authors, rocketing many to bestseller lists and the big screen.

This book was chosen by Michael LaBorn in close collaboration with the Left Unread Books community on Bindery. By inviting tastemakers and their reading communities to participate in publishing, Bindery creates opportunities for deserving authors to reach readers who will love them.

Visit Left Unread Books for a thriving bookish community and bonus content:

leftunreadbooks.binderybooks.com

MICHAEL LABORN is the founder of Left Unread Books, an imprint dedicated to dismantling systems of oppression one book at a time. A Black man in a white-centered world, LaBorn actively makes space for Black and brown writers by challenging systemic barriers in the industry and championing underrepresented authors in bookish spaces. He has a platform of 107K followers on TikTok and has been featured in *Elle* and *Bold Journey*. A book reviewer and passionate advocate for marginalized people, he loves reading anything that challenges him to see the world through a wider lens.

INSTAGRAM.COM/MICHAEL.LABORN

YOUTUBE.COM/@MICHAEL.LABORN